C000003094

A PART OF ME

VIVIEN BROWN

BLOODHOUND
— B O O K S —

Copyright © 2024 Vivien Brown

The right of Vivien Brown to be identified as the Author of the Work has been
asserted by her in accordance with the Copyright, Designs and Patents Act 1988.

First published in 2024 by Bloodhound Books.

Apart from any use permitted under UK copyright law, this publication may only
be reproduced, stored, or transmitted, in any form, or by any means, with prior
permission in writing of the publisher or, in the case of reprographic production,
in accordance with the terms of licences issued by the Copyright Licensing
Agency.
All characters in this publication are fictitious and any resemblance to real
persons, living or dead, is purely coincidental.

www.bloodhoundbooks.com

Print ISBN: 978-1-916978-82-9

To Joe Rees and all who selflessly donate a part of themselves in order to ease the suffering of others.

'Next to creating a life, the finest thing a man can do is save one.'
Abraham Lincoln

PROLOGUE

AUGUST, 2019

The room is too warm, too quiet, too beige. It's nothing but a plain, functional holding area where worried families, unnaturally silent and naturally scared, are herded while they wait for the axe to fall. Or perhaps for a miracle. Surely miracles do come along and surprise everyone, even the doctors, sometimes.

If an accident had to happen, he can't help thinking, then it couldn't have been at a more convenient place. In theory, anyway. It was right outside the hospital, a stone's throw from A&E, not that that made a lot of difference in the end. It wasn't as if a string of eager doctors and nurses came rushing out across the car park, abandoning the other patients inside, lugging all the right equipment along with them. An ambulance still had to be called; the gawpers still stood and watched, some of them taking sneaky photos on their cameras; and the drivers in the traffic backed up along the busy street still leant impatiently on their horns, unaware of what lay ahead.

A clock ticks. Footsteps pass by, squeaking on the just-washed floor in the corridor outside. Magazines lie unread on a table. Coffees go cold in polystyrene cups. There is a vague

1

whiff of antiseptic. They sit together, heads either leant back against the bare wall or bent forwards in trembling hands, eyes closed, tearful and tired, none of them quite touching – they don't all know each other that well, after all – while in the far corner the other family waits too. A woman, the wife of the motorcyclist, and her teenaged son. Their chances of good news are surely better. He had been wearing a crash helmet, a padded leather jacket and big heavy boots. Whereas she...

Should they really all be here, both families, kept together in the same room? He looks across at the others, prepared to be angry, but he sees that they are hurting too, knows that whatever happened out there was not their fault, yet still something about it feels wrong. But then everything about this day was already wrong, wasn't it? The unfairness, the sheer randomness of life, hangs over them all like a cloud, just as it has done for weeks, months, and now this...

How can it be that the world can tip and everything can change in seconds? That on such a seemingly ordinary day, with the sun shining and the traffic lights working, and the little green man beeping to his heart's content, three women can step out into the road, onto a clearly marked crossing, and only two of them reach the other side.

ONE

OCTOBER, 2018

O nly six o'clock, and it was already getting dark outside as Beth Hogan tugged the faded curtains shut, one of the old plastic hooks snapping away from the rail and bouncing down onto the cluttered sideboard beneath. She glanced at the familiar photos in their fake silver frames, picked up one of herself as a child and blew the dust away. Her mother had been too frail in her final weeks to think about cleaning.

'Another cup of tea?' Mrs Fellows from next door, a floral apron pulled over her black jumper and skirt, put a hand on Beth's elbow and guided her back towards the settee. 'I usually find it helps. Warm and comforting, you know... in times of trouble.'

'No, thank you.' Beth allowed herself to be pushed down, gently, into the sagging cushions, the muted hubbub of polite conversation from the last few stragglers seeping in from the hall as Tom took them in search of coats and scarves. 'I think I've had more tea these last two days than I normally drink in weeks. I wouldn't mind a drop of brandy, to tell you the truth, but I don't suppose Mum had any spirits in the house. Sherry's all very well, but some occasions just cry out for something a tad stronger.'

'Ah, yes. Always a bottle or two of sherry in this house, that's for sure! The not-so-secret ingredient in your mum's famous trifles. Our Molly was a real pro when it came to trifle. My custard always turns out a bit on the lumpy side, and it tends to get a nasty skin on the top, and I'm never sure whether you're meant to put jelly in or not, but your mum...' Mrs Fellows shook her head, sadly. 'You know, I don't think I've ever been in this house for any sort of celebration without seeing an enormous bowl of trifle in the middle of the table. In fact, this is the first time...'

'Well, today's not exactly a celebration, is it?' Beth knew she sounded harsh, but this was a funeral, not a party. 'And Mum's not here anymore to make it.'

'Of course.' The old lady backed away, head down as if she were showing a sudden interest in the carpet. 'I didn't mean any offence. Just remembering, that's all. She was a lovely cook, and a lovely woman. Now, let me go and see if I can find that drop of brandy for you, shall I? There may be some stashed away for Christmas puddings and the like. And I'll do the washing up too, before I go. You must be tired, and it will save you the bother.'

'I'm sorry, Mrs Fellows.' Beth put out her hand and stopped her from leaving. 'I'm just on edge today. Obvious reasons, I suppose.'

'That's perfectly understandable, and I've told you before, Beth dear, to call me Hetty. I like to think of us as friends.'

'Of course. And I can't thank you enough for all you've done today, and for Mum these past months. I know I should have done more but I just haven't been able to spend as much time here in Shelling as I would have liked. What with the distance, and work, and Tom just starting at university, and...' She stopped, not wanting to say too much more. It was all still so new and frightening. 'And now we've got Christmas to get through, without her. And there's still all the sorting out to do. Mum's clothes, the furniture, all the photos and ornaments...'

'Don't worry about that now. You have your own lives to lead, and I've been only too happy to step in. And will do again, if you need me to help out in any way. We were great friends, your mum and me; even more so since we've been widowed. I mean, who else could we call on for a bit of backup once we'd lost our menfolk? A jar we couldn't open, a bit of shopping if one of us was out of sorts, a vase of flowers from the garden to brighten the place up, a shoulder to cry on from time to time... In sickness and in health, as they say. That counts just as much among friends as it does in a marriage. Of course, I was here for her, and I know, if things had been the other way round, she would have done exactly the same for me.'

'Thank you.' Beth patted the seat beside her. If only she had had a friend like that to prop her up when Sean went, but she mustn't complain. She had the children and, somehow, they had all managed to keep each other going. 'Please, Hetty, sit down for a while. Leave the washing up. And the booze. It'll only give me a headache anyway, and I have to drive back tomorrow.'

The old lady lowered herself down next to Beth, rubbing at her arthritic knees. She pulled a hankie out from her sleeve and dabbed at her eyes. 'I will miss her dreadfully, but I suppose at our age we can't expect to live forever...'

'Nonsense. You've got years in you yet.'

'I wish that were true, dear.'

Beth smiled and leant in closer, dropping her voice. 'I was hoping to have a quiet chat with you actually, before Emily comes back from her walk.'

'Poor little mite. I can't say I blame her for wanting a bit of time away from all this. She's taken it hard, hasn't she?'

'I think it's all the black clothes, and actually seeing the coffin, you know? It's made it all very real. They were very close, her and her gran. But she's not such a little mite anymore. Hard to believe she's fifteen.' Beth gazed out across the room, remembered images popping into her mind. The children here, when they were younger, their heads bent over the old dining table as they did a jigsaw together on a big wooden tray; in their pyjamas, reading in the big armchair by the fire; toddler Emily scribbling away with her crayons or carefully pulling a comb through her gran's thick grey curls... 'They grow up so fast.'

'They do indeed. So, what was it you wanted to talk to me about, dear?'

Beth glanced towards the doorway, but everyone seemed to have gone now. Only the family remained, although they had all made themselves scarce. Jack had driven off straight after the service, reluctant to miss his shift at the hospital early the next morning, Emily was still out walking, and Tom was already back upstairs, probably texting or Skyping or whatever it was he and his girlfriend did whenever they'd been apart for more than an hour or two. No Mum now. And no Sean, who hadn't even made the effort to turn up for the funeral of the woman who had been his mother-in-law for a quarter of a century. Despite the divorce, a part of her had still thought that he might appear at some point during the day, but things had not been amicable by the end, and it was a long way to come...

At that moment, her family felt so much smaller than it ever had before.

'Well, I'm not sure whether you can help or not, but you'd known Mum for a long time, hadn't you?'

'Oh, yes, we've been friends since long before you were born.' Hetty wiped her eyes with a screwed-up cotton hankie she had pulled from her apron pocket. 'We moved to the village within weeks of each other. Both newlyweds, both in need of someone to have a bit of a chinwag with while our husbands were at work. Women didn't tend to go out to work back then. Our job was to keep our homes spick and span, to cook a nice meal for when the men came home in the evenings, to look after the kiddies when they came along. I know this old house almost as well as I know my own, the times I've spent in it.'

'I didn't want to raise this before, while she was alive.' Beth paused, not really sure that she wanted to raise it even now, but she knew that if she didn't, she probably never would. 'I didn't want to hurt her feelings or make her think for a minute that she wasn't...' She lowered her voice. 'Wasn't enough, if you know what I mean.'

'I'm not sure that I do, dear. What exactly is it that you're asking me?'

'I know that you must know things about... well, about the past, *my* past. Those early days, when I first came here, when I was a child.'

'Yes, of course. As if it were yesterday. A sweet little thing you were too.'

'Then, I suppose what I'm asking is... if you can help me to find my mother. My *other* mother...'

TWO

Geraldine Payne gazed at herself in the mirror on the bedroom wall and adjusted her hat. Was it a bit pretentious, wearing such a big feathery thing? It might be all right for younger women to pull out all the stops on their wedding day, with their flowing lace veils and floor-skimming white dresses and trains that reached back halfway down the aisle, but this really wasn't that kind of a wedding. She was in her sixties, for heaven's sake! And wearing a nice just-below-the-knee cream suit, with a hint of a shimmer through the thread, and a row of heart-shaped pearl buttons down the front. Not to mention the satin high heels that had cost almost as much as her whole outfit had the first time around, and that she already knew would be giving her poor feet hell by the end of the day. But the hat... well, there was something extra special about wearing a posh hat and, no matter how old she was, she had to concede that today was certainly going to be special.

'How are you doing, Geri?' Ruby had appeared behind her, a newly manicured hand resting on her shoulder, their two faces now reflected back, side by side in the glass. It didn't seem so long ago that Geraldine had been preparing for Ruby's own wedding to her son Michael. She had bought a hat then too, a big extravagant blue affair, and had been bursting with excitement and anticipation and plans, but the wedding had never happened. Cold feet might have been understandable, but Michael's reluctance to go ahead with it had turned out to be more warm bed related, and that bed had not been Ruby's.

Still, things had worked out all right in the end. What could she do but forgive? Michael was her son, and a grown-up, and she knew it was not her place to tell him what to do or who to love. She had to admit that, despite her early misgivings, he seemed happy enough with Patsy, whom he had recently married, quietly and without family or fuss, on a foreign beach, so at least poor Ruby's nose had not been rubbed in it, even if it had meant their daughter Lily not being there either. But none of that had stopped Ruby from remaining just as much a part of the family as she ever would have been if she had become her real-life official daughter-in-law. Probably more so, since Ruby had left London and come back down to Brighton to help with the running of the shop, and she and little Lily had moved in with her.

'Ready to go?' Ruby smiled at her.

Geraldine nodded. 'As I'll ever be.'

'The cars are here.'

'I'd better come down then, hadn't I? Are the other bridesmaids ready?'

'Yep. Patsy's looking super-glam as ever, and Lily must have been to the loo at least three times since breakfast, she's so excited, but we're all set.'

'I do feel a fraud, you know. All this fuss, at my age. Three bridesmaids! I only had one at my first wedding, and we had the reception in a chilly church hall and travelled there in my dad's old Mini. It was all I could do to squeeze my dress into the back, let alone make room for Ken.'

'Well, things are different this time. I can't see William making do with a church hall, or driving some old banger. He wants to spoil you, and I don't blame him. You deserve the best.'

Geraldine turned and wrapped her arms around Ruby. 'Thank you. It is rather nice travelling in style, isn't it? It may only be a register office ceremony this time but it's going to be wonderful, isn't it? Doing it all again. There's something quite unreal about it all. As if I'm dreaming. The outfit, the posh shoes, the flowers...'

'Which reminds me.' Ruby pulled herself out of Geraldine's grasp and opened the small velvet handbag that was swinging from her arm. 'You've got the new hat, the old earrings that were your mum's, and Mrs Castle's pearl necklace will do for the borrowed, but you didn't have anything blue, so this is from me. And Lily, of course.'

'Oh!' Geraldine held out her hands and took the garter Ruby was offering, an instant flush rising in her cheeks despite their covering of newly applied make-up. 'I don't know if this is quite me. It is a bit raunchy, isn't it?'

'Nobody's going to see it, Geri. Except William, of course, and I don't think he's likely to complain.'

'Oh, I suppose you're right. Why not? Today's a day for being bold, isn't it?' She raised one leg up onto the bed and slid the frilly garter over her foot and up past her knee, bringing her skirt back down to cover it. 'Better hope we don't get a gust of wind though.'

'The only wind we're likely to get is from Michael if he eats too much wedding cake.'

Geraldine laughed. 'He'd better not! I must say that this being given away lark does seem a bit outdated these days, especially when it's my own son doing the giving, but I'm quite looking forward to being handed over from one big handsome man to another.'

'Come on then. Let's do it. Your carriage awaits.' Ruby proffered an arm and led her towards the stairs.

'Makes me sound like Cinderella.'

'And why not? Today you shall go to the ball, and dance with your prince.'

'I'm not sure I'd call William a prince. A knight in shining armour maybe. Or a saint, to be taking me on.'

'Oh, do shut up. He's bloody lucky to have you, and we all know it.'

They stood together on the landing, Geri taking a moment to catch her breath, her hand shaking a little as she held on to Ruby's arm.

'Wow, Mum! You look great.' Michael was standing at the foot of the stairs as she came down. He was sporting an unseasonal suntan and wearing a new suit and shiny shoes, and held out his hand, ready to walk her to the waiting limousine.

'So do you,' she said, straightening his tie and fighting back the lump that had suddenly come up in her throat.

'And so do I,' said a small indignant voice, as Lily pushed herself forward, grabbed hold of her frilly pink skirt at each side and did a twirl for her gran.

Everybody laughed as Geraldine bent to hug her.

'Mind my hair!' Lily said, her little face crumpling into a frown as she pushed Geraldine off and rearranged her sparkly tiara.

'Diva!' Michael muttered, and everyone laughed again. 'We put you in a posh dress and you think you can get away with anything.'

'Bridesmaid's prerogative,' Geraldine said, laughing as she planted a quick kiss on the top of Lily's head, careful not to touch the tiara again. Then she took a big deep breath, picked up her bouquet from the hall table, and they all stepped outside.

'I don't know why you chose to get married in October. It's freezing.'

'It's a bit chilly, that's all.' Geraldine gripped her new husband's surprisingly warm hand and shook her head at Michael. 'Hardly freezing, although I suppose it comes down to what you're used to. We can't match Portugal for sunshine, I'm afraid, but you grew up here, remember. A bit of bracing sea air never did you any harm before. You may live over there nowadays but you're still a Brighton boy deep down. You just need to re-acclimatise.'

'Still, a warmer day would have been nice.' Michael gazed longingly across at the sanctuary of the posh hotel where a welcoming bar and a hot meal awaited and tried to huddle inside his suit, slipping his hands into the pockets of his jacket until Patsy gave him a playful slap and made him take them out again.

'You know why we had to change the date, Michael,' Geraldine whispered as soon as William had moved off to stand under a particularly attractive tree for a photo with his best man.

'Agnes?'

'Yes, of course, Agnes. We could hardly go ahead with a big showy wedding so soon after she died, could we? I'm sorry you had to change your flights, but it wouldn't have felt right. William needed some time to grieve for his mum, and to get the practical stuff dealt with.'

'The house, you mean?'

'Well, yes, although that will take time, of course. But the rest of her estate. He was her only child, and her executor. There's been a lot to do. Bank accounts, friends to notify, bills to pay, and some charities she wanted to help. Cats and dogs, mostly. There are still so many boxes of possessions and mementoes, and some legacies to sort out from the will, including a few things she's left to Lily actually. She was always so fond of Lily, ever since the day she and William found her on her own like that...'

She saw Michael wince, the memory of that terrible time, just three years earlier, so obviously still raw. Ruby going out just for a few minutes and having that awful accident, his own long-term absence, that awful fear of what might have happened to little Lily if William and his mother had not discovered her in time, all alone in the flat. She knew exactly how he felt because she still felt the same way herself, even now. Guilty. Ruby had been struggling in London since Michael had left her, coping alone with too little money and trying to look after a child when she had been hardly more than a child herself. She had needed help, from both of them, and they should have done so much more. It should never have taken a spell in a hospital bed to make them see that.

'But this isn't the time to talk about any of that. It all turned out okay, didn't it?' Geraldine looked over at Lily, prancing about on the grass, having no trouble at all being the centre of attention. 'Better than okay. They're both safe now, and happy. And you coming for the wedding now meant you could be here while Lily's at home for half term, and for her birthday too. So much nicer than a video call and a present in the post.'

'I'll assume that was meant as a slap on the wrist. But you do know I'll always try to be here for her when I can, don't you? Lily is very important to me. It's just getting time off work...'

'Oh, I know. But this time you managed to kill two birds with one stone, didn't you?'

'Yes, it's been great. A birthday cake and a wedding cake within days of each other. Definitely worth flying over for!'

Geraldine laughed. 'You and your belly! You'll be a great fat lump by the time you're forty. Still, it's hard to believe Lily's six already. She's growing up so fast. Such a shame Agnes isn't here to share in any of it, but this is a day for celebrations. Much as we all miss Agnes, it's not a day for mourning.'

'You're right.' Michael made a big show of lifting his sleeve and looking at his watch. 'And, by the way, it's not morning.' He winked at her, back to his usual cheeky-chappie self as his eyes gleamed with merriment. 'It's afternoon!'

THREE

B eth had always known she was adopted. She could only vaguely remember the day her parents had first sat her down and started to explain, when she was probably about four years old. It had all been so casually introduced, and told in such simple but loving language. About her being extra special, because they had wanted her so badly, and waited for her, and chosen her. She had imagined a long line of babies, like dolls on a toyshop shelf, and her parents-to-be walking along, peering at each one, perhaps picking it up or prodding it, until they had reached her and instantly known, before they had even held her, that she was the one. There were no secrets, no shame, just a matter-of-fact approach in the telling of how her life with them had begun, for which she would always be grateful.

There had been other conversations like that over the years, little bits of information dripped in, as Beth got older and more able to understand. About their own failed attempts to conceive a baby naturally, an early miscarriage, the years of waiting for a miracle that she herself had become. Nothing about it felt unusual or upsetting or strange, although once she was at school with friends who had families of their own, it did occur to her that what her parents had told her was true. She *was* special, or at least different. There were other children who had older parents like hers, some with no brothers or sisters, one or two from broken homes, but she didn't meet any who were adopted, or who knew that they were anyway.

It was only as she entered her teenage years that Beth began to realise that there were secrets involved after all, that there were gaps in the story, bits that had never been explored or explained, bits that her adoptive parents may perhaps have found too upsetting to talk, or even to think, about. It was quite possible, of course, that they had never been given the full details, or that they had chosen not to know, but still the niggling doubts crept in. Where had she come from? Who were her natural parents? Her *real* parents? Why had she been given away? Did they not love her? Want her? The more she pondered these questions, the more she shied away from the possible answers. Whoever they were, whatever their reasons, they had walked away from her, hadn't they? Turned their backs. Abandoned her. But, in doing that, they had brought a new mum and dad into her life, and it was they who had given her a loving home, the sort of life and future she might not otherwise have had.

The more she thought about it, the more she had told herself it might be best not to dig too deeply. Her past was gone, never to be remembered. She had been just a tiny baby. This life was all she knew, and why risk hurting the two people who had wanted her so badly, and chosen her, and made her feel special? They didn't deserve to be upset, or made to feel that what they had given her was somehow lacking or second best. No, she couldn't do that to them, and certainly not to satisfy some occasional inexplicable yearning to find out who her first parents had been, and therefore who she herself might be.

She sat alone, on the night of the funeral, after Hetty

Fellows had finally gone. She felt overwhelmingly tired, yet knew she would not be able to sleep, so she lay back against the cushions and let the familiar sounds of the old house she had grown up in envelop her. The clock above the fireplace ticking, the dying crackle of the fire that her son Tom, with his still boyish love of messing about with matches and logs and scrunched up newspaper, had busied himself lighting just before they'd set off for the church, and the occasional drip from the leaky kitchen tap as water bounced into the washing-up bowl in the sink. A floorboard creaked on the landing as one of the kids went to the bathroom, the same board her teenaged self had learned to step over on the nights she had crept in late and hoped not to be heard.

She was going to miss her mum so much. The wisdom, the warmth, even the trifles! It was the end of an era, and the sale of the house, when it came, would break her bond with this village forever. There would be no need to come back to Shelling after that, not now that both her parents were gone. Her real life was miles away in London these days. Her job at the bank, her friends and workmates, Emily's school. She almost included Sean in the list, but Sean too, of course, was gone. The aftershock of their divorce, just a year ago, and the huge financial strain as she had battled and failed to hang on to her family home, still hung over her some days, like a big dark cloud not quite ready to burst. At least, once her mum's estate was wound up, there would be some inheritance money to ease the burden. She could move out of her small rented place, which was only ever meant to be a stopgap anyway, and find somewhere to buy, a proper home for herself and the kids, somewhere she could really call her own again. But money was just money, when it came down to it. There were bigger, more important things to worry about now.

It was at times like this that needing to know more about her past, her roots, her blood, suddenly seemed to matter, in a way they never had before. Hetty had tried to help her, but her memories revolved around what had happened after she, baby Beth, had arrived. Her mother and father's obvious happiness at bringing this new scrap of a thing home after years of trying for a baby of their own, pretty pink blankets that Hetty and Molly had crocheted together, the big solid second-hand pram, the rows of nappies hanging outside on the line. Steering her back to what went before had proved fruitless. Yes, she remembered that Molly and Arthur had been off to meet with an agency of some kind, talked about a mother and baby home where there might be a child for them, wrung their hands with worry and waited for news... It was all vague and lacking in detail, no real help at all.

'I think your birth mother came from somewhere down south,' was the best she could get, after as much gentle pushing as she felt was appropriate, given that they were both still sitting in their funeral clothes and her poor mum was hardly cold in her grave. 'Not a local. She came up here to Norfolk to stay with a relative, I think, before the birth, hence her being in that nursing home place for a while, but she was expected to go back soon after. I always assumed she was young and unmarried, you know, a schoolgirl possibly, sent away in disgrace, that kind of thing, but they weren't given much information back then, your mum and dad. I don't believe they ever met the girl, or even knew her name. They were just given a little box of keepsakes and suchlike, things to show you when you grew up.'

'But they never did, Hetty. They never showed me anything.'

'Never found the right time, maybe? And the more time went by the harder that would have got. I don't know, love. Sometimes it can be easier to let go of the past. They wanted you to be theirs, if you know what I mean. Not to share you with some shadowy person none of you knew anything about. That's why I think they liked the idea of that bit of distance between them and the natural mother, the fact that she lived miles away, you know, just in case...'

'What? She turned up at the door wanting me back?'

'Oh, I don't think that could ever have happened, dear. Even in those days, things were done properly. Legally, I mean. Once they brought you home, or a while later anyway, once the courts had done their thing, you were theirs, papers all drawn up and rubber-stamped, here to stay. But at least they knew they wouldn't be bumping into the mother by accident.'

So, she'd come from the south. The south was a big place. But it could have been London, couldn't it? For all she knew, she might have passed her own mother in the street once, twice, a hundred times, without knowing it. She could have met her, spoken to her. She was being silly, of course. What were the chances...? Still, there was so much she didn't know. Was her birth mother even still alive? Or her father? And what if there were brothers and sisters that she knew nothing about? And who quite possibly knew nothing about her either.

Beth closed her eyes. It was already gone midnight, and she was almost too tired to drag herself up the stairs to bed. And, with the children taking over the other rooms, that meant sleeping in her mother's room, in her mother's bed, which perhaps should have felt comforting but somehow just felt wrong.

Still, somewhere in this house she felt sure the answers to her own beginnings must be lurking. The mysterious box of keepsakes Hetty remembered, for a start. Where was it, and what might be inside? And why had she never been shown it before? There must be documents too... the kind that would accompany any adoption. Perhaps not her mother's name – she was sure Hetty was right and her parents would never have been told that – but a clue, at least, to where she should start looking if she had any hope at all of finding it out for herself. But nowadays, of course, there was the internet. You could find out almost anything from the internet. Maybe that's where she should start.

Was it the right time to start digging? She knew she should have been grieving the loss of her mum, clinging to her children, rebuilding their lives after Sean's departure, not trying to find a long-lost anonymous family she knew nothing about. But she also knew, deep down, that it had to be now. She had put her questions off for long enough, not wanting to upset her mum or burden her with the weight of her own problems. As if worrying about the divorce and its effect on her grandchildren, and watching her only daughter trying to hang on to enough money to live, hadn't been bad enough for a frail old woman to cope with. No, there were some things Beth felt she'd really had no choice but to keep to herself, but now the time had come. The clock inside her was ticking and this couldn't be put off any longer. She'd spoken to Hetty, and she would find the keepsake box, and the papers, and then... She would finally try to find her other mother, and maybe even discover a whole extended family. They might not want to know her, and they certainly might not want to help her – it was such a big thing she was going to have to ask – but she'd never know unless she tried.

Beth hadn't admitted it until now, not even to herself, but she was scared. Not scared of what her past might hold, but of the big empty unknown space stretching out in front of her that was her future.

FOUR

Geraldine eased herself out from under William's arm and rolled onto her back. The hotel bed was big and warm, a modern version of a four-poster, and she lay for a few moments just gazing up at the elaborate swathes of cloth that were draped artistically over the carved wooden frame above her head, smiling at the discarded blue garter that hung, like a tossed hoopla ring at the fair, at a jaunty angle over the corner of a chair.

She looked across at William, lying beside her, snoring gently. They had really done it. Got married. Said the words in front of all their friends and family, eaten and drunk and laughed and danced, then crept away, while the party carried on without them down below, to this magnificent room, to enjoy the silence and the privacy, and each other. She was sixty-five but she felt like a naughty teenager, sneaking off for a bit of clandestine fun.

The morning after the night before! She was no longer Geraldine Payne, widow. She was Geraldine Munro, wife. It was going to take some getting used to, but this was the start of a whole new phase in her life. A proper retirement at last, and someone – exactly the right someone – to share it with. With Ruby now running the shop for her, and Lily at school all day, there would be time for all the things she really wanted to do. Days when they could just go out, wherever the fancy took them, find a nice pub, have a meal, perhaps come back and walk on the beach or potter about in the garden. It had never felt quite right doing those things alone. And, while William's mother had still been alive, there had always been that need to include her in their plans, or at least to get back early, to check on her. Responsibility. Duty. The maintaining of separate homes, and trying to live between the two. All of that was behind them now. William had packed up most of his own stuff within days of his mother's death and more or less moved in with her. She felt a twinge of guilt, as if Agnes's passing had come as some kind of relief, the lifting of a burden that had somehow set them free, when in fact the sadness of her loss still hung over both of them with no prospect of it disappearing any time soon. But there was no denying that they could do what they liked now, go where they liked. Together.

'Morning, Mrs Munro.' William opened his eyes and reached for her hand. 'Shall we ring for some breakfast? Eggs? Avocado on toast? A little caviar?'

Geraldine leaned over and kissed him. 'Breakfast in bed? You old romantic, you! But it'd probably all be cold by the time they wheeled it up here in the lift. And just think of the crumbs in the sheets...'

'Or we could go down to the dining room and rough it with the plebs?'

'Actually, I think I'd prefer that. A little table for two, by the window. The smell of fresh croissants. A chance to flash my new ring at the waiters.'

'Your wish is my command. We might even see Michael and Patsy, if they're up and about already. He's not one to miss out on a big fry-up if there's one on offer! But, a nice hot shower first? Or a bubbly bath? Might as well take advantage of what's on offer before we have to check out. There's some lovely looking creamy stuff in a posh bottle in there. I had a sniff of it last night. Magnolia and chamomile. And a stack of huge fluffy towels.'

'Mmm, lovely! But there's no hurry, is there?'

'None at all. Breakfast is served until ten and we have the room until eleven. Tea?' He nodded towards the tray, laden with a kettle and cups and little sachets of every kind of tea and coffee imaginable.

'I'd love one.'

'Well, if you won't eat in bed, at least stay there for your cuppa. Plump up the pillows, and I'll look outside the door and see if they've remembered to leave that newspaper I ordered.' William was out of bed and pulling on the complimentary gown he'd found hanging in the wardrobe. 'Want the telly on?'

'Well, this is the life. If this is what marriage is going to be like, I wish we'd done it sooner.'

'I can't promise four-posters and posh toiletries every day of the week, but today is not just any old day, is it?' He retrieved the paper from the carpet in the corridor and closed the door, picking up his glasses from the bedside table and slipping them on. 'Today is the first day of the rest of our lives, and I will be spoiling you rotten, whether you like it or not.'

'I do like it. Very much. Now, how big is that bath?'

He peered into the bathroom. 'Are you thinking what I'm thinking, Mrs Munro?'

'Room for two?'

'Definitely!'

They positioned their cups of tea side by side on the ledge in the corner of the bath and eased themselves down into the soft foamy water, William insisting on taking the taps end, their knees bent up, hers tucked neatly between his hairier ones.

'Look at that. You're getting me all hot and bothered!' he joked as his glasses quickly steamed up and he had to take them off.

'Here, let me take those.' Geraldine balanced them behind her tea and let out a contented sigh. 'It's years since I've shared a bath.' She ran her hands through the bubbles and slowly smoothed them over her arms.

'I don't think I ever have.'

'Really? Not with Susan?'

'She wasn't that sort of a wife.'

'That's a shame.'

'Doesn't matter now, does it? All in the past. I have myself a new wife now, and I've no complaints so far!'

Geraldine laughed. 'Glad to hear it.'

They both sat quietly for a while, eyes closed, neither able to find the room to lie down but relishing the closeness and the warmth. 'Would you like me to wash your hair?'

'I'd love you to wash my hair. Not sure anyone's ever done that before either. I'm not counting being at the barber's, obviously.'

'Your mum must have, surely?'

'Well, yes, but a very long time ago. A quick rub with a bar of carbolic, when I was a kid.'

'I don't believe that for a minute.' Geraldine trickled shampoo into her palm and massaged it over his head. 'She always struck me as being a very loving, caring mother.'

'Only joking. But, yes, she was. The best...'

'It's okay to be sad, you know. I was only thirteen when my mum died. It's so long ago now, but there's still a gaping great hole in my life where she's supposed to be.'

'It really affected you, didn't it? Losing her so young?' He gazed at her; his voice lowered. 'It's not surprising that you...'

Geraldine put her fingers to his lips to stop him saying more. 'Sssh. Let's not go there. Not today. I wish I'd never told you now.'

'Why? No secrets, remember? We all make mistakes; all do things we wish we hadn't. Even boring old me.'

'It was more than fifty years ago, and I just prefer not to think about it anymore, that's all.'

'Sorry. I shouldn't have mentioned it. What's done is done, Geri. We can't forget our past, and we shouldn't, but we can't go back either, can we?'

'No, and I wouldn't want to. As long as she's happy somewhere, with people who love her...'

'I'm sure she is.'

'I'm glad you didn't know me back then. I was a mess... lashing out, answering back, refusing to do anything I was told. My poor dad. As if he didn't have enough to cope with after Mum died, without me going off the rails. I must have been a bloody nightmare.'

'You were grieving, just as much as he was. Just in a different way.'

'Being young's not all it's cracked up to be, is it?'

'God, no! I'd go for experience any day, and a good dose of common sense. We may not be as young as we were, but that doesn't matter. Onwards and upwards, right? Good times ahead. We have time now, to do anything we choose. And, once we sell Mum's house, we'll have the money to go with it.'

'It wasn't just hers though, was it? You bought it together. Are you really sure you don't want to keep it? I could move in there with you, if you wanted me to.'

'No, Geri. It's served its purpose, hasn't it? It wasn't our family home, after all. I didn't grow up there. It doesn't have years of memories attached. It was the right house at the right time. It was a solution for us both. It got us out of London and it gave Mum some independence, having her own space, but still knowing I was there upstairs if she needed me... but I don't want to be there anymore. Half a house. Or a whole house, now she's left her share to me. Makes no difference. You have a lovely home that I know full well you don't want to trade for my ramshackle old place. You want to stay put, and I want to be with you, so your house it is. End of discussion!'

'Even if that means living with Ruby and Lily? I really can't ask them to leave.'

'We've been through this, Geri my love, and I wouldn't expect you to. Or want you to! I love them, almost as much as I love you. One big happy family, right?'

'Right.'

'And Ruby's only twenty-five. She has plenty of time, no rush while she has the shop and little Lily to fuss over, but she'll meet someone and want to set up her own home one day. It's what she deserves. Happiness. But only when she's ready. I will not be chasing her out of the house, believe me.'

'I know. I just wanted to be absolutely sure you're happy.'

'Never happier.'

'Good.' She cupped some water in her hands and dribbled it over his soapy hair. 'That needs proper rinsing. I'll get out now and let you duck under.'

'Trying to drown me already?'

'Never! Just hungry. Come on. Let's get dressed and go in search of eggs, shall we?' She wriggled about, trying to get her footing. 'I just might need a bit of help climbing out. I'm so wedged in, there'll probably be a tsunami when I finally manage it. A hippo rising out of the mud comes to mind.'

He hooked a blob of foam onto his finger and plonked it gently on the end of her nose, laughing as she rested her hands on his upturned knees, made it to a standing position and clambered over the side, slopping puddles onto the tiled floor.

'The water level's dropped so low without you in here, I'm not sure I'll be able to duck under at all!' He laughed.

'See, I told you. I'm a hippo. Diet starts tomorrow.'

'Don't you dare. I love you just as you are. Every last pound of you.'

***

'Come on, Lily. Help me clean up a bit. Anyone would think your gran had already been gone for a week, the amount of mess we've made!' Ruby ran a cloth over the kitchen table to catch the crumbs and handed Lily the milk. 'Back into the fridge with that, please. And then go and get out of those pyjamas and straighten up your bed before you go and feed Flopsy.'

'Do I have to? Can't you do it today?'

'Your rabbit. Your responsibility. Those were the rules, remember? And it's time you changed his straw. Okay?'

'Okay. I suppose.'

As Lily harrumphed her way back up the stairs, Ruby loaded their cereal bowls into the dishwasher. She, too, was still in her pyjamas. It had been a wonderful wedding, but it had been after midnight when they'd got home and she'd had to carry her daughter in from the taxi, the little girl's weary eyes just forcing themselves open long enough to slip out of her bridesmaid dress and into her Disney princess pyjamas before flopping into bed. It was a good job it was a Saturday. No school, and no shop to worry about either, since Geri had insisted she closed up for a few days to let them all not only prepare for the wedding but relax and recover afterwards too.

Ruby yawned. Ten o'clock and they'd only just had breakfast. Yes, she was tired, but when had she last danced like

27

that? Flinging herself into it, arms waving above her head, really enjoying herself? Even having her ex, Michael, and his wife, Patsy, there in the same room hadn't held her back. It really didn't matter what he thought of her anymore. She had had fun, and so had Lily, swirling around the small dance floor, eating far too much cake and so obviously high on sugar.

She looked around the kitchen. It was a mess. Scraps of stray foliage from the bouquets, unwashed mugs and glasses, an open bottle of bubbly, balled-up tissues smudged with make-up, an empty Smarties tube, and a few wedding cards that had arrived in the post in the middle of yesterday's commotion and had been hastily read and tucked back inside their ripped-open envelopes. There was even a pair of shoes, left lying on their sides under the table, far too pointy-toed and gaudy with their polka-dot pattern to be Geraldine's, so they could only belong to Patsy. All the evidence of a family getting ready for a wedding but not having the time nor the inclination to tidy any of it away before setting off, excitedly, for the ceremony.

Geri and William would probably be home from the hotel soon. Only a flying visit, to 'touch base' as Geri called it, park the car safely on the drive and say their goodbyes, before collecting their already-packed cases and heading off for their honeymoon week in the sun. In fact, that meant Michael and Patsy would be here soon too, as their flight left just after Geri and William's and Michael had offered them a lift to the airport in his hire car.

Ruby grabbed a plastic sack and started picking up all the rubbish. She lifted Patsy's ridiculous high heels and held them over the bag, half tempted to drop them in too, but no doubt, even if Patsy waited in the car outside when they got here, Michael would have been given his orders to retrieve them, so she thought better of it. Besides, she was past playing revenge games. He was with Patsy now, and she was welcome to him.

'Mummy?' Lily was back, in a baggy Mickey Mouse T-shirt and leggings, and was standing in the doorway, watching her. 'Can I ask you something?'

'Of course you can. As long as it's not just to put off having to feed the bunny.'

'No. I said I would, didn't I?'

'I know. Sorry, Lil. So, what's up?'

'Is William my grandad now?'

Ruby stopped what she was doing and pulled her daughter into a hug. 'I hadn't really thought about that. Do you want him to be?'

'I don't know. I think so. But he's not really, is he? Just because he's married to Gran now... It's like when Patsy married Daddy, it didn't make her my mum, did it?'

'Families can be a bit complicated, can't they?' Ruby guided Lily into a chair and sat down opposite her. 'But Patsy... well, that's different. Even though your dad and me aren't living together anymore, nothing changes the fact that I'm your mum and always will be. Patsy's your stepmum, and your godmother too. I know I used to say silly things about wicked stepmothers, but she's okay really, isn't she? You like her. She's nice to you, and that just shows that new people, like Patsy, and William too, can come along and fit right in, so you end up with an even bigger family, who all stick together and look after each other, and love you...'

'I haven't though, have I? Got a big family?'

'Big enough.'

'But Lauren at school has two grannies and two grandads and so many cousins she says she can't remember all their names! And I've only got one gran.' She screwed her forehead into a frown. 'And you and Daddy don't have any brothers or sisters, so I won't ever get to have any aunties or uncles or cousins...'

'Not much I can do about that, honey.'

'But you could have another baby, couldn't you? Then I'd have a sister. That would be heaps better than having cousins.'

'That's not going to happen anytime soon.'

'Why not?'

Ruby stood up and went to the fridge, and poured them both a glass of juice. Why did children ask the most awkward questions? 'I'd need a husband first, wouldn't I?'

'So you could have a wedding and I could be a bridesmaid again?' Her eyes lit up with excitement. 'And then I'd have a stepdad as well as a stepmum? That would be good, wouldn't it? More family, to love me?'

'Well, yes, I suppose it would. But, Lily, I can't just marry any old person, can I? Just to have a baby. Which could just as easily be a boy baby, by the way!'

'I didn't mean just any old person, Mummy. He would have to be a nice person. Like Daddy.'

'Yes, he would.' Ruby couldn't help but laugh. 'But finding him could take time. And, while we're waiting, yes, I think we could ask William if he'd like you to call him Grandad.'

FIVE

1968

Geraldine's back ached. She turned over, awkwardly, in the narrow bed and pulled the pillow back over her head. No matter how far down beneath the covers she tried to burrow, no matter how much cotton wool she stuffed into her ears, she still heard them. Night after night, the cries of so many babies, other girls' babies, hungry, restless, in need of a nappy or a cuddle or a breast, echoed through the thin plaster of the cream-painted walls. Sometimes there would be the piercing screams of some other poor girl struggling to push another unplanned baby into the world, or the incessant sobs of those who already had. Deeply distressing sounds that she could not escape from, and that kept her from sleeping. Or maybe it was her own thoughts, her own fears, that were doing that?

She had been here for eight days now and she knew it would be her turn soon. She lay a hand on her enormous belly, protruding between the open buttons of her too-small nightie, the skin stretched tight as a drum. There was no kicking tonight, no little butterfly flutters, no movement at all. Perhaps the baby had managed what she herself was failing to do, and had gone to sleep. Or perhaps it had quietly died? Best for everyone maybe if it did.

She gripped Mr Snuggles tightly, instinctively slipping the tip of his worn woolly arm into her mouth for comfort, but it wasn't working. A bear, even one as warm and familiar as Mr Snuggles, just wasn't enough. It was at times like this that she really missed her mum. Those familiar warm arms around her late at night, a quiet chat in the dark, a cup of hot chocolate in the silence of the kitchen, when she'd had a nightmare or a sore tummy or had been scared by some mysterious shadow on the wall. Even now, more than a year after her mum had died, Geraldine would sometimes wake in the night and be just about to call out for her before remembering that she was gone.

Half of her was only too aware that, if her mum were by some miracle here now, she would be the one who knew exactly what to say, what to do, to comfort her and make everything all right, while the other half felt nothing but a horrible sickening shame. Perhaps it was best that her mum hadn't lived to see any of this. After all, how could she possibly love her now, after what she had done? Her dad certainly didn't, or he wouldn't have sent her here, to face this awful terrifying thing all alone. Even his sister, the thin-faced Aunt Ellen, who had reluctantly agreed to take her in for a couple of months, 'until the dust settled' as she had been overheard to say, had washed her hands of her now, handing her over, battered suitcase and all, 'until the deed was done'.

The wooden sign beside the front door, with 'The Ferns' written in plain black lettering, announced this place as a nursing home, but everyone, inside it and out, knew it was nothing of the sort. They were kind enough here, in their practical no-nonsense way, but there was precious little nursing going on, and the plain dormitories, basic washing facilities and functional kitchen resembled nothing that Geraldine had ever called home. It was a holding bay, nothing more. A place for the unmarried and the 'fallen' to give birth, away from prying eyes, stay for as short a time as possible, then hand over their babies to strangers and slip quietly back into their real lives, as if nothing had ever happened. Reputations still intact, even if their bodies were not.

She just wanted it to be over. To close her eyes and not wake up until it was done, the baby delivered, removed, handed over, forgotten... but that wasn't going to happen. There was no sleep, no drug, that could take any of this away. No mother to hold her hand. No magic wand. No escape.

She tried to imagine how it would be. Would hers be the next in a long line of voices screaming into the night? Would she be the next one torn apart as she pushed out this alien thing she had never asked for in the first place? The whole idea of it made her shudder. The pain, the mess, the blood, and then the milk trickling out of her swollen breasts, her insides left empty, her outsides left saggy and sore. She didn't want this. She was fourteen. She had been so stupid. And she had never been so scared in all her life.

SIX

Beth packed the two big cardboard boxes into the boot of her car. It was a bit of a squeeze, on top of her suitcase and the kids' rucksacks, but taking them home to sort through was the only way. She had only taken a couple of days off work and Emily needed to get back for school. Then there was the hospital appointment on Thursday afternoon, when she would know for sure just how bad things were, although she had tried hard not to think too much about that just yet. There just wasn't time to sift through everything before they set off.

Her mum had not been a great hoarder. Not of the unimportant things in life anyway. Some of her clothes were years old, it was true, but they were all things she had continued to wear. One good warm winter coat, two pairs of plain flat lace-up shoes, and a posh pair of cream court shoes for special occasions, a selection of practical knitwear and skirts, her two Sunday best dresses, one solitary pair of elasticated trousers she rarely wore except when gardening, and her old mac and boots, in regular use in the muddy lanes of Shelling and its surrounding countryside whenever the rain came. Just running her hands over them all brought instant memories flooding into

Beth's head, of the many times when she'd seen her mum wearing them. A trace of her favourite lavender cologne lingered in the folds of one of the dresses, as the material rustled and a mint humbug fell from the pocket.

There were a few pieces of jewellery, mostly of no real value, although Beth had made sure her mum's wedding and engagement rings were rescued and were now safely tucked away in her purse. Perhaps Emily would like to have them one day. She'd taken her dad's watch too, although it hadn't worked for years, and an old threadbare knitted rabbit of her own that her parents had hung on to long after she'd grown up and left home. Pinky, she'd called it, which made no sense at all seeing as it was most definitely brown.

Molly Green hadn't been one for hanging on to books or magazines she had already read either, not when Shelling had a perfectly good little lending library that operated out of the new village hall every Wednesday and had provided all the free reading matter she had needed. So, apart from the many framed photos and ornaments, all with their own sentimental story to be told, sorting through her cupboards and deciding what to do with the contents would probably not take all that long, once Beth was able to find a few spare days to come back here and put her mind to the job.

The two battered old boxes were another matter entirely. As soon as she had located them on the top shelf of the wardrobe and blown the layer of dust off the lids, she knew they were the only possible place where she had any hope of discovering what she was looking for. Stuffed to the brim with papers, just a brief glance had told her that these boxes were her parents' equivalent of a filing cabinet. Not that there seemed to be any actual filing system in place, as everything was just jumbled up together, but somewhere here, among the old certificates and bills, the curling black-and-white photos and faded letters, she felt sure the answers must be lurking. If anything had been retrieved from her previous existence, it would be here.

'Got everything?' Beth asked, as her two silent teenagers slammed the car doors and belted themselves into the back. 'Checked upstairs? Toothbrushes? Dirty clothes? Chargers?'

Emily nodded. 'Yep.'

'Sure?' Beth turned her glare on to Tom, already fiddling with his headphones, ready to push the buds into his ears. 'Because I'm not turning around and coming back if you suddenly miss something when we're miles down the road.'

'Chill, Mum. It's all packed, okay? And it's not as if you won't be coming down here again before the house is sold, is it?' Tom raised his eyebrows as if she was being utterly ridiculous. God, he was so like his father sometimes. 'If I've left a pair of socks under the bed, they'll still be there on the next visit. They're not going anywhere by themselves.'

'You haven't, have you?' Beth pulled a disgusted face. 'Just think of the pong!'

Tom laughed. 'Go back in and check if it worries you that much.'

Beth turned the key in the ignition. He was winding her up, she knew that. And he was right, of course. In the grand scheme of things, dirty socks were a long way down the worry list. She put the car into reverse and eased off the small gravel driveway, sending a flurry of tiny stones up into the air, just as Hetty Fellows came bustling out from next door, waving her arms like a windmill.

'So glad to have caught you,' she said, as Beth stopped and wound down the window.

Hetty was wearing the floral apron again, but now it was liberally splattered with flour. 'I made you a little something for the journey,' she said, holding out a small round tin. 'Melting moments, baked fresh this morning. For when you stop off somewhere...'

'Thank you, that's very kind.' Beth took the tin and passed it back to Emily.

'See you soon, I'm sure. No hurry to return the tin. And don't worry about the house. I'll look in every now and then, check for any post, burst pipes, that sort of thing.'

'Thanks, Hetty. And don't worry if you see anyone going in with a key. I've got an estate agent coming to take photos and value the place, before it goes on the market. And he might need to show people around, if we get as far as finding any potential buyers.'

'Is it young Jim from the village?'

'Yes, I thought I'd use a local firm. But young? Are we thinking of the same person? The man I met must be forty-five easily.'

'Oh, once you get to my age, dear, anyone under sixty's young! Still, you'll be all right with Jim and Gloria. Nice couple. Trustworthy. Only been here about fifteen years, so they're village newcomers really, although they do judge the cake competition at the annual show, which I must say I have never won, despite the lightness of my raspberry sponge. Anyway... you could do worse. They're not the sort to rip you off when it comes to their fees, or to sneak in with the key and pinch the silver.'

Beth laughed. 'I think they'd have trouble finding any worth pinching!'

They all waved as the car moved off. Tom had already lifted the lid from the tin and was inspecting the contents. 'Mum, what exactly is a melting moment?'

'No idea.'

'Only one way to find out.' He lifted one out and took a big bite. 'Mmm, not bad actually.'

'Tom! You've only just had breakfast. And those are supposed to be for when we stop.'

'And they're meant to be for all of us,' Emily said, putting her hand into the tin to claim her share.

'How long till we're home?' Tom asked, through a mouthful of crumbs.

'Ugh, stop spitting!' Emily whacked her brother on the arm, almost spilling the contents of the tin on the floor.

'Honestly, you're like a couple of little kids. Just sit quietly and behave, so I can concentrate on the driving. We'll be back when we're back, okay? Depends on the traffic.'

'Want me to check?' Tom flipped open his smartphone and started jabbing at it with his thumbs.

'If you like. Not that it will get us there any quicker.'

'Might do. Nothing like a bit of prior knowledge. Congestion, accidents, alternative routes, and all that. I still say you should get a satnav.'

Beth clicked the radio on and shuffled in her seat, settling into a more comfortable position. It was a long way home but she didn't need a satnav. After all these years, she knew the way like the back of her hand. The country lanes, the shortcuts, the main road home, where to stop for a coffee or a loo. She took a deep breath and closed her eyes, her hands gripping the wheel to keep it steady as they rolled along the familiar stretch of long straight road. She opened them again quickly and breathed out, feeling the calm wash back over her, watching the trees swish past, listening to the tinny remnants of Tom's music seeping through his headphones and the clack of the lid as Emily replaced it on Hetty's cake tin.

It would be a wrench to sell her mum's house and cut all ties with the village she had grown up in, never to have to drive this route again, but she could really do with the money. How much was a little old-fashioned country cottage worth these days? She had no idea, but with luck it would be enough to finally allow her to put her head above water again after the financial strain of the divorce. If her mum had died earlier, before the divorce, or even in the middle of it, Sean would no doubt have wanted to claim a share of the sale proceeds. Marital assets, fifty–fifty, and all that. His hotshot solicitor would have been all over her inheritance like a rash. But it was all hers now. Their settlement had been fair, and final. No going back, no re-negotiating their deal, no second chances.

Her mum had stood strong for her through it all, offering comfort and advice down the phone, and an occasional shoulder to cry on. She may have been well into her eighties and getting unsteady on her feet but she had given every appearance of having years left in her. Had she known how sick she was, and kept it to herself so Beth wouldn't worry? Like mother, like daughter, she thought, with a sigh, taking a glimpse at her kids in the rear-view mirror. Why say anything unless, or until, she really had to?

Still, it was impossible to know what had been going on with her mum's health, without contacting her doctor, trying to get to her medical records, or questioning poor old Hetty again, but what good would it do to delve into any of that now? If her mum had known that she didn't have long left, then she had certainly hidden it well, but when most of their contact in recent months had been down a phone line, perhaps that wasn't so difficult to do. No, it was best to let things lie, to hope that her mum had simply slipped away without the added stress of knowing what was coming. It would have been so like her though, putting Beth first, protecting her inheritance, wanting only the best for her. And Sean had not turned out to be the best. They had both known that in the end.

SEVEN

R uby loved hearing the little bell tinkle as she turned the key and pushed open the door to the shop. Although she had made quite a few changes to *Bits & Bobs* since Geri had handed over the reins, the bell was one thing she knew she would never want to get rid of. It reminded her of her childhood, when Mrs Castle and the rest of the staff at the children's home had taken them all for an outing in the mini-bus and they'd stop off for sweets at their favourite corner shop on the way home. She could still picture the rows of big glass jars filled with acid drops and rhubarb and custards, coconut mushrooms, and gobstoppers so huge you could choke on them if you weren't careful. Wooden shelving and a counter she could barely see over, and always that little tinkling bell whenever another customer came in or went out through the door. Later, she had been back to try to find that little shop but it had long gone, and a modern glass-fronted newsagents', its confectionery shelves lined with mass-produced Mars Bars and rolls of Polo mints, had taken its place. Still, it was memories like that that had given her the idea to add some old-fashioned sweets to their own stock. It was all very well selling seaside souvenirs and postcards, pretty boxes made out of shells, and tea towels with pictures of the pier on them, but what kids really wanted to take home was sugar, pure and simple.

She stowed her bag under the counter and fired up the till. She had two assistants now, although neither were due in until later. Kerry was only twenty-two but had worked for Geri for a long time. She had been one of what they all laughingly called Geri's waifs and strays, in need of a helping hand and someone to give them a chance when nobody else would, and she'd been more than happy to stay on when Ruby took over. She was very much a do-the-job-take-the-money kind of a girl, more interested in enjoying her social life than in harbouring any ambition to move on or better herself.

Then there was the new girl, Leanne, who Ruby had interviewed herself and taken on just four months ago. She knew Leanne wouldn't stay long. She was bright and bubbly, and had passed her A-levels with flying colours but was holding off on going to university for a year or two while she considered her options, whatever that meant. This job was clearly just a stopgap, a chance to gain some work experience and earn some money while she waited, but Ruby was glad to have her, no matter how short her stay.

Ruby liked Leanne and, if there wasn't that awkward employer/employee thing going on, they would very probably have become real friends. In fact, Leanne had been trying to twist her arm for weeks to go out on some kind of double date with her and her boyfriend Dave, plus whichever of Dave's mates happened to be available, or quite possibly desperate, Ruby thought to herself, but she didn't actually say so.

Leanne's circle of male friends would be much too young for her of course, most of them probably still in their late teens, but in truth the thought of dating anyone at all terrified her. Michael had been her first, and her only, boyfriend. They had met when she was barely out of school, her mooning after him like a lovesick puppy, and when she had unexpectedly fallen pregnant with Lily it had sealed them together for far longer than ever would have happened in the normal course of things. He was older than her, cleverer, more confident, and he hadn't loved her, not properly. Yes, they had moved to London together and talked about getting married, but she knew now that, even if a fancy job in Portugal and a fancy girl like Patsy hadn't come along to rock the boat, it could never have worked long term. He had left her and flown off into the sunset, sending cheques she had been too stubborn to cash and occasional demands for access, but he hadn't cared enough to stay and help look after his own daughter day to day, had he? To be there to tuck her in at night, to read her stories, or to buy her new shoes and teddies and Saturday morning ice creams? Could she trust anyone again, after a betrayal like that? And who would want her now anyway, with her troubled past and her car crash scars and a young daughter in tow?

No, if Lily wanted a baby sister or brother, she would have to look to her father and Patsy to produce one. The idea of career-girl Patsy up to her elbows in dirty nappies and covered in milky sick was so ridiculous it made her laugh. That would put an end to her immaculate gel nails and her hours in front of the make-up mirror!

The bell tinkled, signalling her first customers of the day. It was always quiet early in the week, especially once the high season was over. She watched the two women who had come in as they made their way along the narrow aisles, picking up a few bits and putting them down again, then turned her attention to the accounts book she had pulled from the top drawer and settled down to work.

'Excuse me.' The younger of the women had come up to the counter and was hovering expectantly. She was tall and imposing, with big untamed mousey hair, the buttons on her coat straining to hold it together at the front, as if it were a size too small. 'Are you Ruby, by any chance? Ruby Baxter?'

'Yes, I am.' Ruby looked up into a rounded face she did not immediately recognise. 'Do I know you?'

'You may not remember me, but we knew each other as kids. The times I must have passed this shop and never came in! But it is you, isn't it? I recognised you straight away.'

'I don't...' Ruby stopped and stared harder at the girl's pale face. 'Vicky Dunn? Vix? Without the freckles and pigtails but... Wow, I don't believe it! It must be – what? – ten or twelve years since we've seen each other?'

'More like fifteen. It must be, because that's when I left the children's home, when I was adopted. Did you ever...?'

'No. Nobody was fool enough to take me on!' Ruby forced a laugh, but she had seen enough children come and go, off to their forever homes, while she stayed behind, and the truth of it, of not being chosen, still hurt. 'My mum always refused to sign the papers anyway. When she was sober enough to even think about it, of course. Didn't want me herself but wouldn't properly give me up either. I got a family of my own in the end though. One of Mrs Castle's friends took me in when I got too old to stay. Mrs Payne. Or Geri, I call her now. She used to come for tea, help out with finding work for some of the older girls, remember? This is her shop. Well, mine now, technically! She gave me a job and somewhere to live. She's the closest I've got to a real mum these days.'

'Oh, I'm glad. This is my mum, by the way.' Vicky held on to the older woman's arm. 'Well, adoptive mum, obviously. Joyce.'

'Pleased to meet you, love. Vicky's often talked about you. How you shared a room, and played with your dolls together. Betsy, wasn't it?'

Ruby turned to Vicky. 'You remember that? You remember my Betsy?'

'Of course. Those dolls meant a lot, didn't they? Let's face it, we didn't have much else to love, did we? I bet you can't remember my one's name, can you?'

Ruby didn't even have to think about it. 'Lily,' she said, feeling a lump come up into her throat as if she just might cry. 'I always loved that name, but you'd already nabbed it, so I had to make do with calling mine Betsy. Second best.'

'I didn't know that. I'm sorry. You should have said.'

'Oh, I was pretty much used to second best for everything back then. But I did love Betsy. She gave the best cuddles! I wonder what happened to her?'

'You don't know?'

'No. I think maybe my mother took her, threw her away. One day, after she made one of her rare visits, Betsy just disappeared. I couldn't find her anywhere. Never cried so much in my life. She could be cruel like that, my mother. And jealous. But I have a daughter now, Vix, and guess what I called her? Lily. My real-life Lily, and definitely not second best this time. She's six, and the most beautiful, perfect little girl you could ever imagine. And so much more precious than any doll could ever be.'

'Oh, wow, that's wonderful. So, are you married? Living with...?'

'No, I was with Geri's son for a while but he left. Married someone else.'

'I'm sorry.'

'Don't be. We're okay, Lily and me. Better than okay. How about you?'

'Oh, still single and fancy-free. Well, who'd want to take me on, eh?' She laughed. 'No, I share a flat with a couple of other girls these days, but I'm only a bus ride away. Mum's still here in

Brighton though, so I'm often about. I don't suppose you fancy a proper catch-up, do you? A night out some time? Drinks, maybe? Or a burger or something, if you want to bring Lily along. I'd love to meet her.'

Ruby hesitated. Did she really want to drag it all up again, relive those times? But Vicky had been a good friend back then, and it would be nice to have someone her own age to talk to for a change. She had got friendly with Laura, one of the nurses she'd met in hospital when she'd been in London, but she rarely got the chance to meet up with her nowadays. In fact, she had been spending far too much time lately either here in the shop or surrounded by pensioners and children, with very little in between. Even the mothers at the school gates seemed like alien beings sometimes, gathering in their little cliques, the stay-at-homes hanging about in their jogging bottoms, chatting as if they had nothing much to do for the rest of the day, while the rest, like her, hurried wordlessly away to work as soon as their kids had disappeared into the playground.

'Yeah, okay, why not?'

'I'll give you my number and we'll sort something out. At the weekend maybe? Or whenever you can manage it.' She took the mobile that Ruby held out to her and skilfully navigated her way to the contacts list where she tapped in her number. 'Here, ring me now, then I'll have yours.'

Ruby nodded and did as she was told, watching as Vicky quickly rejected the incoming call and saved the number.

'I'll take a quarter of barley sugars before we go,' Vicky's mum said, pointing to one of the glass jars, and Ruby quickly bagged them up, waving the woman's hand away as she reached for her purse. 'On the house,' she said, coming out from behind the counter and accepting the loose hug that Vicky pulled her into. Vicky's coat might be badly-fitting but it was warm and furry, and she smelled vaguely of grass. Ruby couldn't decide if it was some kind of perfume or the real thing.

'Lovely seeing you,' Vicky said, the little bell tinkling again as they opened the shop door and stepped out into the wind.

'You too.'

'Is Granny in Spain now?' Lily sat at the kitchen table, swinging her legs, her feet still unable to reach the floor.

'Yep. Enjoying all that sun and sea and...' Ruby stopped herself from saying the next word that leapt into her mind, quickly pushing away the thought of Geri and William having sex. Ugh, no! Much as she loved them both, they were over sixty and the mental image was not a pretty one. 'Lots of sand,' she added, picking up Lily's empty plate and taking it to the sink.

'But we've got sea and sand here.'

'Maybe not the sunshine though, eh? Not in October. And they'll be in a lovely hotel, remember, with a big pool, and dancing, and someone else to cook their food and make the beds.'

Lily sat silently for a moment, as if pondering the possibilities. 'Is it near where Daddy lives? Because Daddy has lots of sun and sea and sand too.'

And sex too probably, Ruby thought, trying hard not to. 'Yes, he does, but he's in Portugal, and Portugal's not the same country, Lil.'

'Can we go? You and me? To a hotel with a big pool and someone to make the beds for us? And to see Daddy?'

'Lily, you've only just seen Daddy. Maybe one day, when the warmer weather comes and there's no school, we can sort it out for you to go and stay with him again, when Daddy's got some time off from his job.'

'But I want you to come too.'

'I don't think that's a very good idea, honey. Me and Daddy aren't... well, we're not best friends anymore, and it's nice for you to spend time with him and Patsy, isn't it? I know they love having you there, and they spoil you something rotten. You needed an extra big case last time just to bring all the presents home with you.'

'I suppose.'

'But you're right. You and me should have a holiday together somewhere, just the two of us. But not Portugal, okay?'

'Spain then.'

'I'll think about it, Lil. Let's see Granny's photos when she gets back, and hear all about it before we decide though, okay?'

Lily nodded, digging her spoon into the mound of ice cream Ruby had just put in front of her.

'Can I have strawberry sauce?' Lily looked up, spoon hanging in the air, a vanilla moustache already imprinted around her mouth. 'And sprinkles?'

Oh, how easy it is to distract them at this age, Ruby thought, as all mention of Spain and Daddy and fantasy holidays she probably couldn't afford disappeared into the ether. If only all life's worries could be so easily pushed aside by a big bowl of ice cream.

EIGHT

Beth had been so busy in the days since they'd got back from the funeral that the boxes of paperwork she'd rescued from her mum's wardrobe still lay unopened in the corner of the bedroom. She knew she had been putting off looking through them. Perhaps tonight, when she got home, she could make a start.

Her appointment was not until three thirty but she'd asked for the whole afternoon off work. Sitting worrying as the time to leave the bank approached would not be any good for her concentration, and making mistakes when handling large sums of other people's cash was not generally a very good idea. She pulled on her coat at lunchtime and stepped out through the huge wooden double doors and into the bustling street, taking a big deep breath of damp, chilly air. It was only just November but already some of the shops were preparing their Christmas displays, and she wondered if maybe she should start picking up a few bits early to ease the pressure once the serious Christmas shopping began.

No, she couldn't quite get into the Christmas spirit just yet, not while this big niggling fear hung over her, but there was time to wander for a while, grab a sandwich and a coffee somewhere before heading home to get ready. What exactly did getting ready entail though? A quick shower, a change of clothes, making sure she had loose change for the hospital car park, stuffing her appointment card into her bag. The real preparation lay in sorting things out inside her own head and she wasn't at all sure she had done anywhere near enough of that.

At first, she had put her tiredness and headaches down to the stress at home, the arguments, the awkward nights perched silently on opposite sides of the bed, the inevitable decision to divorce. Sean had not made things easy, and the negotiations and squabbles and toing and froing of solicitors' letters had dragged on for much longer than she had expected. Sean could be very stubborn when he wanted to be. So could she, to be honest. It was only natural that she should feel ill, wasn't it? She'd been having trouble sleeping, which didn't help, but who wouldn't lie awake into the small hours with so much going on in their mind? And she had lost her appetite lately too. For life, as well as food. With a head full of form-filling and finances and failure, how was she supposed to sit back and enjoy either her food or herself? She couldn't remember the last time she'd been out to a restaurant or fancied a juicy steak. If it wasn't for having to cook for Emily, she probably would have settled for beans on toast most nights, just to save all that effort. Besides, the loss of weight that came from eating less could only be a good thing, couldn't it? She'd been meaning to shed a few pounds for ages, so at least something good had come out of the whole sorry business.

It had been Emily who had insisted she go to the doctor. Emily, who she should have been taking care of through all the mess of her broken marriage and beyond, was suddenly the one taking care of *her*. 'You don't look right, Mum,' she'd said, her forehead crinkling into a worried frown. 'You look tired. In fact, even your skin looks tired! Get a check-up, please. For me.' And so Beth had done just that, if only to keep her daughter happy.

It was amazing what doctors could tell about a person just from a few drops of blood. What was working well, and what wasn't. What her body was short of, and what it wasn't. A hospital appointment had followed, and then another, and the news, when it finally came, had not been good. But she hadn't told Emily that. Hadn't told anybody at all. For months now, she had plastered a happy face on, said she was just a bit run-down and in need of some vitamins, and buried her head in the sand. Until today.

'Ah, Mrs Hogan.' The doctor was wearing a white coat and small frameless glasses. He half stood as she came into the room and held out his hand, directing her to sit down opposite him at the desk, upon which was an open file. *Her* file. 'How have you been, since we last spoke? Feeling any better?'

Beth nodded, but it wasn't true. She knew it, and so did he.

'Have you had a chance to read the leaflets I gave you last time? I know it's a lot to take in, but forewarned is forearmed, I always think. There's a lot of information about CKD out there, and support of course. Just avoid trawling the internet, if you can help it. You'll only frighten yourself unnecessarily. Try to stick to the NHS site if you're tempted to search, and the recognised kidney charities. They know what they're talking about. Facts, not scaremongering.'

'I just keep asking myself why.' Beth looked him straight in the eyes, hoping for an answer she knew he wouldn't be able to give. 'Why me? Nothing I've read really tells me that. I mean, is this something I've caused myself, by my diet, or my lifestyle?

I'm not overweight and I don't drink all that much. I'm not diabetic. Well, you know I'm not because that was one of the blood tests, wasn't it? My blood pressure's high, admittedly, but I put that down to the divorce. It's why I went to my GP in the first place. Stress, not sleeping well...'

'Try not to overthink it, Mrs Hogan. Beth...'

'I just don't get it, that's all. That there's a part of me that's just decided to stop working properly. I mean, why? And why now? Was there anything I could have done differently, to prevent it, or anything I can do to slow things down or stop it now that it's started? Or is it...' She stumbled, her mind flipping back to that box of old papers awaiting her in the bedroom at home. 'Is it something I could have inherited?'

'Beth, we talked about all this last time you were here. Certain types of kidney disease can be passed on. Polycystic, or PKD, for instance, where cysts form on the kidneys, but symptoms would normally have shown themselves long before now, and your CT scan showed no sign of cysts, so that's not the case here. I thought you understood...'

'I thought so too, but it's all so much to take in and somehow it doesn't feel real yet. I think I'm probably in denial or something like that. Disbelief...'

'That's not uncommon. This is a chronic, ongoing, condition, but there are often very few signs or symptoms until it's already taken hold. They creep up on you, and you put them down to something else. The tiredness, the lack of appetite, the headaches. They all add up, but finding out what they add up to can come as a real bolt from the blue.' He paused for a moment and took a breath before going on, his voice now slower, calmer, suddenly more serious-sounding. 'I won't lie to you, it's rare for things to get this bad this quickly. A one in fifty chance, maybe. But I'm afraid to say that your kidney function levels have fallen again since your previous test. Your kidneys are struggling to clean your blood and deal with your body's natural waste products. The longer we allow that to continue, the more dangerous the levels and that will inevitably lead to some very nasty symptoms indeed. To be blunt, in the end, if left untreated, these can – *will* – prove fatal. Trying to look for reasons won't help. In fact, in my experience, it will only make things feel worse. It's nobody's fault. Sometimes things just happen. No rhyme nor reason, and this is one of those times. Bad luck, a twist of fate, call it what you will, but your kidneys are failing, Beth. It's a fact. And they're not going to get better. I'm so sorry but we are getting closer now to dialysis, and ultimately the need for a transplant.' He stopped for a moment, took his glasses off and wiped them clean. Beth wondered if he'd done that simply so he wouldn't have to look at her while she tried to digest what he was saying. 'I'm so sorry.'

NINE

1968

Geraldine looked down at the tiny bundle in her arms and cried. Whether she was crying with pain or joy or just sheer relief that it was over she could not be sure. The baby was a girl. She was alive and healthy. A good weight, a good pair of lungs. And beautiful, or so the midwife insisted, although with her face all red and wrinkly and with some sort of slime still damp and sticky on the top of her head, it was difficult to believe.

'There we are, my love,' the woman was saying. 'Just the afterbirth to deliver and that's you all done and dusted.'

There was more? Geraldine wished she'd listened when they'd explained what would happen to her. She'd already been through hours of pain. Everything felt stretched and split and broken. Everything hurt. And still there was more?

She gazed at her baby, hardly able to take it all in, that she had made this totally separate being and brought it into the world. Sandie. The name had come to her, soon after that first piercing cry, when the little girl had been handed to her for inspection, all warm and wriggling, and there had been one tiny white foot sticking out from the bottom of the blanket.

Her baby was barefoot and, if not actually singing, then at least she was keen to be heard. For some silly reason, she thought of Sandie Shaw. Standing there on her TV screen, barefoot and singing "Puppet on a String".

The record was one she had listened to in the common room, one of a stack of forty-fives, mostly sleeveless and scratched, that lay on the top of the sideboard, along with a pile of tatty magazines, left there in some sort of attempt at providing entertainment for the girls. One or two of them, hands cradling their bumps, had got up and danced around the room to the sounds of Cliff or Elvis, and Geraldine had watched them and laughed at their ungainliness, but she had never felt compelled to join them. There was nothing to be happy about, nothing that made her want to dance or sing. Yet there was something about that one song. The words seemed to fit somehow, with this feeling, this strange longing for something she knew she could not have. The feeling that there was a string binding them together somehow, the baby and herself. A string that could never be totally broken. She would so love to be able to promise to always be there, just like in the words of the song, but that was never going to happen. Not for her and baby Sandie. It just wasn't possible...

She ran her fingers over the little feet, separating the tiny toes, all bare and wrinkly and so much softer than she ever could have imagined. I wonder if one day that...

And so Sandie it had to be. Not that she had any right to name her. This baby was not hers to keep. Loving her would make no difference. Madly, gladly, any way at all, would make no difference. She would not be there. She couldn't be.

She loosened her grip as her baby was lifted from her arms. She would be taken from her forever soon enough. Or perhaps not soon enough. The last thing she needed was to start getting attached to a child destined for a life she could never be a part of. It had all been decided, and nothing was going to change that now. She had to accept it, deal with it, get on with her life. Go back to being that carefree teenager she used to be.

The afterbirth came away quickly and easily. She caught a glimpse of it afterwards, lying in a metal dish beside the bed, and felt her stomach heave. It looked like something from a butcher's shop window. Someone came to clean her up, to adjust the bedding, offer her water, tell her to rest. And then she was alone, the tears drying on her cheeks.

She had no idea where the baby had gone. She wouldn't ask. She shouldn't care. She could feed her, she knew that much. If she wanted to. For a while anyway. Best for baby, so they said, to have proper milk from her mother, in the first days, weeks... But what did she know about any of that? She had spoken to the other girls, the ones who had gone before her in the queue. Those who had done it, put their babies to their breasts, had found it so much harder to let go when the time came. In fact, one had flatly refused and had walked out, head held high, and taken her baby with her. Probably best not to, then. No feeding, no holding, no cuddles. Perhaps best not to see her at all. She couldn't allow herself to love her. It would only complicate things.

She wondered if they would have told her aunt Ellen by now. Told her dad? That the deed was done, the baby out of her, the shame over? Would the two of them be on the phone to each other right now, talking about her, deciding how long to leave her here, when to come and collect her, when to send her back to school as if nothing had happened?

If only her mum was still here. Geraldine dug down beneath the scratchy white gown they had put her in, felt for the locket around her neck and flipped it open. Her mum's face smiled up at her, that lovely kind face she remembered so well. If you were here, it all would have been so different, she thought, kissing the picture gently before closing the locket back over it. She had precious little to give to Sandie but she would give her this, and hope she'd be allowed to keep it as a link to her past, to her family. The locket was Geraldine's most valued possession, and she would miss it, but the thought of it staying with the baby comforted her somehow. Maybe her mum would watch over Sandie, just as she knew she still watched over her?

She could hear the babies down the hall. Screaming, howling, whimpering. Was Sandie one of them? Was she crying for her milk, for her mum? A mum she had met for minutes and would never remember? She didn't know. One cry was just the same as another. She didn't recognise her own baby's voice, probably wouldn't even recognise her face by the time she'd been wiped and the wrinkles from all that pushing and sliding had eased themselves out and disappeared from her skin.

This baby had come from her body, but she was not hers. She never could be. She would be taken away, brought up by proper parents, a mummy and a daddy who could give her everything. It was for the best. Everybody said so. She had to let her go. And yet she knew that she would never ever forget her.

TEN

The bus had come quickly and Ruby had arrived at the seafront with time to kill before her six o'clock meet-up with Vix. There were still a lot of people about, mostly young, walking in groups, their arms wrapped around each other and laughing, and a few lone dog walkers striding a lot more purposefully, occasionally stopping while their pets sniffed at something of interest or lifted a leg to pee. There were families too, tired-looking kids trudging along with plastic buckets in their hands at the end of their Sunday at the seaside, some licking at ice creams despite the chilly weather. Near the entrance to the pier a juggler, dressed from head to toe in red and yellow tartan, threw coloured balls into the air and nodded his thanks whenever a few coins landed his way.

That was what she liked about Brighton. There was always activity, even as winter drew near. Life going on, in one form or another. Although the wind was cold and the sea was churning loudly against the pebbles down below her, she felt she had needed a breath of fresh air before heading into what she knew, even so early in the evening, would be a noisy and crowded pub. Geri and William were back from Spain now, and more than happy to sit with Lily, letting her look through all the holiday photos on their phones and sample the over-sugary fruit sweets and giant Toblerone they'd bought at the airport. Rather them than her, Ruby thought, when it came to getting Lily to go to sleep tonight after that lot.

It was odd, but Ruby felt nervous about seeing Vix again. They had shared much more than just a room while they were in care, but that had been a long time ago. Their lives were different now and she couldn't help but worry they would no longer have much in common beyond a lonely motherless childhood she would prefer not to remember, let alone talk about. Still, a rare Lily-less night out was not to be sniffed at and, if it didn't work out, she could leave early, go back on the bus and never have to see Vix again. There was nothing to lose.

She tottered a bit in the heels she rarely wore and pulled her skirt down a fraction as it insisted on riding up her thighs with every few steps she took. She had not had a proper drink since the wedding nine days ago and was looking forward to a couple of glasses, even if it was highly likely to go straight to her head. She smiled as she thought back to when she'd left the house and William had insisted on pressing enough cash into her hand to make sure she could get a cab home later, just in case. She didn't think that would be necessary but it was good of him to care.

She spotted Vix as soon as she pushed the door open. She had nabbed a corner seat near the fire and there was a bottle of white wine and two glasses on the little round table in front of her. She half stood as Ruby pushed her way through the crowd, and leaned forward to hug her.

'Sorry, I started without you. White all right?' Vix pointed at the bottle, already getting on for half empty.

Ruby nodded, slipping out of her coat and hanging it over the back of her chair.

'Say if it's not. I can drink the rest and get you something else, no problem!'

'It's fine, honest.'

'It's not like I actually know your alcohol of choice, is it? We were a bit young for it last time we met!'

'It was all warm milk and weak orange squash back then, if I remember rightly.' Ruby laughed as she made herself comfy next to her childhood friend.

'And that awful Ovaltine stuff at bedtime. We don't really want to talk about any of that though, do we?' Vix lifted her glass, took a swig and immediately topped it up again, pouring one for Ruby too before replacing the bottle on the table.

'No.' Ruby breathed a sigh of relief, happy that she and Vix were clearly thinking alike. 'Best not.'

'So... let's talk about now! I feel like we need to get to know each other all over again. I mean, I don't even know where you live, what you like to watch on TV, what music you listen to...'

'This evening could end up like some crazy twenty questions quiz! A bit like going on a first date!'

'Yeah, exactly. But without the should we or shouldn't we have sex at the end of it!'

Ruby laughed.

'Although I could be up for it if you are!'

'What?'

'Only joking, but I find it's easiest to get the big stuff out of the way early. I'm gay, just so you know. It's not a secret, and it could be tricky to weave it into the conversation later, or a bit awkward when you start talking about blokes and expect me to compare notes, so there we are. Cards on the table.' She lay her hands flat on the table in front of her, as if to emphasise the point. Her nails, Ruby noticed, were nibbled and none too clean. 'Nothing for you to worry about though, I should stress.' She laughed, but clearly nervously. 'I'm really not about to make a pass at you or anything like that, but I do like girls. I'm... out and proud, as they say. Now, tell me something equally shocking about you.'

'Wow. I wasn't expecting that, and not in the first two minutes, definitely! But good for you. If that's who you are, you are totally right to just say it. I'm just not sure what I can possibly tell you to match it.'

'Okay. I'm not trying to make a contest out of it! Come on, let's start with your daughter, shall we? A nice safe topic of conversation. Lily, you said? I bet you've got lots of pics on your phone. Can I...?'

'Of course.' Ruby took her phone out and flicked through her photos. 'This is one of my favourites. Taken last month, on her birthday. She's six.'

'Yeah, you said. But I can see from the number on all the cards too! And the candles on the cake. Big unicorn fan, is she?'

'They all are at the moment, until the next craze comes along. We never really had anything like that, did we?'

'Not going to talk about it, remember?'

'No, you're right. Look, here she is with Geri. That's who I told you about before. My sort of substitute mum. She'd just got married when that one was taken, hence the posh dresses and soppy grins.'

'Married? At her age? There's hope for us all yet!'

'Second time around. Her first husband died a few years back.'

'Right. Sorry. Your Lily's a real little beauty, by the way. You must be so proud of her.'

'I am. How about you, Vix? Do you want kids some day?'

'Got to meet the right girl first. And then there's the question of which one of us does the carrying. And we'd need a sperm donor, of course. Two girls don't have all the necessary equipment. Nature hasn't quite caught up with modern thinking just yet!'

'It's a lot to have to deal with.' Ruby took a sip of her wine, her fingers cool against the glass. 'When I think about how easily I fell pregnant, when I didn't plan to be, or even want to be. Nature has a lot to answer for.'

'Ah, but you wouldn't go back and change things, I bet. Not now you've got her.'

'God, no! I nearly lost her once though.' Ruby hesitated, not sure how much to tell. 'I left her by herself, you see. It was only supposed to be for a few minutes... but I wasn't able to get back for her. She was on her own for far too long. It should never have happened, but I had an accident, hit by a car.' She lifted her hair and tipped her head, revealing what remained of her scar. 'It's a long story, but social services had their eye on me for a while. Everything worked out in the end, and I won't be making that sort of mistake ever again. I've got Geri to thank for that. Speaking up for me, taking us both in, being the family I needed. I sometimes think she was sent specially, to be like my fairy godmother or something. I can't imagine being without her now.'

'Believe me, you're not the only one to do something stupid and still have the scars to show for it. Take a look at this.' She rolled up the sleeve of her jumper. 'Some burn, eh? Had to have skin grafts and everything. Kids and kettles don't mix!'

'Oh, Vix. I'm so sorry. That must have been painful.'

'I hardly remember now. It was a long time ago. And I only had myself to blame. Still, I can't help wondering why we're dwelling on all this negative stuff. A fun night out, we said! Do you want to eat? They do great food here. A bit basic, but tastes good. I can recommend the steak and ale pie. Unless you're veggie, of course.'

'Come on, Vix. For years, we had to eat what we were given.

Couldn't afford to be fussy then, and I'm still not. I eat anything!'

'Me too. Not keen on semolina though, to be honest.'

'Snap! But I somehow don't think that's going to be on the menu here. Come on, you bought the wine, I'll get the food.' She pulled William's twenty pound note out of her purse. She didn't need a taxi, but she could do with a good dinner. She felt sure he wouldn't mind.

'Well, I have to warn you that I eat like a horse and drink like a fish, so I do not come cheap! But, go on then, you've twisted my arm. I will have the pie, and plenty of mash. Might even run to a pudding as it's a special occasion. But, when it comes to a second bottle, I'm paying, seeing as I seem to have already drunk more than my fair share of this one.'

'Sounds fair.'

Ruby got up and squeezed her way to the bar. It didn't take long to make her choice and order for the two of them, and she picked up knives and forks and a bundle of salt and pepper sachets on her way back to the table.

'So, you still haven't told me what you do.'

'Do?'

'For a job, I mean. Let me guess. You're a... librarian, or you work in a bookshop? You always did love to read.'

'No.' Vix laughed. 'You're way out there. All that silence, and dust. I'd be bored to tears.'

'Butcher, baker, candlestick maker?'

'Nope. Try something a bit more... outdoor.'

'Mountaineer? Window cleaner? Oh, no, you were never too fond of heights, were you? Gardener maybe?'

'Nowhere near. Okay, I'll tell you. I work at Sidell's.'

'Never heard of them. What do they do?'

'It's an animal centre.'

'What? Lions and tigers?'

'Not quite that wild! More tortoises and parakeets. It's a little old-fashioned kids' petting zoo. I've been there three years and I love it. Feeding, weeding, breeding. You name it and I'm there, in all weathers, keeping the place tidy, the animals and the visitors happy, up to my elbows in poo half the time.'

'Oh, Lily would love that. Do you have rabbits?'

'Dozens. Turn my back for too long and there are dozens more. They breed like... well, rabbits! Seriously though, bring her along. I can get you both in free and she can come backstage so to speak, see what goes on behind the scenes.'

'Yes, please! She'll be thrilled. She's had a bit of a thing about rabbits for ages. We've got one at home. Flopsy. Not very original as names go, but he's a real sweetie. I dread what she'll do when he dies, because they don't live all that long, do they?'

'That's the worst bit. Most small animals don't. And it's so easy to get attached to them. Anyway, tell me about your job. The shop I found you in, surrounded by postcards and tea towels and sticks of Brighton rock. It's Geri's, you said?'

'Was. She's handed it over to me now. Oh, she's still around, giving advice and popping in every now and then, but it's legally mine. She'd wanted to retire for a while, and Michael, that's her son – my ex – wasn't interested, so she decided to give it to me. She says it's a weight off her mind, that she's enjoying being free of it all, but it was still really generous of her. It's not as if I'm blood or anything...'

'Ah, but Lily is, isn't she? Must have been her way of keeping it in the family, a bit of a nest-egg for the next generation. Making sure you don't up and leave and take Lily with you.'

'I suppose. Not that running a shop is the future I want for Lily. I'm becoming your typical pushy mother lately. I want her to have it all, you know? Because I – *we* – didn't. Ballet lessons, horse riding, piano, pets. And good grades at school, of course, maybe even university, a real career...'

'I think every mum wants that, don't they? Happy and healthy, that's what really counts though. Kids can't all grow up to be brain surgeons or the prime minister, can they? I'm sure my mum – my adopted mum, because my real mum wouldn't have given a shit what I did – wouldn't have chosen for me to be mucking out rabbit hutches. Or to be a lesbian, for that matter. But we have to live our own lives, make our own choices. Even if that does mean dying from an overdose in some filthy hovel somewhere.'

'Is that what happened to her? Your mum?'

'Yeah, so they tell me. Not that I remember much about it, or about her. And as for my real dad, well, who knows? Could be anybody.'

'We really didn't have the best of starts, did we? It's amazing we've survived to be so normal!'

'Speak for yourself.' Vix laughed. She lifted the wine bottle out of the way as a waitress brought their meals to the table. 'Wow, that was quick.'

'Looks lovely.' Ruby picked up a fork and dipped into her mash, popping a dollop into her mouth, then frantically waving her hand about to fan it. 'Ouch. Hot!'

'You always were the one to rush straight in, weren't you? Do it first and think about it afterwards.'

'Story of my life.'

'Well, eat your dinner and then you can tell me all about it. We've got all evening, and I'm not going anywhere.'

Geri was curled up on the sofa when Ruby got home, hugging a mug of hot chocolate and watching some old film on the TV.

'No William?'

'He's already gone up to bed. Lily wore him out!'

'Oh no. She wasn't any trouble, was she?'

'Of course not. A bit overexcited, that's all, but she went out like a light eventually. How about you? Had a good evening?'

'Yeah. I wasn't sure what to expect but Vix hasn't really changed. Still big. Still has hair like a gorgon! She talks a lot, says what she thinks, and drinks a fair bit these days by the look of it, but it was okay. She works at a kids' wildlife place and wants me to take Lily along there, so we'll definitely be meeting up again.'

'That's nice. You don't get out nearly enough, and you need more friends your own age. We're always happy to help out with Lily, you know that, if you fancy another night out without her.'

'Thanks, Geri. What would I do without you?'

'Don't be daft. We love spending time with her. Oh, and William's finally sorted out Lily's inheritance. You know, the bits and pieces his mum wanted her to have. He did a bit more sorting at the old house this afternoon and brought them back here. They were still in his boot when you were getting ready to go out, so he was going to wait and show you in the morning. They're in a couple of boxes, out in the garage now. I'm sure he won't mind you selling them though, or some of them at least, if you don't want to keep them. They're not everybody's cup of tea.' Geri laughed suddenly.

'What's so funny?'

'Unintentional pun there, I'm afraid. No, it's just that she's... oh, come on and see for yourself. If you're not in a rush to get to bed that is.'

Ruby followed Geraldine down the hall and out into the front garden and waited as she slid the garage door up and over and flicked on the light.

'There.'

'Oh, when you said a couple of boxes, I thought you meant... like shoe box size. These are enormous.'

'Perhaps I should have called them crates, but she did have rather a large collection.' Geri pulled at the corner of one of the lids and eased it open, rummaging down into layers of tissue paper and pulling out a big china teapot in the shape of a castle.

'Oh, is that the famous pot that Lily's always on about? The one from her third birthday party, when Agnes had a bouncy castle in her back garden and brought out a teapot to match? She still remembers that day so well, and that she was sick all over the grass and Patsy, of all people, had to clean her up! The only year I've ever missed her birthday, because I was in hospital...'

'You couldn't help that, but yes, I think it probably is that pot, although Agnes had so many different ones. Well, Lily has now, as she's left her the lot. Heaven knows what she – or you – will do with so many teapots. Or where you could possibly keep them!'

'It was lovely of her to think of Lily though, wasn't it? To leave her something so obviously precious to her. It wouldn't feel right to sell them.'

'Well, you'll have no problem next time Lily wants to play at tea parties, will you? Spoilt for choice, in fact. Those dolls won't know how lucky they are!'

'You don't mind storing them here for a while, do you? They are taking up quite a bit of space, and you might want...'

'It's fine, love. Look through them when you have time. No rush. It's not like we don't have half of Agnes's worldly goods stashed away already. William's got the probate documents now and he wants to get on and sell their old house as soon as he can, so I dare say a fair bit more will be coming this way in the next few weeks. It's not as if I ever park the car in here anyway. The driveway's fine.'

'Thanks, Geri. And Lily is a very lucky little girl.'

'They're only old teapots, Ruby. No great value in them.'

'I meant she's lucky to have you. And William. We both are.'

Geri wiped a tear away. 'Oh, stop it. It's what a family's for. Taking care of each other. Agnes loved Lily. And William and me... well, we do too, you must know that. We love both of you. Now, off to bed with you. Someone needs to be up and about for Lily when she wakes up at the crack of dawn, and it's not going to be me! I've done my bit tonight and, much as I love her, I'm in need of a good eight hours. This babysitting lark's exhausting, and I'm not as young as I was, you know.' She turned off the light and closed the garage door, pushing Ruby back into the house ahead of her before heading up the stairs. 'Night, love. I'll leave you to lock up. See you in the morning.'

ELEVEN

Beth put down her magazine. She had only picked it up as a distraction, hoping it might take her mind off things, but she had come across an article about an actress, quite a famous one, who had gone through cancer, an operation and everything, and not said a word to her kids. Why burden them with worries over something they couldn't do anything about? That had been the woman's reasoning. If it had all gone wrong, ended badly, they would have had to find out and deal with it all then, but until that time, which might never come, she had decided to keep quiet. Gone into hospital, told a lie about some minor procedure, and kept all the anguish to herself, unshared, only revealing her secret when she had the all-clear and the whole nightmare was over.

Could Beth do that too? Bear the brunt of it all alone? Carry on as if nothing was happening, explain away her symptoms, as she had already been doing for months now, by blaming them on tiredness, financial worries and grief? But her illness was worsening. It was getting harder to hide, harder to lie, and for her, short of a transplant, there could be no miracle cure. Dialysis would take several hours at a time, as often as three times a week, and that could go on for months or quite possibly for years. Maybe even for the rest of her life. She would have to talk to her boss about time off, or try to get it done in the evenings which would mean not always being there when Emily came home from school. Any length of time spent away from home would be difficult, so holidays would be almost impossible, she would have to be much more careful about what she ate and drank, and there would be times when she might look ill, feel ill...

Could she really hide all that? Yet, the thought of telling them, when they had only recently been through all the upheaval of the divorce and the loss of their beloved gran, was not one she could contemplate. It still felt so unreal, as if it was happening to somebody else, and she would wake up in her own bed and find it was all just a horrible dream.

Jack. If she must do it, then he was the obvious one to talk to first. He was her eldest, and in many ways her most level-headed, sensible child. And he was a nurse. He would be the one least likely to get emotional, the one most able to understand the clinical side of things and to help explain it to the other two.

Transplant lists were long. Everyone knew that. Age, blood, tissue type, urgency, would all be taken into account when a kidney came up for grabs. There was a pecking order, and what realistic hope was there of her reaching the top? There could always be someone more suitable, or more in need. No, a transplant might be a long way off, if it ever happened at all, and in the meantime she – they – had to find a way to live with what was happening to her right now.

Beth had always carried a donor card, never really thinking about when or if it would have to be used. She would be dead by then, after all, so why should she care which bits of her they took, when the rest was headed for the furnace anyway? But now, suddenly, she realised its true importance. It wasn't just a piece of paper in someone's purse, or a promise made online. It was real. *This* was real. Dialysis three times a week forever, unless someone somewhere died to help her live. It was a terrifying prospect.

She kept coming back to the leaflets she had picked up at the hospital weeks ago. There was one about living donors. There were people out there who gave up an organ while they were still alive, donating it to someone they may never have met. How could they consider doing that? And why? But there were countless others who did it for a family member or a friend. Parents, siblings, children. Spouses who sometimes, by some miracle, even without the obvious blood link, turned out to be a match. Could that be the way for her? Finding someone who would consider it at least?

Her parents had adopted her, and were both dead now anyway, and Sean was a definite no-go. As an ex-husband he would feel no obligation. It was all he could do to agree to her taking part of his pension and keeping the dining room table, so a kidney was out of the question. And there was no way she was going to ask any of her kids to take such a big risk, not while they were still so young and healthy and happy, just starting out in life and taking their first steps in their careers. It was her job to look after them, protect them, give them everything she had, not the other way around. And telling them how bad things were... even just telling Jack... would lead to all sorts of trouble. They would want to help, to be tested, if they could, she knew they would. And what if one of them, or all of them, were a match? What then? No, she had to do something to prevent that from happening, and there was only one thing she could think of. The idea of it had been brewing at the back of her mind for a while, and had been slowly growing now that her mum was gone and there was nobody left to hurt. Surely it was worth a shot.

Somewhere out there was another family, a blood family. Who, and where, were her long-lost mother and father? Were they still alive? And were there brothers and sisters out there too, or nieces and nephews? Did they ever think about her, wonder what had happened to her? Maybe they were searching for her, or desperately hoping she might be searching for them...

She knew it was fanciful, that she was allowing her imagination to run away with her. Desperation had a habit of doing that to a person. Because, if they had tried to find her, they would surely have succeeded by now. They had had more than fifty years to go looking and she would have been easy enough to trace. She had only lived in two places in her whole life, and a change of name when she married would surely not have caused too big a problem. Everything was there on the internet these days.

The reality was probably very different. They had no more looked for her than she had for them. The past had been left to lie. And if she did manage to find them, any of them, what then? Would they shun her, or welcome her with open arms? And – she hardly dared to wonder – would just one of them be willing to give up a part of themselves to save her? As a mother herself, she knew only too well the lengths she would go to for her own children, but this mother had broken the bond and walked away, so long ago that any feelings she might still have for her child could not possibly compare to her own for her darling Emily. And to agree to being a donor, to giving up a kidney, to a daughter she had not seen in decades, and when she herself must be quite old by now? It was a huge thing to expect of anybody, and in her heart of hearts she knew it was selfish of her to even consider asking, but she would never know if she didn't try.

She had meant to go through those boxes she'd brought back from Shelling, just in case the answers were there, or a few clues at least. The shock of what the consultant had told her, of how serious this thing was starting to become, had left her feeling muddled and confused, but she had to start looking. She had to know. It was why she had brought all that stuff home in the first place. Why she had collared poor old Hetty on the day of the funeral. These shadowy figures from her past might be related to her by blood, but they were strangers, and no, when she thought about it, she had no qualms about taking something from a stranger. Why should she? Not if it kept her own children – and herself – safe. They had given her up, after all. Turned their backs. Handed her over to others without any idea of what would happen to her, where she would go, whether she would be happy. Perhaps they had even left this awful disease lurking inside her, a genetic throwback that had lain waiting to erupt like some terrible ticking time bomb? For more than fifty years they had abandoned her to an uncertain fate. Didn't they owe her something in return?

———

She waited until Emily had eaten her dinner and finished her art homework. That girl was so talented, had always loved having a pencil or a paintbrush in her hand since she was small, but she seemed to have lost interest since the divorce, as she had in so many things she used to enjoy. And that was her fault. Hers and Sean's.

Keeping up the appearance that everything was normal was hard. It was already draining Beth dry. And tomorrow she was going in to the hospital to have a fistula fitted into her arm, some kind of joining and strengthening of the arteries ready to take the tubes she would need inserted during the gruelling dialysis treatment that was soon to come. Emily would be packed off to her dad's overnight just as she usually was on a Friday, totally unaware of where her mum was, or why. One more secret, one more lie, to add to the growing guilty pile.

Leaning over to plant a gentle kiss on her daughter's forehead once she had finally fallen asleep, Beth stood for a few moments in the dark, absorbing the silence, then crept back towards the door, closed it behind her and crossed the landing to her own room. Piles of removal boxes and crates she had brought with her after the divorce still stood, unopened, in the corner. Somehow this place did not yet feel like home and she doubted that it ever would. It had served its purpose, and put a roof over their heads when Sean had insisted on selling their old house so he could take his share and 'move on' as he'd called it, but she could not imagine staying here for long. It was time to get a mortgage and buy a home of her own, just as soon as she had sold her parents' place and had a decent deposit to put down. Working for the bank helped, with its special staff lending rates and all that expertise on tap, but she was finding it harder and harder to look into the future with any real sense of hope.

Beth closed the bedroom door and sat down wearily on the edge of her bed. Most of whatever was in those big moving-home packing boxes was probably rubbish anyway. If she hadn't needed any of that stuff in all these months, or missed it, then it really couldn't be of any importance. Unlike the contents of the two battered old cardboard boxes she had brought back from her mum's.

A flurry of dust rose up as she lifted the lid from the first one. She was tempted to just tip everything out onto the carpet, rummage through it quickly like a fox delving into someone's rubbish sack, but these were her parents' papers. Things they had regarded as important enough to keep, maybe even to treasure. She took the first envelope from the pile and eased its contents out. Photographs. Old black-and-white ones, square, quite small, already curling a little at the corners. She picked out one of a couple who looked vaguely familiar, sitting in deckchairs on the beach, and turned it over to see if anything had been written on the back. *Molly and me, Southend, 1958.* It was her dad's writing, big and spidery, and when she flipped the photo back over and looked more clearly, she could see that yes, it was him, and her mum, in what must have been the very early days of their marriage. It could even have been taken on their honeymoon. She couldn't remember ever asking where they had spent it, but she knew it would have been somewhere in England, somewhere by the sea. They had not travelled abroad. Well, hardly anybody did back then.

The other photos had similar captions. Dates, places, names. All in her dad's writing. He had always been the one to open the mail, pay the bills, keep records. When she thought back, he was probably the more sentimental of the two of them too, the one most likely to grab the camera at special moments, light the candles on her birthday cakes, carry her up to bed and tell her stories, usually the sort he made up as he went along, without the aid of an actual book. Her mum had been the one who kept the house running, baking cakes, washing and dusting and polishing, and the one who made sure she had a clean uniform and got to school on time. She lifted the beach photo to her lips and kissed her dad's face. She still missed him, just as her mum had, right up to the day she'd died. That was why all this searching for hints to her past seemed so wrong. As if her warm and loving parents had not been enough, as if they could be so easily replaced.

She put the snaps back into their envelope and laid it aside. Their passports were next. Yes, they had eventually travelled overseas. Only to Majorca, and once on a day trip to Calais, and both passports were now long out of date. She almost laughed when she looked at their photos, all very formal and unsmiling, taken in front of a pleated curtain in one of those little booths. Her dad had taken off his glasses, and her mum's hair was stiffly permed, every curl combed neatly into place, and Beth could just see the lacy collar of what had always been her favourite blouse.

Old MOT certificates and car repair bills came next, all relating to cars they no longer owned, and held together with a rusting paperclip. Why had they kept all this stuff? Beth reached for the small bin she kept under her dressing table and dropped them in.

Half an hour later, and with the bin overflowing with unwanted papers, she reached the bottom of the first of the cardboard boxes and the last of its contents – a small rectangular tin, the sort which had probably started out containing biscuits or sweets. It had a picture of a fluffy cat on its lid, and something inside it rattled as she pulled it from the box.

As she prised open the lid of the tin, she could see there were several things inside. A tiny teddy, a bit threadbare, with one eye missing and wearing a stripy knitted jumper with a hole in it. An old-fashioned black vinyl record, what her mum and dad would have called a 45. The label told her it was called "Puppet on a String", by someone called Sandie Shaw. She had a vague recollection that the song might once have won the Eurovision Song Contest, back before she was born, but certainly couldn't remember it ever being played at home. There was a bundle of papers underneath, folded together and held with a rotting rubber band that disintegrated and fell away as she touched it. She would read them in a minute, but first there was something else she just had to investigate.

A locket, hanging from a thin chain. Not real gold, and a bit tarnished, but pretty enough just the same. She dug at the hinges, almost breaking a fingernail, until they clicked open to reveal a photo. A photo of a woman's face, a little faded and not quite in focus, smiling at the camera. Smiling at her. A shiver ran through her. These things were hers, weren't they? These were the things Hetty had spoken about, the things that had come with her as a baby. She looked down at the little teddy, his missing eye giving every impression that he was winking at her. And then she looked again at the picture in the locket, bringing it closer, gazing into the woman's eyes, as clear and blue as her own. Could this be her? Could this be the face of her mother?

TWELVE

Geraldine stood on the pavement and waved as the estate agent's car drove away. She gazed up at the *For Sale* sign attached to a post that had just been hammered into the ground beside the gate.

'Will you be sorry to see it go? The house?'

William put an arm around her shoulders and pulled her in close. It was a chilly day and she'd left her coat inside. 'In a way. But it's no use to me now, is it? A new life with you, that's what I'm looking forward to. And this old house isn't a part of that. It's served its purpose, letting Mum enjoy her final years. A bit of sea air, the independence that meant so much to her, me on hand if she needed help with anything...'

'You were a good son to her.'

'I'm not sure she would have always agreed with that. When Susan and I persuaded her to give up the family home...'

'Which, from what you've told me, was getting far too much for her to manage by herself.'

'It was, but bringing her to live near us in London was a mistake. That flat was a mistake. She hated it from the moment she moved in.'

'Maybe, but you rectified it in the end, didn't you? Got her out of there, away from London and all the noise. She loved living here in Brighton these last couple of years, spending more time with you, being by the sea, getting to know Lily... And from what I can gather, getting her to downsize and take on that London flat in the first place was a lot more Susan's doing than yours.'

'I know. More convenient for us, she said. Easier to visit, not that we did much visiting, to be honest. And it made financial sense too. London flats appreciated in value so much more quickly than run-down old country houses miles from anywhere. As if that mattered to Mum. God, she hated London with a vengeance! I should have been firmer, put my foot down, made sure we really listened to what Mum wanted, not just what we thought she needed, but Susan wasn't one to think with her heart. If she ever had one! Oh, Geri, if only I'd met you years ago, before Susan ever came along, how different my life would have been.'

She smiled up at him. 'We can't go back, love. And I'm not sure what my Ken would have had to say about it, you turning up to whisk me away! But the important thing is that you put things right for your mum in the end, and you made her happy. That's what I love about you. You put everybody else first. You want us all to be happy.'

'And are you? Happy?'

'Of course I am, you daft old thing!'

'Hey, not so much of the old. I am younger than you, remember?'

'As if you'd ever let me forget it. Now, shall we go inside and sort out what's left of your mum's things? There are only a few boxes left to shift, and that man with a van will be here for the rest of the furniture at twelve. Then we can get the walls washed down and the carpets hoovered, ready for the first viewings.'

'Slave driver!'

'I'll let you do it all by yourself if you're not careful.'

William looked up at the newly erected sign. 'Does that look a bit crooked to you?'

'A bit. And none too sturdy. A strong wind and it'll probably come down, but let's hope it's not there too long, eh? A quick sale, the agent said. We might even get a buyer before Christmas. Properties like this are in demand. And once the sale proceeds are in the bank, we can start planning that cruise you've always fancied.'

'Aha! Married me for my money, eh? You'll be telling me you've ordered a Lamborghini next!'

'I thought a Jag might be more suitable, actually. Leather seats, mahogany dashboard, a bit of good old-fashioned luxury. I'm not sure I could climb in and out of a sports car these days, even if I wanted to.'

'You'll get a pushbike and a week in Skegness, and be grateful, my girl,' he joked, leading her back in through the open front door. 'And, if you're really lucky, I might push the boat out and treat you to a Chinese tonight.'

They spent the afternoon in companionable silence, William up to his elbows in soapy water while Geraldine pushed the hoover into every nook and cranny, disturbing the occasional spider and far too many cobwebs. The house looked so much bigger now it was empty. The rooms had those big square dimensions, tall ceilings and old-fashioned picture rails that Agnes had fallen in love with the first time she had walked in. It still had the original fireplace in the living room too, although Agnes had chosen to install an electric fire rather than having to get down on her rickety knees every day with a basket of logs and a box of matches. Geraldine flicked the switch on now and smiled as the fire started to glow red, instantly making the room feel cosier. The cleaning had kept her warm but now she had flopped into a fold-up chair to take a much-needed break she could feel the cold of the evening seeping in.

'Tea!' William handed her a mug, pulled the curtains closed and lowered himself into the second chair beside her.

'Thanks, love.' She wrapped her fingers around the warm china and breathed in the steam. 'Good job you thought to pop these old camping chairs in the boot. I wouldn't have fancied sitting on the floor.'

'That's the boy scout in me, still there after all these years. Always prepared!'

'I didn't know you were a scout.'

'Ah, there's still so much you don't know about me.'

'Like?'

'Now, that would be telling, wouldn't it? A man likes to have his secrets. Where's the fun in telling you everything all at once? I've decided I'm going to hold back a few little juicy snippets for you to wheedle out of me bit by bit as the years go by. Maintain the mystery! But, as for being a scout, I have to confess that my time in the troop didn't go well. Or last long. Let's just say that camping and me were not natural bedfellows.'

'What did you do? Rub two sticks together and set fire to the tent?'

William turned his face away. 'Well...' He tipped his head towards the fireplace. 'Did you ever wonder why Mum preferred electric? Why she was so wary of naked flames?'

'Oh, my God. You did, didn't you? You actually did set fire to something!'

He turned back towards her then and she could see how hard he was trying not to laugh. 'Sometimes, Geri,' he said, 'you can be so gullible. Of course I didn't! I was very good at all that campfire stuff. And very careful. No, it was more the being away from home I couldn't take to.'

'You were homesick?'

'Not just homesick. Actual proper sick. Vomited all over my sleeping bag, and my mate Bill Hanson's too, not to mention the groundsheet, and then again all over Brown Owl from the girls' camp next door when she came rushing over to look after me. I think it was obvious then that scouting was not for me.'

'Oh, dear. What happened? An honourable discharge?'

'More a parting of the ways, by mutual agreement. I just preferred my own bed to all that getting back to nature and eating half-raw sausages stuff. The ground all bumpy and rock hard, creepy-crawlies in your shoes, other kids snoring all night, the cows in the next field a bit too close for comfort... I hated all of it. And, you know as well as I do, I always was a mummy's boy!'

'It's such a shame you never had kids.'

'Where did that come from?'

'Oh, I don't know. I just see you as such a family man, yet you spent so long in a bad marriage, with nobody to give all that love to. You would have made a lovely dad.'

'As you've said yourself, we can't go back, can we? And your family's my family now.'

'For better or worse, eh?'

'They're not so bad, are they? Okay, so we don't see all that much of your Michael but Ruby's as good as ours, and as for Lily, she's such a little charmer, who could fail to love her? Did I tell you, that she asked me last night if she could call me Grandad?'

'No, you didn't. When was that? When you were reading her a bedtime story?'

'Yes. It was that one about the family of pigs, you know? With Grandad pig all jolly and cuddly, and taking them on adventures. That was probably what put the idea in her head. Either that or the thought of extra family members meaning extra pocket money! Nice of her though.'

'Yes, it was. And what did you say?'

'Well, I was well chuffed so I said yes, obviously. Who wouldn't?'

'Come on then, Grandad, drink up and let's get these chairs and boxes stashed in the car. You promised me a takeaway, and I'm starving.'

Christmas crept up suddenly. It seemed as if one minute they had been outside in their wellies, tidying up two gardens ready for winter, and the next they were snuggled indoors and putting up a tinsel-covered tree, the curtains shut against the cold and dark of the longer evenings.

Geraldine had found looking after Agnes's empty house, with all the regular checking for post and burglars, and showing strangers around at odd hours of the day, a lot more stressful than she had expected it to be, but it hadn't been for long. Things had moved quickly. They had a buyer now and all the legal work was sailing along at speed. She crossed her fingers every time she thought about all the things that could still go wrong. The buyer changing his mind, the survey revealing some terrible problem with the electrics or the roof, William having a wobble and deciding he'd rather not sell at all.

'I didn't have you down as such a worrier,' he joked when he had caught her nibbling at her fingernails for the second time that day and she had been forced to admit why. 'And besides, if there did turn out to be anything to worry about, it would be my problem to deal with, not yours.'

'What's yours is mine, right? Doesn't that include the bad stuff as well as the good?'

'Of course. We're a team now, you and me.'

She cuddled into his side, watching the newly installed Christmas lights flash on and off in what appeared to be a totally random pattern.

'What will you do with the money? From the sale?'

'Aha! Now I see where we're going with all the what's yours is mine talk!'

'I didn't mean...'

'No, I know you didn't. But you've asked me that before, and I really don't know. To be honest, it's more money than I know what to do with. Treat my lovely wife to whatever her heart desires, I suppose. Shoes, handbags...'

'You know I don't need anything like that, especially now I don't have to dress up for work. I'm just as happy in a pair of slippers these days.'

'Well, a new conservatory then, or we'll do up the bathroom... I don't know. We could send Ruby and little Lily off on a holiday. They'd love that. Maybe we could go with them, if you'd like to? Or book that cruise we talked about a while back. And put the rest of it away for a rainy day?'

'I hate to think of it wasted, just sitting doing nothing in the bank.'

'Not wasted, Geri. Just there, as insurance. You know, if the roof falls in or something. It's a lot of money and I don't want to just fritter it away.'

'I wasn't thinking of frittering. Just... well, shouldn't we be doing something positive with it? Something good? It's not as if we need so much, is it? Not at our age. What would Agnes have wanted us to do with it, do you think?'

'She never said. Give it to some cats' charity probably, in memory of old Smudge.'

'Oh, God. Smudge! I'd forgotten. He's buried in her garden, isn't he? And we'll be leaving him there when the new people move in. Do you think we should...?'

'What? Dig him up? No, I don't think so. Let him lie. Rest in peace and all that. Under a tree in the sunshine, where she always wanted him to end up. It hardly matters whose tree now, does it? Not now she's gone too.'

'I suppose not.'

'But going back to the subject of your heart's desires... you haven't told me what you want for Christmas yet. You know I'm hopeless at present-buying unless you give me a wish list, or at least a sizeable hint.'

'There's nothing I need.'

'Need doesn't really come into it, Geri. I'm not talking a new packet of M&S knickers or a pair of oven gloves here. It's more a case of choosing something flippant, silly, extravagant... something you'd love to have but would never dream of buying for yourself.'

'Oh, really?' She laughed. 'Ken used to buy me knickers, you know. The practical kind. He'd take a sneaky look in my drawer to see what sort I wore and to check the size, and then go and buy me more of the same. And he got me a casserole dish once. It was a particularly nice casserole dish, as it went, but...'

'Not exactly a gift to make your heart flutter?'

'He wasn't always the most romantic of husbands, but...'

'You did love him? It's okay, I don't mind you saying it. I'm hardly going to be jealous of a dead man, am I?'

'No need anyway. He was then, and you're now. You know, I never would have expected any of this to happen. After I lost Ken, I thought it would just be me, struggling to run the shop, living on my own for the rest of my days. The typical middle-aged widow. And now look at me! How things have changed, and that's all thanks to you, Mr Munro. And to Ruby and Lily, of course. A new phase of my life – of *our* life – is beginning, and we've got so much to look forward to.'

'I won't argue with that.' He turned her face towards him and kissed her full on the lips. 'But I know what you're doing, you know.'

'Oh? And what's that?'

'Changing the subject, that's what.' He made a grab for her feet, pulling them up onto his lap and tugging her slippers off. 'Now tell me what you want for Christmas or the feet get it.'

Geraldine squealed, trying to pull them out of his grasp.

'I will do it, Geri. I'll tickle them to death.'

'You wouldn't dare.'

'Try me.' He gripped both her ankles together in one firm hand and lifted the fingers of the other, wiggling them in the air as he brought them nearer.

'Okay, okay, you win.'

'Good. So, what is it to be then?' He relaxed his hold just enough for her to pull away and jump to her feet.

'Tricked you!' She laughed, stepping back and heading out towards the kitchen. 'Now, I'm going to make us a nice cuppa and then, and only then, without any further torture or duress, I might give your question some serious thought.'

THIRTEEN

It was surprisingly easy, once Beth had read through the papers in the biscuit tin. She knew the name of the place now – *The Ferns* – and the address. It had been some sort of nursing home for unmarried mothers, about twenty miles from Shelling, out towards the coast. She had found the road on a map, but not the home itself. It didn't take too much googling to work out why. It had stopped being a nursing home way back in the seventies, had spent a very short time as some sort of failed hippie yoga retreat, and was now a small middle-grade hotel, called The Fernlea. Thanks to the magic of the internet, she had taken a virtual tour, gazing at the shabby brick and glass frontage, the small car park and grounds, the distant view of the sea, and the rather tired-looking interiors of some of the bedrooms, wondering if one of them might be the one in which she was born.

She was hugely tempted to go there, to book a room, stay for a night or two, try to absorb something of her own history from its walls. She had been putting off the trip to Norfolk for far too long, but she did need to spend some time sorting out her mum's things, having a clear-up and clear-out, ready for the house's eventual sale, whenever that might be. But she knew she couldn't justify the expense of a hotel stay. Not when she could sleep at the cottage itself. Still, a short detour on the way up wouldn't take long, and the pull of curiosity now that she had done her research was hard to ignore.

It was while she had the laptop open that she decided to embark on another search too. One she had put off for long enough. *How can I trace my birth mother?*

There were several sites offering information, promising possible contact, hinting at happy reunions. She chose one, pretty much at random, and started to fill in the boxes, entering her birthdate, the county where she had been born, the fact that she was female, her email address... It all just seemed so matter-of-fact, so clinical, so bloody easy. A simple matter of ticking boxes, refining the search until you arrived at exactly what you were looking for. As if looking for a missing parent was no different from looking for the perfect pair of shoes.

The site asked her for a photo, but she wasn't sure she felt quite ready to go that far. Luckily, she was able to skip that stage. She was not yet sure how any of this worked, and the last thing she wanted was for her birth family to see her photo before she had made any kind of contact or had the chance to see them.

And then there it was. The results of her search, delivered in moments, hovering just out of sight.

View matches...

Tentatively she pressed the button. There were fourteen of them, it said. Fourteen women whose information matched hers. Well, a nine out of ten match anyway. Fourteen possible mothers. And another 234 scoring eight out of ten, but she could leave looking at those until later.

She could feel the excitement starting to mount. Was one of these women her mum? Had she been here, on this very site, registering her own details, waiting for the day that Beth did the same? Could it really be this easy? And, if so, why on earth had she not done this before?

Then the crunch came. She would have to register, pay a regular subscription, give details of her account so they could set up a direct debit. They wanted her money. Of course they did. The promise of information was just the lure, wasn't it? The way to suck her into something they were trying to sell. But why were these hidden women only partial matches? The information she had given was right, accurate, one hundred per cent fact. If nobody matched it exactly, if nobody scored a perfect ten, then their details must have failed to match somewhere along the line. The wrong year, the wrong month, the wrong county. They weren't the right women, were they? Not her mother. They couldn't be.

Beth closed the laptop with a heavy heart. No, this was not the way. It couldn't be. Dubious websites offering instant hope for a price, and only managing to produce half-hearted results. There had to be way, a proper, official way. She just wasn't quite up to looking for it yet.

'What is this place, Mum?' Jack sat beside her, gazing up at the big iron gates as they drove through them on a chilly Friday afternoon and proceeded slowly along the gravel drive, ending in a horseshoe-shape in front of two enormous glass doors. He had a few days off between night shifts and had decided to come up to Norfolk with her, ostensibly for a bit of bracing sea air. Having overheard half a phone conversation the day before, Beth suspected he had had a falling out with his latest girlfriend, one so newly on the scene that she had yet to meet her and now probably never would. He wouldn't normally choose to spend two days sorting through an old lady's cupboards but, whatever his reasons for coming, she was glad of his company.

She pulled the car into a corner space and opened the door, twisting her legs to the side and stretching before stepping out, shivering in the chilly December air.

'The Fernlea Country Hotel.' Jack answered his own question, hopping out beside her and reading the faded sign beside the entrance. 'Why...?'

'Just somewhere I wanted to take a quick look at. I'm sure they probably have a bar if you want a drink while I have a wander about.' She pulled her purse out of her bag and offered him a fiver. 'Here. My treat.'

Jack followed the signs to the Gents over in the corner and would no doubt then find his way to the bar, if there was one.

The foyer was small but cosy, with dark wood panelling, a rather worn green carpet and a real fire burning in the grate. A series of mismatched landscape paintings graced the cream-coloured walls. There was a tall, thin Christmas tree in the corner, covered in red and gold baubles, its lights switched off, and a few strands of tinsel draped across the reception desk which was currently unmanned.

There was a brass bell on the counter but Beth chose not to ring it, preferring to stand for a few moments and take in her surroundings undisturbed, grateful for the warmth from the fire. It was almost impossible to imagine this place as it must once have been. Had her mother stepped in through those very doors, young, pregnant and scared? Stood here, wondering what fate had in store for her and her child? How long had she stayed, Beth wondered, and how long before they had been parted? Remembering the births of her own children, she found it almost impossible to imagine how that must have felt. Putting that little teddy and the record and the locket into a tin, knowing that was all she could give, all that the baby would ever have to link them together. And then the handing over, the saying goodbye...

'Good afternoon. How may I help you?'

The voice seemed to come out of nowhere, making Beth jump. The girl who now stood behind the reception desk looked no more than about seventeen. Probably weekend staff, or a kid working after school, for pin money. She had plastered on the kind of smile that gave every impression she would rather be elsewhere, her voice rather high-pitched and abnormally formal, as if she had been taught exactly what to say and how to say it. Her thin hands were resting on a big book which she had already opened. 'We don't appear to have a reservation...'

'No. Sorry. No reservation. Oh...' She turned as Jack reappeared at her side, shaking his head and still clutching the fiver. 'No bar either, it would seem.'

'We do offer a drinks service. For residents only. In their rooms. If you'd like to...'

'Oh, no, sorry. We're not booking in. Just looking, really.'

'Looking? There's not an awful lot to see.' The girl stared at her challengingly. 'So, if there's nothing else...?'

Beth was about to walk away, aware of Jack hovering next to her with a baffled expression on his face, but it was worth a shot, surely? She would probably never be here again. 'I don't suppose...' she began, not at all sure how to broach the subject. 'I don't suppose you might know anything about the history of this house, before it became a hotel?'

'What? The yoga place, you mean?' The girl's voice, now she was off-script, had quickly reverted to a much more natural Norfolk accent. 'Load of weirdos, from what my gran tells me. Used to parade about in long white robes, chanting and stuff. Lotus position on the lawn and all that. Some film crew came once and made a documentary about it, or it might have been an advert or something. Some of the locals were in it, like as extras, but I've never managed to find it on YouTube. You one of them, were you?'

Jack laughed, as if picturing his mum in a robe with her legs wrapped up around her ears.

'Er, no. I was interested in the house before that. When it was a nursing home.'

'Oh, the mother and baby home, you mean. Yeah, I heard about that. Sad, wasn't it? Having to hide away just because you got up the duff. Like it was shameful or something. Hundreds of them came here, they reckon. Had they never heard of the pill in those days?'

'I'm not sure the pill had actually been invented, to be honest.'

'Really? Not surprising then, really, is it? I mean, they were still going to be at it, weren't they? Pill or no pill.'

Beth wasn't sure whether to laugh or cry. The girl was naïve, opinionated, utterly indiscreet and quite clearly in the wrong job, yet her willingness to talk just might be useful. 'I don't suppose you know anyone around here who might remember those days, might even have worked here?'

'What is this? You researching for a book or something? You look like a writer to me.'

'Yes, I am.' Beth glared at Jack, willing him to keep his mouth shut. 'How clever of you to guess.'

'I have an instinct for these things. I like to guess what our guests do. You know, for a living, like. There's a man staying here now who I'm sure is a private detective. He's always got his phone out, taking pictures. And making notes in a little book. Probably working on a case.'

'Or photographing the wildlife maybe?' Jack cut in. 'Making notes about the birds.'

The girl laughed. 'He's making notes about a bird all right. The one in Room 17, would be my guess. Anyway, the answer to your question is no. Whoever worked here back then is long gone by now. Retired. Or dead, more like. It's fifty or sixty years ago. Like ancient history...'

'Sorry to have troubled you then. But thanks anyway.' Beth walked away, pulling her son with her before he started asking what on earth she was up to. Ancient history indeed! She didn't know whether to be offended or just to have a good laugh about it.

Outside, Jack just shrugged his shoulders as if she had gone quite mad as Beth stood on the gravel and peered up at the windows on the first floor, then walked around to the side and into the small garden at the rear and looked up again. More rooms. One of them was the one, but she would never know which. Never know what being here in those days must have felt like. Oh, yes, she had been here all right, she was sure of that, but she had been so tiny, there were no memories to be had. Yet, this was where she came from. And, since the day she had been taken away, probably by some anonymous do-gooder adoption worker, and handed over to Molly and Arthur Green, it was the closest she had ever been to her real mum.

'So, are you going to tell me what's going on?' Jack put a mug of coffee and a microwaved ready meal down in front of her and joined her on the sofa.

'Going on?'

'Oh, Mum, stop putting on that innocent face. What was that hotel place all about? And you making out you're a writer?' He waited for a response but she wasn't about to confess all. 'Has this got anything to do with you being adopted? I know you never really talk about any of that stuff, but when you start poking about in mother and baby homes from the old days, and trying to find someone who remembers... well, it does kind of add up.'

Beth sighed. 'Yes, actually. I think... no, I'm sure that that was where I was born. The place your gran and grandad got me from.'

'Got you from? You make it sound like they went to pick up a parcel!'

'Well, they did, in a way, didn't they? They wanted a baby, and someone else had one to give away. It was an arrangement that suited everybody. I just wish I knew a bit more about it. I wish I'd asked while I still had the chance.'

'Asked what though? I mean, you are Beth Hogan, daughter, mother, and probably a granny yourself one day. Grew up in Norfolk, moved to London, married, divorced. What else do you need to know? You're you, no matter where you started out. Nothing changes any of that.'

'That all sounds very plausible, Jack, and you're right, of course. Nothing I might find out really changes anything, but I'd still like to know. About the bits that are missing. Who my birth parents were, what they looked like, and... well, *why*, I suppose. What happened in their lives to make them give me up?'

'The usual, I expect. Young girl, pregnant, scared. Her parents not wanting the shame of it all, or trying to do their best for her, make sure she didn't wreck her future. And the father either a kid himself, or a married man, not wanting the responsibility. Same old story, but things were different in those days, weren't they? It was all about reputation.'

'Yes, I'm sure you're right, and I'm the product of some stupid unplanned accident, but I'd like to know more. Dig out some facts, trace my birth mother, maybe even meet her.'

'Like on one of those *Long Lost Family* TV shows, you mean? They don't always end well, you know. But it can't be that hard to track someone down, can it? Lots of people do it.

And if it's what you really want, I can help you. They're my family too, after all. And it's not as if Gran...'

'Yes, I know. I can't upset her now, can I?' She picked up her fork and took a tentative bite of her pasta. There was a blandness to it but it would have to do.

'Is that why you've left it so long? Never tried to do it before?'

'Yes. And because I had nothing to go on before. But now I've had the chance to look through all your gran's old papers and belongings and I found the name of that place, what's now the hotel, and I couldn't resist just taking a peek at it, as it was more or less on our way here. To think I've been there before, that one of those rooms was where I was born. It just makes it feel real, all of a sudden. And there was an old tin as well, of things they'd kept. A teddy, a record, a locket. All things that were hers. My mother's...'

'Can I see?'

'The locket, yes. The rest of it's back at home, so you can have a look when we get back if you'd like to.' Beth slipped her hand down beneath the neck of her T-shirt and pulled out the thin chain.

'You're wearing it?'

Beth nodded, then reached behind her head and undid the clasp, placing the locket down in front of her son.

'So, you think this was hers?' Jack shovelled some food into his mouth before putting his fork down and giving the locket his full attention. 'Your real mum's?'

'Yes, it must have been, and she left it for me, something to link me to her, for me to have when I was older, only your gran never gave it to me.'

'And why do you think that was?'

'I don't know. Let sleeping dogs lie, I guess. Why stir things up? And, Jack... don't call her my real mum. Your gran was my real mum, wasn't she? The one who wanted me, loved me, brought me up. This other woman was just the one who carried me for nine months, then gave me away.'

'Okay, I get that.' Jack fiddled with the catch and finally managed to open it. 'Oh, wow. Is this her? No, it can't be. She's too old, isn't she? This woman must be at least – what? – mid-thirties? Forty? Why would a woman that age have to sneak off to some baby home?'

'I don't know. The baby wasn't her husband's maybe? Or even older women could make mistakes, couldn't they? Get pregnant without being married? Or, God forbid, she was attacked? Raped? Just had to get rid of it – of *me* – and forget I ever existed. It's why I want to know. Who she was, what happened to her. If that's even her. Or if it's not, then who is she? This woman in the picture? Why did my mother want me to have the locket? The teddy I can understand, but the record? I don't even have an old record player so I can listen to it, and there isn't one here. Music was never really your grandparents' thing. It's "Puppet on a String", by the way, by Sandie Shaw. What does that mean, do you think? That she felt like a puppet, being manipulated by other people, not in control of her own life? Is that what she wanted me to know? What she was trying to tell me?'

'You don't think you might be reading a bit too much into it, Mum? Maybe it was just her favourite song? It'll be easy enough to get the lyrics from the internet, or to find an old video clip on YouTube if you want to listen to it. We can do that now if you want.' He reached for his phone and started tapping away at the keys with his thumb. 'And anyway, whoever this woman is...' He stopped tapping for a moment and lifted the locket up to the light, studying the old photo more closely. 'You have to admit she does look a lot like you.'

FOURTEEN

By Saturday evening they had worked their way through the wardrobes, the kitchen cupboards and the sideboard, leaving just the basics in place and piling everything else into boxes which now stood in the corner awaiting their fate. Several filled sacks sat in the small hallway awaiting delivery to a charity shop, and the car boot was stacked with the few bits Beth had decided she definitely wanted to keep. Anything edible was lined up on the kitchen worktop, while several old out-of-date tins and packets from the back of the cupboards along with everything else nobody was likely to want was bagged up and piled up in and around the dustbin outside, ready for collection day. Only the furniture and curtains remained untouched, along with the pictures and mirrors that would have left faded marks on the walls if they'd taken them down. It felt important to leave the place looking lived-in and homely for any potential buyers when the estate agent's viewings began in earnest.

'You look tired, Mum.' Jack washed his hands at the kitchen sink and filled the kettle for yet more tea. 'Time to stop and get ourselves a takeaway, or we could go down to the pub to eat maybe? I wonder if they still do those wonderful steak and kidney pies?'

'I'm sure they probably do. But on a Saturday night? Won't they be packed? Shall we ring and book a table for lunch tomorrow to fill us up for the journey, and just make do with something here this evening? There are plenty of tins to use up, and there's still some of the bread I brought with us. Beans on toast maybe?'

'We had toast for breakfast, and a sandwich for lunch. A man cannot live on bread alone! No, I'll nip out for something. My treat. If I can take the car, that is.'

'Of course. That little supermarket in the petrol station should be open.'

'I know, Mum. But it'll just be more tins and ready meals. If there's one thing I never forget about a place it's where to get the best takeaways! A throwback to my student days. Grandad used to go out on his old bike with the big basket on the front, do you remember? And bring back fish and chips, while Gran warmed up the plates in the oven. All wrapped in newspaper too, the old-fashioned way. No polystyrene containers back then. Can't beat it, can you? Proper English fish and chips. Do you fancy that? Anything extra? A pickled onion? Gherkin? Mushy peas?'

Beth shook her head and smiled. 'Just a very small cod for me. A kid's portion. I'll pinch a few of your chips.' She wasn't sure she had the appetite for a whole plate of fish and chips of her own, let alone extras, and it was hardly on the kidney health diet list, was it? Still, she could always rely on Jack to finish up anything that was left. If he wasn't already twenty-four and six feet two she would say he was still a growing lad! She put her feet up and closed her eyes as he picked up the car keys and let himself out of the house.

The next thing she knew was a gentle nudge in the ribs and a voice in her ear. 'Mum, wake up. Food's ready.'

'Oh, sorry, I must have nodded off. Here, let me sort out the plates.'

'All done. Plates, cutlery, salt, vinegar, tomato sauce, the lot. All you have to do is come to the table.'

'You spoil me!'

'Well, someone has to. Madame...' Jack pulled out a kitchen chair and guided her into it, draping a tea towel over his arm as if he were a waiter showing her to her table. 'And may I get you a drink to accompany your meal? A glass of wine, perhaps?'

'We don't have any wine.' She laughed. 'A cup of tea will do me.'

'Oh, I think we can do better than that.' He produced a bottle of white wine and four cans of lager from a carrier bag on the floor and stood them in the middle of the table. 'Would you believe that little shop in the village was still open? Sells everything in there, that woman. Never stops talking, mind! She'd have had my whole life story out of me if I hadn't had the perfect excuse that I had to rush back because the food was getting cold. Not that she didn't seem to know it already. Knew who I was instantly, asked after you, and how the house sale was going. Anyway, wine or beer?'

'Wine, please, but just a sip. I've got a bit of a headache. Must be all that effort today.'

'Can I get you anything? A couple of pills?'

'No, no, I'll be fine. Now, eat up. I can see you're starving!'

He had given her far too many chips. She pushed them around, nibbling at one and trying to edge the rest into a pile to disguise just how many she would be unable to eat. Should she tell him? That she wasn't really drinking alcohol anymore, that she wasn't meant to use salt, that she was following a special diet plan and trying to eat more healthily, keep her blood pressure down, protect her heart? Anything she could do to improve her lifestyle would surely give her the best possible chance, to fight it, hold it at bay for as long as possible. Maybe she should just tell him everything? About her illness, what the doctor had said? Come clean, ask for help? It was something she had been putting off, but if she was ever going to say anything, then now was the time. Just the two of them here, with the questions about her adoption still hanging in the air, providing the ideal opener to talk about the real reason she was so keen to trace her birth parents. After all, as Jack had said earlier, they were his family too. His ancestors. His roots. Despite what the doctor had told her, if there was any chance at all that she had inherited something deadly, then he may have inherited it too. And so might her other children.

Kidney disease. Dialysis. Fistulas. Transplants. He would know about these things, far more than she did. She had simply read the leaflets. He would have seen it for real, maybe treated patients who had something similar, seen the symptoms, the operations, the successes and the failures. He would understand.

'Jack...'

He pushed another chip into his mouth and munched, stopping to wipe a dribble of ketchup from his chin. He looked at her, a frown settling across his forehead. 'What's up, Mum? You know, you really do look shattered. An early night for you, with a hot water bottle. Nurse's orders!'

'Yes, I think you're right, but first, there's something I have to tell you.'

'Sounds ominous.'

'Yes, it is really.'

'You're worrying me now. I haven't seen you looking like this since you sat us all down to tell us you and dad were getting divorced.'

'Not something I enjoyed doing, believe me, but you had to be told, and your father wasn't going to do it, was he? Always the coward.'

'So? What is it this time? Have you met someone? Because, I wouldn't mind, you know. In fact, I'd be pleased. We all would. So long as he made you happy.'

'No. There's no one. Might be nice if there was, but no. Not yet.'

She hesitated, feeling the tears starting to well up.

'Mum? Whatever's the matter?' Jack stood up and came to her side of the table, knelt down on the floor beside her and threw an arm around her shoulders.

'I'm ill, Jack. I have something called CKD.'

'Kidney disease? What?! No! How could I not know about this?'

She shook her head slowly and rested her head into his shoulder, finding it hard to speak. 'Because I didn't want to tell you. Didn't know how.'

'Oh, Mum. How long have you known?'

'A few months. Well, getting on for a year, I suppose, but it wasn't so bad at first.' She pulled herself up straight and took a deep breath. 'I didn't want to say anything until I knew the facts, until I understood more about it, you know. If I could beat it. Or how bad it might get. But now that I know... well, it explains a lot. My tiredness, headaches, losing weight. I just put it all down to stress at first. Your dad going, your gran getting ill. But...'

'But it was your kidneys all the time? God, Mum, how could I not have noticed? What do they say? The doctors? Can it be treated with meds?'

She shook her head. 'I am taking tablets, yes, but they're not going to be enough.'

'What are you saying? That you're going to need dialysis?'

She nodded. 'And sooner rather than later. My...' She tried to remember the word, the technical term the doctor had used, but she couldn't. 'My rating or whatever you call it. You know, the reading, the number they get, from the blood tests, is dropping. Getting worse.' She lifted her sleeve. 'This thing... this fistula... Oh, you'll know more about that than I do, but it means it's bad. Too bad to ever put itself right anyway. It's dialysis, and then a kidney transplant, or I die. Look, to be honest with you, all this interest in finding my birth mother – I know it seems sudden – but it started out because of my kidneys. I had this crazy notion about finding her to see if she could help me. Or if someone I might be related to might be able to help me. I don't have anyone else, do I?'

'You have me. Tom. Emily...'

'I know that, and I'm grateful. You'll never know how much having the support of you three got me through splitting up with your father, but that's not the sort of help I mean. Not this time.'

'Then what do you mean exactly?'

'I'm going to need a donor, Jack. The only long-term solution to this whole illness, other than waiting for some random stranger to die, is to find a donor. A living donor. A match...'

'You wanted to waltz up to a mum you haven't seen since you were days old and ask her for a kidney? Are you mad?'

'I think desperate is more the right word. But I've had time to think about it and it was never going to work, was it? I just have to wait on the list like everybody else.'

'And what about us? Your kids? Surely, we're just as likely to be a match. Maybe one of us can do it. I'll get tested as soon as we're back home.'

'No. No, you won't.' She gripped his hand so hard he

winced as her nails cut into his skin. 'It's too risky and I won't let you. Any of you. You're too young, and far too precious to me. I'll wait, and I'll hope. It will be okay, you'll see. No tests. No heroics. You have to promise me, okay? End of discussion.'

They sat in silence for a while, the rest of their meal cooling on the plates in front of them. 'Oh, Mum.' Jack pulled her in towards him. 'As discussions go, there's no way this is the end. It's just the beginning. And I'm not promising anything. Not until I've had time to think about all of this.' He let out a huge sigh. 'It really has been a weekend of revelations, hasn't it?'

When Beth got up on Sunday morning, Jack was already sitting in the kitchen, his head bent over his phone. He put his hands around the teapot, clearly decided its contents were still hot enough and poured her a cup.

'Right. Let's look for your mum. You wanted to know about her, who she was, how to find her, so that's what we're going to do.' He pushed the old locket across the table towards her. She had forgotten she was no longer wearing it.

'But we don't have a laptop with us.'

'You can do just about anything on a phone these days, and I've got a good signal. I had a quick search through for an image that matches the locket photo, but nothing, I'm afraid. Now I'm trying to find out about tracing long-lost mothers!'

'Okay.' She sipped at her tea and watched him tapping away at his screen.

'From what I can gather here, things changed in the mid-seventies. Before that it was all kept secret, and it would have been much harder to get what we need. But there was a new Act, with more emphasis on the child's rights, and that's sort of allowed things to be backdated a bit, to include getting info about an earlier adoption, I hope.' He stopped and swallowed the last mouthful of his tea. 'The birth certificate you've got at home can't be the original, can it? It's a sort of edited, adoption replacement version, that doesn't really give you the full picture. Like these ones here, see?' He held the phone up for her to look at but quickly took it away again. 'There has to be an original, something with your birth parents' names on it. And yours too, if it was changed. Imagine if you turn out to be a Gladys or a Gertrude or something!'

'Not funny, Jack.'

'No, I know. Sorry. But it looks like we can apply for your birth records. You may have to talk to someone first though. Like a counselling session thing with a social worker, so you know what's involved and to make sure you understand the implications.'

'Implications?'

'Of her not wanting to meet you, maybe? Or of dragging up things you might not want to find? How it could all make you feel. Or make *her* feel. But, if that goes okay, you can apply for your birth certificate, and find out which adoption agency was used so you can actually go there if you want to know more. I doubt much of it was held on a computer back then. It will all be paper records, and after fifty odd years, to be honest, they've probably archived everything. Filed it all away in some old dungeon, covered in dust, but I don't think they will have thrown any of it away. That sort of information's too important, isn't it? The whole story. The big decisions and why they were taken. Peoples' lives, you know...'

'You're probably right. But that means having to come to Norfolk, doesn't it?'

'Ever heard of telephones, Mum? And emails? Good old-fashioned post even, if you have to sign forms or anything. I reckon we can at least get things started without rolling up anywhere in person. We've got a birthdate, a place, the names of the parents who adopted you. We're only missing that final piece of the puzzle, aren't we? It has to be worth it. You could find out you're in line for a big inheritance or that your mum was a princess or something! It's quite exciting really.'

'Or that she was raped and my real dad's still serving life in Pentonville.'

'Oh, stop it! I have a good feeling about this. And look at the locket. Don't you want to know who that woman is? I know I do. And coming back to Norfolk's not impossible. You'll probably have to anyway at some point, until Gran's house is sold.'

'But even if we do all that, and they tell us who she was, where she came from, why she gave me up, what are the chances she still has the same name now or lives in the same place as she did then?'

'One step at a time, Mum. It would give us a starting point, wouldn't it? Look, if you're serious about this, we have to at least try. Are you? Serious, I mean? Do you want to find her?'

'Yes, I think I do.'

'Right then.'

'And not as a potential life saver, but as my mother. I'm curious now, and I think – no, I know – that I want to meet her and maybe get to know her, if she'll let me. So, do your bit. Go and find her for me, okay? I'm hopeless at all this stuff and it helps a lot, knowing I've got you on the case.'

'You make me sound like Inspector Morse or something!'

'Nothing wrong with that. When did any of those stories ever end in failure? The detective always gets the right answers in the end. I have every faith in you!'

'Let's just hope our suspect is still alive and well somewhere then, eh? And that she wants to be found. The last thing we want is a load of red herrings or to follow a dead-end trail that leads to a body in the library!'

'I think that's more Miss Marple than Morse. And you don't really have the right clothes or hairstyle to be her! Although I could lend you the locket. Not her usual pearl necklace, but close enough.' Beth laughed. 'Now, come on, let's make some toast to soak up this tea and then finish what we came for. Boxes to be carried out, a quick dust, push the hoover round. Then how about a stroll around the village, and buy a paper maybe?'

'Okay. Funny to think this could be the last time I'm ever going to be here in this house. End of an era. Unless we get a lead about your mum, of course. You know I'll come back here with you, don't you? Shifts permitting. I mean, if they want to talk to you or show you papers and stuff, or if you want to try and meet up with her?'

Beth nodded. 'I don't think she was a local girl. Not according to Hetty Fellows next door. Which reminds me, we should call in and say goodbye before we go, and give her back her cake tin. I'm amazed she wasn't knocking on our door the minute she saw us arrive on Friday.'

'Not wanting to intrude, probably. I expect she misses Gran as much as we do. Must feel odd to her, coming in here and not seeing her. I know it does to me. Don't forget the pub lunch though. I'll ring up now and book it. I'm looking forward to that.'

'Of course. And then back to London straight after. I don't want to be picking Emily up too late from your dad's. She does have school tomorrow. And, Jack... not a word to her, or to anybody yet, about this adoption business, or my illness. Especially my illness, okay? Tom's only just settling in at uni and I know he'd want to come dashing home if he knew I was ill, but what good would it do? I want him to do well, find new friends, put all the divorce stresses behind him. He's got a bright future ahead of him and the last thing I want to do is spoil that, take his mind off his studies, stop him finally letting his hair down. So, our secret for now, all right?'

'If you insist. But I want to be there, when you start the dialysis. It's not something you should have to face on your own. Deal?'

'Deal.'

FIFTEEN

Lily held the rabbit very gently on her lap and ran one hand over its fluffy fur while trying to entice it to eat the carrot she held in the other.

'Thanks for this,' Ruby said, as she and Vicky stood close by, sipping coffee from cardboard cups.

'It's fine. We're not exactly busy at this time of year, even on a Saturday, so I have plenty of time to walk you round. You sure it's not too cold for her?'

'Oh, she doesn't feel the cold. Kids never do! Not when they're having fun. And she's got her gloves if she needs them.'

'You can't feed animals, or stroke them, with gloves on, Ruby. It's just not the same. Skin on skin, it's the only way!'

'Mummy, look! This one's called Benji and he's three. That's right, isn't it, Vix?'

Vicky nodded. 'Yep. Is he your favourite?'

'I like all of them. It's not fair to have favourites. Mummy, can we take him home to play with Flopsy?'

'Put them together for five minutes and you'll end up with babies all over the place,' Vix muttered under her breath. 'They're randy little buggers.'

Ruby tried not to laugh. 'Flopsy's a boy, remember, so it's not gonna happen! Anyway, I don't think that's a very good idea, Lil. He likes it here, with all his friends. He might get a bit scared if we take him away from what he's used to.'

'But Flopsy doesn't have any friends. Do you think he gets lonely in Granny's shed all by himself?'

'Not when he's got you. And you play with him every day, don't you? Now, come on, shall we put Benji back in his run and go and meet some other animals? The pigs, maybe?'

'Can I feed them some carrots too?'

With some reluctance, Lily handed the big white rabbit over to Vicky and stood up, brushing straw from her lap.

'Piggies eat just about anything. Come on, they're over here. Would you like to see?' Vicky held out her hand and took hold of Lily's, giving it a rub for warmth, and led her away to the opposite side of the barn, stooping to whisper something in her ear.

Lily giggled. 'No, they don't!' she squealed. 'I don't believe you.'

'I told you, Lily. They eat anything... and everything.' Vicky turned round and winked at Ruby. Whatever she had told Lily that pigs like to eat it was obviously something outrageous, and probably rude. Still the same old Vicky Dunn!

Ruby finished her coffee, dropped the cup into a wire bin in the corner and followed the smell all the way to the pigs.

Ruby loved Christmas. There was something very contradictory about being here by the sea, watching the cold grey water swilling about at the foot of the pier, when all the usual images were of roaring fires and snow-covered hills and bright bouncing robins. The only birds she could see were the gulls, swooping low, ever hopeful of a morsel of easy food dropped by one of the hardy locals, wrapped up warm and taking a stroll after lunch.

There were quite a few people about, despite the bitter wind. Lily was walking up ahead, her small hand enveloped in William's much larger one as she skipped along at his side, a fluffy unicorn toy with tinsel round its neck tucked lovingly under her arm. She was wearing a new red hat and a matching scarf with pompoms swinging from its ends, both of which Geri had recently knitted in secret, picking up her needles every evening once Lily was in bed. Ruby had never seen Geri knit before, let alone have to figure out how to make the pompoms, winding the wool around little cardboard circles she had cut from a cereal packet. Patience had been tested and progress had been slow, but this was the newly retired, relaxed, contented Geri, the one who had slowly begun to replace the much more uptight anxious version Ruby had first come to live with all those years ago. William was undeniably a calming influence, not only on Geri but on all of them. The father figure Ruby had never had before.

'Penny for them,' Geraldine said, linking her arm through Ruby's as they turned a corner and wandered up into town, away from the sea.

'Oh, just thinking how much things have changed. How happy we all are!'

'Nothing wrong with that. I'm all for happiness. Especially at Christmas.'

'I wonder how Laura's doing?' Ruby could picture her friend now, taking a few days leave from her stressful job in A&E and recently settled in her new home in London. 'Her first Christmas as a vicar's wife!'

'Busy, I expect. What with nativities and midnight mass and carol services. And she's still nursing too, isn't she?'

'Yeah, and loving it, although she's cut her hours back a bit now. I must try to go and see her in the New Year. Take Lily with me.'

'Or leave her here with us. You know you can do that, don't you? We're more than happy to babysit, overnight if you like. It's time you had more of a life of your own, a chance to go out and see friends... or boyfriends.'

Ruby laughed. 'Are you trying to matchmake?'

'Not at all. But, you know, if there was someone...'

'There isn't.'

'There's no need to feel awkward about it, that's all I'm saying. Just because you and Michael were once together doesn't stop me wanting to see you happy and settled with someone else. The right someone, obviously. I am not in the business of taking sides, although, if I did, it would probably be yours. That son of mine did not treat you well, but it's all behind us now. All I care about is making a better future, for all of us. And what William is making us for our tea, of course!'

'Geri, you can't possibly be hungry. Not after that huge Christmas lunch!'

'Ah, but I cooked that. Making our tea is William's territory today, and there's something especially appealing about food someone else has slaved over.'

'It'll probably just be a turkey sandwich and a slice of cake. Not a lot of slaving involved.'

'Sounds perfect. Now, how about a quick bit of window shopping before we get back to the car? I have an M&S voucher from my old friend Brenda Castle that's burning a hole in my purse.'

'You'll spend it on bath stuff like you always do, and that won't be on show in the window.'

'Oh, I know, but it's always fun to look, isn't it? Nothing quite like new clothes. I was hoping William might get me that winter coat I've been hinting about, but he had his heart set on buying me fancy jewellery. Diamonds, no less.' She held up her arm, lifted the sleeve and flashed her wrist. 'And in a watch! I feel almost scared to wear it, but it beats my old Timex any day.'

'He loves you, Geri. Let him show it.'

'Oh, I will. No harm in him seeing me staring at the coat too though, eh? It'll be the sales soon, so they might cut the price, and he does love a bargain.'

***

The living room carpet was still strewn with screwed-up wrapping paper and empty cardboard toy packaging when they got home. Geraldine slipped off her shoes in the hall and made straight for the kitchen and the kettle, while Lily made a grab for the remote control and William pulled the curtains shut, sunk into the sofa and closed his eyes. The lights on the tree twinkled gently in the corner and the mingled smells of lunchtime's roast turkey, Christmas pudding and warm brandy still lingered in the air. A typical family Christmas. There had been a time in her life when Ruby had never expected to experience anything like it. Growing up without a family, she had always longed for days just like this. An easy shared existence, someone to care about and to rely on, that feeling of closing the door and knowing everything and everybody you loved were all there together, inside. Snug. Safe.

They settled down to watch a Disney film. Lily's choice, but if Christmas wasn't for kids she didn't know what was. And, while Lily still believed in magic, Ruby wanted nothing more than to believe in it too. She had a family now, a home and a shop, and one of her oldest friends had come bouncing back into her life. All she needed now was a man to make it all complete. Her very own Prince Charming. Ruby smiled to herself. As if!

'Anyone for a mince pie?' Geraldine was back, balancing a

tray bearing three cups of tea and a glass of squash, which she carefully placed on the coffee table in front of the fireplace.

William's eyes eased open and he yawned and stretched exaggeratedly. 'I was meant to do that. Why did you let me nod off?'

'Oh, this isn't tea, love. Not *tea* tea, just a cup of tea and a little pre-tea snack. Your turn will come, don't you worry. I have high hopes for whatever you're going to rustle up later. And I've stacked the dishwasher as full as it will go but there are still a few pans that wouldn't fit.'

'You mean you want me to wash up as well?'

'All part of the kitchen duties you volunteered for, my sweet! You do lunch and leave the rest to me, that's what you said. I distinctly remember.'

'I'd better say yes to that mince pie then, to sustain me for the work ahead.'

'Well, you know where they are, in the cake tin. I couldn't carry that in as well as the tea, could I?' Geraldine sat down in her favourite armchair and reached for her cup. 'Now, what are we watching? Oh, *Cinderella*! My favourite.'

Ruby laughed at the indignant look that crossed William's face. 'I'd like a mince pie too, please,' she said. 'If you're going that way. And warmed up in the microwave would be nice.'

'And can I have an ice cream?' Lily said, looking away from the screen for a moment.

'In December?' Geraldine sounded horrified.

'Can I?' Lily put on her best begging face.

'I suppose so. If you ask nicely,' said Geraldine, giving in as she usually did.

'Please, Grandad.'

'This is what comes of living in a house full of women,' William muttered, hauling himself up and heading for the kitchen. 'Nagged and put upon, to within an inch of my life!' He turned and winked at Ruby. 'But I wouldn't have it any other way.'

SIXTEEN

1968

Margaret was nice. Of all of them, she was the one who seemed to care the most, listening, explaining, throwing an arm around anyone who got scared or angry or upset. She hadn't been on duty the day Sandie was born but made a special point of coming to find Geri the next morning, fussing around her and making sure she was comfy.

When she brought the baby to her, wrapped in what looked like the same blanket as before, Margaret cooed and chucked and gurgled in that funny high voice grown-ups always seemed to use when talking to babies, and told Geri how beautiful her daughter was, and how good she had been during the night.

'Are you sure you won't try feeding Baby, my lovey?' she said, holding the baby out towards her as if she was handing over a delicate package that might very easily break. 'Bottles are all very well, but...'

'Sandie. Her name's not Baby, it's Sandie.'

'That's nice.'

'And she'll have to get used to bottles, won't she? When she goes to her new place?'

'She will, yes. And she's already feeding really well from them. But you might like to try... you know, just for the closeness, the comfort?'

Geri turned her head away and kept her arms firmly under the covers. 'Who is it meant to comfort? Her? Or me?'

'I'm sorry, lovey. It's your choice. Some of the girls like to do it, have cuddles while they can. Something to remember afterwards, you know. But if you don't want to...'

Geri felt the tightening in her tummy, the heaviness in her throat. She wanted to. Of course she did. But she couldn't, could she? Not if she had any hope of walking away from this without a broken heart.

'I don't want to feed her. Or hold her,' she said.

'Okay. If you're sure.'

'Do they have anyone yet, ready to take her? Do you know who they are?'

'You know I can't tell you anything about that, but it won't be long now. I can tell you that much. I believe there will be someone from the adoption agency coming to take the little one on Friday.'

'The new parents won't come here?'

'No, lovey. Best you don't see them. I know how it would be, you trying to get a peek at them through the office doorway or out of the window as they drive away. Trying to work out if they're good enough for her, if they're going to love her and look after her properly. Last minute nerves and changes of heart. I've seen it happen. Best you don't get that chance. No, someone will come and take her, and she'll be handed over to her new family somewhere else. She'll still be legally yours for a while, until the adoption is finalised, but you won't see her again. I know it will be hard, but it's what you wanted, isn't it? Best to have that clean break. And then you can go home, put it all behind you. I understand from matron that your father is planning on collecting you on Saturday, so we'd better work on getting you ready, eh?'

Ready? What did that mean? Wash her hair, pack her bag, ignore the blood in her underwear and the soreness when she sat down, the milk leaking from her breasts, paint on a stupid smile? Ready to go back to her other life, be a schoolgirl again, pretend none of it ever happened? Ready to forget?

'You can put a few things together for her, you know. Things her new family can keep for her, for when she's older. Well, you know that already, don't you? I think you said you want to give her this little teddy...' Margaret glanced at the small bear sitting at the end of the bed.

'Yes. And my locket. Will that be all right?'

'Nothing that identifies you, lovey. You do know that your identity has to stay a secret, don't you?'

'It's not my photo inside. And there's no name or anything. It's a picture of my mother.'

'That should be all right then. If you're sure about parting with it. You do know you can never get it back?'

Geri nodded. 'And one more thing. There's a record, in the lounge. Do you think anyone would notice if I pinched it? I'd like her to have that too. "Puppet on a String". It's the song I was listening to the evening before she was born. Sandie Shaw. That's what gave me her name.'

'Well, I'm happy to turn a blind eye if it disappears! Some of those old singles have been around a while and they're getting pretty scratched. One less won't make much difference. I'll help you put a little package of her things together on Friday morning, so nobody else will see what's in it anyway.' She rocked the sleeping baby gently in her arms. 'But the adoptive parents will want to choose their own name for her, Geri. She won't actually grow up being called Sandie. You do understand that?'

'I know.' She watched the woman cradling her sleeping baby and fought the almost overwhelming urge to reach out and take her, hold her close and never let her go. 'But she'll always be Sandie to me.'

SEVENTEEN

SPRING, 2019

Beth lay back in the hospital chair and tried to read her book. This was her second dialysis session but she still wasn't used to it. She was finding it hard to concentrate on anything much apart from all the noises from the equipment and the coughs and conversations from the other patients in the busy room, not to mention the strange sensations as the machine beside her drew her blood out, ran it through its tubes and sent it swishing back inside her.

Jack had come with her for her first visit, just as he had promised. It was lucky that the dialysis unit was in the same hospital where Jack worked and he had not been working a shift that day, but he had a busy life, a demanding job, patients of his own to care for, and she knew she had to start getting used to doing this on her own. It would soon become routine, a fact of life, to be endured three times a week for who knew how long. Until they found her a new kidney, she supposed. Or she managed to find one for herself. She had not yet fully abandoned the idea of asking for help from her long-lost family, but now she was one step nearer to finding them she had to admit it was starting to feel like a pretty stupid plan. And a selfish one. 'Hello,' she would say. 'You don't know me but I'm your daughter. Can I have one of your organs, please?' Ridiculous. Impossible. Crazy. What had she been thinking?

The interview, talking to a specialist social worker about the process of reuniting with her birth mother, had not gone quite the way she had expected it to. The questions had been about her expectations, and her feelings, as well as those of the mysterious stranger she was hoping to find. A stranger who, she had been made to realise for the first time, was unlikely to be a selfish woman who callously gave her away but a strong, brave woman who may well have made the ultimate heartbreaking sacrifice in order to give her child a better life.

The whole meeting had felt incredibly intrusive at first, forcing her to dig down into her own feelings and preconceptions and to question them, but slowly she had begun to understand its purpose. She was about to do a big thing. It was life-changing and potentially very emotional for everyone concerned, and the possibility of rejection had to be faced head-on. Her mother, if she was still alive, might be overjoyed at being contacted. Then again, she might be horrified and be unwilling to accept her at all. She would have moved on, made a new life. There could be a partner, other children, things she had no wish to drag back up from a long-ago past, a long-ago mistake, and to have dropped right back in the centre of the life she had now. The spectre of failure hung over Beth's head all through the discussion, like the elephant nobody really wanted in the room while at the same time being totally unable to deny its presence.

Maybe she should just give up the whole idea. Talking had made her begin to really think about her reasons, her purpose, what could happen if she went ahead, and she knew it was already going way beyond just looking for a donor. She would be seeking, finding, meeting a real flesh and blood person, a woman who could look like her, think like her, a woman she could never then *un*-find. It was beginning to feel too real, too personal, too emotional...

When the birth records finally arrived through the post, Beth had found herself unable to even open the envelope. She had phoned Jack and waited two days until he had been free to come, late one evening after his shift, when they knew Emily would be asleep.

He peeled back the flap in silence and drew out the contents carefully, unfolding the paper and laying it out in front of her on the table. Still she dared not look.

'Do you want me to...?' Jack asked.

Beth nodded. 'It's at times like this I wish I could drink. A large brandy might help.'

'I don't think so, Mum.'

'No, I know.' She sat in silence for a moment, just staring at the paper in front of her.

'Okay. Here goes.' He picked it up again and read through it slowly. 'Her name is Geraldine Pamela Clark and she lives – *lived* – in Brighton. No occupation listed.'

'And the father?'

'Sorry.' Jack shook his head. 'That bit's blank. Probably because he wasn't there when the birth was registered. They'd need his permission to name him, wouldn't they?'

'Not there because he'd already washed his hands of me, you mean. Didn't want to know.'

'Or because he was never told. Or maybe nobody knew who he was.'

'Not even my mother?'

'It's possible. You've seen *Mamma Mia*. More than one suspect. It happens.'

Beth sank back into her chair. She hadn't realised just how

A PART OF ME

tense she had been, how straight she had been sitting, her fists clenched on her lap. 'Anything else? My real name?'

'Well, your first names are the same as they've always been. You're registered as Elizabeth Jane, but the form's dated a good two weeks after you were born, so the new parents – Gran and Grandad – were probably in the driving seat by then. Their pick of names, not Geraldine's, maybe? Unless she'd named you already and they stuck with her choices. Who knows?'

'Elizabeth Jane Clark. Sounds funny, doesn't it? When I always knew myself as Beth Green. Just think, all those silly jokes I had to put up with at school. Bethnal Green, they used to call me. You wouldn't think kids in Norfolk would have ever heard of Bethnal Green! And to think I was really a Clark all along. It kind of rolls off the tongue though, don't you think? Elizabeth Clark. Beth Clark...I could go back to it. I don't really fancy staying as a Hogan, now your dad and I are divorced. What do you think?'

'Don't be too hasty, Mum. I kind of like us all having the same surname. And you might decide to change it again one day. If you ever get remarried, I mean.' Jack half-laughed, but she didn't react. Hitching up with another man was way down her wish list right now.

'So, what do we do now?'

'That's up to you, Mum. We know who she is now, or *was*. We have a town, an address, enough to get started. If you still want to?'

And that was how they had left it, just ten days ago. Left it because other things seemed, for now at least, more important.

The nurse came over and asked if she was all right, if she needed anything.

'I'm fine.' Beth lowered her head and returned to her book, and the paragraph she had already read at least twice without taking a word in, but it was no good. She had too much flitting through her mind to read.

In some ways, she thought, it was actually quite handy that she and Sean were no longer together. It gave Emily somewhere to be, having a meal and watching TV with her dad after school or spending time with him at the weekends. So long as she timed it right, making school-time or weekend appointments, she could be here at the hospital for several hours at a time and Emily would never know. Work was a different kettle of fish though. She had had no option but to explain things to her boss, ask for time off, a kind of ongoing sick leave by appointment. He had been sympathetic, of course, on the face of it at least, while still managing to mutter about rotas and whether he was going to need some kind of part-timer to fill in when she was absent. She left his office knowing her job was safe – for now – but feeling as if she was creating a terrible inconvenience too. She had sobbed silently in the Ladies for a good fifteen minutes afterwards.

There was no escaping it though. She had to do this, no matter how difficult or inconvenient or downright frightening it was. The treatment would keep her healthy, keep her alive until...

'Did you know they're thinking about changing the law?' A woman lying back in the next chair, who had briefly introduced herself earlier as Maggie, was trying to catch her attention, putting down the magazine she had been looking at and moving carefully so as not to dislodge the tubes in her arm. Well, it was boring just sitting here hour after hour, Beth had to admit. She might as well humour the woman and have a chat.

'Pardon?'

'The law.' Maggie pulled herself up into a sitting position. She was small and round and homely-looking, probably in her mid-fifties, and wearing a huge pair of fluffy pink slippers, as if she was making herself comfy on her own sofa at home. 'You know, about being a donor. It's a new system, see, like they have in other countries. Everyone's going to be one now, unless they opt out. Didn't you know? Oh, but you're new to all this, aren't you?'

'Yes. Only my second session.'

'Thought so. I can tell. As I was saying... donors. There'll be no need to carry a card anymore, and no excuse for folk to dither about, wondering should they or shouldn't they? Much simpler. Much fairer. I mean, who needs to hang on to their organs once they're gone? When they can do so much good.'

'No, I didn't know that. Are you sure?'

'Oh, yes. They'll still have to clear it with the relatives and all that once you pop your clogs, but it'll be just assumed that when you die, you're willing. You can bet your life...' She stopped and laughed at her own unintended joke. 'Bet everyone's life, I should say, there'll be loads of people who can't be arsed either way. They won't go to all the bother of opting out. I mean, when you're gone, you're gone. Into the earth, or the flames. So many people don't think about it, or don't want to. And every organ retrieved is a life given back, isn't it?' She nodded towards the machine at her side. 'Should give us a better chance. In theory anyway.'

'Yes. Yes, I guess it will. Thank you.'

'What for, lovey?'

'For the ray of hope, I suppose.'

'Oh, there's always been hope. Just got to keep our chins up and keep on keeping on, haven't we?' She lifted a finger to her own chubby chin and gave the skin a little wobble. 'I mean, what's the alternative? Lie down and give up? Not me. You got kids?'

'Yes. Three.'

'There we are then. You keep at it for them, don't you? I've got two. Both grown-up now, of course, and a couple of grandsons too, but they still need you, don't they? Always will. And it's not so bad here, you know, once you get used to it. Just treat it like an appointment at the hairdressers or a trip to Tesco's. Or the dreaded ironing! Something you have to do every few days. Once you plan it, time flies, believe me. I knitted a scarf for my youngest, just sitting here.'

'Knitting? With the needles in your arm?'

'Well, no, I used the long plastic ones. Size four!'

Beth laughed. 'You know what I meant!'

'Yes, I know. I don't let these buggers get in the way.' She tilted her head towards her arm. 'They're pretty secure, you know. Not about to pop out if you sneeze! But, yes, I managed it somehow. Where's there's a will there's a way. You really only need one good arm to do all the work with knitting. The other one is pretty much just holding it steady. I saw it as a bit of a challenge to tell you the truth, and it's not as if I was tackling some complicated cable pattern or anything like that. Just a straight stocking stitch, and all one colour. It gave me something to do. And her over there, Sandra, with the headphones on, she's teaching herself Spanish. She'll probably never use it. It's not like it's easy to pop over to Madrid when you've got to be here every other day. But time's precious, so don't waste it, lovey, that's what I say. Use it well. Find something you've always wanted to do, never had time for. A bit of multi-tasking. It's what we women are so good at, so they say.'

'Not sure there is anything really.'

'Just have a think about it. You can't just lie there every time, staring at the ceiling. Something good has to come out of our time in here, that's all. Well, I'm sorry if I've kept you from your book. Good, is it?'

Beth turned it over and looked at the cover. 'I have no idea. Can't get into it at all.'

They sat quietly for a few moments, both watching the nurse as she moved about the room, her flat black shoes squeaking on the shiny floor.

'Fancy a game of I-Spy?'

'Yeah, why not?' Beth was starting to like Maggie. 'You go first.'

'Okey dokey. I spy with my little eye, something beginning with... D.'

'That's too easy!'

'What? You think I mean dialysis? Oh no, it's something much less obvious than that.'

'Door?'

'Nope.'

'Doctor?'

'Can't see one. Unless he's hiding in the office and you've got X-ray eyes.'

'I give up then. Dog. Daisy Duck. Daniel Craig...'

'Now you're just being silly, but I like silly.' Maggie giggled like a teenager. 'And I quite like Daniel Craig, although you can't really beat Sean Connery as Bond.'

'What was it then? This thing starting with D?'

'Doughnuts!'

'Where?' Beth laughed. 'That has to count as cheating, waving imaginary cakes in front of my eyes when I'm craving sugar!'

'No, really, they're not imaginary. I have two right here.' Maggie pulled a white cardboard bakery box out from her cavernous tote bag. 'Want one?'

Beth's eyes widened. 'God, I'd love one, but we're not meant to eat, are we?'

'Save it for later. That's what I do. A reward, for when we get out of here.' Maggie gave her an encouraging grin. 'A little of what you fancy. What the hell? Life has to have some little pleasures. Right! I-Spy. Your turn next. Unless you'd prefer to help me do my crossword. I've got a pen somewhere here in my bag.'

Beth nodded. 'You're on.'

It was going to be all right. Manageable. As Maggie had said, just a regular chore, like doing the ironing or having her hair done. And she was going to knuckle down and get on with it, no matter how tedious and inconvenient and bloody uncomfortable it was, and come out at the other side of all this with a donor, a transplant and at least one healthy, fully functioning, very real life-saving kidney. If it was the last thing she ever did.

EIGHTEEN

Ruby had never left Lily before. Well, not intentionally, knowing she wouldn't see her for days. As she climbed into William's car and closed the door, she couldn't help feeling uneasy. What if something happened while she was gone? To Lily, or to her? Her mind shot back to her road accident three years earlier, and to Lily left all alone while she was in hospital, in a coma. How would she ever forgive herself if she wasn't here for her daughter and something terrible were to happen again?

When the invitation had come from Laura in London, Geri had insisted that she accept it. A few days away would do her good, she had said, and both Lily and the shop would survive without her. She was more than happy to pop in once or twice and oversee things if there were any problems her assistants couldn't handle. Ruby was entitled to a break every now and then. It had all made perfect sense until this morning when the reality of leaving Lily behind had hit her.

Lily was standing on the step now, still in her school uniform, her hand in Geri's, and waving frantically with the other, as they pulled out of the drive and headed for the station. Ruby turned her head, thrust her arm out of the open window and waved back, her gaze fixed on Lily's little pale face until they had turned the corner and she was no longer in sight. Lily was smiling, happy, safe. Ruby knew that. With Geri and William to take care of her, nothing bad was going to happen. Not this time.

Laura and her husband Paul had finally redecorated the old-fashioned vicarage they had moved into last year, including what she had described on the phone as a dreamy nursery that she just had to show her before it turned into the chaotic mess she knew it would as soon as it was filled with babies and all that went with them. Laura had been excited but obviously more than a little shellshocked at finding herself pregnant with twins. Two for the price of one, she had joked when she had announced the news, sending Ruby a photo of her growing belly and her hands wrapped protectively around it. Laura would be okay. A good mum. And her babies would have a loving and secure home. Just as she and Lily did now, at long last.

There was to be a belated housewarming party this evening, nothing too raucous, just a few friends, followed by a baby shower on Saturday afternoon, when Laura was going to reveal the sex of her babies, and then a lazy Sunday, perhaps a gentle stroll and a coffee somewhere, nothing too taxing for Laura now she was getting bigger, while vicar Paul went off to do his thing at the church, and a late lunch which Paul had promised to cook before Ruby and Vicky caught the evening train back to Brighton.

She wasn't sure whose idea it had been for Vicky to come with her as a sort of plus-one (sad old Ruby without a boyfriend in tow), but Laura had seemed happy enough with the arrangement and Ruby was glad about it now. Company for the journey, someone to steady her nerves at being back in London after so long, and Laura would welcome Vicky, and would like her, she was sure.

She also knew she could always rely on Vicky to liven up any party. Being with her for a whole weekend and sharing a room again would be fun. Just like old times, but a whole lot better. She just hoped Vicky would remember that their host was a vicar and behave herself once the vodka shots started to kick in.

Vicky was already there on the platform when Ruby trundled her small weekend case along towards her, checking her ticket for the right carriage and seat number for at least the third time since leaving the house.

'Hey, you made it!' Vicky said, drawing her into a hug. 'I'd have felt a bit of a dick having to go on my own when I don't even know these people.'

'It's a long time since you've felt a dick,' Ruby quipped. 'If you ever have...'

'Now, now, none of that smutty talk. I'm a good girl, I am.' Vicky roared with laughter.

'Seriously though, I'm not late, am I?'

'Of course not. Another ten minutes yet. Looks like we've got good weather too. It's ages since I've been to London, which is mad when it's only an hour away. But I want to do it all. All the touristy stuff. Buckingham Palace, Oxford Street, Big Ben...'

'We won't have time. We're only there for two days, and Laura has plans.'

'Oh, come on, Rubes. The party's not until tonight, is it? We can at least take a bit of a peek around when we get there. We'll only get in the way if we turn up too early, won't we? Your mate's going to be busy organising stuff and she won't want to have to feed us.'

'There'll be food at the party.'

'Yeah, right. Sausage rolls and nibbly bits. I need a proper dinner. A burger and chips, at least. We can have a wander. Get a bit of atmosphere, grab something to eat, before we head over to hers.'

'Atmosphere? The only atmosphere's likely to be petrol fumes and sweat! And we've got cases with us.'

'Oh, you are such a spoilsport. So, London's not your favourite place. I get that. Not the happiest time of your life being stuck there on your own with a kid, but give it a chance, eh? Let's enjoy ourselves, pack loads in. How often do you get to be childfree for a whole forty-eight hours?'

'Well, I suppose we could just walk along to the Tower or somewhere. It's not that far from the station.'

'Brilliant. And there's tomorrow morning too, before the shower thingy.'

'You'll probably have a raging hangover and not get out of bed until lunchtime!'

'I'll have you know I have the constitution of an ox. It'll take more than a drop of alcohol to keep me from the changing of the guard.'

'We'll see.'

***

'Just like old times,' Vicky said, lying back on one of the two small single beds, beneath the window, the contents of her case emptied out all around her. 'Us together, sharing a room.'

'God, I hope not, or we'll have old Mrs Castle bringing us our Ovaltine and telling us to put the lights out by eight o'clock!' Ruby lifted the edge of the curtain and peered out into the back garden. 'It's a nice house, isn't it? And the garden's tiny but quite pretty.'

'What did you expect in London? Land costs a fortune here. Looks like you'll have to bag yourself a vicar if you fancy cheap accommodation and a job for life around these parts.'

'Oh, no. Not me. Too high a price to pay. I'm really not religious at all. I had Lily christened, obviously. It was Paul who did that, after I first met him and Laura at the hospital. It felt like the right thing at the time, like thanking God for letting her be found, and letting me live, but we don't go to church or anything. Not now. Anyway, a London house isn't for me, you know that, with or without a vicar in tow. And can you imagine all the stuff a vicar's wife must have to do? Be nice all the time, for one. Open the door to everyone who knocks, basically, at any time of the day or night. Smile, be helpful, caring. People wanting weddings and christenings and funerals, people crying, or dying even... but I'm sure Laura being a nurse for so long must help her with all of that.'

'Yeah, and you'd be on show all the time too. It wouldn't do to wear your skirts too short or get caught having a sneaky fag or singing along to Barry Manilow.'

'What's Barry Manilow got to do with anything?'

'Oh, you know, gay icon and all that. But I mean just letting your hair down, having a laugh. It could be Take That or Kaiser Chiefs or anybody really. It's just not how you think of vicars or their wives, is it? I bet they sing hymns when they get drunk. If they ever do get drunk...'

'Ha, you are so wrong! Didn't I tell you Paul's in a rock band?'

'No!'

'Honestly. He plays guitar, got a motorbike and everything. Well, you'll meet him later. Come on. Let's get our glad rags on and go downstairs, see if we can help with anything. Laura said the others will be here around half past eight.'

'Shame we didn't get to go inside the Tower. I would have liked to see the ravens.'

'No time. And did you see the prices? We'd have to stay all

day to make it worthwhile. We got to see the outside though, didn't we? And the bridge. Enough history for you, surely?'

'I suppose. We'll go again another time maybe? And to London Zoo. I'd love to go round there again. I don't think I've been since I was first adopted. You know, Mum and Dad trying a bit too hard to make me happy, take me everywhere, give me everything all at once. All crammed into that first year or so before...'

Vicky stopped and sat up, pulling a bright red dress from the heap on the floor and whipping off her jeans. She never did finish her sentence.

The balloons were still strung around the ceiling and hung in corners. Some pink, some blue. They had added a childlike quality to last night's party, so much so that Vicky had whispered something about expecting jelly and ice cream next, or a game of Pin the Tail on the Donkey. Ruby had slapped her on the wrist and told her to ssshh before anyone heard her.

Laura had been up since the crack of dawn, tidying and cleaning after the party, with all the nesting instinct of a proudly pregnant woman, and was now going round gathering the balloons together, cutting strings and letting them float down to the carpet before bundling them into plastic sacks and carrying them all up the stairs. The occasional loud popping sound told them that not all had survived the trip.

'What exactly is she doing?' Vicky said, coming in from the kitchen, bleary-eyed and yawning, carrying a mug of coffee, black, steaming and clearly a lot stronger than the constitution she had so confidently boasted about yesterday.

'It's something to do with whether she's having boys or girls, or one of each, I think.'

'Bit of a stereotype thing though, isn't it? Pink for a girl, blue for a boy, and all that. What if it ends up trans or bi or something?'

'A bit soon to be thinking about that, isn't it? It's traditional, the colour thing. And sort of cute in its way.'

Vicky huffed. 'Did *you* know? What you were having, before Lily was born?'

'Yeah. They asked us, at the scan, if we wanted to know, and it seemed silly not to. Helps with what to buy.'

'What? More pink stuff, you mean? And dolls instead of train sets?'

'Nothing wrong with dolls. Ours were lifesavers in their way when we were kids, weren't they? We could hardly cuddle a train at night, could we?'

'I suppose. Still, I've brought something totally non-gender specific as my gift for this afternoon.'

'You didn't have to bring anything. Laura won't be expecting...'

'Ha ha, but she is very definitely expecting, isn't she?' Vicky puffed out her cheeks and stuck her belly out, spilling a drop of coffee onto her T-shirt as she laughed.

'You know what I meant. You didn't have to bring a gift.'

'After she invited me and let me stay over? Anyway, it's not much. Just something from the gift shop at work. A year's sponsorship of a piglet. Never too young to get children involved with animals and, with a bit of luck, the parents will renew it next year and keep supporting us.'

'You love your job, don't you?'

'I do, yes.' Vicky swallowed the rest of her coffee and curled her bare feet up beneath her on the sofa. 'It's only a tiny place but it makes kids happy. And it makes *me* happy. Animals don't let you down like people do. They don't judge you, or walk out on you. You can trust them and, once they take to you, it's unconditional. I sometimes think I'll end up as one of those mad old spinster cat ladies, surrounded by fur and fleas, but happy as Larry.'

'Right. What do you think?' Laura was back, with two square packages tucked under her arms, each wrapped in silver paper. She threw them haphazardly across the room, one aimed at each of them, although only Ruby managed to catch one. It was surprisingly light.

'Balloons,' Laura said, plonking herself down in a shabby armchair and resting her legs on a pouffe. 'For the big reveal. One box per baby, but what's inside? Both pink, both blue, or one of each? That is the question!'

'I thought that was to be or not to be!'

'More like what's it to be?'

'Can't you tell us? Let us into the secret early?'

'No, I cannot! You will find out when everybody else does, when we open the boxes later and the contents come bobbing out. Now, who's for breakfast? We've got cereal, toast, eggs...'

'Any hair of the dog?' Vicky said, closing her eyes. 'Or a couple of aspirin at least?'

'Oh dear. A bit too much to drink last night?'

'You could say that.'

'Not something I have to worry about these days,' Laura said, holding her tummy protectively. 'I've not touched a drop since I found out.'

'There you are. See. Another reason to stay single and childless.' Vicky opened her eyes and grinned. 'Babies are all very well, but I think I prefer sticking with the beer and settling for a couple of tabbies, to be honest.'

Geraldine had made fish fingers for Lily's tea. Not just bought the frozen kind, but actually flaked up some cod and mashed a few potatoes to mix in with it, and made her own breadcrumb coating. Was it any healthier? She wasn't sure, but at least there would be no hidden additives or E numbers. She had thought about cooking a traditional Sunday roast, but William was out and she wasn't sure what time he'd be back, and Lily liked to eat early. Keeping a plate back and reheating it for him later never really seemed to work. There was something about beef, especially pink in the middle the way he liked it best, that only ever looked and tasted perfect when it was eaten straight from the oven.

She had never been a particularly adventurous cook. Not particularly adventurous about anything, to be honest. Michael had been her only child – well, the only one she had had any hand in raising – and back then, when he was small, she had always been so busy helping Ken run the shop that meals had necessarily been quick and easy and based on convenience. She had never been the sort of mother to bake her own bread or spend hours poring over cookery books. It was a shame, but life was what it was. They had left it late enough having Michael in the first place. Partly financial, partly the fear of going through another labour, wondering if she could allow herself to really love a child after the heartbreak of letting Sandie go. And Ken… knowing how it made him feel, that she had done all this before. Sex, pregnancy, childbirth, all the things they should have explored for the first time together, but never could because she had been a stupid teenager who couldn't wait to get herself into trouble.

But they had gone ahead in the end, having just the one child, before it was too late, each knowing they might regret it if they didn't. In a way, it was a good thing they had had a boy. Not so easy to compare. What she might have looked like. What she might be doing now. It was probably why Geraldine had become so involved in the local children's home, helping to find the girls jobs and places to stay as they came into adulthood, trying to give back whatever it was she had been unable to give to Sandie, her own daughter, once she knew she would never have another.

Michael was different. Boys were different. Yet in so many ways just the same. The little feet under the blanket. The screwed-up wrinkly face. Crying for his milk, and his mum.

He had been the kind of child who would eat anything. He still was! It had never been difficult trying to get him to accept school lunchboxes packed with healthy salads, although she did worry sometimes that he was eating a few too many chips to make up for it when he got home. He was never fussy though. He just ate it all, whatever she put in front of him, shovelling it down as fast as she could supply it and, miracle though it was, he'd turned out okay. She had no idea what sort of meals Patsy gave him nowadays, or even which of them did the cooking, but he looked well enough on it.

Lily was a different matter. She loved having Lily around, and having the time to spend with her. And Lily was going to eat well, live well. Good healthy food, the sun on her skin, the beach to play on, pretty clothes, a bike, lots of little friends. The happiest childhood anyone could ever experience. She owed her that after the terrible start the poor child had had in life. Parents who didn't get along, all that time in London with just Ruby, struggling to make ends meet, the days spent alone when Ruby had her accident. No, never again. No child was going to be lonely or scared, or get too fat or end up with rotten teeth, on her watch.

She took the plates through to the sink, glad to see that every mouthful had been eaten and Lily's plate scraped clean. She had made a fruit salad for afters, a big bowl of cut-up melon and halved grapes and fat juicy strawberries, but they were both feeling too full to tackle it just yet. Ruby gave her too much chocolate, too much ice cream, let her stay up too late. But Geraldine had to remember that Lily was not her child. She was Ruby's, and Ruby was allowed to make her own rules, and her own mistakes, just as she herself had undoubtedly done all those years ago. But for now, for this weekend, and for a few more hours, Lily was hers, and that gave her a very good feeling. A warm feeling, of being needed, that even being with William could never quite manage to match.

'Can we play tea parties now, Granny?' Lily was pulling various dolls and teddies from her toy box in the corner of the dining room. They had eaten at the proper table, not in the kitchen as Ruby always did. And now Lily was pushing the salt and pepper and the little bowl of untouched tartar sauce aside and starting to arrange her dolls around the table, each one with a cushion placed to prop it upright on a chair. 'With one of Aggiss's special teapots?'

Geraldine laughed. Lily never had mastered how to say Agnes's name, but she remembered her and that was all that mattered.

'Of course. Which one would you like?'

'The castle!'

'Say please then, and we'll go and find it.'

'Please, Granny.'

Lily always chose the castle, the teapot she had first encountered in William's old London garden when he and his mother had thrown a birthday party for her the one year Ruby had not been able to. A bouncy castle, lots of cake, and the promise of a rabbit. What more could a three-year-old want? Lily had been so happy she'd been sick! Geraldine smiled to herself. It had been a special day for her too. The day William had first kissed her, in the kitchen when everyone else had gone.

She could never have imagined then where it would lead. To this... bliss.

'Come on then, let's go into the garage and dig it out from the box, shall we? I'm beginning to think we should bring it in and keep it here in the cupboard, it gets used so often. But we must be very careful. We don't want to break it, do we?'

Lily followed her into the hall. William was just coming in through the front door. 'Well, I've done it,' he said, a distinct look of pride spreading across his face. 'I've signed up for the Amateur Dramatics Society at last. And they're going to let me have a go at being in charge of the scenery and props for the next show, in July. Plenty of woodwork and painting to be done, and I said I'd do the prompting, as I'm backstage anyway, just in case anyone forgets their lines, so I'll be going along to the rehearsals too. That should keep me out of your hair for a couple of nights a week.'

'That's great.'

'What? Happy to get rid of me, are you?' he teased.

'You know I didn't mean that. No, it's great that you've found something you love doing. And they're lucky to have you. I knew they'd snap you up.'

'I don't know about that. I was the only volunteer! Everyone else seems keen to get onto the stage. Fighting over the parts, they were. But me, well, I'm more than happy to stay out of the spotlight, and away from the microphones, especially as it's a musical and I can't sing to save my life! Now, where are you two off to? And what's for tea?'

The train home was packed. Ruby glanced through a magazine she'd picked up at the station while Vicky half-dozed beside her,

her over-large hips encroaching into the space that was meant to be her seat.

'Two boys! Can you imagine it?' Vicky had opened her eyes and was gazing out of the window into the darkness. 'Still, Paul looked pleased, didn't he? What is it with men and sons, eh? Someone to play football with, I suppose. To take fishing, and teach them about engines and stuff.'

'I don't quite see Paul as an engines type somehow. He might ride a motorbike but I don't think he takes it apart.'

'Maybe not. But don't they realise girls can do all that too? I'm pretty good with a football as it happens. And I know my camshaft from my big end.'

'Big end, eh? You have to have one to recognise one, I guess.' Ruby laughed, swivelling her eyes towards her friend's bottom. 'To be fair though, I think Paul would have looked just as happy whatever sex they are. He was just being a proud dad-to-be, that's all.'

'Maybe. I wonder what they've done with all those other balloons though? The pink ones, I mean. Now that all the blues are hanging round the door of the vicarage like a bloody great *Look at me, I'm having boys* beacon. She might as well put up a neon sign.'

'Ah, don't be mean. She just wants to shout it from the rooftops, and who can blame her?'

'What did you say their surname is again?'

'Thomas. Why?'

'Oh, just thinking about names. I bet they pick biblical ones, like Isaiah or Benjamin or something like that. Or Timothy. Timothy Thomas. Ha, that's a good one!'

'Well, they won't pick Thomas, will they? Thomas Thomas... can you imagine that?'

'Just as long as it's not John.' Vicky pulled a disgusted face, and it took Ruby a moment to realise why. 'Now, that would be unfortunate.'

Ruby laughed. It had been fun spending time away, but she was looking forward to getting back to Lily. Perhaps she should have nabbed a handful of those pink balloons. They might have been a bit hard to keep hold of on the train but Lily would have loved them.

NINETEEN

'I'm going to go there.' Jack had a determined look on his face. 'Later this week. Maybe on Friday when I'm off duty.'

'Go where?' Beth sat with her feet up in front of the TV, still feeling tired and a little sick from her latest treatment.

'Brighton. Now, don't you give me that look. One of us has to make the first move and there's no way you're up to it.'

'But...' Beth stopped. She wasn't sure what to say. Knowing her mother's name and where she came from was one thing but actually turning up on her doorstep was quite another. All the things she had talked about with the social worker came flooding back into her head. The possible shock, fear, anger, upset that her mother might feel, not to mention the possibility of outright denial or rejection. Who knew how Geraldine Clark might react when confronted with the living embodiment of her past? And then there was the thing – the really big crucial kidney hunt thing – that she had not told the social worker about at all, the thing that would almost definitely send this Geraldine woman running for the hills.

'You wanted to do this. It was your idea to find her. I can't see any point in stopping now, can you? You're sick, Mum, and whether or not you're still thinking of asking this woman to help you, sheer curiosity must make you want to go ahead, surely? Shared genes, the gaps in our family history, so much we don't know. And I'd like to know, even if you don't.'

'Would you?'

'Of course. The picture in the locket, that woman who even you must see looks so much like you. The birth certificate, the name, the address. We've got almost everything now except actually getting down there and finding her, and that's what I intend to do.'

'On your own? No girlfriend tagging along?'

'If that's you fishing for information, then no. No girlfriend.'

'I thought there was someone...'

'It was nothing serious. We decided to call it a day. No biggie, okay?'

'Sorry. I didn't mean to pry. It just seems to be all work and no play for you lately, that's all.'

'I love my job, and I'm only twenty-four. There's still plenty of time for all the love and romance stuff. Besides, I don't tell you everything, you know.' Jack winked at her. 'But you could come if you like. To Brighton. We can time it between dialysis appointments.'

'But I've got work. I'm already taking more time off than feels fair.'

'You're not well, Mum. It's nothing to do with being fair. You're entitled.'

'Oh, I know, but...'

'Will you please stop saying *but* all the time. Now, I have a four-day gap between shifts and I intend to spend at least a couple of those days in Brighton. You can pack your sunglasses and your bucket and spade and come with me, or you can stay here. Your choice.'

'And what about Emily?'

'Pull her out of school on a sickie and bring her with us, or leave her with Dad.'

Beth closed her eyes. Should she?

'No.' It was just too complicated. Emily was no toddler, happy to be whisked away for a holiday at a moment's notice. She would want to know why, and Beth did not yet feel ready to tell her. 'You go, if you must. I'll stay here. Let's keep things as normal for Emily as we can for now, okay?'

'You're going to have to tell her some time, Mum. And Tom. They're not babies. You're sick and they have a right to know. And about the mother hunt too, for that matter. This woman we might be about to meet is just as much their grandmother as she is mine.'

'They had a grandmother, and they've only just lost her. It's too soon to thrust some kind of replacement in front of them.'

'You know that's not what this is about.'

'I'm not even sure what it is about anymore. Do I really want to rake it all up, after fifty years or more? Disrupt this poor woman's life, and ours, on a whim? It's not as if I can really go in there and just boldly ask for a kidney, is it? The whole idea was ridiculous right from the start. It was just me panicking, clutching at straws, and I already feel bad about it, without even going through with it. I wish I'd never started any of this now.'

'So, you don't want me to go? Don't want to at least find out if she's still alive? What she's like? If she's been longing for you to turn up all this time? Because she might have, you know. You coming back into her life might be the most wonderful thing ever.'

'Or the worst.'

'Will you stop being so bloody negative!' Jack crossed the room and sat down heavily beside her, grabbing her hand and squeezing it in his. 'I'm sorry. I shouldn't be swearing at you, but it's all just so frustrating, when we've come this far... Look, at

143

best, this is going to give you a whole new family. At worst, we get sent away with a flea in our ear and we're no worse off than we are now. I know what I want to do.'

Beth gazed up at her son. 'Okay,' she said, her voice hardly more than a whisper. 'Go and see what you can find out. Try to get a look at her. But you won't approach her, will you? Don't go knocking on her door and making some big long-lost grandson announcement. If we do this, we need to do it slowly, do it right.'

'I'm not sure there is a right way. Whatever we do, it's going to be a bit traumatic, for all of us, but I'll go carefully, I promise.'

Jack swung his bag off the overhead shelf and onto his shoulder and followed his fellow passengers off the train.

It was mid-morning and still only early May but the sun was shining hot and strong as he stepped outside. He drank some water from his now almost empty bottle and brought up a street map on his phone. The road Geraldine had lived on was a good twenty minutes' walk away, and so was the beach, in completely the opposite direction, and for now that seemed like the best bet. A look at the sea, a bun or something to keep him going until he decided what to eat later, and time to make a plan which, despite having had several days to think about it, he still hadn't managed to do.

He passed a couple of Bed and Breakfasts on the way down, each with a big *Vacancies* sign hanging in the window. It was tempting to stop at one of them, make a reservation, perhaps leave his bag to save lugging it about all day, and then come back later when he was ready to sleep. But it was May, not August. There would be plenty of choice, some places probably tucked away down the smaller streets and therefore cheaper, and there was no hurry. Better to play it by ear. For all he knew, he might find all the answers he needed quickly and be back on the train home by the evening. Or be welcomed into this Geraldine's life and home, with the offer of dinner and a night in the spare room. Wouldn't that be amazing? But no, he had promised his mum he wouldn't just turn up uninvited, so he'd better stick to it.

He could smell the sea long before he saw it, drawing its fresh brininess into his lungs and feeling the tension begin to slip from his back and shoulders. Nursing was much more of a physical job than most people realised, and being the only male nurse on the ward meant it was often him doing the lifting and pushing that he hated watching his smaller female colleagues struggle with. 'You're too much of a gentleman,' the ward sister had said to him on more than one occasion. 'Nobody expects you to do their work for them.' But he did it anyway, rushing to help when someone fell out of bed or there was no porter available to wheel someone down to X-ray.

He tried to push all thoughts of work and hospitals out of his head. Knowing that his own mother was now a regular visitor to the dialysis unit just two floors below his own ward and that, sooner or later, she would probably be under the surgeon's knife, was not easy to deal with, no matter how professional and practical he was trying to be, for her sake as well as his own.

The promenade was quite busy with a mix of what looked like locals going about their usual business and the more obvious holidaymakers, clutching beach bags and towels and wearing sun hats and sandals, the children – all under school age as it was still term time – licking ice creams or trying to ride their scooters without bumping into the legs of the passers-by.

Jack found himself a spot to stop and gazed out over the mounds of pebbles to the rolling grey waves. Now that he was here, he felt suddenly apprehensive, unsure of himself. Whatever he did in this next day or two could make a huge difference to a lot of people's lives. He just wasn't sure what he was going to get for his trouble. A pat on the back, or a kick in the teeth? It really could go either way.

———

He found it after lunch. A small ordinary-looking terraced house, probably pre-war, the bricks painted white, the door blue. A row of straggly roses lined the path, where a few weeds were pushing their way up through the gravel. There was no garage and no driveway, but a small black Renault was parked outside, sandwiched between lots of other cars, each with some kind of residents' permit showing through the windscreen.

Jack crossed to the other side of the road and stood on the pavement, crouching for a moment, pretending to tie his shoelace. What now? He had promised his mum he wouldn't just knock and announce who he was, but he had to do something, say something. Door-to-door salesman? Jehovah's Witness? Window cleaner touting for business? There were any number of excuses he could come up with if he needed them, enough to get as far as the step anyway, and to get a glimpse at whoever was living here. He'd know if it was her, wouldn't he? Recognise her eyes, from the photo in the locket, see some resemblance to his mum, or to Emily or himself?

He was kidding himself if he really believed it would be that easy, and that recognising her would be that instant. Anyone could answer the door. Man or woman, black or white, someone far too young or far too old...

This wasn't going to help in any way, was it? But he was here now, a chance, however slim, presenting itself, so he did it anyway. Walked across the road, opened the gate, went up the path and rang the bell.

'I'm sorry to bother you...' He had got that far, working out in his head what he was going to say, but he was struggling to get much further. But then he didn't have to. Nobody came to the door. He rang again, took a step back, peered up at the windows above him, listened for the sound of footsteps that never came.

He walked back to the gate and out onto the pavement, putting his bag down at his feet while he pondered his next move.

'Hello?' An old woman, grey-haired, stooped, was peering out at him from the open doorway of the house next door. 'Can I help you?'

Jack put on his best smile, turning on the natural charm he was so famous for on the ward. 'I do hope you can,' he said, taking a step towards her along the pavement and waiting to see what she would do. Returning his smile, she wandered slowly down her path, limping a little, and stood looking up at him from the other side of her gate. Not much of a safety barrier, he thought, if I was intending to do her any harm. Why were the elderly so trusting?

'A bit of a long shot I know, but I was looking for someone who used to live here. At number 62. Maybe they still do?'

'And who would that be?' She peered at him, the first sign of suspicion creeping across her small wrinkled face.

'A family called Clark. This would have been a long time ago, mind. In the late sixties, early seventies?'

'And why would you be wanting to know?'

It came to him in a sudden flash of inspiration. 'I'm researching,' he said. 'Trying to trace the family of someone who's died, people who might be in line for an inheritance.'

'Ooh, like that programme on the telly, you mean?' Her eyes lit up. '*Heir Hunters*, looking for people who've been left a fortune?'

'Just like that, yes. I don't suppose you know where I might find them? A Miss Geraldine Clark in particular.'

'Young Geri? Do you know, I've not seen her in years. Not since her father died. The mother went early, you know. Cancer. Not even forty.'

'Oh, that's sad.'

'It was. But they're not here now, my duck. No, Geri moved out long ago, when she got married. They never owned this place, you know, the Clarks. Just rented. Not seen her since her dad passed on, about ten or twelve years back it must have been, and then only from the window, not to talk to. Bit of a miserable old bugger, he was, her father. Kept himself to himself. It's a single lady living in there now. A dentist, would you believe? Not been here long. It was a taxi driver and his wife before that. Too noisy by half, those kids of theirs.'

'So,' Jack tried to steer the conversation back towards Geraldine Clark. 'I don't suppose you know where I might find her now?'

'Who? The dentist? At work probably. Leaves the car here and walks to the surgery. It's just up the road there.'

'No. No, not the dentist. Geraldine – Geri – Clark. Although you said she was married, so maybe not a Clark anymore...'

'Oh, yes, of course. They had a shop, down near the sea. Her husband's family. Baines or Haynes, or some such name. I can't quite remember now. I think young Geri may have worked there for a while. Now, what was it called? *Bits & Bobs*, yes, that was it. My husband was called Bob, you see. That's how it's stuck in my mind. God rest his soul. I think it's still there, the shop, but I have no idea who runs it now. Not the sort of place I ever go in, all seashells and sticks of rock for the tourists.'

'Thank you, that's very helpful, Mrs...?'

'Oh, I'm not telling you my name. You could be anybody.' The old woman's expression changed, and she shuffled back towards her door, muttering to herself. 'Trying to bluff your way in and steal my purse for all I know.'

'I assure you, I'm not...'

She stepped back into the safety of her hallway and peered back at him through the half-closed door.

'Thank you, anyway. You've been very helpful.'

'I'll be expecting a share, you know. Of that will money, if she gets it. You wouldn't have known where to find her, would you? If it wasn't for me.'

'Of course. But I can't arrange that without knowing your name...'

'It's Higgins. Elsie Higgins.' She took a last look at him, shook her head and closed the door as Jack waved politely, picked up his bag and walked away, laughing.

Ruby had come back from London a few days ago, but there was still a ripple of excitement running through her. Much as she loved Lily – of course she did – it had been so good to be able to stay up late, have a few drinks, and talk about adult, girly things, without the constant interruptions and questions that the presence of a six-year-old inevitably involved.

Laura and Vicky couldn't be more different from each other, or from Ruby herself if she was honest about it, but that didn't seem to matter. So, Vicky liked girls and Ruby liked boys, and Laura was so safely married and pregnant she was well out of the market for either, but that hadn't stopped them comparing notes, giggling about past relationships, sharing their dreams and drawing up ridiculous plans for their very different futures.

Since Michael had left her, Ruby had never felt a strong need to replace him. Her one and only experience of loving a man had ended badly and it was easy to tar them all with the same brush. Unreliable, uncaring, prone to follow their dicks rather than their hearts, if they even had such a thing. But watching Laura with Paul had opened her eyes to something else, something she was beginning to think she would not say no to if she were lucky enough to find it for herself. Okay, so Paul was a vicar. Not necessarily your typical man, and obviously far more likely to be the faithful kind, but she had seen such a genuine connection between them.

There was a lot of affection between Geri and William too, she was certain, but they were old, and it had taken them a long time to find it. It was more of the cosy, comfy kind, all cuddles and cups of cocoa, or that was how she liked to think of it. She couldn't even begin to imagine there being any actual sexual thing going on, but she supposed there must be. Just not too enthusiastic or exciting, and probably not very often.

She sat behind the counter in the shop, which was very busy today now the sun was shining and the first tourists of the season were out in force. She was waiting for Kerry to come back from her very late lunch break, which Ruby was only too aware tended to revolve less around food these days – she was getting way too thin – and more around having a sneaky cigarette or two and sending lengthy texts to whoever her latest boyfriend happened to be. This new one was married, despite his protestations that it was 'complicated' and he was just waiting for the right time to leave, but there was nothing Ruby could say or do to make the girl see sense. She was her boss, not her mother, and it really was none of her business. Still, as soon as Kerry came back to take over in the shop, Ruby would take a break of her own and escape for a while down to the beach. She had always done her best thinking on the beach, the crunch of the pebbles underfoot, and the rhythmic sound of the sea calming her and somehow putting everything into perspective. Whatever small worries she might have were always easier to cope with once she let the wind and the waves blow them away. Not that she had worries exactly, more just a restlessness, a niggling need for something to change. And that could only happen if she let it.

It was hard now to believe that she had ever lived in London when Brighton was so clearly where she belonged. Another black mark against Michael's name, for not only dragging her there but leaving her there to rot. And look at him now, sunning himself in Portugal. He was no more a natural city dweller than she was. London was only ever a stepping stone for him, a way to advance his career, yet he had abandoned her there, pulled along in his wake and left stranded like a lump of seaweed on the shore.

She shook her head. Why on earth was she wasting any more time thinking about Michael? He had Patsy now, and she had a home and a job and Lily, all the things she would never have thought possible before he – and his wonderfully generous mother – had come into her life.

'Excuse me.'

She looked up, startled by the proximity of the voice, and straight into the face of what could quite possibly be the most handsome man she had ever seen. He was tall and sandy-haired and he had kind brown eyes.

'Oh, hi. Sorry, I was daydreaming there for a moment. What can I help you with?'

He didn't answer straight away.

'A souvenir maybe? Postcards? Or some sweets? I've got all the traditional ones. Barley sugars, rhubarb and custards, acid drops...'

His gaze travelled slowly along the rows of sweets behind her. 'Well, maybe a bag of peppermint creams. Always been my favourites.' He smiled, showing a set of even white teeth that didn't give the impression of ever having eaten a sugar-laden sweet in their entire lifetime.

'Of course. Small or large?'

'The peppermints or the bag?'

'The bag! I still weigh them in ounces. People like the old-fashioned ways. Antique scales and all. Are four ounces enough?' She lifted the jar down from the shelf and unscrewed the lid.

'Perfect.'

'So, what brings you to Brighton?' She poured the sweets carefully onto the scales, then slid them into a small pink and white striped paper bag and rolled down the top.

He handed over a five-pound note and she gave him back his change. His fingers were big and warm as they took the coins from her hand and slipped them into his pocket.

'How do you know I'm not a local?'

I'd definitely have spotted you before now if you were, she thought, but out loud she said, 'The overnight bag, I guess. Looks like you've just got off the train.'

'About four hours ago actually. But very observant of you. Yeah, I'm here on a sort of holiday. Just for a day or two.'

'Sort of holiday?'

'Combined with a fact-finding mission. Which I'm hoping you might be able to help me with. I'm looking for someone, you see. Someone who I'm told might have worked here, in this shop.'

Oh, God, Ruby thought. Don't say he's looking for Kerry. Not another of her exes. But if he was, then she'd have been mad to let this one slip away. Unless... no, surely this wasn't her married man. She took a sneaky look at his left hand, still holding the bag of sweets. No, no ring.

'Well, we don't have a lot of staff.'

'Oh, I don't mean current staff. I'm talking a way back. Like fifty years ago.'

Ruby felt herself relax. Not Kerry then. 'Well, we're a family business, and always have been, so if she – or he – has worked here and I don't know about it, then Geri certainly will.'

'Geri?' He was looking at her very intently all of a sudden.

'Yeah, Geraldine Munro, my sort of mother-in-law.'

'Sort of mother-in-law?'

He was teasing her now, tilting his head to one side, imitating her own earlier response.

'It's a long story. Not my actual mother-in-law, as I'm not actually married.' Why on earth had she told him that? She could feel her face redden. 'Anyway, Geri's been here since the year dot, and her husband's family even longer than that, so if you're looking for someone from way back, she's probably the best person to ask.'

'And where might I find this Geri... Munro, did you say?'

'I'm not sure I should tell you that.'

'You're the second person to say something like that to me today.'

'Just being careful. Maybe you should tell me exactly who it is you're after and why, and then we'll see.'

'What is it? Do I look like some kind of axe murderer or something? It's just a family history thing. You know, tracing the ancestors. There's an old photo I'd like to show her too. I tell you what...' He hesitated for a moment, just as the door flew open and Kerry came rushing back in, muttering apologies and dropping her bag down on the floor behind the counter.

'I was about to say,' the man continued, lowering his voice as Kerry beckoned a customer forward and rang her purchases through the till, 'that you might like to pop out for a coffee or something. If you've got a few minutes. Then I can tell you more about it.' He held his hands up. 'Look, no axe, I promise.'

Ruby thought about it, but not for long. After all, how often did a gorgeous man drop in out of the blue and offer to take her out? Well, outside anyway. A week ago she would probably have said no, been over-cautious and suspicious. But now, with Vicky's influence still fresh in her mind and buoyed by her own decision to make more of a grab at life, she knew she had to say yes.

'Okay. I'd like that. Thank you.' It was a warm day, but she grabbed her jacket anyway, reached for her bag, hung it over her shoulder, and followed him across the shop floor.

He held the door open for her to go ahead of him, and they walked, slightly apart and without any discussion about it, towards the sea. The seagulls were soaring overhead, loud as ever, but there were a few clouds looming. People were still sitting on the pebbles in family groups, although most seemed to be wearing jumpers or anoraks now. There was a definite feel of rain on the way.

'Where shall we go? You're the local.'

'A takeaway coffee and a walk along the pier?'

'Sounds good. It's nearly three. Have you eaten? We could get a burger or something?'

'Thanks, but I had a sandwich earlier. Coffee's fine. And I could do with the walk. I get a bit stiff sitting in the shop all day.'

He bought two coffees and they wandered along the wooden boards that stretched out over the sea, warming their hands around the cups.

'There's something lovely about an old-fashioned pier, isn't there? I hope they've got fruit machines and deck chairs, and old men with fishing rods sitting at the end.'

Ruby laughed. 'Something like that. And funfair rides, but you can see those from here, obviously.'

'And hear them. All that squealing!' He stopped for a

moment and leant on the rail, gazing out at the water. 'So, I don't even know your name. I'm Jack.'

'Ruby.'

'Look, this is tricky, and a bit hard to know where to start. I was telling the truth back there. I am looking at family history, in a way. *My* family, to be precise. The thing is... well, I'm looking for a woman I've never met. Her name was – *is* – Geraldine, and I believe she's my grandmother.'

'Geraldine? *My* Geraldine?'

'I don't know, but when you said her name... well, a bit of a coincidence, don't you think, if it's not? Working in the same shop I know she has connections to. And it's not that common a name.'

'No, it can't be her. You've got that wrong. My Geraldine only has one child, a son, Michael, and he's not that much older than you. And there's only one grandchild, and that's his daughter – *my* daughter – Lily.'

'I've got a photo, if that helps to sort this out at all. It was taken more than fifty years ago, but perhaps you could take a look at it? See if it's her?' He pulled a necklace out of his inside pocket and prised it open with his fingernails. 'Here...'

Ruby took it from him. The picture was small and faded, and she had to tilt it towards the light to see it properly. She felt a flood of relief when she realised it was not Geri.

'No. Sorry, that's not her. Not the Geri I know. Even though she would have changed over the years, it's definitely not her. The woman you're after must be someone else.'

'Are you sure?'

'Totally.'

'And your Geri. Do you know what her maiden name was?'

'She's always been Geraldine Payne as long as I've known her.'

'Payne? Only someone told me it might be Baines? Close enough, I suppose.'

'Payne, yes. But not now. She recently remarried and became a Munro. Before that, I'm not sure. I don't think I ever asked.'

'Does the name Clark ring any bells?'

'No, sorry. Why do you want to find her anyway, this long-lost granny of yours?'

'Like I said before, it's a long story, and it happened ages ago, but it's probably fair that I don't say any more. She might not want me to talk about it.'

'Intriguing.'

'Not really. Just personal. Best discussed with her, if I can find her.'

'Which you haven't. If that's her in the photo, then it looks like you've been on a wild goose chase. Geri's not her, not the woman you're after. So, what will you do now? Go home to... Where did you say you come from?'

'I didn't, and it's London, but I think I'll stick around, do a bit more digging. I'd still like to talk to Geri Munro if I can. She might know something. So, I'm going to stay for a night or two, I think.' He nodded towards the bag slung over his shoulder. 'I came prepared.'

'Well, I hope you've got a mac rolled up in there. It looks like it might rain at any minute. I hope you get lucky with your search, but I suppose I should be getting back to the shop. Drop in again tomorrow if you're around. I'll talk to Geri tonight, if you like, and see if she knows anything.'

'No. Don't do that.' He looked alarmed. 'Please. I'd rather speak to her myself, if that's all right with you.'

'Oh, okay.'

'Maybe you could just try to get her to meet me, without saying what it's about?'

'I can try, I suppose. It's not as if I even know what it is about really. Can I at least tell her your name?'

'Yes, that's fine. Just say it's Jack, not that she'll know who I am. Maybe I can give you my number and you can ask her to call me? Or see if she'll come and meet me somewhere? At the shop, or the pier?'

'You're a real man of mystery, aren't you?'

'Not really. I'm happy to tell you whatever you want to know about me. No dark secrets. But you will try, won't you? Just a chat with her, that's all I want.' He held out his phone. 'Can we swap numbers? I promise not to stalk you.'

'Yeah, why not? I can always block you if you do.'

'Thanks, Ruby. It is important, honestly. But, like I said, it's private.'

'I'll see what I can do. Come about lunchtime. And there'll be a bag of peppermint creams on the house waiting for you, to repay you for the coffee.'

TWENTY

1968

'So where have you been then?' A group of girls in navy uniform hung around her in the playground on her first day back. 'Someone said you were sick. Not catching, is it?'

Geraldine shook her head. 'Rheumatic fever. The doctor said I needed lots of rest to get better but I couldn't be left on my own, and Dad had to go to work, so I went to my auntie's, at the seaside. I stayed in her spare room.'

'All right for some. Months off school and sitting about on some beach. I wish I had caught it now, so I could do that too!'

'You wouldn't have wanted what I had, believe me. It was horrible.'

It was easy to lie, but that part was the truth. She wouldn't wish what had happened to her on anyone.

In a few more weeks it would all be final and legal and there would be no going back. But then, it already was final, wasn't it? The decision had been made, the baby taken from her, and she knew perfectly well that there could be no changing that now.

Her dad had cried the day she came home. She couldn't

remember him ever crying before. Not even when Mum had died, when he had tried so hard to be strong and brave and find ways to fill the gap in their lives that they both knew could never really be filled. And, seeing him like that, crying, for her or the baby, she wasn't sure which, had made her decide something. No more playing up, no more sneaking out, no staying out late, no more giving him cheek. She had punished him enough, and it wasn't as if there was anything to punish him for. He had done his best, and she had let him down. Let her mum down too. From now on, she would knuckle down at school, do her homework, make him proud. There would be no more messing about with boys. No more stupid mistakes. And there would be no more babies. Not for a very long time. Maybe never.

TWENTY-ONE

The house in Shelling still hadn't sold. Beth put the phone down after talking to the estate agent and poured herself a second cup of tea. While properties in London cost the earth but still seemed to go like hot cakes, whatever their condition, it would appear that the housing market in a small country village in the back of beyond was very different.

'We do get retirees, moving out of town, downsizing, and the weekenders looking for a holiday home, although most want to be nearer the sea. And businesspeople, craving the rural life and willing to commute to Norwich or further afield,' he had said. 'But your mother's house doesn't really fit what they're after. Most buyers tend to want either the modern new builds they can walk straight into or the chocolate box roses-round-the-door dream. The house is rather outdated, as I'm sure you realise. It needs time, work, vision...'

'How many viewings have you had?'

'Not nearly as many as I would have liked, I'm afraid. Only five so far, and it wasn't the right house for any of them, but it's spring now. Things always perk up a bit when the sun comes out.'

'So, what if we drop the price?'

'We can certainly do that if you'd like to, Mrs Hogan. A cheaper price for a quicker sale, or hold out for what it's worth. The choice is yours.'

Was there any choice, really? Keeping an empty house, miles away, was pointless, not to mention stressful. There were still bills to pay, maintenance to think about, a garden to keep on top of. How could she keep doing all of that from a distance? And it was a waste, a home standing empty when someone could be living there, breathing new life into it. And, besides, she could do with the money. 'We'll drop it. See if it makes any difference. What do you suggest? Ten thousand?'

'I think that would be a very good start.'

Start? Beth said her thank-yous and hung up. It sounded like he thought even a reduction of that size might not be enough. She allowed herself to think of the ten thousand pounds she had just said goodbye to, and what it could buy. A car. Furniture. Paying off Tom's student loan…

'Mum?' Emily had just come thundering down the uncarpeted stairs, still dressed in her school uniform. Ten thousand pounds could carpet a whole house, easily, and with cash left over, she was sure.

'Yes, love?'

'Can I get a Saturday job?'

'Where's that idea suddenly come from?'

'It's not sudden. Everybody does it. And maybe work in the summer holidays too. There are loads of shops and other places that need people part-time.'

'But you're still only fifteen.'

'Not for much longer. It's my birthday in two weeks.'

'I do know that, Em. I was there when you were born!'

'So, can I? When I'm sixteen. I mean, that's practically an adult, isn't it? I'm allowed to do all sorts then.'

'Like what?' Beth's imagination flew straight to an image she would rather not have to think about. Sixteen, the legal age of consent. Her baby, having sex? Legally allowed to have sex? No, no, no! Was this where the conversation was really leading? She hoped not.

'Well, okay, so I won't be old enough to vote, or buy booze or cigarettes, but I could get married if you and dad said yes, couldn't I? How stupid is that? I can have a husband but still not be allowed to buy my own glass of wine! But if I was earning some money of my own, I wouldn't have to keep asking you for stuff, would I? And I don't mean alcohol. I mean shoes and magazines and cinema tickets...'

'Well, I'm not against it, Em. It would do you good to get out there and start working, get a taste of the real world. But school comes first. Studying, homework, exams. Your brothers didn't get holiday jobs until their A-levels were out of the way.'

'That's because boys are lazy. And Dad was still with us back then, and we went on proper holidays and for days out and stuff. I know it's not your fault, Mum, but we don't have as much money now, do we? You'll be at work, and even when Tom comes home you know he'll be out with his mates all the time, or he'll get his old job back at the pub for the summer. And I don't want to just sit around bored when school breaks up. And I need some independence. Practice at being a grown-up!'

Beth had to hand it to her daughter. She pleaded a good case.

'Okay. I suppose so.'

'Thanks, Mum.' Emily threw herself at her, flinging her thin arms around her neck.

'You'll have to do the legwork though. Go out and find somewhere.'

'Oh, I've already got a good idea about somewhere, actually.'

'You have?'

'Tell you later.' And she was gone again, at least kicking off her shoes this time before bounding, noisily, back up the stairs.

Beth hated the idea of her daughter growing up. She missed the days when she could bath her and tuck her up in bed with a story and a cuddle. Buy her pretty little frilly dresses and take her to parties where the kids played musical chairs and pass the parcel, and ate platefuls of mini sausages and sugary birthday cake, half of which ended up on the floor. The weekly swimming lessons and the ballet classes that had all gradually slipped away when the novelty wore off. Not that she could afford any of those things now.

She was proud of her boys, but there was something special about a daughter. Someone in her own image, she supposed. Someone to do all the things she hadn't done herself, or to do the same things but do them better. It seemed like only yesterday that Emily was starting at school, yet here she was now, with periods and breasts and talking about work and independence, even marriage. She would have to keep a close eye on Emily, be the guiding hand, the voice of reason and authority, especially now that Sean wasn't living with them anymore. Sixteen was a dangerous age. There would be temptations, experiments, mistakes. She had made enough of those herself in her time. The last thing she wanted to think about was her daughter doing the same, kissing some spotty boy, being taken advantage of, having sex. Ending up the way her own birth mother had. No, not Emily. The daughter she would do anything for, fight to protect, die for if she had to...

Death. Why did her thoughts keep coming back to death? Yes, her kidneys were failing but that didn't mean she was going to die. She was dealing with it, having the treatment, being careful. Yet, still, the visions haunted her, of a time when she could be gone and her children left alone. She did not have to die for her daughter, she didn't have to die at all, because what mattered more than anything was living for her daughter. For all of her children. And for herself. And not just living, but living well. Recovering. Leading a full and active, healthy life. But to do that she had to get a new kidney. They had to find her a donor. Or she had to find one for herself.

'I think I know who she is.' Jack sounded excited when he called later.

'You've seen her?'

'No, not yet, but I've spoken to people who know her and I'm pretty sure I've got the right woman. Geraldine Munro, she's called these days. And, Mum, she's got a son, and a granddaughter.'

'Oh.'

'Is that a good oh?'

'I think so. It just feels strange to know I might have a brother. Or half-brother anyway. And a niece.'

'Well, let's not jump the gun. I have to do a bit more digging tomorrow. It looks like the picture in the locket might not be her, so that's one mystery still to be solved, but I'm on the right track, I know I am. So, I'm going to stay over tonight. And then...'

'What will you do, Jack? If you find her, I mean. You can't just jump on the poor woman.'

'No, but I can't just walk away either, can I?'

'Go easy. Don't frighten her away.'

'Of course not. The very definition of diplomacy and tact, that's me. I've already had two women eating out of my hand today. I had to promise one of them a small fortune, and the other cost me a coffee, but I'm on a promise of free peppermint creams tomorrow. Can't be bad.'

Beth laughed. 'I have no idea what you're talking about, you do know that?'

'Don't worry about it. Now, I'm off to find a bed for the night, and a decent fish and chip place. Talk tomorrow, okay? After your dialysis. Look after yourself, Mum.'

'I'll try to. And I'll have Maggie there to talk to, so it will be okay. We're going to play draughts. She's bringing a fold-up board. We only need one working arm each for that, so as long as our chairs are close to each other.... I just have to see if I can remember the rules.'

'It's easy, Mum. Very straightforward. Very black and white.'

'Ha, ha, very funny. Night, Jack.'

Geri pulled a deck chair out from among the cobwebs in the shed and opened it on the grass. Summer weather seemed to have come early this year, but who knew how long it might last. Best to make the most of it before it rained again as it had the day before. Ah, the English seaside in the rain. Nothing quite like it!

She ran a damp cloth over the wooden arms of the chair, brushed a few specks of dried-on dirt from the fabric and sat down, tilting her face up towards the sun. William had headed off to the shops, armed with a long list of items the am-dram company were going to need for the upcoming play, and with a firm budget in mind as the funds in the coffers, mainly the small profit left over from ticket sales at the previous production, were apparently running low. He was going to start with the charity shops, he had told her, and then move on to the pound shop, and look for offcuts and end-of-lines at the DIY place. Bound to be something of use there and, if not exactly what he needed, then he would get what he could and find ways to improvise. She could tell he was really looking forward to it all.

Marriage the second time around was turning out to be very different from the first. With Ken there had never been time for anything she could honestly call fun. Working at the shop, running the home, looking after Michael, and her charity work at the children's home, had filled her days, while the nights offered little more than the fulfilment of her desperate need for sleep. She had never really had what she would call a hobby, unless her inexpert attempts at knitting counted. And neither had Ken. Never been sailing, even though they lived so close to the sea. Never learned to ballroom dance, although she would love to be able to waltz. It was such a romantic dance. Never taken up embroidery or watercolour painting. Never even ridden a bike or put on a pair of skates. Her dad had always said it was unladylike, and too dangerous.

Now, as she closed her eyes and felt the warmth of a beautiful May morning on her skin, her mind turned to Ruby's mystery visitor. Jack, he'd said he was called, down from London for a few days, but Ruby didn't seem to know much more. Why on earth would some handsome (Ruby's word) young man from London be so keen to speak to her?

She tried to run through some possibilities, but all she kept coming back to was Michael. He was her only real connection to London. Maybe someone her son had worked with, been friends with while he lived there? She couldn't help wondering if there was something more sinister involved though. Had Michael got involved in something he shouldn't? Drugs? No, he wouldn't. Did he owe money? Possibly. Had this Jack person tracked him down here to Brighton, remembered something Michael had said about his childhood home, his family, the shop? What did he want? All her instincts told her to steer clear of this, whatever it was. To keep her head down and tell Ruby she was not going to meet this man. Michael was old enough to sort out his own problems, pay his own debts. And if there was anything criminal, anything unsavoury going on, then she had her family to think of. Lily to protect. The fun part of her life was just beginning. Nothing Michael might have got mixed up in was going to spoil that. She couldn't let it.

William had talked of them going on a cruise, but she wasn't sure it really appealed. It was just another way of seeing the oh-so familiar sea from a different angle, with the possibility of seasickness thrown in for good measure. Maybe an African safari, or a visit to Borneo to see the orangutans, if she was brave enough to navigate all that jungle and the heat. Or Disneyland. That sounded good. They could take Ruby and Lily. How she would love to see Lily's little face light up with the excitement of it all. Meeting Minnie Mouse and Daisy Duck, and all those beautiful princesses in their shiny dresses. The rides would be so much bigger and better than the ones at the end of the pier. They even had fireworks every night, so she had heard. And they had the time now, she and William. And the money. It was all possible. Anything was possible. She just had to decide what it was she wanted to do, and then do it. Whoever Jack was, she didn't want to get involved. He could sling his hook.

She must have dozed off for a while because when she woke up, to the sound of footsteps crunching on the path, it was gone lunchtime and William was back.

'You'll never guess who I've just seen,' he said, a hint of intrigue in his voice as if he was giving her three guesses but none of them would turn out to be right. 'Sitting in the window of that little café that does the really good Danish pastries.'

'Well, you'll have to give me more than that to go on. Let's see now... Brad Pitt? Tony Blair? Elvis?'

'Now you're being silly. You know Elvis is dead, and what

would the other two be doing in a little backstreet café in Brighton?'

'Well, it has to be somebody unexpected, or you wouldn't be so thrilled about it, would you?'

'Thrilled? Who said I was thrilled? Just pleasantly surprised. And it's not so much the who, but the who she was with...'

'Ah, so the who is a female then? That narrows things down a bit. Princess Anne?'

'Okay, spoilsport, if you're not prepared to guess sensibly, I shall have to just tell you. It was Ruby!'

'Ruby? Our Ruby? What exactly is so unusual about that?'

'I told you, Geri. Aren't you listening? It's the who she was with that caught my eye. It was a man, and they were... how should I describe it? Looking kind of cosy, if you know what I mean. Deep in conversation. Hands across the table and all that.'

'Ruby and a man? Like on a date, do you mean?'

'I have no idea, but wouldn't it be nice if she was? About time, if you ask me. A lovely young girl like that deserves a bit of romance.'

───────────

'So, she wouldn't come?'

Ruby shook her head. 'I'm sorry, but she doesn't know you, or what you want. What did you expect?'

'Well, you don't know me, but that didn't stop you talking to me, did it? Or coming out for lunch?'

'That's different.'

'Is it?' He took a sip from his coffee and gazed out of the window. Two thick sandwiches sat untouched on floral plates in front of them. 'Did you say how important it was?'

'How could I? You told me not to tell her anything, so I didn't.'

'True. I'm going to have to rethink this, aren't I?'

'Well, it might help if you were to explain it to me, then I can try her again. Whatever it is, it can't be that personal, surely? Unless you're telling me Geri's got a secret family somewhere.' She smiled at him, as if the whole idea was ridiculous. 'Other kids and grandkids I know nothing about.'

He stared at her in silence.

'Hang on, that's not it, is it? Jack, tell me. Does Geri have another child? Children? Apart from Michael?'

'I'm not even sure it's her yet, am I? Not if she won't talk to me.'

'But, if it is her, then you're saying Geri – *my* Geri – could actually be your grandmother?'

He nodded. 'She – or Geraldine Clark anyway – had a baby a long time ago. She was probably only a teenager at the time. A daughter. She gave her up for adoption.'

'And that baby…?'

'Is my mother, yes. Her name's Elizabeth. She was born in Norfolk in 1968.'

'Geri's never been to Norfolk.'

'How can you possibly know that?' He reached across the table and placed his hand over hers. She didn't pull it away. 'It was long before you knew her, Ruby. Before you were born. Who knows what her life was like back then? Where she went, or why?'

'But she would have told me if she'd had a daughter, wouldn't she? Told Michael?'

'Obviously not.'

'Oh my God. I wonder if Ken knew? Her first husband. Assuming he wasn't the father, of course. Do you know who…?'

'No. That bit's blank on the birth certificate.'

'And William. Her husband. They've only just got married. Does he know, I wonder?'

'Who knows, Ruby? That's why I was trying to tread carefully. If she's kept it a secret all these years, she might want it to stay that way. I can't just barge in and assume I'm going to be welcomed with open arms. Same goes for my mum. She really wants to find her family. Her blood family. But it's awkward, isn't it? Finding them. Announcing yourself. Not knowing if they wanted to be found?'

'But...' Ruby stopped. She really didn't know what else to say. She had thought she knew Geri so well, knew all there was to know about her uneventful life. Her mum's early death, her marriage to Ken, a son, the shop. She had never even lived anywhere but Brighton. Geri just wasn't the sort of person to have secrets. Not that kind of secret.

'I need to see her, Ruby, and so does my mum. You do get that, don't you? I mean, if you hadn't ever met your family, or you'd not seen your own mother for years, you'd want to, wouldn't you? Or to try to, at least.'

'I haven't. Seen my mum for years, I mean. I spent most of my childhood in care.'

'Oh, I'm sorry. I didn't know.'

'She was a drinker. She never wanted a kid, and she walked away as soon as she could. Or staggered away, more like. It's complicated, isn't it, when children are separated from their parents? Brought up by someone else? Believe me, I do understand. There's always something missing. Some feeling of not being wanted, not being good enough. Does your mum feel like that?'

'I don't know. I don't think so. Maybe it's more just about wanting to fill in the blanks, join the dots, you know. She had a good childhood. Her adoptive parents are dead now, but they looked after her well, loved her. Loved all of us.'

'All of you?'

'Yes, I have a brother and a sister.'

'The big family Lily's always wanted.'

'Lily?'

'My little girl. She's so desperate for aunties, uncles, cousins, babies...'

'Looks like she's had them all along, she just didn't know it.'

'It may not be her, Jack. The Geri you're looking for, it might not be her.'

He folded his fingers over hers. 'I think we both know that's not true. It's her, Ruby, I just know it is.'

TWENTY-TWO

Vicky climbed over the low wall that surrounded the enclosure and back onto the path, leaving the three old tortoises happily munching on a fresh supply of cabbage leaves and carrot tops.

Time to go into the small staff room and eat her own lunch, a sandwich with almost as much green stuff packed inside it as she'd just fed to the tortoises. That was her mum's influence, meeting her outside this morning and handing her a lunch box packed with healthy food she would never have chosen for herself. Still, she had to admit that her usual diet was nowhere near as good as it should be and, despite being on her feet all day, she was piling on the pounds lately. Standing next to Ruby, all small and slim, she had felt like a misplaced elephant. Her size was something neither of them mentioned, but she was acutely aware of it, the topic not to be talked about, the elephant in the room.

She had not spoken to Ruby for almost a week, since they had parted at the station on Sunday night, when she'd refused a lift home as Ruby had jumped into William's car, in a hurry to get back and see Lily before bedtime. Not that she minded getting the bus. There was a particularly attractive bus driver she had her eye on, although sadly she had not been the one who pulled up at the stop that night, and the grumpy male driver she had been saddled with instead had not even been polite enough to say thank you as she paid her fare.

It had been good spending time in London, meeting new people, even if most of those who had turned up for Laura's party and baby shower were either pregnant or vicars or, in one case, both. Unlike many of her age, Vicky didn't have a wide circle of old and loyal friends. In the early years following her adoption she had been quite shy, withdrawn, lonely, never feeling as though she had much in common with the other girls at school. They had a shared history, had been classmates for years, whereas she had only just arrived. She wasn't into music and going to gigs, or particularly bothered about fashion and make-up. She had eventually got quite friendly with a girl called Joanne who kept guinea pigs and had a big soppy boxer dog called Tyson, and they'd spent many happy hours playing with the animals, cleaning out cages and dog-walking in the park, but Joanne's family had moved away and nobody had quite managed to fill the gap.

Vicky had left school at sixteen with very few qualifications and a burning desire to work with animals, not people. She often thought that, if a ten-ton lorry were to be out of control and hurtling towards a person and a dog, and there was only time to make a grab for one of them, it would be the dog she would save first. Unless the person in question was a gorgeous redhead with big boobs, of course, in which case she might think again.

There was no one else in the staff room, which suited her just fine. She had left taking her lunch break until late, and sometimes it was nice to have a bit of peace and quiet rather than have to join in with all the holiday talk and what the others were watching on TV. She sat facing out through the window and opened the tin foil wrapping from around her sandwich, biting into the bread as she watched a sparrow hop along the top of the fence outside. She would make sure to leave a few crumbs to feed to him on her way back. And pull out the limp lettuce too. Plenty of animals here would be glad of that.

She ate most of the bread and cottage cheese and had a couple of bites from the apple her mum had provided, before slipping it into the pocket of her fleece. She knew a few greedy rabbits who would happily finish that off for her later. All this healthy stuff would be the death of her! Good job the little zoo gift shop sold chocolate, so she could still enjoy a few sinful calories without the parent police making a song and dance about it. When she was sure no one was going to come in she went to her locker and pulled out the drinks bottle she kept tucked inside her bag. That was the good thing about vodka. It looked pretty innocent when it was poured into a clear bottle. Just like water. She took a long swig and closed the lid. That should be enough to see her through the afternoon. Enough to deaden things a bit without actually getting her the sack.

'All right, Vix?' Stan, who had worked there longer than she had been alive, called out to her as she passed him on the path.

'Great thanks, Stan. Just off to do the reptile talk.'

'Can't be doing with them snakes,' he muttered. 'Rather you than me, girl.' And then he went back to the task he seemed to do best, swishing his old broom along the many meandering pathways, pushing leaves and wastepaper into heaps he would then scoop up and dispose of before starting the whole process all over again. Like painting the Forth Bridge, a never-ending task. She couldn't imagine how he always appeared to be so content, whistling away to himself, but it took all sorts to make a world, as her dad always said. He hadn't said that when she'd told him she was gay, of course, but what had she expected really? Banners? Balloons? An announcement in *The Times*? She was what she was, and he would never understand that. They were too different. It was just the way things were.

There had been a quiet but grudging acceptance in the end, because it was something he knew he couldn't change, but there was clearly nothing to be welcomed either. Nothing to be embraced or celebrated. Nothing to rejoice in. Her mum had tried her best to smooth things over but the hurt cut deep. She was an outsider again. Not what he had wanted, or expected when he had taken her on. No mention of love. No warm hug to show he cared. The flicker of shame that showed in his face was something she could never forget. He was a bigot, and she was a disappointment. Home had never felt the same since that night. No longer the safe harbour she craved. And so she had moved out, taken a room in a flat with strangers, where she could be whoever she wanted to be, no questions asked.

The booze helped to dull the edges, but she knew she needed more. The loneliness had crept back into her life, and she needed... Affection? Attention? She wasn't even sure what she needed, only that it was missing.

Every time she went into the kitchen the kettle beckoned, like an old but dangerous friend waiting silently and patiently for her to give in to it again.

Ruby sat behind the counter in the shop and fiddled with her nails. There were things she should be doing but she couldn't concentrate, her mind constantly going over what Jack had told her. She could not be sure that Geri was the woman he was looking for, but the evidence did seem to add up. It would be easy enough to go home later, or even right now, and get Geri on her own, then ask her outright. She might deny it all, of course, either because it was totally untrue or because she preferred to lie. Or she might just admit it straight away, and be thrilled to know that her long-lost daughter was alive and well and keen to meet her.

Whatever happened, Ruby knew she could not just ignore this. If she did nothing, said nothing, the truth would catch up with them anyway. Jack was not going to let this go. He would get in touch sooner or later, or his mum would. His detective work had brought him this far. He was determined to see it through. It was only a matter of time.

No, she would have to bring Geri and Jack together somehow, but not by sneakily pretending he was someone else, accidentally-on-purpose bumping into him in the street, engineering some meeting where only one of the two knew what was going on. That would not be right. She would have to talk to Geri. The best way, the only fair way, was to explain who Jack was and what he wanted, to tell the truth. And if Geri said no, if she chose not to see him, that would have to be the end of it. Jack and his mum would just have to accept that whatever had happened all those years ago had to stay right where it was. In the past.

Ruby hoped that didn't happen. She liked Jack. She liked Jack a lot, and she liked the thought of seeing him again, getting to know him better, as part of the family. Or maybe even as something more, something quite separate to all of this. She had his number and he had hers. It was a start, at least.

'Geri?' Ruby came into the kitchen and sat down at the table, glad to see that Lily was not around.

Geraldine was peeling potatoes at the sink. She had her back to her and didn't turn round. 'Yes, love?'

'There's something I need to talk to you about. Something... private.'

'Well, now you have me intrigued.' She put her peeler down and wiped her hands on a cloth, then pulled out a chair and sat down.

'Where's Lily?'

'Upstairs. I said she could play for a while before her tea. Why?'

'It's just that I'd rather she didn't hear what I'm going to say, that's all.'

'Have you met someone?'

'What?'

'Oh, I know you probably think we're nosey old buggers, but William happened to spot you at lunchtime. With someone. A young man.'

'Oh.'

'None of our business, I know. But, if you have, well, I just want you to know that I'm happy for you, and he will be very welcome here. As any friend of yours is welcome here.'

'No. Oh, Geri, no, you've got the wrong end of the stick. Yes, I did have lunch with someone today, but it's not what you think.'

'No?'

'It was Jack, the one I told you about yesterday.'

'The bloke from London?'

'Yes. I'm sorry, Geri. I know you said you didn't want to get involved, and I respected that, but that was before.'

'Before what?'

'Before he told me exactly what it's all about. Why he so desperately wants to meet you.'

'Is it to do with Michael? Is he in some kind of trouble? Money?'

Ruby reached across the table and held Geri's hand. 'It's not about Michael. It's about... Elizabeth.'

'Who's Elizabeth? Ruby, I have no idea what you're talking about. And who exactly is this Jack?'

'He says... he says he might be your grandson.'

Ruby watched the puzzlement in Geri's face turn slowly to something almost like fear. Her hand, caught underneath her own, clenched suddenly and Ruby was sure it had started to tremble a little.

'My grandson?'

'He says... oh, Geri, I don't even like to ask, but did you have a baby? A little girl? One you gave up for adoption?'

Geraldine closed her eyes but it didn't stop a tear from escaping as she slowly nodded her head. 'Yes. Yes, I did. It was so long ago. I suppose I always knew that she might come looking for me some day, but it's been more than fifty years, Ruby. I thought it was never going to happen. I thought that part of my life was over. That I would never know what happened to her...'

'But you never forgot her?'

'Of course not. How could I ever forget? My little Sandie. So beautiful, so small...'

'She's called Elizabeth now. Did you know that?'

Geraldine shook her head. 'Her new parents were going to choose her name. That seemed only fair if they were going to look after her. But she'll always be Sandie to me. I named her after a singer. One with bare feet!' She smiled to herself as she remembered. 'And this Jack, he's her son? I have a grandson?'

'Elizabeth has three children, Geri. Two boys and a girl. And she wants to make contact. Her adoptive parents are dead now, and Jack says it's time. She'd really like to meet you, and so would he. He's still here, in Brighton, waiting. He'd like to meet you soon, tomorrow, or today even, and try to pave the way for his mum and the others, but only if you want to. You don't have to, Geri. You don't have to do anything if you don't want to. And there's no rush. This must all be such a shock for you.'

'It's a shock all right. But it's a good one. I always hoped that one day...'

'Well, it looks like that day has come.'

They sat quietly, Geraldine occasionally dabbing at the corners of her eyes as she tried to take it all in. Ruby really didn't know what she could say that might help, that could possibly make any difference, so for now she said nothing, just letting it all sink in. From upstairs, the sound of little Lily thumping about as she dropped something on the landing brought them back to the here and now.

'She'll be back down in a minute. Don't say anything in front of her.'

'No, of course not. But what about William? Does he know?'

'Oh, yes. We don't have secrets. And we do talk about it sometimes. About *her*. It's not something he thinks I should feel guilty about.'

'No, you shouldn't. And Ken?'

'Yes, he knew. I couldn't have married him without telling him that, could I? It wouldn't have been fair. We were young when we met, and he just naturally expected that I was... well, a virgin, just as he was. It would have been very wrong of me not to tell him the truth, and he did accept it. A bit grudgingly, I suppose, but what was done couldn't be undone, could it? And he did love me. Enough not to leave me because of it.'

'It can't have been easy.'

'It came up from time to time, my past thrown back at me in the middle of an argument, that sort of thing, but on the whole it faded, you know. It took us a long time to have a baby of our own, but I think if it hadn't happened then things would have been a lot worse, with Ken knowing I'd already been with someone else, had a child, experienced all that without him. But then we had Michael and everything was all right again.'

'Oh, Geri. You poor thing. I can't imagine having to give up a baby. When we had all that stuff going on with social services and I thought they might take Lily off me... Losing her would have broken me. I don't know how you coped.'

'No choice, love. I was fourteen. Can you imagine? Only fourteen, still a kid myself, and suddenly carrying this baby I hadn't planned or wanted. My mum not long dead, my dad ashamed of me, probably as scared as I was, not really knowing what to do, just wanting to make it all stop, pretend it wasn't happening.'

'So he sent you away?'

'Yes, to an aunt in Norfolk, and then to a nursing home place for the actual birth. I had the baby. And then I came home, went back to school, and she didn't come with me. I never saw her again.'

'And the father?'

'I don't like to think about him, Ruby. Let's just say he wasn't involved in any of it. Oh, at the conception, keen as can be, of course, but not after. When it came down to it, it was just me and my dad. And my auntie, but she was not exactly what you'd call warm or sympathetic.' She shook her head. 'Do you think I should do it, Ruby? Meet my daughter? And her children? I mean, they don't know me at all. I'm not the mum or the gran they grew up with. I'm just a stranger. What if I'm not what they're expecting? Not who they hope I am?'

'Seems like they're willing to risk it.' Ruby squeezed her hand. 'If you are...'

TWENTY-THREE

1971

Geraldine met Ken on her second day working in the shop. Her dad had finally started to allow her off the leash a little after her fall from grace, and had agreed to her taking a Saturday job, so long as it didn't interfere with her studies. The new decimal currency had just been introduced and she and her new boss, Betty Payne, had spent the morning re-pricing everything, clicking little sticky labels over the existing ones. She felt sure she would never get used to calling two shillings 'ten new pence', especially as the coin itself looked just the same as it always had and Betty still called it a 'florin'.

Ken was Betty's son, a good-looking lad a little older than Geraldine, and his sudden arrival in the shop that lunchtime, excitedly talking about a Rolling Stones concert due to take place just down the road at the hall known as The Big Apple, had sent unexpected flutters through her. Whether it was the thought of a famous group coming to her home town or meeting Ken himself she wasn't sure, but the effect was quite electrifying. When he suggested they go outside and share a bag of chips on the pier, she could hardly get out of the shop quickly enough.

She never did get to see the Stones. As far as her dad was concerned, that would have been a step too far, and she was still eager to prove how changed she was, that the foolish mistake she had made that had led her to Norfolk and back was behind her now, and never to be repeated.

Being with Ken was a revelation. He was polite and respectful. He asked her dad's permission before taking her to the pictures, promised to get her home by eleven and stuck to it. He held her hand tightly whenever they walked together and was quick to help her put on her coat, laughing when she struggled because one sleeve was inside out. He often complimented her on her hair or a new dress, where most boys his age wouldn't notice such things. Her friends nodded their approval. One or two made no secret of their envy. So protective. Such a nice smile. Funny too, when he chose to be. And a family business to secure his future. If only they could find a boyfriend as nice as Ken...

Ken's kisses were tentative and usually preceded by a squirt of breath freshener or a Polo mint and, even after they had been seeing each other for six months, her knickers were still very much in place.

'I think you have a real gentleman there,' her dad had said one evening after Ken had delivered her safely home. 'I do believe there could be wedding bells ahead.'

'Not just yet, Dad.' Geraldine had never really considered the possibility of marriage. She was still young. She didn't even have a proper job yet, only her few hours in Ken's parents' shop, and she had her A-level exams to think of. And she knew, even if Ken did not, that she was damaged goods. If things were going to go any further, as she was starting to hope they might, she knew she would have to tell him.

They were sitting on a bench in a park when she chose her moment. Or was forced into choosing it, more like. Ken had brought a bottle of cheap white wine and some plastic beakers, and she had made sandwiches with his favourite cheese and pickle. They were watching a big waddly duck emerge from the pond and make its way towards them, looking for bread. Ken picked an edge of crust from the sandwich in his hand and broke it into crumbs, at which point half a dozen others, some of them little more than babies, came quacking towards them, as if someone had just rung the dinner gong.

'Always hungry, aren't they?' Ken had said, laughing.

'Like children.'

'Yeah, but when we have ours, I hope we can give them something a bit better than dry bread.'

'Ours?'

'Well, we will one day, won't we? Settle down, I mean. Raise a family?'

Geraldine had felt something inside her tighten, her stomach clench with nerves. Now. Now was the time to say it. To tell him she was not what he thought she was. Not the innocent girl he believed her to be. To tell him what she had done. Before he did something ridiculous, like propose to her, which just would not be fair when he did not have all the facts. She owed him the right to back out, back away, before it was too late.

She had never told anyone before. Her friends at school knew nothing, only that she had been ill and had taken time off to recover at the seaside. She had certainly never mentioned anything at the shop, no matter how kind Mrs Payne had always been. And, until now, there had been no need to confide in Ken. Boys came and went. Took what they wanted and then turned their backs, shrugged, moved on. She knew that only too well. But now here was Ken, not walking away, talking of a future they might end up spending together, and about having kids of their own.

Did she want to do it again? Go through another pregnancy, another labour, all the heartache and pain and emotion that went with it? She had not believed she ever would, but with Ken beside her maybe it was possible after all. If only he knew...

This was the moment. When she told him she would watch his face and she would know. Instantly, she would know. How shocked he was, how disappointed, how revulsed. Whether he really loved her enough to take the truth and live with it. Live with her. Forgive her. Or whether he would pick up his plastic beakers and what was left of the wine, turn his back just as his predecessor had done, and walk away.

TWENTY-FOUR

Beth let out a little cheer as her king leapt over Maggie's remaining pieces like a hurdler leaping its way across the board, and her second win was in the bag. It was surprising how something as simple as playing draughts could take her mind off what was happening all around her, and inside her.

'All done.' The nurse had reappeared and was unhooking her tubes. 'Have a nice day.'

'They sound like they work in some American burger bar sometimes, don't they?' Maggie chuckled as she folded up the board and bundled the pieces back into their box.

'They mean well. I've got no complaints.'

'Oh, no, of course not. Angels the lot of them, and where would we be without them, eh?'

'You've put the idea of a burger in my head now, or some sort of food anyway. Fancy joining me for something to eat in the canteen? There's nowhere I need to rush off to today.'

'That'd be nice.'

They left the small ward together, nodding their goodbyes to their fellow patients, and headed for the lift.

'No news?'

Beth didn't have to ask what Maggie was talking about. Asking for news, when they were here, was never about family or work. It meant news of treatment, or better still a potential transplant.

'No. You?'

'Not a dickie bird. Makes you wonder who gets all the kidneys, doesn't it? How they pick. It just seems I've been waiting so long it will never happen.'

'Oh, come on, Maggie. You know only too well it's about finding a match. And helping those who are the sickest. It's not first come, first served.' She held the lift door open and ushered her friend in ahead of her. 'I certainly don't expect to jump to top of the list for a good while yet.'

'I saw a lovely one yesterday.'

'A lovely what?'

'Kidney! In the window at the butcher's, it was. A really healthy bright red colour too. Sitting in a little puddle of blood. Lamb's, probably. A bit small for you or me, but I'm sure it was just perfect for its original owner. And now it's only good for going in a pie!' Maggie sighed and pushed the button for the ground floor. 'If only we could just go out and buy one as easily as that, eh?'

'You can, apparently. In some countries, if you're rich enough, there are people who will sell you one.'

'Ugh. Can you imagine it? Being so desperate for money you'd let them slice you open and sell a part of your own body. And what if anything happens to the one you've got left? I'm sure God gave us two for a reason.'

'Two arms, two legs... eyes, ears, boobs. We've all got built-in spare parts, haven't we? Plenty of people manage with just the one though. If they have to, I mean.'

'One good kidney will do me, so long as it does the job. I just hope they find it for me before it's too late.'

'Don't say that, Mags. Our day will come.'

'I've got a brother I haven't seen in years. Did I tell you that? Lives in Australia. Turns out he's willing to be tested. Actually prepared to offer me one of his if it suits. Can you believe that? I'm not sure I'd do the same if it was the other way round.'

'I bet you would.'

'For my own kids I would. In a heartbeat. But for Jim? He's been out there since I was a teenager. We hardly know each other. And he's almost sixty! I'm not sure they'd even allow it at his age. The operation, the risk, and he'd have to travel halfway round the world to get here, and to get back again. No, I can't see it happening.'

'Don't say no though. Promise me, if there's even a chance, that you'll take it.'

Maggie nodded. 'I suppose so. What about you? No family able to help you?'

'No.'

'That's a shame. But I hope you've asked them, whoever they are. This isn't the time to be all proud and noble. Not when your life's at stake. And you can't go making me promise to take what I can if you won't do the same.'

'It's complicated.'

'Isn't it always? Now, come on, let's find us a nice cup of tea and a bite to eat and you can tell me all about it.'

'Sunday used to be the day for church.' Geraldine sipped the last of her morning coffee and peered out of the kitchen window. 'Come rain or shine, my mother would drag me there, in my best dress and my polished shoes, and her always wearing a hat. Sunday school in the little side room, with Bible stories and orange squash, while she sat through the service in the main church. Dad never went. His one real day of rest, he'd say, and the only chance he had to do the garden. I think in reality he just liked having those couple of hours to himself, a bit of peace and a packet of Woodbines. There was never much evidence of the grass having been mown while we were gone.'

'When did you stop?' Ruby asked. 'Going to church?'

'When my mum got sick. She kept going, for as long as she could, but not me. It's hard to believe in a God who lets one of his own suffer like that. Oh, I got married in a church, of course. That same church, in fact. First time around, that is. It's what was expected, and the vicar knew nothing about my little indiscretion, so there was no reason not to.'

'Don't call it that, Geri. Your so-called indiscretion created a life, gave you a baby.'

'And I gave her away.'

'You can't change that now, but you can welcome her back, can't you? Welcome a whole new family you knew nothing about.'

'I hope so.'

'Are you scared?'

'What do you think? Petrified.'

'Are you sure you don't want me to come with you? Or William?'

'No, I need to do this on my own. For now, at least.'

'If you're sure. You know we're all here for you, right? Whatever happens. Now, are you ready?'

'As I'm ever going to be. I'll just pop upstairs and say goodbye to William and Lily. Keep everything as normal as I can.'

'I'll call Jack, and tell him you're on your way, okay?'

Geraldine nodded. 'He knows where to meet?'

'Yep, he's looked it up. Don't worry, he'll be there, looking out for you. And he's nice, Geri. Really nice. A grandson for you to be proud of, trust me.'

It only took Geraldine a few minutes to run upstairs and back again, grab her handbag and be on her way.

She drove slowly, pulled into the little car park behind the pond and took a last look at herself in the mirror. Just a little more lipstick, perhaps, and a comb to tame her hair. It somehow felt very important that she should look her best.

Being here again, she couldn't help remembering that day, so many years ago, when she had confessed all to Ken. There had been a group of ducks gathered at their feet and she had swallowed a big glug of wine for Dutch courage, but it had gone down the wrong way and made her cough. Ken's arm had come around her, instinctively, and patted her on the back. Amazingly it had stayed there as she told her tale.

That had worked out okay, hadn't it? Big moments acted out on a small stage. Secrets and revelations shared in a simple park, with nothing but the trees and the birds as witnesses. That was why she had chosen to meet here now, in a place where she could look at her new grandson and he could look at her, and they could take their time to say whatever it was they each needed to say. Slowly, quietly, privately. No busy pub or coffee shop, but still neutral territory, surrounded by nature, a safe place she was free to walk away from at any time if it all got too much.

She knew as soon as she saw him sitting there on a bench by the water, that this must be him. Long legs, tousled hair, big kind eyes. He stood up as she approached.

'Geri?' he said, holding out a hand for her to take, but almost immediately changing his mind and wrapping his arms around her instead.

She nodded, easing herself away far enough to be able to look up at his face. 'Hello... Jack?'

'Yes. And I know this must feel awkward, strange, but believe me it does to me too. So, we'll just take it slowly, okay? Come on, sit down by me and we'll talk. I've brought water, and juice. I avoided coffee. Didn't know how you take it, or you might be late and it wouldn't stay hot.'

'Thank you.'

'First of all, thanks for agreeing to this. I know me turning up out of the blue must be a bit of a shock.'

'It is.'

'Not too unpleasant a one, I hope?'

'No.'

'Don't worry. I'm not going to suddenly expect to call you Grandma or Nan, or anything like that. Just Geri for now, if that's okay?'

'Of course.'

Jack felt around for something in his pocket. 'Just in case you think I could be some sort of imposter, there's something I think you should see. Or keep, even.' He lay something round and smooth in her hand. 'Do you recognise this?'

Geri looked down. The locket. She could hardly believe it. It was the locket she had put into the box on the day Sandie was taken away from her. Her fingers went straight to the little clasp at the side and clicked it open, and there was the picture of her mother. Just as she remembered her, smiling, and wearing her best Sunday hat.

'This is my mother,' she said, quietly. 'I haven't seen this picture for more than fifty years. It was the only copy I had.'

'We did wonder, who she might be. Especially when Ruby took a look and said it wasn't you. That was when I started to doubt whether I'd found the right Geraldine.'

'I would never have been allowed to send Sandie away with a picture of me. Rules, you see. All about being anonymous. Sending my mother to watch over her was the next best thing.'

'Sandie?'

'Your mum. She was Sandie then, before they took her away. Elizabeth now, I'm told?'

Jack nodded. 'Or Beth. She prefers Beth.'

'And Mr Snuggles?' she said, holding back the tears as best she could. 'What happened to him? My bear? Do you have him too?'

'The one-eyed teddy in a holey jumper? Yes, we have him too.'

'Oh, Jack,' she said. 'It's really you, isn't it? There's no mistake. You're my grandson. My family.'

'Looks like I am, yes.' He moved closer to her on the bench and waited. It was only seconds before she threw her arms around him and hugged him, her happy tears soaking into his shirt.

'When can I see her? Sandie? Sorry, I mean Beth. Oh, I do so want to see her.'

'You know it won't be easy for me to go down to Brighton.' Beth sat next to Jack on the sofa and played with a loose strand of wool at the hem of her jumper.

'Why? It's hardly any distance on the train.'

'Well, there's my treatment. And Emily...'

'You're making excuses, Mum. You know you are. We could start with a phone call if you prefer. Maybe a video call so you can see each other?'

'No. That would feel too detached somehow. If we're going to do it, it should be face to face.'

'I agree, so let's do it. I know it's scary, but it won't get any easier by putting it off, will it? We can easily fit a trip down there in between dialysis days, and be back again the same day.

I'll come with you, hold your hand all the way. No need to stay overnight. And we can go while Emily's at school, or leave her with Dad for a while. Or...'

'Or what?'

'Or we could tell her what's going on and take her with us. I really don't see any need to be secretive about it now, do you? She's always known you were adopted, and this is just the next step. Finding your family... isn't it what every adopted kid wants to do at some time or another? And they're her family just as much as yours or mine. Tom's too.'

'I don't know, Jack. It's all a bit... well, huge, isn't it? Overwhelming. I know how nervous I feel about it, so who knows how she'll feel. She did love her gran.'

'We all did, but meeting Geri makes no difference to that, does it?'

'No, but let's be honest, I might not even be doing this at all if it wasn't for my illness. I only really started looking for her and whatever family I might have in the ridiculous hope that one of them might be a kidney match. And that all just sounds so cold and calculating now. I mean, you've met her, and you say how nice she is, and there she is all excited about seeing me again, when all the time I've only really been thinking about her as a donor, not as a mother, or even as a real person, with feelings. What does that say about me?'

'That you were scared, not thinking straight, desperate? That you were looking for any way possible to get the help you needed.'

'That's true, but now I'm not so sure. I've been thinking about her, about meeting her, and what I want out of it. They told me that at the counselling session, that I had to work out why I was doing it, be ready for rejection, disappointment, but they never told me how to feel if she said yes, if she was really keen to see me. This woman sounds like she really cares, Jack, but how do I feel? I have no idea. It's just been so long. Do I really need her in my life? As some kind of second mother? Because even thinking about asking her to donate a kidney is off the table, isn't it? It was just me being selfish and unfair, and not thinking at all about her, or what she needs from me rather than what I might need from her. I mean, she's too old to give up a kidney anyway, isn't she? Even if she was willing? Maggie was saying only yesterday that her brother's probably too old and he's not even sixty yet. I just need to be patient, wait for a donor to come up on the list, wait my turn.'

'Or let us help you. You've got three kids, Mum. Young, healthy kids who you won't even consider for testing. But the chances are that one of us will match, right? We're your flesh and blood. We're the obvious choice.'

'No!'

'Why the hell not? Okay, maybe not Emily. She's still a kid, but Tom and me, we're grown-ups, able to understand what we're doing, make our own choices. I really do think it's time to tell them now. Both of them. It's not as if you can hide your illness forever. What if it gets worse? What if Emily wants the two of you to go away on a holiday and you have to say you can't? What if a kidney suddenly becomes available and you have to go straight to the hospital? She's living with you. She needs to know. Be prepared. Understand. We're a family, and we have to stick together, face this together.'

'I thought we were talking about Geraldine, about going to meet her. Not about transplants.'

'All part of the same problem though, isn't it? One secret born out of another secret. Finding out about one led to finding out about the other. But now it's time for the truth. All of it. Then we can decide, as a family, what we're going to do about it.'

TWENTY-FIVE

'I really like him, Vix.' Ruby put down her glass of wine. 'It will be so strange having all these new members of the family to get used to, and he's one of them, but that shouldn't stop me from... well, liking him, should it?'

'Fancying him, you mean? Of course not. You're not blood related, are you? So, he's... what? Your ex's nephew? Your daughter's cousin. Hardly crime of the century.'

'I know, but it still feels a bit awkward. And, to be honest, I know so little about him. He's a bit younger than me, I think, and he could have a girlfriend already for all I know. He could even be gay!'

'Not sure I like the way you said that. What do you mean by *even*? There's nothing wrong with being gay, Ruby.'

'I know that. I just don't want *him* to be gay, that's all.'

'And was there any indication at all that he might be?'

'I don't think so. He did sort of hold my hand in the café. And the way he looked at me...'

'There we are then. Put your rather faulty gaydar away and trust in your instincts. He was interested, right?'

'I hope so.'

'So, when's he coming back? When's the big family reunion?'

'Nothing's organised yet. He's talking to his mum, sorting out a day to come back down.'

'But you do have his number, right?'

'Yeah, but I'm not going to ring it! He might think I was chasing him or something.'

'As if!' Vicky said, raising her eyebrows. 'No wonder you're still single, Ruby Baxter. Have a bit more gumption, why don't you?'

'Gumption? When did you start using words like that? You sound about seventy!'

'Sort of thing my dad says all the time. Pull your socks up, stiff upper lip, nose to the grindstone, and all that. He's that sort of a man. Full of advice and pep talks. Very old-fashioned, you know?'

'No, I don't, because you never talk about him.'

'Nothing to tell.'

'Don't you get on?'

'You could say that.' Vicky picked up her drink and downed what was left of it in one big gulp. She was drinking pints today and this was her third. She didn't want to think about her dad, let alone have to talk about him. 'Now, enough about your half-hearted love life. When are you bringing Lily to see me at work again? We've got some new piglets, just two days old. A litter of five. I know she'd love them. I might even be able to wangle it so she can pick a name for one of them.'

'Oh, she'd be so up for that! You do know she'd want to call it Peppa though, don't you?'

'Even if it's a boy?'

'There must be at least one girl among them, mustn't there?'

'Yeah, probably, but we haven't sexed them yet. Maybe we could try to ease her towards something a bit more original though. Kids always seem to think piggie names have to start with a P. We've done naming competitions loads of times and you wouldn't believe how many children have picked Percy or Penny or Porky. And all the rabbits end up as Roger or Rocky. Or Peter, of course.'

Ruby laughed. 'Can I bring her at the weekend? Sunday afternoon?'

'Yeah, that's fine. I'll leave you a couple of free tickets at the gate. Make sure you come and find me. Lily can help me make up some tubs of feed. And she can get in among the piglets, give them a stroke or a brushing. Bring wellies. There may be mud... or worse.'

'Ugh! Spending my day off up to my knees in shit. Why did nobody tell me that having kids could end up so messy?'

'Nothing a hosepipe can't fix. Don't be such a wimp. Now, I have to love you and leave you, I'm afraid. Oh, God, that's another of my dad's favourite phrases. If I ever turn into him, just shoot me, okay?' She stood up and pulled on her coat, and Ruby followed her to the door. 'See you Sunday, unless your new cuz calls, in which case you have my permission to blow me out. Can't have you missing out on a hot date just to play with a bunch of pigs. I know my place.'

'Not likely.'

'You never know. And me and the porkers will still be there, whatever day you come.'

Vicky waved goodbye and walked away, taking the sea road towards her usual bus stop. There was no queue. She had obviously just missed a bus. With twenty minutes to wait for the next, she decided to walk for a bit, get some exercise and fresh air to help clear her head. She was definitely drinking too much. She was only meant to have been meeting Ruby for a quick drink after work, then she had promised to go back to the flat and cook. It was a Tuesday tradition. The so-called Flat

Meeting. Food, a chance to catch up, discuss anything important, like who hadn't cleaned the bath or the oven, and making sure they had all paid their share of the rent and the bills. And it was her turn to cook, apparently, as her flatmates had reminded her, quite pointedly, when she'd left that morning.

Was there anything edible left in the fridge? Any pasta in the cupboard? Potatoes that weren't starting to go green or send out little spindly shoots? She had no idea. Food had become a bit of a chore lately, just something to shovel in as fuel. Left to her own devices she would happily get by on packets of crisps or a chunk of cheese, or yet another wander down to the nearest chip shop, but she knew that would not get her off the hook when it came to feeding the five thousand. Well, there were only three of them actually, but it was not unusual for there to be hangers-on too. Boyfriends, mates, brothers and sisters, passing through before going out for the evening or settling themselves, like sardines, on the crowded sofa. Word had got out somehow, that there was always food to be had on a Tuesday. When it was their turn, the others seemed to have no problem producing big vats of chilli, dishes of lasagne, stir fries, some sort of stew. Enough to go round, to share, with leftovers to spare, no matter how many people turned up at the table. It was expected.

Vicky sighed. Once every three weeks she had to think about the others, make something for them all to share, and then sit down together and talk. That was all she had to do. It should have been easy. But she didn't want to. Didn't enjoy it. Didn't really fit. She knew that only too well. All she wanted was a room of her own, privacy, being allowed to keep herself to herself. Eat what she wanted to eat, when she wanted to eat it. Alone. Or perhaps with Ruby, in a pub somewhere. All this big happy family stuff, the noise and bustle of too many people crammed between the same four walls, all talking at once, all pretending to care about each other, had never felt right, comfortable, normal. Before her adoption, or after.

There was a small supermarket on the corner. She went in, trawling the aisles quickly, with no idea of what to buy. Chicken pieces, pasta shapes, a jar of sauce, a packet of frozen garlic bread. Or two, just in case they were extra hungry. That would have to do. And, at the till, as she waited to pay, she spotted a big chocolate cake reduced to half price. On its use-by date, a bit squashed. She popped that into her basket too. It might make it as far as the kitchen table. Then again, it could just as likely end up hidden in her room. Something to comfort herself with later, if it all got too much.

Emily came bounding in from school, threw her bag down in the hall and went straight for the biscuit tin.

'Mum?'

'Yes, love?'

'You know I said I might have a Saturday job lined up?'

'Did you? You said you had an idea of what you might like to do, but I'm sure you never told me there was something actually lined up.'

'Oh, I thought I did.' Emily stuffed a whole chocolate chip cookie into her mouth and Beth waited for her to swallow it before the conversation could continue. 'Anyway... they say I can start next week. As soon as I'm sixteen. It's local, so I won't need a lift there or anything.'

'I don't remember offering you one.'

'Oh, Mum! I could hardly go to work on the bus, could I? That would mean getting up at like the crack of dawn or something. Anyway, I can walk there, so that's lucky, but I still have to start at half past eight. Can you believe that? It's like going to school. Will I be able to have some breakfast before I go, do you think?'

'You know where the cereal's kept. And the bread.'

'No bacon and eggs? We always have bacon and eggs at the weekend.'

'Fine, if you want to cook them yourself. On the Saturdays I'm not working I look forward to having a nice lie-in. Breakfast at ten, no problem. Breakfast at half past seven, no way. If you're going to be a working girl, it's time you learnt to look after yourself.'

Emily grumbled under her breath. 'Huh. Well, aren't you going to ask me what the job is?'

'I'm sure you're about to tell me.'

'Well...' Emily sat down at the small kitchen table and kicked off her shoes, one of them flying across the room and bouncing off the oven door. 'Oops. Sorry about that.'

'The job, Em? Tell me about the job.'

'It's at Cut Above, the hairdressers. Just sorting out the towels and sweeping up the hair and stuff like that to start with, but they say it's all good practice, you know, for a proper career later on.'

'A career? Are you telling me you want to be a hairdresser now? I thought you had your heart set on being a vet? And, before that, I seem to remember you saying something about being a marine biologist. After we went to the water park and watched the dolphins.'

'It's cruel keeping dolphins in captivity. I know that now. And it takes seven years to be a vet. Seven! Can you believe it? That's like a lifetime before you actually earn any money. And all those exams!'

'And then there was the TV presenter phase, when all you wanted was to be the next Davina.'

'I like that programme she did about people finding their long-lost children, that's all. And the money drop thing she used to be on. But I'm not sure I've got the right face for the telly. That's why I think I'd be better the other side of the camera. Doing beauty, make-up, that sort of thing.'

'And sweeping up hair from the floor will be a start, will it?'

'Yes! Everybody knows that all the really top people started at the bottom. Find out all about the business from the ground up, that's what Alan Sugar says. I can watch and learn, can't I? And they do beauty treatments and manicures there too. Not just hair. Besides, it's quite artistic, isn't it? And you know how much I like art at school.'

'Fair enough. At least you'll be out of my hair all day!' Beth laughed at her own joke, but Emily just groaned.

'And I'll be earning some money at last.'

'Yes, that too.' Beth took a deep breath. 'Emily...'

'Yeah?'

'While we're sitting here, there's something else I need to tell you. Something I should have talked to you about a while ago, but it's... difficult.'

'Oh God, Mum, it's not the birds and the bees stuff, is it?'

Beth couldn't help but laugh. 'No. Why? Is there anything you need to ask me about any of that?' She watched Emily squirm, her cheeks turning almost instantly pink. 'It's okay, Em. No yukky embarrassing talk, I promise.'

'What then?'

'Well, something you said just then, about that programme. People tracking down their families... You remember that I was adopted, don't you?'

'Yeah.'

'Not something we've ever talked about much, not while Granny and Grandad were still with us anyway, but just lately... well, I've been wondering about them. My birth parents. Where they are, who they might be, why they decided to give me up.'

'Oh.'

'Is that it? Just oh?'

'What do you want me to say? I mean, for anybody to give up their baby and never see it again, it's not right, is it? I know I could never do it.'

'You can't know that, love. What you might do. What reasons you might have. Or they had. We don't know what their circumstances were, what pressures they might have been under. And it was a different time, different attitudes.'

'So, what are you saying? That you want to find them? The people who abandoned you?'

'That's a harsh word, Em. But, yes, I'm curious.'

'So, what have you done? Written in to the programme? Are we going to meet Davina? Are we going to be on TV? Ooh, I might get to meet the make-up people. See how it's done...'

'No, Emily. No TV, but I have... well, no, to be honest, it's Jack who's done all the digging. And he's found her, Em. My birth mother. I won't say your real gran, because that's not fair to the gran you've known all your life, but your... biological gran.'

'What? How come I don't know about this? Why is big brother always the one to know all the secrets? I'm not a little kid, you know.'

'I'm beginning to realise that. But, don't worry. Nothing's happened yet. Well, I haven't spoken to her, I mean. Or met her.'

'But you're going to?'

'Yes, I think I am, but I'd like it if we all did it together. Safety in numbers!'

'Why? Oh, Mum, she's not, like, in prison or in a mental hospital or something, is she?'

'No, of course not! Jack says she's just a very nice, ordinary woman. With a husband and a son and a little granddaughter who's only six. They live by the sea, in Brighton.'

'He's been there? Met her?'

'Yes.'

'See what I mean? It's always Jack this and Jack that. What about me?'

'Jack's the oldest, Em. Since your dad and me split up, I have to have someone to talk to sometimes. Someone I can lean on a bit, and Jack's just been there for me, that's all.'

'I'm here for you!'

'I know that, love, but you're still so young. It's my job to look after you, not the other way round. I could hardly send you off by yourself to somewhere miles away to meet strangers, could I? And he offered. He wants to get to know them as much as I do.'

'So, what else aren't you telling me? What else does Saint Jack know that I don't?'

Beth swallowed hard. If she was going to say anything about her health, now was the time to do it.

'There is something, but I don't want you to worry, or to get upset.'

'Well, saying that is just going to make sure I do worry now, isn't it?'

'I'm sorry, Em. That's the last thing I wanted to happen. It's why I've kept quiet for so long.'

'So long? What are you talking about? What's going on, Mum?' Emily reached her hand across the tabletop and closed it around her mother's. 'Mum? Are you crying? Why are you crying?'

Beth lowered her head and stared at the floor, at the crumbs under the table, at the one abandoned school shoe, at Emily's grey school tights, bunched at her ankles. The words wouldn't come, but the tears did.

'I'm sorry, Em, but I'm not very well.' Beth saw the shock on her daughter's pale face, felt her fingers tighten over her own. She wasn't sure what to say to make any sense of it all, to make everything all right. 'You spotted it first and you were right. But it turns out it's not just tiredness, not the stress of the divorce, or losing your gran. It's a bit more than that.'

'You haven't got cancer, have you?'

She shook her head, slowly. 'No. God, no.' She couldn't do this on her own. She wasn't sure she could do any of it on her own. Not anymore. 'Could you call Jack for me? See if he's free to come over? And we'll call Tom as well, maybe try to get him on FaceTime, then we can all talk about it together. About the people in Brighton, and my illness, and what happens next... not just to me, but to all of us.'

TWENTY-SIX

'Can I come with you to the animal park?' Geraldine had found it hard to settle to anything over the last few days since meeting Jack, and an afternoon out was just what she needed.

'Of course you can,' Ruby said. 'I'll be glad of the company. Once Lily gets into the pen with those piglets, I'll just be a spare part!'

'We can take the car, save you using the bus. And I can finally meet your friend Vicky. You've talked so much about her.'

'That's fine. I'm sure she'd like to meet you too. I get the impression she's a bit short of friends. We've probably only got the two free tickets though.'

'Oh, I don't mind paying to get in. I'm sure it all goes towards helping the animals. And it's only a few miles away but I've never actually been there. I don't think the place can have existed when our Michael was small or I probably would have known about it.'

'Michael's not really much of an animal lover though, is he?'

'No, you're right there. He was always more into cars and

football when he was a child, but I did my best to get him interested in wildlife and nature. Took him on cliff walks and birdwatching trips, and to the zoo a few times. I don't think he ever really enjoyed it much, but I did!'

'Well, you'll have no such trouble with Lily. I have yet to find an animal she didn't fall in love with. She won't even let me kill a spider.'

'Good for her! Shall I make us a snack to take with us? Or a flask of tea?'

'No, let's use the café there, shall we? Help boost the funds, like you said. Lily will probably want an ice cream and Vicky says they do good cakes. Give Lily a sandwich and she'll only feed it to some passing bird.'

'Right. Let me just go up and run a comb through my hair and we'll go.'

Vicky was inside a big wire-fronted cage, surrounded by budgies, when they arrived.

'Be with you in a minute,' she called over her shoulder, just as a little green bird decided to settle there, happily opening its beak and taking a seed from her hand. She eased him onto her finger and gently relocated him onto the nearest branch, picked up her bucket and let herself out through the double doors, careful that none of the birds had decided to try following her in a bid to escape.

'How's things?' Ruby asked, laughing as Vicky pulled a feather from her hair.

'Good, thanks. Busy, as usual. I know Sundays are meant to be days of rest, but I never mind working. It gets me out of the flat. And it's a nice day. Not quite so much fun when it's raining.'

'Well, Lily's come prepared for all weathers.' Ruby pointed to the rolled-up raincoat sticking out of her bag and the Minnie Mouse wellie boots and matching sun hat Lily had insisted on wearing. 'Nothing's going to keep her away from those piglets! And this is Geraldine, by the way.'

'Call me Geri. Everyone does.'

'Hello, Geri.' Vicky held out a hand, quickly withdrew it to wipe it down her overalls, then held it out again. 'Sorry. You don't want bird poo all over you.'

'Could be worse,' Ruby joked. 'Best to get the handshakes out of the way before we get to the pigs.'

Geraldine did a pretend shudder. 'Oh, definitely.' She laughed. 'Pleased to meet you, love.'

They all followed Vicky along the path towards the pig barn, Lily skipping along excitedly between her mum and her gran, one hand in each of theirs.

'Can we take lots of photos, Mummy?' she said. 'Then we can send some to show Daddy.'

'Yes, we can.'

'Do they have pigs in Portugal?'

'I'm sure they do.'

'And Vicky says I can choose a name for one of them. I can, can't I?'

Vicky turned round and nodded, reaching into her pocket for a key. 'Come on, they're still inside at the moment, having some quiet time before we let them out for the public to see. Special privileges for you, my little one. First look, first pick. You decide which piggie you like the best, and that's the one you can name, okay?'

It was quite dark inside, with only one small window to the outside world, and there was a strong smell of stale straw and rotting vegetables and poo. The enormous mother pig lay on her side, seemingly asleep, and the babies were all rootling about along the length of her, sucking and snorting contentedly.

'Ah, they're so cute,' Lily whispered, gazing at them in awe.

'They certainly are.' Geraldine held her hand over her nose and smiled at her granddaughter. 'It's not going to be easy to choose one, is it?'

'Which ones are boys and which ones are girls?'

Vicky laughed. 'I'd have to get down underneath to check that,' she said, looking to Ruby for guidance.

'It's okay. She knows the difference.'

'Well, to be honest, Lily, we don't know yet. They're only a week old and we haven't wanted to take them away from their mum yet. It's not all that easy to tell while they're so small. Maybe you can pick a name that would suit either a boy or a girl.'

'No Peppa then, eh, Lil?' Ruby said, giving Vicky a knowing look.

'Oh.' Lily pointed at the smallest piglet, who had unlatched itself from the teat and had come over towards the fence, where it was now gazing up at Lily curiously. 'All right then. I like this one, because she's the littlest, and because she likes me.'

'She?'

'Well, I think she's a girl.'

'Could be. Fifty–fifty chance you're right,' Vicky said, shrugging her shoulders.

'She's got a girl face. She's too pretty to be a boy.'

'Pretty?' Ruby looked closely at the little hairy face, half black, half white, and the squashed-looking snout. 'Really?'

'Yes,' Lily said, indignantly. 'I think she's very pretty, like a princess.'

'Princess Fiona maybe, while she was still an ogre.'

'Don't be mean, Mummy.'

'Sorry, Lil. I'm sure she is very pretty. For a pig. So, is that what you're going to call her? Princess?'

Lily pondered. 'No. I'm going to call her... Portugal.'

'Hmm, Portugal Pig,' Vicky said. 'That's a new one!'

'Had to start with a P though, didn't it?' Ruby laughed.

'Had to.'

They spent the next ten minutes watching the piglets do pretty much nothing but feed and snuffle around, then Vicky led them back out into the sunlight.

'Right! Who's for helping me sort out some tortoise food?'

'Yes, please! I like the tortoises, but one of them did try to eat my finger last time we came.'

'I'm not sure that's quite true, Lily,' Ruby said, trying not to laugh. 'They are vegetarian, aren't they, Vix?'

'Certainly are. I think he was probably just giving your finger a little nibble to say hello, Lily. Or a little kiss, maybe.'

'Ah, that's so cute,' Lily said, for the second, and probably not the last, time that day, as she skipped off ahead, gripping Vicky's hand. 'What are they having for their dinner?'

'Well, I've got some lovely cabbage leaves, and some Brussels sprouts.'

'Yuk. I hate Brussels sprouts.'

'Good job we have some ice creams then, for the human babies.'

'I'm not a baby. I'm six!'

'Shall we leave them to it and go and get that cup of tea?' Geraldine whispered. 'I could just murder one of those cakes you mentioned.'

'Why not? It's not as if we're needed here, is it?' Ruby said. 'See you later, girls,' she called as Vicky and Lily climbed over the low fence into the tortoise enclosure. 'Come and find us in the café when you're done. And you be a good girl now, Lil, or there'll be no ice cream.'

'She's always a good girl,' Vicky said. 'And a great little helper. Give us half an hour, okay?'

'Yeah, that's fine.' Ruby led Geraldine back along the little winding path, waving goodbye over their shoulders as they went.

'She seems nice,' Geraldine said, as they went inside the little café, ordered drinks and chose their cakes. 'Good with kids. None of her own yet, I assume?'

'No, and not likely to be for a while yet.'

'No nice man in her life then?'

'Or woman!' Ruby said, sipping her coffee and quickly putting the cup down again. 'Ooh, that's hot.'

'Oh, I see. You mean she's gay?'

'Yep, gay, and proud of it. But lonely too, I think. I get the impression things aren't good between her and her dad. Adoptive dad, that is. She gets on well enough with her mum but Vicky's not living at home with them anymore. She shares a flat with a couple of other girls now, although she never really talks about them. I think she finds it hard to make friends. It's what being in care does. You either come out desperate to be loved and to fit in, so you throw yourself at the first person who comes along, or you put up barriers and try to protect yourself, because you know you don't fit at all, however much you might want to.'

'Is that how you felt? Because I did try, really hard, to give you a home, a family. If only Michael hadn't...'

'Geri, you were great. You *are* great! I couldn't have asked for a better life than the one you've given me, with or without Michael. And yes, I did throw myself at him, as you well know, but that's in the past now. I don't need him. I've got you, and Lily. But Vicky hasn't been so lucky. I wonder if she likes seeing me because I come from the same place, had the same start in life. I know who she really is, what she's been through, so I understand her in a way her new friends don't. And Lily... well, Lily gives her the chance to spend time with a child, and have some fun. She clearly loves kids. No threat, I suppose. All that innocence and trust, soaking up information like a sponge, and there's no judging, is there? Lily doesn't care about Vicky being gay or growing up in a home. None of that means a thing to her. And I'm sure it helps that Lily loves the same things that Vicky loves. Animals, and chocolate, basically. We won't mention the wine!'

'We'll have to invite her over. For tea maybe, and to meet Flopsy. Has Lily actually cleaned out his cage this week, by the way? A visit from Vicky could be just the spur she needs to get it done, to prove what a good animal keeper she can be.'

'Good idea. Although I have a suspicion we're going to be asked if she can have another rabbit after today, or if she can take a tortoise home. Or a piglet!'

'You'll just have to be strong and say no, love. We can't have the back garden turned into a mini zoo. Not when William's just planted all those vegetables. They'd be gobbled up as soon as they pop out of the ground. No, if Lily wants animals, she can come here to see them. We'll have to find out if they do some sort of annual membership discount or one of those adopt-an-animal schemes, to encourage her to get more involved.'

'I don't think she's going to need much encouragement. Just try keeping her away!'

'Mmm, these really are delicious cakes. I'm quite tempted to become a regular visitor myself.' Geraldine licked the last crumbs from her fingers, just as her phone started to ring in the bottom of her bag.

'Now, who can that be? William, not knowing where his clean shirt is, probably. He's got a rehearsal later this afternoon.' She found the phone and stared at the screen for a moment, her fingers hovering over it as if reluctant to accept the call. 'Oh...

It's not William.' She could feel her hand starting to tremble. 'It's Jack.'

'Oh, do you think he's sorted out a day to come down, with his mum?'

'Only one way to find out.' Geraldine pressed Accept and put the phone to her ear. 'Hello? Jack, how lovely to hear from you. How are you?'

At that moment, the door flew open, as if blown by a hurricane, and Lily came bounding in, Vicky putting her bucket down outside and trailing in behind her.

'I saw a tortoise having a poo,' Lily announced, loudly, to the entire room. 'And one climbed right up on top of another one's back. Vicky said they were playing leap frog.' She plonked herself down on an empty chair just as Geraldine stood up and slipped away outside in search of a quiet place to talk. 'Can I have an ice cream now, Mummy?'

'Please.'

'Please,' she mimicked. 'With a flake in it. And lots of red sauce.'

Ruby watched Geraldine through the window, sitting on a wall with her back turned towards them, and wished she could hear what was being said, so she did not immediately respond.

'Please,' Lily said again, kicking her legs against the side of her chair. 'I have washed my hands.'

'Glad to hear it. Right, ice cream it is. Can I get you one, Vix?'

'No, I'm okay, thanks. Just nipping into the staff room to get my drink. Not worth paying café prices when I can bring my own. Give me a few minutes, then we can all go over to the reptile house. Lily wants to see the snakes.'

Ruby shuddered. 'I think I'll give them a miss.'

'Not still scared of slithery things, are you? Remember that time I brought a big fat worm in from the garden? I got a knife out of the drawer and chopped it in half because one of the boys had said both halves would grow back again, and we'd have two worms. One each. You ran out of the kitchen screaming like I'd just murdered my granny or something. Mrs Castle had a fit. Thought you'd hurt yourself. And she told me off for playing with knives. Not that I was playing. It was a serious experiment. Science!'

'Go on, go and get your drink. I can do without all the reminiscing, thanks very much.'

'Chicken,' Vicky muttered, under her breath, but not quietly enough that Ruby didn't hear it. There was definitely a cruel streak running through Vicky Dunn and right now it had brought a very uncomfortable vision of that revolting worm back into her head. It was all very well Vicky still living in the past, but there were big chunks of it that Ruby would really much rather forget.

'I like chickens,' Lily said, still kicking at the legs of her chair. 'If we had a chicken in the garden, we could have eggs for breakfast every day.'

'They're coming down next weekend,' Geraldine said, returning to the table with a smile on her face.

'Who's coming?' Lily asked, her eyes still trained on the big colourful pictures of ice creams on the wall behind the counter.

Ruby and Geraldine looked at each other and Ruby shook her head. She would have to explain things to Lily but not right here, right now. Not when ice cream and a visit to the snakes were all Lily was really interested in.

Vicky sat in the corner of the staff room, her locker door open, and took a swig from her bottle. This was getting ridiculous. She should be able to get through a few hours without the need for a drink. But it helped. And what harm could it do? It was not as if she was about to drive, or operate heavy machinery, or be asked to walk in a straight line. The animals wouldn't notice, or care, if she'd had a drop of vodka. And the only person likely to come close enough to smell it was Lily. She allowed herself a smile. Lily would probably be smothered in ice cream by now, and eager to wrap herself up in the nearest snake. She would never understand why Ruby was so scared of them. Snakes weren't the evil, slimy creatures their reputation made them out to be. Unlike some men she could mention, her father being top of the list.

She screwed the top back onto her bottle and slipped it back into her bag, quickly locking it away. Maybe when she caught the bus home tonight, that pretty bus driver would be on duty. It was time she made a move, found herself someone, dug herself out of this self-pitying hole she was slowly sinking into. She wanted what Ruby had. People who cared about her. A home. A life, away from this place. Love. But those things didn't just drop into your lap, did they? If she wanted things to change, it was going to be up to her to do something about it. She rubbed at the scars on her arm and pulled her sleeve back down over them. Those scars were what despair looked like. She could not go back there.

TWENTY-SEVEN

The train was crowded. Well, Beth thought, what could she expect, travelling down to the seaside on a sunny weekend? They had been lucky to find seats together, she and Jack sitting side by side, with her younger kids across the aisle, already squabbling over the last biscuit in the packet. They had taken the news of her illness remarkably well, helped greatly by Jack's calming presence and his explanations of the medical side of things, which made it all sound so easy and matter-of-fact and unfrightening. Strangely, it had been the rest of it that had elicited the worst reaction, from Emily anyway.

'But I had a granny,' she had said, her voice slipping into a childish wail as if she might at any moment start stamping her foot like a toddler.

'You had two, actually.'

'I know that, but Dad's mum died so long ago I don't properly remember her at all. Granny Molly was my granny. My only real granny. I don't want another one. Some stranger, trying to take her place.'

'Nobody is trying to take her place, Em. She was my mum, and always will be, but this other lady is important too. She gave birth to me, when she was hardly more than a child herself, and if she hadn't done that, and hadn't decided to give me up for adoption, then we would never have had Granny, would we? Or Grandad? They would have been the strangers. Yes, she gave me away, but in doing that she gave me – *us* – a family. Finding her was something I always had somewhere in the back of my mind and now just seems like the right time to do it. Can you understand that?'

Emily had thought about it for a moment and then nodded, noncommittally. 'I suppose. So, if we go there, to Brighton, will we have time to go to the beach? And on the pier?'

'Of course we will. Call it an early birthday celebration. Oh, don't look so horrified. You can still have your mates over on the day, do all the pizza and sleepover stuff you're getting way too old for!'

'I am not!'

'I'm not complaining. There are far worse things sixteen-year-olds can get up to. No, we'll treat Sunday as a bonus. Fish and chips and amusement arcades and sticks of rock. Even buckets and spades if you like! How could we even think of going to Brighton and not doing all that stuff? And a birthday makes it absolutely essential, I'd say. I don't expect meeting her to take very long, no more than a couple of hours, and you don't even have to come with us for that bit if you don't want to.' Why was she finding it so hard to mention the woman's name? 'You can wait for us somewhere and we'll meet up again after.'

'But Jack's going with you?'

'Yes. He's met her already, remember. I'm relying on your brother to help break the ice a bit, hang on tight to me and stop me from shaking... or running away!'

'I'll come.'

'Are you sure?'

'Yep.'

'And you, Tom? Fancy coming along for a day at the sea? And to meet your long-lost family?'

'Well, I can't be the only one left out, can I? I don't have anything to rush back for. And I'm curious. There are all these relatives we know nothing about. I wonder if any of them look like us?'

'God help them if they look like you, Big Ears!' Emily said, quickly dodging as her brother rolled up a piece of paper and aimed it at her head.

And so they had all piled onto the train and, whatever they might each be feeling about the meeting to come, it was easier just to pretend they were on a fun family day out to the beach. Beth had packed towels and her sun hat, sharing bag space with that funny little striped teddy she had found in the box with the locket and that Jack had told her the woman – Geri – was so keen to see again. Geri. It felt odd calling her that, this woman she knew so little about. But Geri it had to be. She might have given birth to her, but calling her Mum was not really an option. Not yet. In fact, it probably never would be.

Geraldine paced around the room like a caged lion.

'Stop it, love. You'll wear a hole in the carpet.' William reached out and touched her arm, guiding her into an armchair. 'They won't be here for a while yet. Have a cup of tea or something. A gin even, to settle your nerves.'

'I don't want to meet my daughter reeking of booze. And too much tea will just make me want the loo.'

'It will be all right, you know. We're all here for you.'

'I know. I don't even know why I'm getting so het up about it. It must be so much worse for her, mustn't it? I mean, I was there. I know what happened. She was just a baby. She'll have no memories of it at all. Or of me. She'll be the one with all the questions.'

'Which I'm sure you will answer as honestly as you can. There's nothing to feel ashamed about, or guilty. You did what you had to do.'

'Yes, I did, but she won't know that, will she? It makes me feel like a terrible mother, walking away from my own flesh and blood. Whatever is she going to think? That I didn't care about her?'

'But you did, Geri, and what you did was as much for her as it was for you. You were still at school, with no mum of your own to help you, no support from the father, and you gave that little baby a life with people who could take care of her properly.'

She gave him a watery smile. 'I know, but...'

'No buts, love. What's done is done. No going back, no changing things. We just have to do the right thing now, don't we? Deal with the present, not the past. Welcome her, answer her questions, take things slowly. It will take a while, getting to know each other again.'

'If she even wants that. Who knows what she might be feeling, what she expects to come out of all this? She might take one look and run a mile. We may never see her again.'

William laughed. 'You're not that scary, love.'

'Was it a good idea inviting her here? Maybe neutral territory might have been best. The park again, where I met Jack?'

'We've been through all this. She's family. It's only right we welcome her here, into our home. It's time for the personal touch, don't you think? Show her who we really are, how we live...'

'Yes, you're right. We are family, but I don't expect her to just suddenly fit in. Or to instantly love me, or even necessarily like me. She's a grown woman, a middle-aged woman, not some lost and lonely kid. She's led her life and I've led mine. We're bound to be different. We're not going to be instantly bonded, are we? Not like a real mother and daughter, but I do hope we get on, that we might become friends. In time, anyway.'

'Time to find out, love. I think they're here.'

'Already? Oh, William...'

He gave her a reassuring smile, walked over to the window and peered out through the curtains at the little group walking slowly up the path. 'And she has all three kids with her, by the look of things.'

The doorbell rang, and Geraldine's hand went straight up to tidy her hair.

'Are you ready?'

She nodded. 'As I'll ever be.'

'Want me to go to the door?'

'No, it has to be me.'

Jack's face was the first she saw as she opened the door. He was standing on the step, a few paces ahead of the others, like some sort of advance party, sent ahead to test the waters.

'Hello again, Geri.'

'Jack.' Oh God, why was her voice so wobbly? She must not cry. She really mustn't. Her eyes were drawn to the woman standing behind him. 'Come in. Please. All of you.'

'This is my mum, Beth.' Jack urged his mum forward. Neither woman seemed to know quite how to greet each other, yet each was staring at the other's face.

'Beth. I'm so pleased you've come.' Geraldine stood aside and beckoned them all in to the hall, before closing the door behind them. 'We're in here,' she said, a bit too formally, pointing the way into the lounge.

'Jack, I'd like you to meet my husband, William.'

William stepped forward, placing one hand on his wife's back for support as he shook hands with Jack with the other.

'And this is my mum, Beth,' Jack said. 'And my brother and sister, Tom and Emily.'

Everyone stood in silence for a moment.

'I'm sorry. This feels strange, almost unreal somehow. I'm sure it must be the same for you.' Geri could feel herself shaking but hoped it wasn't too obvious. 'Please, sit down, all of you. Let me get you all a drink, and some cake.'

'Sit down yourself, love.' William was taking charge, thank God. 'I can get the tea.' And then he left the room and she was alone with them, with absolutely no idea what to do or say.

'So, Elizabeth. Beth...' She walked to the sofa and lowered herself down on the edge, next to her daughter. 'I'm sorry. It's going to take me a while to get used to that. In my head you're Sandie. You've always been Sandie. It's the name I gave you, you see, but your... mum and dad chose another name for you. The truth is, I never really expected this day to come. Never expected you to turn up after all this time. I suppose I had hopes, early on, but as the years went by... But here you are. It would be silly to say I recognise you, but your eyes are so like my mother's, and your hair is exactly the colour mine used to be, before the grey set in and I resorted to the dye bottle!' She smiled and was pleased to see her daughter smile too. 'Oh, there's just so much I want to say, but I have no idea where to begin.'

'Me too.' The woman reached out a hand and placed it over hers. 'I suppose all we can do is try. My mum and dad are dead now. Well, I know Jack's already told you that. I couldn't do it before, not while they were still here. It would have felt wrong somehow. But now, it's... well, like a whole chapter of my life that I know so little about, and it's time I did. I want to fill in the blanks.'

'Of course you do.'

'Right,' said William, coming back in with a tray. 'Teas all round? Or can I get you young ones anything else? We have juice, lemonade...'

'Tea's great, thanks,' Beth said, looking around to check with the others. 'Except for Emily, maybe?'

'Lemonade please, if that's okay.' Emily looked up, shyly, before returning her gaze to the carpet.

'Of course. Coming right up. I have to go back for the cake anyway.'

'You have him very well trained,' Beth said, nodding at William's retreating back.

'He's still on probation! We've not been married long.'

'Right. So, he's not... my father?'

'Oh, no. Sorry, no, definitely not. William's my second husband. My first, Ken, died a few years back. But he wasn't around either, when... well, when I fell pregnant. I don't know how much you've been told, but I was only fourteen then. The old story. Stupid teenage stuff, taking risks, falling in with the wrong crowd, suddenly finding myself expecting and trying to pretend it wasn't happening. Your father and I weren't together, not going out or anything, not *an item* as you'd probably say today. Nothing loving or romantic about any of it. It was just a stupid one-off. A fumble. A mistake, and a drunken one, I'm ashamed to say. I never told him I was pregnant. Or my friends. Never told anyone, except my dad, and when I did finally get the courage he went berserk, and who could blame him? We'd not long lost my mum and he just couldn't deal with it. I realise that now. I got the full-on angry, disappointed, bringing shame on the family speech, and then he packed me away in disgrace, to an aunt in Norfolk, and I wasn't allowed back until it was all over.'

'Sounds awful.'

'It was a very frightening, horrible time in my life. Oh, I don't mean that the way it sounds. You certainly weren't horrible. Quite the opposite. I just felt very alone, totally abandoned, and that I had no real choice about anything. I had no idea about babies, or how to look after them. I'd never even held one before. And then, there you were, so small and so beautiful, and all I knew was that I had to give you away. It had been decided, and who was I to argue? Somewhere there was another woman who would take care of you, give you what I couldn't. It made sense. Not that sense comes into it very much at moments like that. All these feelings rushing about in my head, the hormones kicking in and telling me you were mine, that I should be cuddling you, talking to you, feeding you...'

'One lemonade.' William was back, handing a glass to Emily, then hovering over the teapot. 'Now, who wants sugar?'

The room fell temporarily silent again as everyone concentrated on drinking their tea and nibbling cake.

'So, Tom, Emily, we know Jack here is a nurse, so tell us what you do,' William said, putting his cup down and trying his hardest to keep the conversation going.

'I'm at uni. Just finishing my first year. Computer science.' Tom licked a last crumb from his fingers. 'Em's still at school—'

'Studying for my GCSEs. But about to start a Saturday job,' she interrupted, indignantly. 'I'll be sixteen next week.'

'Yeah, whatever. Still a kid though.'

'Tom! Don't be so rude. And let your sister speak for herself.'

'As I was saying,' Emily went on. 'I'm going to work in a salon, to start learning about hair and beauty. I think I might like to be a make-up artist one day.'

'Sounds lovely,' Geraldine said, encouragingly. 'Shame you live so far away or I'd know who to come to when I next need my hair done.'

'Or some sweeping up,' Tom added, edging away just in time as the kick from Emily's foot missed his ankle by inches.

'I apologise for my children,' Beth said, the colour rising in her face. 'Perhaps I shouldn't have brought them.'

'Oh, no, it's fine, really. My son, Michael, is working abroad, but otherwise I would have liked him to be here too. It's lovely for us all to meet, but it's bound to be a bit awkward, isn't it? For all of us. Hard to realise I have grown-up grandchildren. Or that I know so little about them. Or you, of course. Perhaps, when we've had our tea, we could all go out for a little walk or something? Get some fresh air. Lily will be home soon, and her mum, Ruby, who Jack has already met, of course. Lily was invited to a party and didn't want to miss it, but I know she'd love to meet you all. It's a bit of a trek to the sea, and it will be crowded down there on a day like this, but perhaps we could just walk down to the swings. She'd like that.'

'Sounds a lovely idea. Oh, and I've brought Lily a present. It's not much, just a little hello gift really.' Beth reached down and opened her bag. 'I know little girls love presents!'

'You didn't have to do that.'

'I know, but it's not every day I acquire a six-year-old niece I didn't know I had. Or a mum, for that matter, but that's different, isn't it? I always knew you existed, even if I didn't know your name. So, this is for Lily, when she gets home.' She pulled out a small pink parcel and laid it on the coffee table in front of her. 'And there's this too...' She took something else, loosely wrapped in tissue paper, from her bag, and handed it to Geraldine. 'Yours, I believe?'

The little teddy was exactly as she remembered him. The knitted jumper with a hole in it, the stripes, the missing eye. The last time she had seen him was when she had handed him over to that nurse, Margaret, along with the old scratched record she'd pinched from the common room, and her mother's locket.

'Mr Snuggles,' she said, so quietly that only Beth, sitting beside her, could hear. And, whether a woman in her sixties should cry over an old tatty toy or not suddenly didn't seem to matter at all. She could not have stopped the tears that crept down her cheeks if she had tried.

———

Having Lily along certainly helped to break the ice as they all walked down towards the small local playground and its surrounding patch of grass. She had pounced on her present as soon as she had arrived home, declaring how much she loved the pink wrapping paper even before she had got to the unicorn colouring book and pencils she had found inside, and then throwing her arms around Beth's neck in a huge hug.

'Are you my aunty now?' she said, grinning from ear to ear. 'I've never had an aunty before.'

It was Beth's hand she had insisted on holding as they set off down the road, with Geraldine walking on the other side, leaving William to follow them, sandwiched between two slightly bored and wary teenagers, and Ruby and Jack to bring up the rear.

'Nice to see you again, Ruby,' Jack said, bumping against her as she stopped to bend down and fiddle with one of her trainers and lost her balance for a moment. 'You okay there?' He slipped a hand under her elbow to steady her. 'Need help with anything?'

'No, just a lace coming undone. Hang on a sec while I re-tie it.'

The others had moved even further ahead by the time the shoe was sorted out, but neither of them rushed to catch up.

'I'm glad you got your mum to come. Geri's been so nervous about it, but she really, really wanted to meet her.'

'It's mutual, I'm sure. Mum's been pretty scared about it all too, but it was her idea to track Geri down in the first place, and here we are, so I guess it's up to them what happens next, isn't it?'

'A happy ending, I hope. It's nice when families reunite. The times I wished my own mum had got her act together and come back for me, but I know now that was never going to happen. But if this goes well today, it might become a regular thing, don't you think? Keeping in touch. All of us finding out more about each other. Meeting up sometimes. I bet we'll be cracking open the family photo albums when we get back to the house. Geri will want to show your mum a picture of Michael, I'm sure. He is her brother, after all. Or half-brother anyway. And some of Lily as a baby. And her own wedding pictures, of course.'

'I'd be quite interested in all that myself, actually.'

'Having a big family's good. And something Lily's wanted for ages. So many of her friends have brothers and sisters, cousins...'

'Her dad's not on the scene though?'

'He's in Portugal, so it's hard to be from that distance. We never did quite make it down the aisle, but he's married now. To Poison Patsy, as I call her!'

'Oh dear. No love lost there then?'

'She's okay, actually. I mean, she took Michael away from me so we're never going to be best buddies, but he seems to love her and she's good to Lily, so good luck to them. He comes over here maybe two or three times a year, and they keep saying they're happy to have Lily visit them, which only works if someone travels with her on the plane, so it's only actually happened twice.'

'You're pretty much a single parent then?'

'Yeah, I suppose, although Geri and William have been a

godsend. They're my family now. Geri gave me a place to live and a job, and that means I have willing babysitters on tap twenty-four hours a day. Free ones, too! What more could I want?'

'No boyfriend?'

She could feel herself colour. 'No, not at the moment.'

'Sorry. Just being nosey, but it seems a shame. Pretty girl like you.'

'Thanks.' Ruby lowered her eyes to the pavement as they walked on. She wasn't used to compliments, especially from good-looking men. 'Lily keeps me busy. And the shop. I don't really have the time...'

'Ruby, lots of women, lots of mums, manage to work and bring up kids, but still find time for themselves. Everyone needs a bit of me-time, and a bit of fun. And we all need some romance in our lives, don't we?'

'And you? Do you have a bit of romance in your life?' She raised her eyes to meet his, hoping to have embarrassed him as much as he had her.

'If you mean do I have a girlfriend waiting for me at home, no I don't. Which is why I'm going to take a chance and say this, while the others are out of earshot. Do you fancy going out later? With me? On a date? We're not planning on going back to London until late, and Mum and the others will be off buying Kiss Me Quick hats and stuffing their faces with ice cream on the pier once we leave here. I just thought that maybe we could get to know each other a bit better. Seeing as we're both free as birds and in need of a bit of romance! What do you say?'

'I say...' What could she say, other than yes? 'Okay then, thanks. I'd like that. If Geri will babysit, of course.'

'On call twenty-four hours, you said! So, no excuses. We'll grab something to eat and have a drink somewhere. You're the local. You tell me where's good, where you'd like to go. Only, nowhere too posh as I'm on a nurse's pay and I haven't brought my tux!'

———

Beth took a sideways glance at Geri. It was hard to believe this was her mother. They sat side by side on a small painted bench at the edge of the playground and watched as Tom and Emily larked about on the swings they were much too old for, and William span Lily around, faster and faster, on the roundabout until she squealed for him to stop.

'You haven't said anything about your children's father,' Geraldine said. 'Are you...?'

'Divorced. Just last year. He's around still. Emily goes to stay with him some weekends. But, as marriages go, we weren't really the happiest of couples. Best apart. Though I can't say it's been easy. Financially, as well as everything else. We had to give up the family house, so we're renting, at least for now. And since my mum died... sorry, I know you're my mum, but...'

'It's all right. Don't apologise. She was your mum in so many ways I can never be.'

'Well, since she died, there's been even more to have to deal with. I haven't managed to sell her house, which is still standing empty after all these months, and it's in Norfolk so it's not as if I can just pop round there easily to check on things.'

'We had the same with William's mum, having to sell the house when she died, I mean, so I know what a worry it can be. And that was local, so I can imagine how hard it must be when it's miles away. Have you thought about renting it out? Having someone living there would at least keep it safe.'

'To be honest, I could do with the money. A lump sum from a sale, I mean, rather than just a monthly income from a tenant. It could make all the difference to us being able to buy a permanent home. Although Jack's already moved out. He lives in nurses' accommodation, and Tom's away at uni most of the year, so it's just Emily and me really. But I suppose I just crave some stability. A place to call my own again.'

'I wish you luck with that then, love. And I'm sure it will all work out all right. Most things usually do, given time.'

'I hope you're right.'

'Now, I know we agreed to keep this first meeting brief. It's a lot to take in, for all of us. But do let me make you all a bit of lunch before you go. Just a sandwich, or something on toast?'

'That's kind of you, but I did promise Em some chips down by the sea. And a stroll along the pier. You're welcome to come with us, if you'd like to.'

'Oh, no. I don't want to intrude. This is your family day out. And, by the look of what's going on over there, I have a feeling I may be needed to keep an eye on Lily this afternoon!' She nodded towards a bench about twenty yards away, where Ruby and Jack appeared to be getting along rather well.

'You could be right. He has been talking about your Ruby quite a bit since he came down here last.'

'She's a lovely girl. He could do a lot worse.'

'There speaks a matchmaker if ever I heard one!'

'Oh God, no. I love Ruby like she's my own, and your Jack seems like a very nice boy, but I'll let them work it out for themselves. Never let it be said that I'm one of those interfering old busybodies who always knows best.'

'I don't think anyone would accuse you of that, Geri, even if you are technically his granny. You seem a very... caring person. Not many women your age would sob over a tatty little teddy.'

'Tatty? My Mr Snuggles? He's adorable, and even more so after all our years apart.'

Beth laughed. 'I think I'm going to enjoy getting to know you better, Geri. Maybe next time you could come up to

London to see us? I'm sure by then I'll have thought of so many more things I want to ask you. It's just that today's been a bit overwhelming. I'm finding it hard to think straight at the moment.'

'Same here, love.' Geraldine reached out and touched Beth's hand. 'But we can always talk on the phone, can't we? I'll be more than happy to answer any questions at all.'

'About my dad? The drunken mistake? I think I'd like to know more about him.'

'I'll try. But, like I said, we weren't a couple, so I hardly knew him at all really. Never met his family or anything like that. Still, you have a right to know who he was, but I'm afraid you won't be able to find him, or meet him.' She paused, lowering her voice. 'He died, you see, a long time ago. Heroin, when he was only twenty-two. They don't think he meant to overdose, but I doubt he was thinking straight. It was the kind of people he mixed with, you see. Drink, drugs, parties. Everything to excess.'

'Oh.'

'I'm sorry. Probably not what you wanted to hear.'

'I can't feel too sad about someone I never met, I suppose, but that's not a nice end, not for anyone.'

'I know. He'd moved away, was working for some band or other, latest in a long line of bands he swore were about to make it big, but of course they didn't. He was squatting somewhere, living rough. The drummer died that same night too. A bad batch or something like that. It was in the papers, apparently, but I was a teenager. I didn't read papers back then. Not the news pages anyway. That was something my dad did, not me. I didn't hear about it until quite a long time after.'

'Do you have a picture?'

'In a locket close to my heart?' Geraldine sighed, fingering the locket with her mum's photo inside that she had fastened around her neck as soon as it had been returned to her. 'No, love. I'm sorry. Like I said, we weren't close. We hardly knew each other. You could probably find the old news report. Library records or something. That would tell you more, and there might be a photo. Not something I ever wanted to dig out, but you might, if you really want to know.'

'I'll have to think about that. Jack could probably research it for me if I asked him to.'

'Well, I can tell you that your father's name was Russell, if that helps. Russell Hawkins, but everyone called him Sprout.'

'Sprouts?' Lily had come running over towards them and caught the end of the conversation. 'Yuk! I hate sprouts. We're not having them for tea, are we?'

Both women laughed.

'No, Lily. Now, come on, let's walk back, shall we? Our visitors will be wanting to be on their way.'

'Oh, do they have to? I want them to stay and meet Flopsy.'

'Flopsy?' Beth asked, winking at Geraldine. 'I didn't know you had a sister, Lily.'

Lily giggled. 'Flopsy's my rabbit,' she said, squeezing between them on the bench. 'I don't like sprouts but he does.'

'Right, we'd better meet him then, but then we really do have to go. Your cousins will be wanting to get down to the pier and onto some of those scary rides.'

'Cousins?' Lily beamed with excitement. 'Do I have cousins?'

'Tom and Emily and Jack, they're all your cousins now.'

'Oh, wow! I have real live cousins!' And she was off again, bounding across the playground to tell William about the latest additions to her ever-growing family.

TWENTY-EIGHT

1967

It was only a small hall, more of a wooden hut than a proper venue for gigs, but Geri loved coming here, sneaking out of the house in the evenings while her dad watched his boring programmes or read his boring newspaper. It wasn't as if he would notice she'd gone. He was the old-fashioned buttoned-up type, who never went into a girl's room in case he was to see something he shouldn't. Once she had said goodnight and retreated up the stairs, she knew she was safe to do whatever she wanted, and he'd be none the wiser. She'd even mastered navigating around the creaky floorboards and figured out how to close the front door with hardly a click. It was easy enough with the noise of the telly to cover her tracks. Luckily, her dad wasn't one for bolting the door when he went up to bed. Or checking for open windows. That had always been her mum's job and, like the ironing and the cooking, one he had not taken to at all, so getting back in was easy enough, so long as he was asleep and she was extra quiet.

She had not managed to get out of the house as early as usual this week, and the band was already on the stage as she crept in at the back of the hall, the way Russell had shown her last time. Picking her way through the darkness of the storeroom and over a mound of cardboard boxes, she opened the inner door that led into the hall and slunk through it, trying to get her bearings in the crowded room. In the dim light a single beam picked out the pale face and long lank hair of the lead guitarist as he banged his head up and down to the heavy thud of the music. A hand landed just as heavily on her bottom and squeezed it roughly, making her jump, as a voice close to her ear said, 'Hello, sexy,' and asked if she wanted a drink. She nodded as he pushed his way back through the crowds of teenagers, many of them jumping up and down in an echo of the movements on stage. She felt behind her and adjusted her miniskirt back into position to make sure her knickers weren't on show.

Russell was not the sort to have deep and meaningful conversations. Those two words of greeting were probably about all she would be getting out of him tonight, if you didn't count the kissing and the hands that wandered a bit too freely while the lights were down that she was sure would be coming her way later on. She had not been sure about any of that when they'd met for the first time the week before, but all around them the older kids seemed to be doing much the same and she had ended up quite liking it, once she'd had a sip or two of beer and her mouth had started to taste just the same as his.

Russell was definitely one of those people she was sure all the girls would be after and, amazingly, he had turned his attention on her. 'Don't pay to get in next week,' he'd said, as if bestowing a special favour, and then he had shown her the door down a side alley that nobody else seemed to know anything about. 'I'll make sure it's not locked. If you're a good girl I might even let you meet the band after their set. We can hang out. Have a drink. And a fag.'

Of course, she hadn't told him she was only fourteen. How humiliating would that have been? None of her school friends were here. They would never have been allowed to come. So, nobody was about to recognise her. And with her make-up carefully applied and her breasts pushed up, not to mention the lack of light, she was pretty sure he wouldn't guess. She took the plastic cup from his hand and leaned into him as the music grew even louder and the floor throbbed beneath her feet.

The drink only covered the bottom of the cup but it was strong. She didn't know what it was, but not beer this time. It hit the back of her throat like fire. It was all she could do not to gag on it and spit it back out, but she didn't.

'Hey, Sprout!' A couple of other lads had crept in the secret way and were slapping Russell on the back. 'Thanks, mate. We owe ya.'

'Sprout? Why do they call you that?' she said, struggling to be heard.

'My nickname, isn't it? You know, Russell. Brussel. It rhymes, see?'

'Oh, okay. Is that what I should call you then?'

He nodded. 'Everyone does. Except my mum and dad, obviously. What about you? What do they call you?'

That was when she realised that, despite having had his tongue halfway down her throat last week, he had never actually asked her name.

'Geri,' she said.

'Like Gerry and the Pacemakers. Isn't that a bloke's name?' He laughed, right into her ear, and then started to nibble it.

'How come you know the band then?' she asked, trying to divert his face away from her neck where he was doing a good job of sucking it to death.

'Roadie, aren't I?' he mumbled. 'And they're gonna be big, this lot. Going places, and I'm going with them.'

A roadie? She wasn't totally sure what that was, but she'd heard the word somewhere.

'Going where? To London, do you mean?'

'London, America, you name it. They're gonna be bigger than the Beatles, you'll see.'

'Not the same sort of music though, is it?'

'Beatles are old hat now, Terry. These lads are the future.'

She was about to tell him he'd got her name wrong but the music was so loud now she doubted he would hear her, and it hardly mattered anyway.

Half an hour and another drink later, and with her ears ringing, the music came to an end and Sprout was pulling her towards the small backstage area. 'C'mon, let's go and meet them, eh? I can get you an autograph but it'll cost ya.' He smirked, running his fingers down her back and sliding them up under the hem of her skirt.

There were four of them in the band and they were already swilling from cans and lighting up cigarettes by the time Sprout had found a corner and pushed her down onto a pile of bags and coats. She half sat and half lay watching them as he helped to shove their equipment away into cases and they all congratulated each other on a great gig. The cigarettes smelt funny and the drummer swayed a bit as he made his way out to the Gents. From the main hall she could hear people starting to leave, see the lights coming back on. It must be almost eleven, the time she knew the hall had to be vacated, and she wondered if her dad was asleep yet or if she'd have to stay out a while longer to make sure he was before creeping back in.

Someone offered her another drink and she nodded, glad to see it was just beer this time.

'Well now, Terry, have you enjoyed yourself? Up for a bit more fun?' Sprout sat down beside her and tipped her can towards her lips. 'Have another swig. It will help loosen you up.'

She wasn't sure she wanted to be loosened up, but she drank anyway.

'Got to go. Things to do,' the drummer drawled, staggering back from the toilet with his shirt hanging out.

'It's okay. You get off. All of you. I'll sort out the gear.' Sprout grinned at them as they each found their coats, pulling them out from under her, and left.

The guitarist laughed loudly. 'The gear? Is that what you call it these days?' and leered at her knowingly. 'Don't do anything I wouldn't do.'

'That doesn't leave much,' Sprout said back.

It was very quiet when everyone had gone.

'I can't stop long.' Geri tried to stand, but the drink from earlier, whatever it was, must have gone to her head. The room seemed to spin and she dropped back down, giggling with surprise.

'Had a drop too much?' he asked, looming over her. 'You know what you need. A nice lie down.'

And then he had lain down beside her, or was it on top of her? And everything after that had been a bit of a blur. A warm, wet, painful blur.

TWENTY-NINE

'I sn't it time you told Michael what's going on?' William sat next to Geraldine on the sofa and absent-mindedly massaged her feet. 'It's not every day a secret sister comes out of the woodwork. It won't go down too well if he hears it from someone else.'

'Who's going to tell him? Ruby? They're not exactly in constant touch, are they?'

'No, but he does ring to talk to Lily sometimes, and kids aren't known for their discretion. She's so excited she suddenly has cousins, it'll be the first thing she blurts out. It would be much better coming from you.'

'I know, but... well, all these years I've said nothing, so what's he going to think? That his mother was some sort of wayward slut who went around sleeping with virtual strangers and getting pregnant while she was still at school? And then not only gave the baby away but never thought to mention it to him? It makes it sound like I'm ashamed of what I did, that I feel guilty...'

'Well, I certainly hope you don't. And, besides, it's not his place to judge you, Geri. It's not as if he hasn't made mistakes

235

himself, is it? Running off and leaving Ruby, and his own child. Isn't that just as bad?'

'But he has a big sister. One old enough to be his mother, which he's bound to find weird. And he has nephews and a niece that he has no inkling about. It's going to come as a shock, isn't it? That he's not an only child.'

'Geri, he's not a child at all, let alone an only one. He's a grown man, and perfectly capable of understanding how hard it must have been for you, that you did what you had to do. It was all long before he was born, and you're not that person anymore. None of it changes your relationship with him, or the family life you gave him. You didn't know Beth would come looking for you, that you'd ever see her again. Leaving it all locked up in the past was your coping mechanism, and you had every right to keep your secret, but it's not a secret anymore. He has to be told.'

'Not today though, eh? It's been emotional enough, meeting them all, and having to tell my own daughter that the father she had hoped to find is dead. Not that he would have been the least bit interested in the fact that she existed, or in getting to know her.'

'You don't know that for sure.'

'No, I don't, but, believe me, Russell Hawkins was not the loving kind. He took what he was after and buggered off to London and that was that. I'm sorry he died, just as I would be for anyone whose life ended that way, but he didn't mean anything to me, and in my head it's still all his fault. I was young and stupid. What did I know about booze or contraceptives, or pretty much anything really? I was a fourteen-year-old kid still grieving for her mother, and all it took was someone to show an interest in me...'

'Enough! Now stop all this wallowing and I'll make us a hot drink. Then we can watch something on the TV and take our minds off all of this before bed. It's been a lot to deal with today and, you're right, there's no rush to do anything, is there? Nobody's going to blab to Michael before tomorrow. And, if I'm not much mistaken, that sounds like Ruby coming in. And I know you're dying to know how she got on with Jack, so I'll be off to the kitchen and leave you to it for a while.'

'Thanks, love. You always know just what to say.'

'What? That a bit of girly gossip is just what the doctor ordered? It's about time Ruby found herself a nice boy, and if he turns out to be your own grandson, all the better. Keep it in the family, eh?' He smiled at her as he lowered her feet from his lap and stood up. 'Now, what do you fancy?'

'You, of course!'

'I meant tea or coffee, but you can have me too. As a bonus. And a biscuit, if you're good.'

'Actually, I wouldn't mind a cup of cocoa. And a Hobnob, if we've got one left.'

'Your wish is my command.' He gave an exaggerated bow and backed out of the room, leaving her with a ridiculously big smile on her face.

'What did I miss?' Ruby said, coming in and flopping into an armchair.

'Oh, nothing. Just William being William.'

'Lily all right?'

'Yes, out like a light as soon as her head hit the pillow. Must be all the excitement. And, talking of excitement… how was it? Your date?'

Ruby lowered her head but not before Geraldine saw the gleam in her eyes. 'Okay. No, better than okay. It was only a meal and a drink in a pub but I had a good time. Jack's really nice.'

'Well, of course he is. He's my own flesh and blood.'

'Does it feel strange, saying that?'

'No. It feels bloody marvellous, actually. I have a daughter. I have three extra grandchildren. They're a part of me, and always have been, even if I didn't know some of them existed. It all feels so unreal, too good to be true really, as if I'm going to wake up any minute and find out it's all been nothing but a dream.'

'It's not a dream though. It's all very much real.'

'Yes, it is, isn't it? And Sand... I mean Beth... said that I could visit her in London next time. Well, that we all could. I bet you'd like that, wouldn't you? A chance to see Jack again.'

'I am seeing him again, as it happens.' Ruby was definitely blushing now. 'It turns out he works at the same hospital as Laura. Can you believe that? He doesn't think he knows her. Different wards. But I thought I might go up and visit her again soon, and I can meet up with Jack while I'm there, if I time it right between his shifts. His idea, not mine, before you think I'm stalking him or something.'

'Why would I think that? He wants to see you again. That's a good sign, isn't it? And if he likes you as much as you obviously like him...'

'Cocoa!' William was back, bearing a tray. 'I made you one too, Rubes.'

'Thanks.'

William handed them each a mug and settled himself back next to Geraldine, lifting her feet back up onto his lap. 'So, what are you two looking so coy about?'

'Nothing!' the two women both said at once, grinning so much they almost choked on their cocoa.

'Good news.' Beth put the phone down and let out a satisfied sigh.

'Have they found you a kidney?' Emily had only just come in from school and had not been taking much notice of who her mum was speaking to. Now her face reflected a mixture of excitement and fear.

'No. Oh, God no. I wish...'

'What then?' Emily went straight to the biscuit tin and pulled off the lid. 'Oh, Mum, custard creams. Why do you always buy custard creams? Nobody likes them.'

'I do.'

'So, what's the news then?' She slumped down into a kitchen chair and bit hungrily into the first of the three biscuits she had piled up on the table in front of her. So much for not liking them!

'The house. Your gran's. They've found us a buyer.'

'Oh. Right. So, what happens now? Do you have to go back up there, like to sign stuff and all that?'

'I don't think so. I can probably get the papers through the post or do them by email, but I will have to go and have a final clear-out before the new people move in.'

'Who are they? Do you know?'

'I do actually. It's the village vet. Not the old one, Mr Harris. Or do we call vets doctor? I'm never sure about that. Do you remember Mr Harris? Probably not. He came out to the house when your gran's old dog had to be put down, years ago now, but you were only small at the time.'

Emily shook her head. 'Not sure I even remember the dog, let alone the vet.'

'Anyway, this is the junior partner, a man called Ralph Barton. He's taking over the practice now Mr Harris is retiring, apparently. He and his wife have been renting but the owner's recently told them she's coming back to the village and wants to reclaim her house. They really need to stay local, for the business, and the agent tells me they're over the moon they can take on Gran's place. The timing's perfect for them and they've got nothing to sell, so it should all happen quite quickly. They're sorting out a mortgage this week, and there's a baby on the way too. Lovely to think of the old place as a family home again.'

'Can I come? When you go there? I'd like a last look.'

'I thought you'd had a last look. When we all went up there for the funeral.'

'Well, I'd like another last look. A last last look. You know, to say goodbye.'

'It won't be for a few weeks yet, Em. These things take time, all the searches and legal stuff, even when it all goes smoothly. But you can't miss school, so any visit will probably have to be at a weekend. What about your job at the salon?'

'I'll call in sick.'

'That won't go down too well. You don't want to get the sack after only a few weeks on the job.'

'They can't do that. It's not legal to sack someone for being ill. That would be discrimination.'

'But you're not, are you? Ill, I mean.'

'Well, they won't know that, will they?' Emily stared at her defiantly, as if daring her to ring her boss and tell tales.

'We'll make it a Sunday, to avoid any trouble, shall we? There and back in a day. It's possible, if we get up early. Or we can drive up on a Saturday night, as soon as you finish, grab a burger on the way up, sleep at Gran's and make an early start the next morning. Yes, I think that can work. I'll organise for one of those house clearance firms to meet us there and take all the old furniture away, and we can pop any other bits and pieces in the back of the car and sort them out back here. You sure it won't upset you? Seeing everything being carted off?'

'Nah. Gran's gone now. It's not as if her stuff matters anymore, is it?'

'Okay then. Let's wait until we have a definite completion

date and we'll plan a trip for a couple of weekends before. And, thanks for offering to come, Em. I'll be glad of the company.'

'I want to. Like I said, it's the last time, isn't it? It's funny to think I might never see Shelling ever again.'

'I'm sure you will. It's not as if the village is going anywhere. We can always go back, any time. It is still my childhood home, and always will be.'

'I thought our old house was my home and always would be, but then you and dad split up and suddenly it wasn't. Nothing lasts forever, does it?'

'No, it doesn't, and I'm sorry. That we had to move, that things had to change. But when Gran's place is sold we'll have some money again. We can give up renting this place, find somewhere new, somewhere more permanent that we can call our own, put down new roots...'

'I'd like that. With room for Jack and Tom as well, anytime they want to come back?'

'I don't know if they will come back. Not for good, anyway, but yes, we'll make sure there's a place for them if they do. Always.'

Emily moved closer and lay her head on her mum's shoulder. 'Then maybe we'll feel like a real family again at last,' she said.

Beth closed her eyes and breathed in her daughter's scent. Of lemony shampooed hair and biscuits and just a hint of post-school sweat, a reminder that it was PE day. She forgot sometimes just how hard the divorce had been for all her kids, but especially hard for Emily, the youngest, the one still living at home, torn between two parents she loved equally, trying so hard not to take sides.

'An even bigger family than before, now we've found Geri and little Lily.'

'And don't forget Ruby. She might not be proper family, but I think Jack's got his eye on her, so she could be one day.'

Beth laughed. 'Don't let him hear you say that. I'm not sure marriage is really on his radar. Not for a few years yet, anyway.'

'Who said anything about them getting married? You are so old-fashioned sometimes! Who needs to get married these days anyway? Or even live together? They could just have sex and have babies, then split up any time they wanted to. Keep up the family tradition. If it's good enough for Geri...'

'Emily! That was very different, and you know it. Now, go and make a start on your homework while I make the tea. And no more biscuits! Thank heavens they were only custard creams, that you say you hate so much. I dread to think how many you'd have scoffed by now if they were the chocolate ones you actually like.'

'Portugal?' William looked astonished. 'You want to go all the way to Portugal just to tell Michael about Beth?'

Geraldine nodded. 'I think I'd like to do it face to face.'

'You make it sound like it's some terrible news and he's going to react badly. It's not as if anyone's died.'

'I know, but we haven't seen him for ages. I'd like to go. We could take Lily!'

'And what about school?'

'We'll go in the holidays. The beginning of August.'

'You do know that the flights will probably cost double in August, don't you? And the hotels.'

'It's not as if we can't afford it, is it? When we lost your mum, we talked about spending some of your inheritance on a holiday. A cruise, you said! But I'd much rather go out to see my son. And if Lily came with us it would give Ruby a bit of a break. Adult time.'

'To spend with Jack, you mean? You're matchmaking, Geri, which is exactly what you've been saying you wouldn't do. Let them find their own way.'

'Of course. But a bit of time with no Lily to worry about couldn't do her any harm though, could it? She could go up to London, or invite Jack down here.'

'And the shop?'

'Oh, the shop will survive. She can put one of her young assistants in charge, or close up for a few days, for all I care.'

'In August? Peak trading season?'

'There are more important things, William. That shop ruled my life for too long. I'm not going to stand by and see it rule hers. Real life comes first.'

'Fair enough. And the show at the community centre will be finished by then too. Opening night next Thursday, can you believe? I could probably do with a break myself after three nights of all that stress!'

'Is it getting too much for you?'

'Oh God, no. It's actually quite amusing, watching all the drama going on, and I don't just mean what's happening on the stage. Highly strung, I think is the word for some of those actors. The play's meant to be a light-hearted musical comedy but they take it all so seriously. I just hide behind my props and keep my head down.'

'I'm still coming to watch though?'

'Of course. Front row seat already reserved for you.' He smiled and put his arm around her shoulders. 'So, Portugal... August it is then, if Ruby's happy for us to take Lily and doesn't fancy coming along too.'

'She'd be very welcome, you know that, and so does she, but Michael's not exactly her favourite person.'

'We wouldn't be with him all the time. And she needn't be with him at all.'

'True. We'll ask her, but she'll say no. I'm sure she will.'

'You'd best check with Michael too, make sure he's going to be there, not away on business or on a holiday of his own.'

'I will, and we can pick a date to fit in with him, can't we? It will be lovely to see him. It's been a long while since he was here for the wedding. Good for Lily too. You can see how much it means to her to have a family around her, and she's seen so little of him. He'd love to see her, I'm sure, but the distance and his job...'

'He should have thought of that before swanning off and leaving her, so don't you go making excuses for him.'

'I know, and I'm not.' Geraldine sighed. 'I'm only too aware of his faults, but he is my son and all I can do is try to help when I can. I think taking Lily out to see him would be a good thing, don't you?'

'Soften the blow when you tell him about Beth, you mean?'

'Yes, that as well. Parents and kids living apart. It happens for lots of reasons, and he should understand that better than anyone. I'll ring him this evening.'

Beth settled herself on the dialysis ward and reached for her book. Despite Maggie's suggestions that she try to knit or crochet something or have a go at learning a language, she still preferred to just sit quietly and lose herself in a book. Or have a chat or a game of something with her friend, who usually had a pack of cards or a pad of paper in her bag. Anything to keep her mind off what was going on inside her body as the fluids whooshed through her, giving her what Maggie called a 'good clear out'. Where was Maggie anyway? They had fallen into the habit lately of arranging their appointments so they coincided, but there was no sign of her.

She closed her eyes for a while and let the book fall shut. It had been a busy few weeks, what with their trip to Brighton, closely followed by Emily's birthday and a house full of hungry teenagers. She was still finding pizza crumbs in corners and paper plates under the bed but it had been worth it to see her daughter so happy. The paperwork was sailing ahead on the sale of her mum's place, and the promised trip to Shelling to give the house its own 'good clear out' was fast approaching. She had sorted out a friendly local clearance company who would take everything she didn't need and either sell it on or dump it, so that was one less worry to deal with. Now that she had decided to stop juggling requests for sick leave and officially reduce her hours at the bank to help her cope with her treatment, her stress levels had fallen considerably but money was feeling a bit tight and she would be glad of the proceeds from the sale, then maybe they could get started in earnest on searching for their new home.

She must have nodded off because the next thing she knew there was a nurse leaning over her, gently nudging her awake. 'All done for today, Beth. See you again soon.'

'God, I'm getting so used to all this I can actually sleep right through it.'

'That's a good thing, surely?'

'Getting used to it? I suppose. I'd much rather not have to though. Get a kidney and get out of here, that's the plan, isn't it?'

'Of course. You've heard about your friend, Maggie?'

'No. What?' Beth felt a sudden shiver of fear run through her. 'She's all right, isn't she?'

'Well, you know I can't tell you too much, love, but yes, let's just say her ship may have come in.'

'A transplant? She's got a donor?'

'I can't really say.' She gave a small, not so secret, nod. 'I should let her tell you her news. You've got her number?'

'Yes, I have.'

'Maybe don't call her today though, as she may not be able to get to the phone, if you know what I mean. Later in the week maybe?' She grinned. 'I'm sure she'll have a lot to tell you by then.'

'Thank you. Thank you so much. There really is hope, isn't there?' She gazed around the small room, at her fellow patients. 'For all of us.'

THIRTY

Laura's babies came three weeks early. The first Ruby knew about it was a lovely photo on Facebook, of Laura, sitting up in a hospital bed, looking tired but radiant, a wrapped bundle cradled in each arm. It had only been posted fifteen minutes earlier but there were already more than a hundred likes and hugs and messages of congratulations. Ruby added her own message to the list, added two little blue baby bottle emojis, before calling for Lily to come downstairs and take a look.

'What are their names?' Lily asked, peering at the photo and trying to enlarge it on her mum's phone so she could get a better look at their tiny faces.

'I don't know. Laura and Paul have probably chosen their names but they haven't told anybody else yet.'

'They look very small.'

'I think twins often are, Lil. They've been born a bit sooner than a single baby would.'

'They probably didn't have room to move in there,' Lily said, very matter-of-factly. 'Like two children having to share a bedroom. They'd keep bumping into each other and getting in each other's way.'

'Yes, a bit like that!'

'I like babies. Can we go and see them? Like we did with the baby pigs?'

'Maybe we can, but not for a little while yet. And don't go thinking you can help choose their names. Not this time.'

'Can we go and see the piggies then? See how Portugal is, and feed him his dinner?'

'Soon. But, talking about Portugal, I think there's something granny wants to tell you this morning. She may have a nice surprise for you. But only if you're good.'

'I'm always good,' Lily said, indignantly.

'I can vouch for that.' Geraldine had come into the kitchen and put her arms around Lily's shoulders. 'And that is why Grandad William and I would like to take you away on a little holiday.'

Her head bobbed up from looking at the phone. 'A holiday? Really? Where to?'

'How does going to visit your dad sound? Just you, me and William?'

Lily turned towards Ruby. 'Isn't Mummy coming too?'

'Do you mind if I don't, Lil?'

Lily looked uncertain.

'I know Granny would love to look after you and have you all to herself, and Daddy will have lots of nice surprises lined up for you.'

'Will it be sunny?'

'Very. Lots of lovely sandy beaches to play on. And the sea will be much warmer than it is here. Granny's going to book a proper hotel for you all, so you won't have to sleep on Daddy's sofa like the last time you stayed.'

'A hotel? With waiters and people who make the beds? And chocolates on the pillows?'

'Yes, I'm sure there'll be all of that. So, what do you think?'

'Can I miss school?'

Ruby laughed. 'Good try, but no. It will be in the holidays, so there's no school to miss.'

'Can I take my teddies?'

'Well, maybe not all of them, but one or two maybe.'

'I'm going upstairs to tell them!' she squealed and ran out of the room.

'I think we can take that as a yes! But where on earth did she get that bit about the chocolates on pillows?' Ruby laughed.

'From me talking about our honeymoon hotel, I expect. It may have been months ago, but she doesn't miss a thing, that one!'

'And if the hotel doesn't happen to provide chocs on demand?'

'Then I'm sure I can manage a little treat or two from the local shop. Portugal may be a foreign country but I'm sure they've heard of Cadburys!'

'You won't let her eat too much of it though, will you?'

'Ruby, you don't have to worry. I know how to look after her. She won't be living on toffees and chips or staying up late nightclubbing. You can trust me, you know.'

'I know I can. There's nobody I trust more. And thanks for doing this.'

'Just you make sure you have a good time while we're gone. Have some fun.'

'I intend to.'

'Jack?'

Ruby blushed. 'That would be nice. I'll ask him, see if he's free at all. Would you mind...?'

'What? If he came here? Stayed at the house? Of course not. I've already told you that. One room or two, whatever feels right. I don't mind. In fact, I can honestly say I am one hundred per cent in favour. He's a lovely boy, and if he makes you happy...'

'Too soon to say that, Geri. We've talked and texted a lot, and I'm meeting him again soon, I hope, but I'm not going to rush anything. I have Lily to think about.'

'Right. I can understand that. And, if it doesn't work out, or you change your mind for any reason, then you can jump on a plane and join us in Portugal. We'll be able to squeeze you in, I'm sure.'

'Not necessary, Geri. I'll be fine here, with or without Jack.'

'Okay, love. Let's get this trip all booked then, shall we? Flights, hotel, a nice family room with a view of the sea. Internet, here I come. Do you know, I'm really looking forward to it already.'

'And to telling Michael about Beth?'

'Not so much, but it has to be done. Talking of which, I must ring her. I said I'd keep in touch, and I meant it. Now that I've found her – or she's found me – I have no intention of ever letting her go again. Mothers and daughters...' She reached for the locket around her neck and stroked it. 'There's something special about it all, isn't there? I know you weren't lucky with that waste of space mother of yours but you and Lily, well, you couldn't be closer.'

'I love her more than anything or anyone. I just want to protect her, keep her safe. She's the one person in the world I'd happily die for.'

'Let's hope you never have to, love. But I know exactly what you mean.'

Geraldine settled in her wooden seat in the front row and wished she'd thought to bring a cushion. She looked around as the rest of the audience filed in around her. It was a small hall and, as she quickly counted chairs and rows, she estimated that it probably held no more than about eighty people. Not exactly theatre standards, but William and his thespian colleagues had certainly put many weeks of rehearsals and a good part of their hearts and souls into making their show a success, so she hoped everything would go well.

A curtain shivered in the corner of the stage as someone moved about behind it, and lights came on and quickly went off again, no doubt in a practice run for when the show began. She could picture William now, hovering out there somewhere, his dog-eared script at the ready for prompting duties, a screwdriver in his back pocket in case of props failure. He had promised to come and find her during the interval and buy her a cup of tea. She would much rather have had a glass of wine but the hall did not have a licence, so she'd have to wait until the end when a mass cast outing to the nearest pub was planned. It would probably turn into some kind of post-mortem examination of all the things that went wrong or could be improved upon, but that was what opening nights were for, she assumed. A chance to get it all right by the time they got through to the final show.

Blinds had been pulled down over the windows and the main lights went off as a music track blared out, a little too loudly. Someone from behind the stage curtains let out a bossy-sounding 'Sshhh!' and everyone started to settle down for the show. As her eyes scanned the now darkened room, she was sure she could see Vicky Dunn, that friend of Ruby's who worked at Sidell's animal park, sitting right at the back, huddled up to another young woman and whispering something in her ear. The two of them laughed before Vicky turned her attention to peering at the flimsy programme she held in her lap. The girl did not look up again so Geraldine wasn't able to wave at her, but maybe she would catch up with her later when the tea urn came out.

Geraldine looked at her own programme, just about readable under the dimmed lighting. It did not take long to skip through it as it was made up of just two printed A4 sheets folded in half and stapled together, listing the names of the cast and crew, with a brief summary of the scenes and a solitary black and white image across the back. Even she, with her very limited IT skills, could have done better and she made a mental note to offer her services when the planning of the next production began. Or perhaps she and William could give some kind of sponsorship so a professional could tackle the job.

The show turned out to be more entertaining than she had expected. Yes, some of the singers were a bit off-key, and one woman missed her entrance and rushed on into the expectant silence, all red in the face and almost tripping over her own feet but, on the whole, it was a fun performance. She was able to recognise some of the bits and pieces of scenery William had either shown her or talked about, and she was sure she heard his voice at one point, gently guiding one of the more nervous actors back on course with a few whispered words.

It was while they were finishing their tea and biscuits during the interval that she saw Vicky Dunn again, but alone this time and red-eyed, hugging a hankie and clearly upset about something. She would have gone over to talk to her and check that everything was all right, but the audience were being called back to their seats and then, with a rather dramatic slam of the outer door, Vicky was gone.

Beth stepped out of the car in front of the cottage and stretched her legs. Emily had been allowed to leave work an hour early, so long as she worked through lunch, and the traffic had been surprisingly light, so it had been an easy drive to Norfolk but still a long one, and they had managed it without having to stop.

'I need the loo,' Emily said, climbing out and heading towards the front door, jigging up and down impatiently. 'Hurry up with the key.'

Although it was the end of July, it felt chilly inside. The curtains had been left partially closed, preventing the usual shafts of sunlight from beaming in during the day, and there was a haze of dust particles floating in the air as Beth stepped into the hall and put the lights on, Emily dashing past her and hurtling up the stairs.

Beth stood still for a moment, waiting for the echoes of her mum bustling around in the kitchen, the whistle of the kettle, the comforting smells of something baking, but none came. She would never get used to this house being empty. Luckily, it would not be for much longer. She liked the idea of it buzzing with young life again. The thought helped to ease the barely suppressed sorrow she knew was going to hit her hard when they drove away for the last time.

'I'm starving,' Emily said, coming back down the stairs. 'You said we could have burgers on the way, but then we didn't stop.'

'Can we at least bring our bags in first?'

'But it's nearly half past seven. I haven't had anything since my sandwich at lunchtime, and I had to eat that standing up, in between hair washes.'

'Don't they give you an afternoon tea break in that salon of yours?'

'Well, yes, okay, I might have had a bit of cake someone had brought in but that doesn't count. I need a proper meal, not a snack. I'm a growing girl.'

Beth laughed. 'Growing? Or just greedy? I don't know where you put it all. You must have hollow legs. But, okay, we'll walk down to the pub. We're bound to find something there. I can't guarantee they'll have burgers though.'

'Mum! It's a pub. Pubs always, always have burgers.'

Beth wondered how her sixteen-year-old daughter was suddenly so knowledgeable about what went on inside pubs, but thought it best not to ask.

The Brown Cow was just as Beth remembered it. Cosy, not too crowded, and there were still a few tables available even though it was a Saturday night and they hadn't booked. They were given a spot near the window, from which she had a good view of the street outside but could still watch who came and went inside too. There were three older men huddled together on high stools at the end of the bar, one of whom she was fairly sure she recognised as Mr Harris, the vet. The old one, that was, not the younger partner who would very soon be the new owner of her old childhood home. And a few tables away, tucking into one of the pub's famous pies, was the little woman who ran the village shop, gossiping nineteen to the dozen with... yes, it was Hetty Fellows from next door. She would have to go over and say hello at some point, for fear of looking rude if she didn't.

'I'm going to have the chicken and mushroom pie,' Emily said, putting the oversized menu down on the table and looking around for a waitress.

'What happened to the desperate need for a burger?'

'Oh, I can have one of those anytime. If these pies are as brilliant as the menu says they are – award winning and all that – it would be criminal not to try one.'

'I should probably join you then, although I think I'll go for the steak and kidney.'

'Mum!'

'What?'

'Are you that desperate to get a kidney, you're going to eat one?' Emily laughed out loud, then quickly stopped herself. 'Oh, that's probably not funny really, is it? Sorry.'

'Don't be daft. If we can't laugh about these things, we'd have to cry, and we don't want that, do we? Still, I must say, now you've put the thought into my head of eating a kidney, even if it's a pig's, I have gone off it a bit, so maybe I'll have the chicken and mushroom after all.'

'We don't talk about it much, do we? Your illness, a transplant, what happens when they do find you a kidney of your own. I mean, where it's going to come from, like out of a dead body and all that...'

'Best not to think about it that way. Yes, somebody will have to die for me to get a donor, unless we can find someone – someone alive I mean – willing to donate one. I did have this stupid idea about asking Geri or one of her family. To be honest, Em, it was half the reason I wanted to track them down, but now I've met them I know I can't do that. Geri's probably too old anyway, and too nice. Lily's way too young, and I haven't even met this new brother of mine. No, it's too much to ask of virtual strangers, and there's no knowing if any of them would be a match anyway. Just being family won't mean that's a definite. And now my friend Maggie's been lucky, I'm feeling a lot more positive about the whole thing. She's doing really well, says she feels she's got her life back. And it could happen to me. Just like that, right out of the blue. Any day now, when we're least expecting it, I could get the call.'

'That tells you someone's died.'

'Yes, I suppose so. It's easier to think of it as a gift, something they no longer need but have been kind enough to pass on. And, for the family left behind, maybe it can be seen as something good to come out of something so awful.'

'Can I do it? Say that I want to donate my organs, after I die?'

'I think you're still too young to make that decision, Em.'

'Or donate one now, while I'm still alive?'

'No.'

'Too young, too old, too nice. There's always something, isn't there?'

'I said no and I mean no.'

'No what? That I can't? Or that you won't let me?'

'Too right I won't. There's no way I would ever consider letting you do that for me, or for anyone else. Same goes for your brothers. Your own lives, your own health, are too important to me to be put at risk. I'm fine, Em. I'm on dialysis, I'm not at death's door, I have time on my side. I can wait.'

'But maybe you won't have to.'

The waitress arrived then, bringing the conversation to an abrupt stop. Beth placed her hand over Emily's as they gave their order, and squeezed it. She loved the fact that her daughter was willing to make the offer, but as she'd told herself, and them, right from the start, it was one she could not accept.

'Beth, dear, I thought it was you. And little Emily!' Hetty Fellows came bustling across the space between their tables and plonked herself down, uninvited, in one of the two spare chairs. 'How lovely. I heard the house had been sold, so that must be why you're here.'

Beth nodded. 'Yes, we've got someone coming to clear it out tomorrow. Luckily, they're happy to work on Sundays! Anyway, it's nice to see you, Mrs Fellows.'

'Hetty! I've told you a thousand times.'

'Sorry, yes, Hetty. We're only on a flying visit, just to get the old place cleared and ready for its new family. We'll be off again tomorrow evening.'

'Anything I can do?'

'Thanks, but no, it's all in hand. Unless... I wonder if there might be anything you'd like? An ornament or a mirror or something, as a keepsake? I know how close you and Mum were.'

'Oh, what a lovely thought, but I wouldn't want to take anything that's rightly yours.'

'Jack and I took what we wanted last time we were here, Hetty. Honestly, if there's anything at all amongst what's left that takes your fancy, you'd be very welcome to it. Why don't you pop round in the morning? Before eleven, when the van's coming.'

'Yes, dear, I'll do that. Shame to see anything useful thrown away, and there might be one or two little bits I could take off your hands. I'll bring cake, of course!'

'That would be lovely. Oh, I think your pudding has just been delivered to your table.'

'So it has,' Hetty said, craning her neck round and nodding to her dining companion. 'Can't keep a good sticky toffee waiting.'

'She'll probably want so much of Gran's stuff that she'll clear the whole house, Mum,' Emily whispered as soon as Hetty was out of earshot.

'That's fine by me. Less for us to worry about.'

'Then you'll have paid the man to come for nothing.'

'I don't think she'll be wanting the sofa or Mum's old bed, or a pile of tatty second-hand towels, do you?'

'Who knows? If they're better than the things she already has she might.'

'Then our man with a van can take away her old stuff instead. Really, Em, I don't mind. Let the old dear have whatever she wants. She was a good friend to your gran for years. And she's bringing cake, remember.'

'That's true. She always did make very nice cakes.'

'If you've got room in your tummy once you've scoffed the enormous pie and chips I can see heading our way.'

'Mum! She's not coming until tomorrow. I'll be hungry again by then.'

By the time the van arrived on the dot of eleven o'clock, Hetty Fellows had made three trips down the path and back in through her own front door, each time laden with things that 'just might come in handy'. A pile of mismatched plates, four scatter cushions, a feather pillow and an omelette pan vied for space with innumerable sheets and pillowcases retrieved from the airing cupboard Beth had forgotten to look in last time she was here, and the old kitchen curtains which Hetty said she had helped to make years ago and, as their homes were identical in shape and size, were, she insisted, bound to fit.

'Don't forget your cake plate,' Beth called after her as Emily helped to carry the heavier things, including an armchair that only just managed to squeeze through the door, tilted on its side with its covers hanging off.

'I'll be back for it in a mo,' Hetty called over her shoulder. 'I'll take the last of the cake back with me too, if that's all right? I'm not sure the fresh cream would survive your long trip home. And I wouldn't say no to the teapot once you've given it a rinse through.'

Beth laughed. So much for a little keepsake!

By twelve thirty everything was gone. She watched the van drive away before retreating back inside and flopping down onto the carpet, her back against the wall.

'It looks so much bigger, doesn't it?' Emily said, standing in the middle of the living room. 'Now that it's empty.'

'It does. Hardly recognisable as the same house. I suppose we should clean round the edges a bit before we think about going. I kept hold of the hoover and a few cloths, and there's still hot water, although I must remember to turn that off when we leave.'

'Do you want more tea? It'll have to be teabags in cups now the pot's gone though.' Emily giggled. 'At least she left the kettle.'

'Her sister bought her a new one for Christmas, luckily, so she didn't need it.' Beth shook her head. 'But, yes, tea would be good. Then what? Straight home, or do you fancy a trip out somewhere? It's not too far to the beach. Or we could go into Norwich and hit the shops. Find lunch somewhere before the drive back.'

'Are you up to it, Mum? I know you get tired, and it's a long drive. We should do the journey in stages maybe. Stop for lunch in one of those roadside places on the way. I'm not bothered about the beach. It's not that long since we were in Brighton, and shops are pretty much the same everywhere.'

'Since when did you get so grown-up? Saying no to a shopping trip! A year ago, you'd have been trying to get me to buy you a new top or some computer game or other.'

'I'm sixteen now, and I've got a job. And, besides, you still owe me a burger. They do great ones in that place we've stopped at before. The glass place with the jazzy loos and all the potted plants, remember? And I wouldn't mind a milkshake while we're at it.'

'You're on!'

———

She was not going to cry. She had known for months that the house had to go, that that part of her life was over, and that there were far more important things in life, especially now, than getting all nostalgic and weepy about it. Still, she had had happy times here, growing up in the village, catching the bus to school, playing in the fields, watching neighbours come and go. Nothing stayed the same. Why would it? This had stopped being her home when she had left for London, started her job at the bank, met and married Sean. And now, with both her parents gone, it really was just an empty shell, suddenly unrecognisable without all the furniture and knick-knacks that had been such an important part of it for so long and had made it home. It was time.

She piled the last of her mum's things into the back of the car, flung the hoover, now bursting with dust and fluff, into the boot and locked the front door for the last time.

'Bye, little cottage,' Emily said, in her most dramatic voice, waving at it from the passenger window. 'It's been nice knowing you.'

'Bye, Shelling,' Beth echoed, climbing into the front seat of the car and starting the engine.

'At least someone will love it again,' Emily said. 'I didn't really like seeing it all empty like nobody cared.'

'Me neither.'

'Do you think we should go and see them? The new people? As they're right here in the village. It might be nice to actually see who's going to be living here. It would help us to picture it, you know, in the future, when it's not ours anymore.'

'I hadn't thought. I suppose we could. But we don't know where they live, do we?'

'Not hard to find out. If he's the vet, somebody will know. Probably everybody will know.'

'Shall we?'

'Well, I vote yes.'

'Okay then. Where shall we ask? Village shop?'

'If it's open.'

'Believe me, Em, that place is always open. If we hadn't seen her in the pub last night, I would have bet any money that woman never leaves the premises.'

They drove the short distance and parked outside the shop, its stock piled up high behind the windows and spilling out onto the pavement, and a few remaining Sunday papers fluttering in the stand on the wall.

'Oh, yes,' the cheerful little woman behind the counter said, in answer to their enquiry, and instantly knowing who they were. 'You'll be wanting Snowdrop Cottage, Prue's place. I heard the young Bartons were moving out and buying your mum's. Suit them lovely, that will. They should be in. Vet surgery shuts at twelve on a Sunday. I should do the same really. Trade's always slow at this time of day, but you never know, do you? Who might run out of milk or get a hankering for a Battenberg? Not as if I've got much else to do on a Sunday.'

'Thank you. Er... Snowdrop Cottage?'

'Just out of the door, turn right, go past the turning for the church and it's the... let me think now... yes, the fourth house along. Little gate, red door, you can't miss it, my loves.'

'Ah, yes, I know the house you mean. Thank you for your help. Bye.'

Emily giggled as they reached the pavement, almost knocking over a pile of plastic buckets. 'A hankering for a Battenberg?' she spluttered. 'Whoever gets a hankering for a Battenberg?'

'Don't mock, Em. She means well. Now, come on, let's walk down and see if the vet's at home. Just a quick hello, mind. We're not going to impose. We've got a long ride back.'

'Not even if they invite us in for tea and a nice slice of Battenberg?'

'Oh, stop it, you!'

They reached Snowdrop Cottage in a matter of minutes.

'I'd forgotten just how small this village is,' Beth said. 'It always seemed so much bigger when I was a child.'

'Things always do, Mum. I snuck into my old primary school when they did one of those open day things, and it's really tiny. I used to think the playground was massive, but it's not much bigger than our old back garden.'

'You only left five years ago!'

'Seems like forever. And the loos in the Infants! They look like they were designed for midgets.'

'Little kids have little bums.'

'And the sinks were so low you could bang your knees on them!'

'It was a lovely little school. They looked after you well there. It's a shame that things have to change, isn't it? That we all have to grow up and move on. What I wouldn't give to be a child again, back living here, with not a care in the world.'

'Ah, but then you wouldn't have us, would you? Me and the boys. We wouldn't exist.'

'True. But you'd still be there, wouldn't you? Sort of waiting in my future, all that love and joy just waiting to jump out at me...'

'Okay, Mum, come down from your cloud. We're here.'

They opened the gate and walked up the path. Everything was quiet, just a few birds singing in a nearby tree. The church bells they had heard ringing out tunelessly earlier that morning were now silenced, the service long over, and there was not a car to be seen.

'Oh, I do miss this sometimes,' Beth sighed. 'The sheer peace of it all.'

They rang the doorbell and waited, then rang again, but nobody came.

'Must be out somewhere,' Beth conceded, as they turned and walked away.

'Shows that the old girl in the shop doesn't know everything after all. Imagine living somewhere where your every move is part of village gossip.'

'Ah, but I did live here, remember.' Beth looked back over her shoulder as they climbed back into the car, taking a last look at what was once her home. 'For eighteen years! And, actually, it has a lot going for it. Being part of a caring community. London may be home nowadays but it's not a patch on good old Shelling.'

THIRTY-ONE

Vicky crawled under the covers and closed her eyes, but she knew she wouldn't be able to sleep. Life was a bitch. It was cold and cruel and so bloody unfair.

She had given her all to that job, loved each animal as if it were her own family pet, gone home so many times covered in grass and mud and shit and not minded at all. And now it was over. Lack of funds, falling visitor numbers, rising bills, so many families preferring to go to the much bigger zoos at Cromer or Banham. The old place virtually falling apart and no one to fix it. They had all been called together earlier today and given the news that, short of some miracle, their days were numbered. Sidell's would plod along until the end of the summer season but, after that, the owners, Sid and Ellen, who were in their late seventies now, wanted to give it all up and retire. Unless a last-minute buyer came along, which was looking unlikely, they would be closing the place down, the animals would be rehomed and the land would more than likely be turned into allotments or a car park or something.

Sid and Ellen were animal lovers and the wildlife centre had been their dream, but, as they told the staff, they couldn't see themselves doing it forever, not as they approached their eighties. Closing it wasn't what they wanted, much preferring to see the place carry on as it was for as long as possible, but it was starting to fall into serious disrepair and was having trouble competing with the bigger flashier places. Best for all of them that they faced up to the harsh realities and called it a day.

Everybody was shocked, stunned. Many of the older ones were volunteers who, now they were retired, did it for love, not money, and just stood there in silence, shaking their heads in disbelief, while some of the younger staff were in tears. Even Sid himself had looked like he might cry at any moment as he ushered them all home and slipped his key into the gate. The end of an era. And, for Vicky, the end of life as she knew it. The only life she had ever really loved.

She sniffed into her sheets, wiped her nose on the pillowcase, and wondered why all the bad shit in life had such a habit of coming at once, and, not only that, but always landing on the same target. Her. Hadn't she already had enough thrown at her during her short life? Growing up in a children's home, finding herself living with a bigot of a father, being fat and friendless and as good as broke. And she was gay, for God's sake. Not that there was anything at all wrong in that, but it didn't help. It was just one more thing to make her feel different, when all she had ever wanted was to fit in, to be accepted, and loved.

Rose Allen had seemed too good to be true. Beautiful, funny, confident enough to drive a bloody great bus. Just for once in her life Vicky thought she had landed on her feet, found someone who liked her, who actually cared, but who was she kidding? Rose had gone with her to that stupid musical play the other night, but it turned out it was only so she could lust after her ex, some skinny girl in the chorus. It had all been just some pathetic attempt to make the girl jealous, and it appeared to have worked when the girl had swept out from behind the curtains during the interval and whisked Rose away to look at her costumes, though it might as well have been her bloody etchings, and left Vicky standing by herself like some sad wallflower of a Johnny-No-Mates.

She had stumbled out of that hall and straight into the nearest pub, only leaving an hour and a half and four neat whiskies later when the cast of the show and their hangers-on had come rolling in, Rose among them, laughing and congratulating themselves and each other, and Rose had not even noticed she was there.

And then there was Ruby. She liked Ruby. They shared a bond, a history, an understanding. But she hadn't seen Ruby in ages. Too caught up in her shop and her daughter and that lad from London who she couldn't stop talking about. She'd had a text from her just a few days ago, telling her that Laura had had the babies, but that was all. Babies. Huh! Why should she care about someone else's babies, when the chances were she would never ever have one of her own? And two, for God's sake. Why was it fair that someone should get two at a time when people like her had none? And Laura and her vicar were bound to call them some godawful Bible names and make them go to church all the time. Mumbo-jumbo and candles and hypocrisy. What sort of a life was that for a kid?

She thought about little Lily. A sweet girl, really interested in the animals. Rabbits, piglets, snakes, unicorns! She'd have to try to persuade Ruby to let Lily have another pet rabbit, because rehoming so many animals quickly was not going to be easy and Vicky had the horrible suspicion that some of those poor animals were going to have to die. She'd read about what happened in the war, when zoos had to make horrible decisions to protect their animals from the bombings and the possibility of escape. Elephants evacuated, snakes chloroformed to death, aquariums emptied so they couldn't be blown up and shed gallons of water everywhere, even household pets killed in their hundreds of thousands to save them from what was to come.

When she finally slept, her dreams were filled with darkness and dread, a terrifying, faceless fear, that loomed at her and refused to go away. She woke up at two in the morning, drenched in sweat and shaking under the weight of old memories suddenly alive again in her head. She could feel the water, not cold and gushing from a giant aquarium, but boiling hot and belching out of a kettle, raining down on her, drowning her arm in heat and excruciating pain. As she lay in the silence of her room, it was all she could do not to scream, but in that moment, snatched back from all those years ago, she remembered just what true power felt like, finally getting the attention she craved and had always felt she deserved. Taking control. That was what she had to do again. Make her own decisions instead of just sitting back and letting others make them for her.

There were four packets in her bedside drawer. Just ordinary painkillers, no prescription stuff. They had been easy enough to get hold of, two packets at a time, because that was all you were allowed to buy at once. Stupid bloody law. How hard was it to walk a few shops along or wait until later in the day, and buy two more? And then another two, and another? A person could accumulate hundreds of the things in no time at all.

She wondered now if four packets would be enough. If she should have got more, just to make sure? If she was going to do this, then she wanted to do it properly, the way her mother had done so long ago, with a perfect finality to it. No half measures. No waking up again, having buggered up her liver or her kidneys or something equally horrible. Just a long peaceful, painless sleep that drifted into something else, without her even knowing about it. That was all she wanted. It made so much more sense than slit wrists or jumping in front of a train. Or boiling water. But then, this time she wasn't looking for attention or sympathy. If she could do this one simple thing, she would never have to worry about that stuff, or about anything, ever again.

She reached out to her bedside lamp and switched it on. Her fingers fumbled at the first packet, pulling out a silver foil sheet and pushing a tablet out from the back. Then a second, and a third. Slowly, a small pile of round white tablets built up on the sheet beside her, one or two rolling off and disappearing under the bed along with the discarded packaging. They looked like mints, little harmless mints like the ones they gave out after you'd eaten in the Indian restaurant up the road. It was no surprise that kids swallowed things like that, mistaking them for sweets. Ruby had told her that Lily had done it once, when she'd found some in her mum's bag. Long ago, and no harm done, but kids just did stupid things sometimes, didn't they? Without knowing what they were doing. Without really understanding the consequences. She glanced at her bare arm, at the scars that would always be with her, then tugged the sleeve of her pyjamas down and carried on piling up the pills. At least this time it wouldn't have to hurt.

Jack opened his arms and pulled Ruby into them, forcing at least three hurrying passengers to divert around them on the station concourse.

'So good to see you,' he said, giving her a squeeze before letting go and reaching for her bag. 'Here. Let me carry that. God, it weighs a ton. What have you brought with you? The kitchen sink?'

Ruby laughed. 'Not quite. Overnight stuff for my stay at

Laura's – Lily's fine with Geri, and I've got one of the girls to open the shop in the morning, so I don't have to rush back tonight – and presents for the babies, of course.'

'No present for me?'

'Oh. I'm sorry, I...' Ruby felt embarrassed for a moment, until she realised he was teasing her. 'Stop it. You had me going for a minute there.'

'Just lovely that you're here. You are present enough!'

Now she really was embarrassed. She quickly turned her face away so he wouldn't see it colouring up, and pulled him along towards the exit. 'So, what have you got planned? Laura's not expecting me until this evening, so I'm all yours until then.'

'Sounds like an offer I can't refuse. See a few sights? Have a drink somewhere? Food?'

'That all sounds great. Especially the food bit.'

'Are you hungry? Now, I mean?'

'Starving. I only had a quick breakfast so I could get the early train, and have you seen the stuff they sell on board? Or the prices?'

Jack swung her bag up onto his shoulder. 'Well, I'm always up for eating, so let's go and find something, but after that I really do think we'll need to drop your bag off somewhere. I don't fancy lugging it around all day. My place? It's only nurses' accommodation, nothing fancy, but I'd quite like you to see it. And it's not far away.'

Ruby nodded. 'Sounds fine. If we pick it up later, you could come with me to see Laura. I know she won't mind. In fact, she'd like to meet you.'

'Ah, told her all about me, have you?'

'A bit. About you being Lily's long-lost family, anyway. Nothing... well, personal, you know.'

'Like how devastatingly handsome I am, you mean?'

Ruby laughed. 'Or how big-headed? No, Laura's not the

269

type to be swayed by looks. She'll want to see that you're a good person, kind, loyal, all that stuff.'

'Ah, so it's her approval we're after, is it? I am to be vetted to find out if I'm worthy. A second opinion is being sought.'

'Well, you're both nurses. You'll know how important second opinions can be.'

'When there's doubt maybe. There isn't, is there? Any doubt, about me? Because I don't have any hidden agenda, you know. We may have met under unusual circumstances, and we're almost, but I'm pleased to say not quite, related, but I do like you, Ruby. If we can leave all this adoption stuff out of it and forget about Mum and her illness and everything, I just want to get to know you better. That's all.'

'Illness? Your mum's ill? You never said.'

Just for once, it was Jack who looked embarrassed. 'Didn't I?'

'You know you didn't.'

They had stopped outside a small café and Jack was making a great show of peering at the menu stuck to the inside of the steamy window. 'Will this do? It's a bit early for a full-on meal but they do a fine-looking brunch.'

'Whatever you want.'

'Right, in we go then.' He opened the door and a fug of warmth and cooking smells pulled them in.

'Table for two?' A busy waitress bustled by, pointing them to a table in the window. 'Be with you in a sec.'

'You said your mum's ill.' Ruby slipped her jacket off and hung it on the back of her chair. 'I know it's none of my business, but is it something serious? Something Geri should know about? I'd hate for her to find her daughter and then lose her again.'

'Serious, yes, but not about to kill her, and of course it's your business. Geri's too. Not something any of us has any need to be secretive about. Mum has something wrong with her kidneys. She's felt ill for a while but it was only diagnosed about a year ago. She's getting treatment but what she really needs is a transplant.'

'Oh my God! That sounds awful.'

'It all came as a bit of a shock to us all, so soon after the divorce, and then losing Gran. My other gran that is, the real one... oh, you know what I mean, but she's coping with it all really well. She gets tired and she has to go into hospital for dialysis every few days, so she's cut down her hours at work. She's been a bit stressed about Gran's old place, what with it standing empty and being so far away, but she's found a buyer, so that will ease the worry a bit, and there'll be some money coming in soon from the sale. She's looking forward to the future now, to finding a house to buy for her and Em to settle down in. And as a sort of home base for Tom and me too, I suppose. Her life's not all doom and gloom, Ruby. Not totally dominated by her health, even if it could so easily be. A friend of hers, a fellow patient, has recently struck lucky and got herself a new kidney, so she can see it's possible. And, of course, she's found Geri, and all of you. The last thing she'd want is for you to feel sorry for her.'

They gave their order and Ruby found herself gazing out of the window as people streamed by. 'Was she going to tell us?'

'In her own time, I expect. Not really the done thing, is it, to turn up and meet your blood family and immediately land news like that on them?'

'I guess not. Not that there is really a done thing. It's not every day mums and daughters meet up after fifty years, is it?'

'No. It's unexpected and daunting, but nice too, in its own odd way, don't you think? No matter how long apart, there's something special about finding each other again. For Mum, anyway.'

Ruby nodded. 'I can see that. For Geri too. It's like it's filled a gap, answered questions she was too scared to ever think about. Or talk about.'

'Do you mind me asking...' Jack reached for her hand across the table and stroked it gently. 'You told me about being in care. When did you last see *your* mum?'

'Oh, I don't know. She used to drift in and out. Not since before I left the children's home. Fourteen or fifteen years maybe?'

'And do you miss her?'

'Nothing to miss. She wasn't the kissy cuddly sort of mum. I never felt she actually cared about me. There was no affection, no love. I don't think she ever really gave me anything worth having.'

'Life. She gave you life, Ruby. Just like Geri did for Mum. Was that not worth having?'

'If you put it that way, yes. And I'm healthy, amazingly. Despite my mum never looking after me, or herself, properly. She was more or less an alcoholic, even before I was born. It's surprising I didn't pop out with whisky running through my veins instead of blood!'

Two plates appeared, piled high with eggs and bacon, hash browns and baked beans, and Ruby dug in hungrily.

'So, your mum?' she said, putting her fork down for a moment while she reached for her mug of tea. 'What are the chances of a transplant?'

'Average, I guess. So many factors are involved. How ill she gets, where she is on the list, what becomes available, compatibility...'

'But she doesn't have to wait for some random stranger to die, does she? I mean, you hear all the time about people giving a kidney to save their husband or kids or whatever. Have you been tested? Surely family are most likely to be a match, aren't they?'

'She won't hear of it. I would happily help her, and so would Tom, although Emily's still too young for us to even think about letting her make a decision like that. But Mum is adamant she wouldn't take one from any of us. As far as she's concerned, we're young and healthy, with our whole lives ahead of us, and all that...'

'I get that, I suppose. I can't imagine anyone mutilating my Lily, cutting bits of her out, even if it was to help me. It's that mother-child thing again, isn't it? We'd do anything to protect them, give up anything to save them from pain. Our babies are the most precious thing, and I'm sure that feeling never stops, however grown-up they might be. Is there nobody else your mum could ask though? Your dad, maybe?'

'They hardly give each other the time of day anymore, let alone body organs. The divorce was quite bitter in the end and, although Tom and I still see him from time to time and Em goes to stay every other weekend, Mum and Dad don't see each other at all. He's got a new woman lurking in the shadows anyway. I can't see her being over-keen on him making that sort of sacrifice, even if by some miracle he turned out to be suitable. It was hard enough prising any money out of him. A fair share of the house and savings, and his pensions. It had to go to a judge, which took months and cost a fortune in barrister's fees. I've never seen Mum so stressed.'

'That can't have helped. With her being ill, I mean.'

'No.'

Ruby went back to eating her meal, and neither of them spoke again for a while.

'Jack...' A sudden thought had popped into her mind and now it wouldn't go away. 'Being adopted, and with her real dad being long dead, well, it means your mum doesn't have any other relatives, doesn't it? Blood ones, I mean. Except Geri and Michael and Lily.'

'That's right.'

'I hate to ask this, but that's not why she came looking for them, is it?'

He didn't answer straight away. 'Not exactly.'

'What do you mean, not exactly? Is it, or isn't it? After all, fifty years is a long time to do nothing, and then suddenly start searching the minute you're in need of a kidney! Did Beth only start this whole birth mother thing because she needed to find a match?'

'She didn't start searching before because Gran and Grandad were still alive. I've told you that. She didn't want to hurt their feelings.'

'That doesn't really answer the question though, does it? Was she hoping for a bit more from Geri than just a reunion?'

Jack fiddled with his mug, then flicked a few grains of salt from the tablecloth. She could tell he was finding it hard to look at her.

'Jack?'

'Okay, yes. It was mentioned, all right? That finding her real family might throw light on a few things. Provide some answers. That maybe we'd find there was a history of kidney disease, or maybe there'd be someone who might be able to help her...'

'Help her? Give up a kidney for her, you mean? Oh my God! How could anyone do that? How could *you* do that? Turn up in Brighton like you did, tug on poor Geri's heartstrings, rake up all her hidden secrets and sadness, and all that guilt she's been carrying about for so long, just to get a bloody kidney?' She pulled the napkin from her lap and threw it down on the table, grabbed her bag from the floor and stood up. 'I trusted you, Jack. I genuinely believed you'd come looking for your family because you wanted to get to know us. Because you cared. And that your mum did too. But you've played us, haven't you? Geri especially. Have you got any idea how happy she is to have seen her daughter again? To have the chance to let her back into her life? And, as for you... I expected more. Honesty, at least. You're not the man I thought you were, Jack. I'm going to Laura's now, and I don't expect you to follow me.' She swallowed down the lump that was rapidly forming in her throat and threatening to make her cry. 'Whatever this was between us, it's been a mistake. If you can keep something so important from me, from all of us, how can I ever believe a word you say? I don't need a second opinion, Jack. I'm going to trust my own. I don't want to see you again. Goodbye.' And then she stumbled outside and started to run, her bag bumping hard against her leg, leaving him to stare at her unfinished food and pay the bill.

The babies were beautiful. Ruby sat on Laura's sofa with one tucked into the crook of each arm as they slept, not at all sure how she was supposed to reach the drink Laura had put down on the table in front of her, let alone actually drink it.

'So, however do you tell them apart?' Ruby peered at their angelic little faces. 'I know you said they're not identical, but they might as well be. They look exactly the same!'

'It's funny. Everyone says that, but they look different to me. A mother's eyes, I suppose. But, look, Andrew's got this little crinkle above his nose, and his eyes are a bit darker blue, not that you can see that while he's asleep. And Max has got a tiny bit more hair, and longer fingers.'

'If you say so!'

'Ruby, is that your phone again? I know you've put it on silent, but if it's going to vibrate anyway, what's the point? For heaven's sake, answer it. Whatever Jack's got to say for himself, you'll never know if you don't let him explain. Just read his messages. Or, better still, call him back and talk to him.'

'I don't have a spare hand.'

'That's an excuse and you know it.'

'It can wait, Laura. Honestly. If I talk to him now, I'll probably just end up losing my temper with him or hanging up.'

'But it's not his fault, is it? Whatever his mum may or may not have done, it's down to her, not him.'

'Not if he knew about it. He should have told me everything, and he definitely should have told Geri. Them finding her like that, and coming to see her, it means the world to her and I'd hate it all to have been a lie, just an exercise to track down possible donors. It's all just so... well, mercenary.'

'And you're sure that's what it was? Not a woman finally deciding to look for her birth family?'

'After more than fifty years?'

'But you said Jack had explained that. Waiting until her adoptive parents had died...'

'It's very suspicious timing though, isn't it? She gets ill and suddenly her long-lost relatives might come in useful.'

'You could give her the benefit of the doubt. Jack too. From what you've said, you were really beginning to like him. It would be such a shame if...'

'What? I stop seeing him? We'd only just started. He's hardly the love of my life and, besides, I don't want to be with someone I can't trust. I did that with Michael, and look how that ended up.'

'Fair enough. Your decision.' Laura leaned forward and slid Max out of Ruby's arms. 'Here. Let me take one so you can at least drink your tea. And check your phone. Any man who tries that many times has to be worth listening to, surely?'

Ruby reached for her cup and took a sip, carefully replacing it on the table so she wouldn't drip anything hot on the still sleeping Andrew. Reluctantly, she picked up her phone and glanced at the screen. 'Four missed calls. Two voice messages. Three texts.'

'He's keen, I'll give him that.'

'Oh, hang on. One of these isn't from Jack.'

'PPI? Accident claims? I get loads of those.'

'No.' Ruby frowned. 'It's a message from Vicky's mum. Joyce. I only met her the once, and I didn't even know she had my number. She's asking me to call her urgently.'

'That's strange. Maybe you'd better do it. I mean, if Vicky can't call you herself, that has to mean something's wrong, doesn't it?'

'It must do. Do you mind taking the baby?'

'Of course not. He is mine! Probably time for another feed soon anyway.'

'How do you manage it? One on each boob, or do they take it in turns?'

'Whatever they demand. Believe me, my body's not my own anymore.' Laura laid Max down in one of two Moses baskets at the side of the sofa and took Andrew from her friend, slipping him gently into the other. 'I'll pop out to the kitchen and make Paul his lunch before these two wake up. He'll be back soon. And that will give you a bit of privacy to make your call.'

Ruby couldn't help worrying as she waited for Joyce to pick up. She hadn't seen or spoken to Vicky in a while, and that was unusual. Somewhere at the back of her mind a little alarm bell was ringing.

'Ruby?' Joyce sounded very quiet. 'Thanks so much for calling back, only I didn't know who else to contact. Our Vicky doesn't have many friends but she always talks about you, and she really needs someone right now.'

'What's happened? Is she okay?'

'No, love, she's not, I'm afraid.' There was a long pause.

'She's done something very... silly. An accident or a cry for help, maybe, I don't know. I don't like to think that she really meant to do it, but she took an overdose, love. Paracetamols. One of her flatmates found her unconscious.'

'Oh my God! How is she? Will she be all right?'

'Physically, yes, they seem to think so. It's all been pumped out of her, or whatever it is they do. But I'm more concerned with her mental state. It seems she'd been told she was going to lose her job, and that place meant the world to her. It's what's kept her going these last few years. And then there was some business with a girl. I wish she'd come home for a while, but she won't hear of it. She and her father... oh, he loves her all right, but there's been friction in the past and, as you probably know, this isn't the first time she's done something like this. She's very... troubled is the word, I suppose. It was scalding water last time. Years ago now, but the scars are still there, and I can't risk her doing anything else. I'm at my wits' end, I can tell you.'

She'd done it before? Vicky had never fully explained about that long scar running down her arm. She had always assumed it had been an accident. Perhaps she should have asked.

'What can I do?'

'Talk to her. Please, Ruby, just talk to her. There's something about your shared history, something that makes her trust you more than anybody. I think there are things still there, you know, from her past, about being abandoned and not feeling wanted, things that only someone like you might be able to understand. I may be her mother, but sometimes it feels like it's in name only. And I've tried my best, really I have.'

'Of course you have. So, where is she now? Is she back at her flat?'

'No, love. Not yet. They're keeping her in hospital for a couple of days. She's still weak, and sick, and they're talking about a psychiatric assessment before they release her.'

'I'm actually in London at the moment. I was meant to be coming back tomorrow, but my plans have changed, so I don't have to stay now.' She pushed any thought of Jack, and having to listen to his lies and excuses, out of her head. This was more important. 'I'm going to catch the next train back. I'll try talking to her, I promise. I only hope it will do some good.'

'Thanks, love. It's all any of us can do, isn't it? Try.'

THIRTY-TWO

AUGUST, 2019

'So, Jack's not coming down to stay while we're away?' Geraldine was only too aware that something had gone wrong between Ruby and her grandson while they were together in London last week, but she wasn't going to push for the details. Ruby would tell her in her own good time, she felt sure.

'No. So, if you don't mind, I was wondering if I could ask Vicky to come instead.'

'Is that a good idea, Ruby? The poor girl's still in hospital and she must be in a fragile state or they'd have discharged her by now.'

'Exactly. Even more reason why she needs a friend right now. A bit of support.'

'Expert support though, surely? Or help from her family? It's a lot of responsibility to take on, having someone in the house who...'

'What? Might try to kill herself again?'

'Well, yes, to be blunt. And, with us away in Portugal, it will be just you here having to cope with that by yourself.'

'Okay, I know I can't watch her twenty-four hours a day, but she's got a better chance here with me than stuck in that room of hers, all alone, dwelling on things. I'm going to worry myself sick about her so she might as well be here, safely under my nose, especially while I'm off work for a week. And, if anything does happen, there's always 999, isn't there? Nobody knew what she was thinking or planning when she swallowed those pills, nobody knew what was about to happen, so it was only by sheer luck that she was found in time, but next time – if there is a next time – I'll be prepared for it, won't I? Making sure she doesn't get her hands on any more drugs. Listening to her. Keeping an eye on her. Her first few days back out in the world could be crucial.'

'Well, if you're sure. This is your home, Ruby, and I'm not going to start dictating who you can or can't invite here, but just be careful, okay? William and I care about you. We feel protective of you, just as you do about your friend.'

'I know that, Geri, but I'm a big girl now. Just let me do this, okay?'

'Of course. And we're always at the end of a phone if you need us. Always will be.'

'Thanks. And, Geri...'

'Yes?'

'I know I don't say this often enough, but you really are like a mother to me. So much more than my real mum ever was.'

'And it's been a pleasure. I couldn't love you more if you really were my daughter. Which reminds me, I want to ring Beth before we go away. See if there's anything she'd like me to say to her brother, or anything she'd like me to ask him. Sounds funny saying that, when they've never met. I wonder how Michael's going to take the news he's had a secret sister all this time? I have to admit I'm feeling a bit nervous about telling him.'

'Before you talk to Beth, and definitely before you say

anything about her to Michael, there's something I need to tell you, Geri.'

'Sounds ominous.'

'It's something that Jack told me, when I went to London. I probably should have said something as soon as I knew, but I wasn't sure whether to, and I had to deal with the whole Vicky situation first. Anyway... it's complicated, and I might have got it wrong, but if I haven't... well, you're not going to like it.'

'Okay. You're really starting to worry me now. Come on, spill the beans.'

'There's no easy way to say it, but there might be a reason Beth turned up when she did. Why she needed to track us down. Well, you and Michael, anyway.'

'Yes, she wanted to find her family, learn more about where she came from.'

'More than that. Jack says she's not well. She has kidney disease, and it's quite bad. She's having dialysis.'

Ruby could see the shock on Geri's face. 'No! Oh, my poor girl. Why didn't she say anything? And what do you mean, a reason she had to find us? You don't mean before it's too late, do you? She's not dying, is she?'

Ruby put her arm around Geri's shoulders. 'She's not at that stage, no, or I don't think she is. But she needs a transplant. She's on a waiting list, but these things can take time. Years sometimes.'

'And is there no other option?'

'Yes, there is. I'm sorry, Geri, but it looks suspiciously like you could be that other option. Or Michael could. She's looking for a donor. Someone with the same blood type or tissue type or whatever it is that has to match. I'm worried that's why she came here after all these years. Just think about it. Suddenly searching for her family, her real blood family, when she'd never bothered before. It might not really be you she was looking for, Geri. It might just have been a kidney.'

———

'Don't you tell me you're considering it.' William waited until the stewardess had gone past with her trolley. He rarely raised his voice, and he was trying hard not to do it now, but this was too big a thing to keep quiet about any longer. Geri had known about Beth for two days but had only thought to tell him last night. He had hardly slept a wink all night for worrying about it. It was so typical of her to want to do what she would regard as the right thing, but there was no way he was going to let his wife take such a huge and dangerous step to help someone who was little more than a stranger.

'Of course I'm considering it. She's my daughter and she's ill, and if there's any way I can help her...'

'Help her? We're not talking about lending her a few quid or doing a bit of babysitting, Geri. This is serious life-changing stuff we're talking about here. And she hasn't asked you for help, has she? She hasn't actually mentioned anything about it to you. Getting you to help, as you call it, might not be on her agenda at all. Whatever Jack may have said, it's quite likely Ruby misinterpreted it, got things wrong, and now you won't even ring Beth up and ask her. This is not the time to be cautious, Geri, or to worry about her feelings. You need the truth. Answers.'

'I can't.'

'Can't what? Have an honest open discussion with her about why she came looking for you, what it is she wants or expects?'

'You make it all sound so mercenary.'

'Maybe it is. Maybe it's not. We have no idea what her

motives were for finding you when she did, but how are we ever going to know if we don't ask? And it sounds like she's on the waiting list anyway, so it really doesn't have to be your problem, does it? She'll get her kidney sooner or later. Obviously, I hope it's sooner, but that doesn't mean she's getting one from you.'

'It's my body, and it's up to me what I do with it.'

'Oh, for God's sake, woman, stop being so damn stubborn. This is not about women's rights or any of that nonsense. This is about me wanting to protect you, keep you safe, keep you alive...'

'People don't die from giving up a kidney.'

'And how do you know that? Done the research, have you? Looked at the statistics? Weighed up all the risks? Which, let's be honest, are bound to be higher at your age. In fact, will they even let you do it at your age? I hope to God the answer's no.'

Geri turned her head away from him and gazed out of the window at the clouds below. This was the first time she and William had ever truly disagreed about anything, the rumblings of their first argument, and she knew it was going to be a big one. Thankfully, Lily had dozed off in the seat between them, as this was one topic of conversation she had no intention of letting her overhear. 'Let's not talk about it now. I don't want this to ruin our holiday, and I certainly don't want Michael or Lily to know anything about it. A week's truce, okay?'

'During which you'll be thinking about it all the time and probably quietly making up your mind anyway. I know you, Geraldine Munro, and this thing needs to be nipped in the bud right now. You're my wife and I love you.'

'And Beth's my daughter and I love her too.'

'You love the idea of her, that's all. You've met her once. You hardly know her.'

'And whose fault is that? Mine, not hers. Don't you think I owe her, after giving her up, as good as abandoning her for all these years? If she really has come looking for me because she needs help, then I want to give it to her. Or at least try to. It's what mothers do.'

'What? Risk their own health, their own lives, when they don't have to?'

'Yes.' Geraldine lay her hand on Lily's head and gently stroked her hair, her voice dropping almost to a whisper. 'That's exactly what mothers do. And don't you tell me Agnes wouldn't have done exactly the same for you in a heartbeat, because I know damn well she would.'

THIRTY-THREE

1967

Her mum didn't look like her mum anymore. Her skin was a horrible pale colour, almost grey, and her hands were so thin they looked like a bird's, lying still on top of the bedspread as she slept.

Dad had set up a small bed downstairs, in what used to be the dining room. Not that they needed a dining room now. Nobody ever came to dinner, and whatever simple meals Dad managed to rustle up were eaten in the tiny kitchen and largely in silence.

The nurse had been in again. She came more often now, and once she had done whatever it was she did, Geraldine was allowed in for a few minutes, as she always was, to sit by the bed in this gloomy, musty room, before being ushered out again to do her homework or go up to bed, so Mum could 'rest'. It was all Mum did these days. Rest. Sleep. When she did open her eyes there was no life in them, no joy.

Nobody explained anything to her. They didn't have to. The mum that Geraldine knew and loved with all her heart was slipping away from her. They all thought she was too young to understand, but of course she wasn't. Her mum was dying. It was going to happen soon, and there was nothing she could do to stop it.

She reached out a hand and stroked her mum's hair. The perm she always wore had started to grow out, and a few long straggly hairs lay spread across the pillow. Mum would hate to see herself looking this way. Her hair unset, her cheeks devoid of their usual powder, her nails in need of polish. This would not do. It wouldn't do at all.

Geraldine ran up to her parents' room and found the bottle of her mum's favourite Pearly Pink, standing on a lace doily on the dressing table. It was a struggle to force the lid off. It had been so long since it had been used that a film of tacky polish had stuck it down.

Back beside the little makeshift bed, she finally eased the lid off the bottle and waggled the brush around in the gloopy fluid inside. The familiar varnishy smell wafted out at her as she took her mum's hand in hers and carefully painted a pink stripe down the centre of her thumb nail, then worked her way along, from one nail and one hand to the next, blowing a gentle stream of her own warm breath onto them until they dried.

Her mum's own breath came in a ragged way. Slow. Laboured.

'Don't die, Mummy,' she whispered, bending her head and resting it on the bedspread, pulling her mum's newly manicured hand up and placing it onto the back of her own neck, but it didn't move, didn't stroke her the way it always had.

'Come on now, Geraldine.' Her dad was standing in the doorway. She had no idea how long he had been there. 'That homework won't do itself. Let Mum rest now. You can see her again in the morning.'

But she didn't. She never saw her again because by

morning it was over, and someone had already come to take her mother's body away before Geraldine had even made it down the stairs. No last look, last kiss, last touch. No goodbye. She had known this was coming, but that made no difference to the huge empty feelings of utter unmanageable loss that descended on her like a big black raincloud. It certainly didn't make anything any easier, any more bearable, in the painful, grief-stricken days, or the terrible rebellious year, that came afterwards.

It was only much later, when she handed baby Sandie over, knowing she would never see her again, that she finally understood. Not just how hard it had been to let her mother go, but how hard it must have been for her mother too, knowing she had no choice but to leave her only daughter behind.

THIRTY-FOUR

Michael watched through the window as Patsy and Lily sat on plastic chairs on the balcony, a tray of coloured beads laid out in front of them, Patsy trying her best to braid his daughter's hair. As she lifted each strand, he could see how pale Lily's tiny neck was. A week in the Mediterranean sun and some fun on the beach now school had broken up for the summer would do her good, put some glow back into her.

'So, what was it you wanted to tell me that you didn't want them to hear?' He nodded towards his girls, pleased to see how well they got on with each other now. He'd never expected Patsy to be particularly maternal. When they'd first met all she'd really been interested in was her career, but Lily seemed to bring out that warm, caring side of her. He turned back towards his mother and smiled. 'Because there's something quite important that I'd like to tell you too.'

'Perhaps you two should sit down.' William, ever practical, nudged Geraldine down into a squidgy sofa and gestured for Michael to do the same. 'I'll nip into the kitchen and make us some tea. You do have tea, I suppose?'

'Yes, we have tea. I might not live in England now but I was brought up on tea and biscuits, and swiss roll if I was a good boy! There will always be tea in any kitchen of mine. And I've remembered to get some squash in for Lily. You shouldn't have any trouble finding everything.'

'Right-o!'

'How've you been, Mum?' Michael sat down next to her as William left the room. 'It's been ages since the wedding, and I know I should have come back to see you before now, but...'

'I know, love. Work. Time. Busy, busy, busy. It's okay. I'm not about to have a go at you. It's just lovely to be here now and to be able to spend some time with you. I know Lily's missed you.'

'And I've missed her. And I will try harder to see more of her, I promise.'

'Good.'

'So? Something important, you said?'

'I did, yes.'

'Well?' Whatever it was, he was starting to get a bad feeling about it. She and William seemed happy enough, and they'd come away on holiday together, so it wasn't an imminent divorce. Maybe she was ill? No, she looked the picture of health. 'Spit it out, Mum.'

'Oh God, I don't know where to start.'

'At the beginning maybe?'

'Yes, you're right. At the beginning. Well, it started a long time ago – I'm trying not to slip into *Once upon a time* here. When I was a teenager. I'd not long lost my mum and I was being incredibly stupid and selfish and not caring about anybody but myself, and I... well, I went off the rails a bit. More than a bit, actually. Hung about with the wrong people, stayed out late, let my school work suffer, did some ridiculously reckless things...'

'What are you trying to say? That you fell into a life of sex, drugs and rock and roll?' Michael laughed at the very idea of it.

'Well, yes, I suppose I did. Sort of. There was this boy, you see. Man, I suppose I should say, as he was a good bit older than me. He worked with some bands. Pop groups, as a lot of people called them back then. Backstage, shifting and carrying. I suppose I found it all a bit exciting and glamorous, which it really wasn't at all, but I was young and my head was far too easily turned. Besides which, there was drink involved. Far too much of it, and I wasn't used to it at all. And one thing led to another... What I'm trying to tell you, Michael, is that I knew very little about life, real life, the birds and the bees and all that, and I... well, I got pregnant. When I was just fourteen.'

'What?' He sat forward, his back suddenly straight, his gaze flicking towards the balcony to make sure that Patsy and Lily couldn't hear.

'You heard me.'

'Well, I wasn't expecting you to say that. So, what did you do about it? Did you have an abortion?'

'No, I didn't. Your grandad was appalled, and he was pretty strict, as you know, but even he didn't push me to take that route. No, I had the baby. A little girl.'

He didn't speak for a moment. Couldn't. 'So, I had a sister?'

Geraldine nodded, although he wasn't looking at her. 'You still do.'

'So, where has she been all this time? Hidden in the broom cupboard? My God, that's some secret to have kept all these years. A sister!'

'Yes, I know, and I should have told you long ago, but I didn't, okay? I'd pushed it all away, to the back of my mind, tried to pretend it never happened. But it did happen, and she was taken away, quickly, and adopted. She went to live with a couple who couldn't have kids of their own. In Norfolk.'

'I assume Dad knew about this? Or did you keep it a secret from him too?'

'Yes, he knew. It wouldn't have been fair to marry him without telling him everything. And he... well, he didn't like it, but he forgave me.'

'Forgave you? You make it sound like you cheated on him or something. This was all before you met, I guess?'

'Yes, it was. But for a long time, even after we were married, it changed things. It bothered him that I'd had that experience already, and with someone else. And it made me wary of doing it again. Another pregnancy, another baby. I didn't think I'd be able to handle it. Too painful, too many memories. But in the end, we took the decision to try, and then, eventually, we had you. And it was nothing like the first time. I wasn't on my own, for a start, and it was all planned, and I was older, much better able to cope. And you were a boy! The most adorable little baby boy...'

'Hang on, Mum. This isn't about me, is it? It's about her. This sister of mine, and why you've suddenly decided to tell me about her. If you were fourteen, then she must be... what? Over fifty by now. What's happened? Have you found her? Met her? Has she died? Because something's brought all this up after so long.'

'I didn't find her, no, but she's found me. Tracked me down through some agency, and she's been to see me; and Lily and Ruby too. I've been worried Lily might blurt it out and say something to you on the phone, before I had the chance to. But, Beth... She has children, Michael, and she brought them with her. Two boys – the younger one even looks a bit like you – and a girl.'

'I see.' He took a big breath and turned to face her at last. 'And how do you feel about it all? Meeting her? Them?'

'I have to admit I was a bit unnerved by it at first. Scared, even.' Geraldine was biting down on her bottom lip, her fingers picking at an imaginary speck on her top. 'It's not often something from your past turns up like that out of the blue. Or someone...'

'No.' He stared at her, trying to absorb what she was telling him. 'You haven't told me her name yet, Mum.'

'I'd called her Sandie, but she's Beth now. Elizabeth Hogan, to give her her full name. She's nice, Michael. Technically a stranger, but it doesn't feel that way. She's still got a locket and a record and a little teddy, things I'd boxed up to stay with her, and they did. And seeing her has made me happy. Knowing she's okay, that she's had a good life. That I have grandchildren I knew nothing about.'

'Well, I'm pleased for you, Mum. But it has taken some of the gloss off what I was about to tell you myself.'

'Oh?'

The door opened and William backed through it, carrying a tray. 'All clear?' he asked, a little too cheerily.

'Yes.' Geraldine smiled up at her husband. 'He knows now.'

'I do.' Michael stood up and took the tray from William's hands, setting it down on a small coffee table in front of the sofa. 'And I think, now we have drinks, this is a good time to call the others in. Although I'm not sure about the tea now. I think champagne might be more in order.'

'To celebrate having a sister?' Geraldine peered at him curiously.

'No, Mum. To celebrate yet another new member of the family. One you certainly haven't met yet.'

He walked to the glass doors that led to the balcony and pulled them open.

'Come on in, girls,' he said, sliding an arm around Patsy's back as she stood up, her loose blouse swinging open to reveal an only just noticeable baby bump. 'And let's tell Granny Geri our news.'

Vicky put her small bag down beside the sofa in Geraldine's living room and sank down to sit beside it on the carpet.

'We do have chairs, you know.' Ruby tried to inject some jolliness into her voice but she had to admit she was worried. She had never seen her friend looking quite so lifeless. It was as if a light had gone out in her.

'Yeah, I know, but I like sitting on the floor. Not so far to fall.'

'What?'

'Oh, nothing. Don't look so scared. I'm not about to pass out or anything. It's just something I remember my mum saying, when she was going through a spate of dizzy spells. Menopause, I think, and that's what she'd say. If I'm going to faint, I'd rather be on the ground already! Anticipate disaster and you lessen it, make it easier to manage. It's like if you feel really sick, you might as well sit with your head over the loo. Too late to get there once it starts.'

'Vix, what are you talking about? Do you feel sick, or about to faint?'

'No, I'm fine, honestly. I'm a bit of a sprawler, that's all. I often flop out on the carpet. And it's good for your posture. Far less chance of slumping when you've got a solid floor under your bum.'

'I'll join you, then.' Ruby plonked down next to her, and they sat for a while with their backs against the edge of the sofa.

'I'm glad you're here,' Ruby said. 'It'll give us a chance to catch up. Properly, I mean. It's not as if you can have a real conversation in hospital, is it? Just a curtain around the bed and all those people walking past. And you munching through that huge bag of grapes!'

'I happen to like grapes.'

'Good. That's why I brought them.'

'Thanks, Ruby. And not just for the grapes. Thanks for coming to see me, and for this.' She swept her arm around to encompass the room, the house. 'For giving me a safe haven, even if it is only for a few days. I'm not sure I could have faced going home just yet.'

'By home do you mean your parents' place, or the flat?'

'Either. I'd be watched all the time, I know I would. Let's all keep an eye on the crazy girl who tried to top herself...'

'Nobody thinks you're crazy, Vix, but you did, didn't you? You did swallow all those pills, far too many of them, and I still don't understand why.'

'Not sure I do either. It just felt like the only way somehow. Do you get that?'

'No, I don't. Whatever was happening in your life, or still is, I'm not sure that was the way to deal with it.'

'Probably not, but that's me, isn't it? I bottle stuff up. Bury my head for as long as I can until I have no option but to face up to things. And then... bam! Act first, think later.'

'I wish you'd talked to me.'

'I hadn't seen you.'

'You could have rung.'

'But I didn't, okay? There was the news about work closing down and not knowing what might happen to the animals when it does, and then my so-called love life going tits-up. I'd have a few drinks and then realise they made no difference to anything and it was all still there, waiting to drag me down. Calling for help was the last thing on my mind really. It's like admitting defeat, isn't it? Having to tell people you can't cope. And, besides, I knew you were busy with the shop and Lily and whatever was brewing between you and Jack, and I wasn't sure you'd have time to listen to my troubles. And I certainly didn't think there'd be much you could do about them if you did.'

'I'm sorry. I should have been there, seen that something was wrong.'

'You had no way of knowing, Ruby, so let's not go there, eh? What's done is done, and I'm still here. Alive and kicking.'

'I'm glad.'

'So, your folks are away, you've got someone looking after the shop, and there's no Lily to worry about. We're free as birds. What are we going to do with ourselves?'

'Not sure. I thought maybe you just needed some quiet time. You know, to chill, recover, talk or whatever.'

'Boring! Got any booze?'

Ruby laughed. 'You don't change, do you? You can have a beer, and that's all. Just one. No getting drunk, you hear? I'm not going to be the one who helps you to self-destruct. And, just so you know, there are absolutely no tablets in the house. Not so much as an aspirin, so however low you might feel, the only answer on offer around here is a good strong cup of tea and a listening ear, okay?'

Vicky nodded her head and grinned. 'Yes, boss. I hear you, loud and clear.'

'Right. You want that beer now, or shall we ration it? Keep it for this evening? To be honest with you, at three in the afternoon I'd rather have tea and biscuits.'

'Ruby, I swear you're sixty-six, not twenty-six! Oh, go on then. Tea, it is. Three sugars. And only if the biscuits are chocolate. A good biscuit has to be chocolate.'

'I'll see what I can do. And, please, let's sit up on the sofa. This floor's killing my back.'

'Wimp! But okay then, seeing as you're being so nice to me,

I will agree to your demands. Unless you come back with a packet of rich teas, in which case all bets are off!'

There was an unopened packet of Bourbons in the cupboard and Vicky pounced on it as if she hadn't eaten for a week. Thinking about the state of Vicky's mind lately and the sort of mushy slop that hospitals tended to serve up, Ruby concluded that she probably hadn't, so she took a couple for herself and just let her friend get on with demolishing the rest.

'Is there nothing that can be done, to save Sidell's?' Ruby wrapped her hands around her mug of tea and laid her head back, gratefully, against the soft sofa cushions. 'I dread to think what Lily's going to say when she hears that she can't visit her little Portugal Piglet anymore, or that all the animals she loves are going to have to find new homes.'

'Be realistic, Ruby. Do you really believe they're all going to scamper off into the sunset and find wonderful new places to live? Oh, the rabbits will probably be okay, and the guinea pigs. They've got the cuddle factor, haven't they? But who wants to take on an elderly tortoise or a smelly parrot that swears, or stick a spider or a snake in a glass case in the corner of their living room? Where are the pigs going to go except to some farm to end up as roast pork or a pound of sausages? The big zoos won't want them, and any small petting zoos that are still in existence are struggling to hang on with the animals they already have.'

'So, what's the answer? To find a buyer who'll take on the whole place just as it is?'

'In an ideal world, yes. But it's not ideal, is it? If the owners who love it can't make it work anymore, how is anyone else going to? It's a tiny out-of-the-way mini zoo that kids love but even Geri had never heard of it and she's lived around here for years. The place is going to need a ton of money thrown at it before it has a hope of surviving, let alone thriving. It needs a lot of TLC, Ruby. A facelift, advertising, the works, just to bring it into the twenty-first century and get people to notice it. Let's face it, it's never going to attract the big business types. What it needs is someone who cares, someone with passion. Passion for animals, not profits.'

'Someone like you, you mean?'

'Yes, someone exactly like me, but people like me don't have that kind of money.'

Ruby sipped at her tea. 'What if there were a lot of people like you?'

'What are you getting at?'

'How many staff are there? Not counting Sid and Ellen.'

'Seven. Why?'

'Are they all as upset as you are? As keen to try to save the place? All as dedicated to the animals?'

'I should think so. None of us can see ourselves working anywhere else. In a supermarket or a factory or something. We're there because we love what we do. The outside life. Caring for the animals. Talking to the kids who come in. I don't know what any of us are going to do now.'

'Buy the place?'

'Don't be stupid. How could we afford to do that? It may only be a plot of land with a wooden shack of a shop and a few cages dotted about, but we're talking thousands. Tens of thousands, at least. Hundreds, even. I don't know... And we're not earning much above minimum wage, any of us. Some don't get paid at all. Work experience and volunteers...'

'Okay, you couldn't do it on your own, I know that, but together? You must have seen it before, in the papers or on TV. Libraries, pubs... whole villages coming together to save them from closing down because they care about them and don't want to lose them, then running them themselves, with donations and fundraisers, everyone getting the paintbrushes out...'

'And I thought I was the crazy one around here!'

'It's not as crazy as it sounds. It's doable, Vix, I'm sure it is. You just need to get some figures, find out what the place is worth, see if Sid will let you have it a bit cheaper, for the sake of the animals and because he knows you and trusts you. And then, if you can get the others on board, it's just a case of all of you finding your share of the cash. A bank loan, a crowdfunding campaign, borrowing it from family...'

'Well, you can stop right there. Who's going to lend me a bean? I'm high risk, Ruby. Unqualified, thick as a brick, with no savings and a dodgy mental health record. I'm hardly businesswoman of the year. My dad can hardly look at me, so there's no way he's going to help, and I'd have to rob a bloody bank, not go cap in hand to one!'

'You are very negative sometimes, do you know that? Where's your fighting spirit?'

'The only spirit I know anything about is vodka, Ruby. No, it's a great idea, and thanks for trying, but it would never work.'

'Why not at least make a few enquiries first? And talk to the others. You may not have the money – yet – but between you you've got the expertise. You know how the place operates, and you've got that passion you said was so important. Do it for the animals, Vix. For Portugal and all the others. And for Lily. The last thing you want to do is break her little heart if you don't have to.'

'That is emotional blackmail, and you know it!'

'Maybe, but if it makes you think...'

'What do I know about running a business, Ruby? None of us do. Just because we know what to feed the animals, how to lock up and sweep up, how to work a till in the café, doesn't mean we understand wages and invoices and taxes, does it? You had Geri to help you, to show you the ropes, when you took over at your shop. Who would we have?'

'William!' It came to Ruby in a flash. 'That's who. Did you

know he used to be an accountant? Small businesses, tax returns and all that. He'd be perfect, Vix. Oh, not full time. They're enjoying being retired, but to give advice when you need it, be a guiding hand. I think he'd love it. Keeping his hand in, doing his bit for the animals, especially when he finds out how much Lily loves the place. I'll ask him, as soon as they get back.'

'That still leaves one big question though, doesn't it? Where to find the money.'

THIRTY-FIVE

Beth read the letter from the solicitor again and allowed herself a smile. The sale of her mother's house had finally gone through, and without a hitch. There was a final statement enclosed, showing the sale price minus various fees and deductions, but the net sum, when added to the money she still had left from her divorce settlement, was enough for a very sizeable deposit on a house of her own. She should feel elated but, right now, deflated was more like the right word to describe her mood.

She sipped at her tea and pushed the uneaten half of her lunchtime sandwich aside. Despite the good news about the sale, and having a few days off work to use up some of her annual leave before the end of the summer, she didn't feel too good today. She hadn't realised just how much her failing kidneys and the constant dialysis treatments would take it out of her, often leaving her feeling tired and drained, or waking up in the night with cramp in her legs that took ages to go away, no matter how much she rubbed at them or paced about on the landing. Was this it now? The way her life was going to be? Watching what she ate? Counting cups of tea so she didn't take in more fluid than the machine could cope with? Everything having to be planned around hospital visits? It was becoming depressing, and making it so difficult to think too far ahead. Even the prospect of house hunting was a daunting one that she was no longer sure she had the energy for.

She'd had another appointment with her consultant the day before, but the news was no more encouraging than it had ever been. Dialysis was, at best, a temporary fix, and her life expectancy was almost certainly going to be reduced unless the more permanent fix could be found. A transplant. It felt like the Holy Grail sometimes. The carrot being waved at the end of a very long stick. She was still on the list and nobody knew when she might reach the top.

The doctor had again talked about living donors, and how transplanted organs collected that way were far more likely to succeed than ones taken from dead bodies. Collected! He had made it sound as simple as collecting stamps or the latest football cards. Just ask your nearest and dearest to come up with what your set was missing and hand it over. As if!

He had urged her again to approach her family for testing, but she was still reluctant to take that route. Her children... definitely no. Geri and Michael, the brother she had not even met... well, the jury was still out on that one.

'It's been a great week.' William pulled his hat down over his forehead and lay back on the sunbed, closing his eyes against the bright afternoon sun.

'It has. We should do it more often. Take holidays, come out here to visit Michael and Patsy.' Geraldine kept her eyes trained on Lily who was splashing about in the kids' pool just a few yards away. She had her armbands on and the water was only a couple of feet deep but accidents could still happen and Geraldine was taking no chances.

'Especially now there's a baby on the way, eh?'

'Well, yes. If I'm to have another grandchild, then I want to see it. Often. And Lily will too. You know how much she's longed for a baby brother or sister.'

'She has. But we can't keep whisking her away, can we? There's school, and Ruby to consider.'

'True, but who knows? Perhaps they'll come home. Patsy may not want to keep working once she's a mother. And she might want to be nearer to her own mum. Having a baby can change things, how a woman feels, what her priorities are. Even a high-powered businesswoman like her!'

'Now, don't you go getting your hopes up, love.' William pulled himself to his feet. 'I fancy an ice cream. Can I get you anything?'

'I wouldn't say no.'

As if picking up on some magical ice-cream radar, Lily clambered out of the pool and came running over towards them, dripping cold water onto Geraldine's legs as she waited for the towel she knew her gran would wrap around her the moment she stood still. 'Can I have an ice cream too, Grandad?'

'And what do you say?' Geraldine waggled her finger, playfully, then pulled the towel over Lily's shivering shoulders.

'Please. Can I have an ice cream, *please*? A pink one?'

'For you, Lily... anything!' William gave her a little bow and went off in search of supplies.

When he came back with the ice creams, Lily had already fallen asleep, curled into a wet towel-swaddled ball on Geri's lap.

'I don't like to wake her,' Geri whispered.

'Well, unless you want to eat two ice creams, you're going to have to, love. Hers'll be a melted mess by the time we wait for her to wake up otherwise. Go on, have both. You know you want to! She'll have forgotten all about having asked for an ice cream by the time she wakes up, and I won't tell her if you don't!'

'Are you trying to get me fat? No, go on, don't be daft. Give her a little nudge.'

He handed a cone to Geri and gently touched Lily on the arm, bending down to whisper in her ear. 'Here we are, Lil. Strawberry, just like you asked for.'

It was funny how kids could do that. Just snap out of sleep in an instant. Her hand was out and reaching for the ice cream before he had even straightened up.

'What do you say, Lily?' Geri was at it again, like the manners police. He did wish sometimes that she could just leave the girl alone. She was growing into a lovely, kind, polite kid, all by herself, and he was sure she didn't need constant reminders about how to behave, but it wasn't his place to say anything. Once his wife had set her mind on something, he knew full well he'd have his work cut out trying to change it.

William assumed that Lily was saying 'Thank you' but, with her mouth already busy slurping up the pink drips that were sliding their way down the side of the cone, it sounded a lot more like 'Agoo.'

'You're very welcome.'

He gazed across at Geri, who, with Lily now safely out of the water, had picked up her book again. There was so much he wanted to say, whether she wanted to listen or not, but he knew this was not the time. He had held his tongue all week and, for the sake of a fun holiday, and for fear of little ears picking up too much information, they had managed to avoid the subject of Beth's illness and the inevitable argument that he knew was quietly brewing, but it couldn't be put off much longer. As soon as they arrived home tomorrow, his wife would be back on her ridiculous crusade to do what she could, to pay back whatever long-ago failings she still felt guilty of. To give up a kidney, at her age? He could not allow it to happen. Her health, her wish to spend time with her new grandchild, their shared hopes for a long and happy future, were on the line here. And if she wouldn't talk to Beth and put her straight, then he was just going to have to do it himself.

———————

Jack hesitated at the end of the street. Had he been a bit rash, coming here without warning? What if Ruby refused to see him? What if Geraldine did? He had heard nothing from either of them since his ill-fated meeting with Ruby in London and, as far as he knew, neither had his mum. It would be such a shame if they all lost touch again, especially if it was because of something he had said, a misunderstanding that could so easily be ironed out if only they could just get together and talk it through.

He stood on the front path, his hand poised to ring the bell but holding back for a moment while he gathered his thoughts. This reminded him of that day he had first come down to Brighton in search of his family and had hovered outside what had once been Geraldine's childhood home. The old lady he had met, so suspicious yet eager to help as soon as she'd thought there could be an inheritance involved. He almost felt bad for lying to her, leading her on, but there had been no harm done. He was still smiling at the memory when the door suddenly opened and he was faced with Ruby, casually dressed in a floppy T-shirt and jeans, her feet bare on the thick pile carpet, and staring at him as if he was the devil himself.

'I saw you from the window,' she said, her voice lacking its usual warmth. 'What do you want?'

'To come in, to talk, to explain...'

'Who is it, Ruby?' A female voice he didn't recognise rang out from somewhere inside the house.

'Nobody,' Ruby shouted back, adding more quietly so only he could hear, 'Well, nobody important anyway.'

'Oh, Ruby, that's not fair. The last thing I wanted was to upset you, for our friendship to end like it did.'

'You should have thought of that before you tricked me. Tricked *us*. You know, I really thought that Beth came here to meet us for all the right reasons. I thought *you* did. But all the time she was ill and desperate for a donor, and both of you seemed to very conveniently forget to mention that.'

'It wasn't like that, Ruby. Honestly. Please, let me come in. I want to set things straight. Give me a chance...'

'Ah, so this is nobody, is it?' A tall woman, with wild hair, and about the same age as Ruby, had appeared behind her in the hall. 'He looks like a somebody to me! Aren't you going to introduce me?'

'This is Jack,' Ruby said, clearly grudgingly. 'But he's not staying.'

'Oh, so this is Jack!' The woman turned her attention towards him. 'The infamous Jack. I have heard so much about you. All good, until recently, but then not so good, I'm afraid.' She squeezed past Ruby to stand in the open doorway and held out her hand. 'Nice to meet you at last. I'm Ruby's friend, Vicky.'

'Vix, please don't...'

'Oh, stop being so bloody stubborn, Ruby Baxter, and let the man in. He's come a long way, so at least play fair and hear him out. You'll have the neighbours out earwigging if you carry on talking on the step. And I don't think your Geri would like that, do you? People knowing her business?'

'Oh, come on then. But only for a few minutes. I really have nothing to say to you.' Ruby stood aside and ushered him into the same room they had all sat in the last time he had been here. Vicky had already made herself scarce and disappeared up the stairs.

'Geri not in?' he said, picking a chair and sitting down on it.

'She's away, visiting Michael in Portugal. I think she was planning on telling him all about you, and your Mum and everything. Well, probably not everything, actually. Not the bit about the kidney.'

'I wish I'd never said anything. It was never...'

'What? Your master plan? To seek out blood relatives, see what they might be persuaded to give you? I told Geri all about it, what you said to me in London, what obviously slipped out of your devious, lying mouth, but do you know what? She's okay with it. A lot more than I am, that's for sure. She actually feels sorry for Beth, has some mad idea about helping her. That's what you've done, Jack, with your nasty little secret quest for a donor. You've shamed a good, kind woman, a pensioner, into wanting to give back all the love and care she feels she deprived your mum of. Fifty years' worth of it, all paid back with a kidney. So when Vicky here tells me I'm not being fair to you, I hope you'll understand why, because doing that to Geri is not just unfair, it's downright evil.'

Jack shook his head. 'I am so sorry, Ruby. I didn't mean for this to happen. Yes, Mum started out with some vague plan of tracking down a family who might be able to help her, but that was before... before she met any of you, talked to you, saw you as real people, nice people. Geri was just some name on a certificate back then. A stranger. Believe me, Ruby, that stopped being the case as soon as she met her. The locket, the teddy... She just wants to get to know her now, to know all of you, just the same as I do. There is no ulterior motive, no master plan to rob anyone of their body parts. The last thing she would want now is to make Geri feel obliged in some way. This is not payback time. Not at all.'

'Try telling Geri that.'

'I would if I could. When's she back?'

'Tomorrow. Not that you'll still be here then to tell her anything. I want you gone. Like, in the next five minutes.'

'Oh, Ruby. Please, can't we sort this out? We were getting on so well. I thought...'

'Thought what? That I was going to forget all about it, forgive you, that we were going to fall into each other's arms? Live happily ever after? What could I possibly have that you'd be interested in, anyway? I'm not blood, remember, or were you hoping to get me onside so you could line Lily up as a future donor too?'

'Now you're being ridiculous.'

'Maybe, but I'm not sure I can trust you anymore, Jack, so best we stop this right now, don't you think?'

'No. No, I don't. I like you, Ruby. I like you a lot, and if Geri and my mum are going to keep seeing each other, it will make things a lot easier if we stay friends.'

'Easier for who?'

'All of us. Look, I can put this right, I'm sure I can, if you'll just let me.'

'And how exactly are you planning on doing that?'

'There's only one way I can think of and I should have done it ages ago.' Jack took a deep breath. He would be going against his mum's wishes, but what the hell? This was her health, her future, her life at stake here. 'I don't care what my mum has to say about it, I'm going to get tested. And I'm pretty sure Tom will too. There'll be no need for Geri to even think about offering to help if one of us can do it instead.'

THIRTY-SIX

'William, what are you doing?'

William jumped at the sound of his wife's voice behind him. He could have sworn she was safely downstairs, loading the washing from their cases into the machine.

'Nothing,' he mumbled, quickly pushing her mobile phone away under the pillows.

'Doesn't look like nothing from where I'm standing. I know that guilty look. What are you up to?'

'Just sorting out a few holiday bits. You know, putting my toothbrush away...'

'Under the pillow? Is that where you usually keep it?' Geraldine pushed past him and made a grab for the nearest pillow, before he could reach it himself.

'Okay, okay. I own up. It's not my toothbrush.'

'I can see that. And what would you want with my phone? Trying to root out my dating app history or my secret porn habit?' She made it sound as if she was joking but there was a hard edge to her voice, and he knew he'd been rumbled.

'Of course not. Look, if you must know, I wanted to check your contacts. There was a number I needed.'

'Dentist? As you seem to have lost your toothbrush?'

'No need for sarcasm. It was Beth, actually.'

'Oh, and why would you need Beth's number? And, assuming you have a good reason, why couldn't you have just asked me for it? You're acting suspiciously, William, and I don't like it.'

'Sorry, and you're right. I should have asked you, told you...'

'Told me what? That you're going to have it out with her, have a go at her for coming here looking for my help, tell her off for having the nerve to try to save her own life?'

'Oh, Geri.' He sank down onto the bed and patted the place beside him, beckoning for her to do the same. 'Please, can we put an end to this nonsense? We need to talk to Beth. Together. Get the truth about all of this, and then decide what to do about it. Together. I hate the idea of you taking any sort of risk, and it's not as if we know if she wants you to help her, as you call it, or if you'd even be allowed to.'

'No, we don't. Which is exactly why I was going to call her this evening, as soon as we'd finished the unpacking and had our tea. I'm a grown woman, of increasingly advanced years, and I don't need you fighting my battles for me, or jumping in, all guns blazing. You are not a knight in shining armour, much as you might like to think you are.' She smiled then, for the first time since she had come into the room. 'So, let's get the facts, shall we? See what she needs, see what we can do, if anything. And then, if you really believe that I need saving, be my guest.'

'Agreed.' He held her hand for a moment. He was so lucky to have found this amazingly strong and caring woman. If anything, she was the one rushing in all guns blazing, not him, and it was his job to rein her in, be the voice of reason. Because he was not going to let her do anything reckless or stupid, not going to let anything bad happen to her, that was for sure. Not on his watch.

They didn't need to call Beth that evening, because she called them first.

'Geri, I'm so sorry.' It was the first thing she said. No 'Hello', no 'How are you?' Just straight in with an apology.

'Beth? Are you okay, love? And what have you got to be sorry about?'

'Jack's told me what happened. How he let something slip to your Ruby about me being ill, and how angry she is. And now you're going to think so badly of me, and of him. Oh, I should have told you. I know I should. But we'd only just met for the first time since I was a baby, and it didn't seem the right time, not what you'd want to hear...'

'Calm down, Beth. It's okay, really. Of course you weren't going to tell me everything at our very first meeting. Nor would I have wanted you to. I just needed to see you, make sure you'd had a good life, with good parents. Just looking at you, and your beautiful children, that was enough. Honestly. I didn't expect a potted history of everything life had ever thrown your way, a blow-by-blow account of your divorce, a look through your medical records. None of that is my business, is it, unless you choose to tell me about it? I like to hope that you would have done, in time, once we got to know each other better, but you have nothing to be sorry for, believe me.'

'Can we start again, do you think? Meet up again? I'd love you to come up here, to London. Soon. To visit me, and go for afternoon tea or something. Then perhaps we can have a proper conversation, warts and all.'

'I'd like that. But I have to tell you I don't have any warts. A few wrinkles maybe, and the odd mole!'

Beth laughed down the phone line. 'Ah, so I have you to blame, do I? For the wrinkles? And the little brown mole at the

311

top of my leg? It's funny what you inherit without even realising it.'

'Well, you seem to have got my sense of humour anyway! Not sure about the mole. I don't remember that from when you were born. Maybe they took the wrong baby and mine's still there in that mother and baby home, waiting to be collected?'

'Oh, I'm yours all right. Had the locket to prove it, didn't I?'

'You did, love, and here it is, still round my neck. Thanks for bringing it back to me. I've missed my mum all these years and it's nice to have her back.'

'Not quite the same, I know, but it's nice to have you back too, Geri.'

Geri could feel the tears starting to well up and did her best to quash them. 'So, yes, I would love to come and visit, but I don't want to wait for a proper chat. About your illness, I mean. Tell me, now. I'd like to know more about it, about how it affects your life. Look, love, do you mind if William listens in? We tell each other everything, so I'd only be relaying it all again to him later... If you're okay with that, obviously?'

'Of course. It's no secret.'

'Kidney disease, have I got that right? And you're having dialysis?' Geraldine looked across at William, sitting on the other side of the room, and flicked the switch to speakerphone so he could hear what was being said.

'Yes, I'm afraid so. Three times a week. It does kind of restrict what I can do, where I can go. We timed our trip to Brighton for in between treatments and I made sure I took things as slowly as I could. Had to sit down on that bench when we walked to the swings, remember? I had to do the same when we made it to the pier as well, but the kids wanted to go on the rides so they were fine without me tagging along. I do get tired, you see, and a bit breathless, and my legs ache a fair bit if I do too much. Otherwise, well, I'm still working part-time, being careful what I eat and drink, just taking life as it comes, one day at a time.'

'Oh, you poor thing. It must be awful. I do wish you'd confided in me.'

'Sorry.'

'Please stop saying that. You can't help being ill, can you? But, tell me, what have the doctors said about it all? Is it a genetic thing? As far as I know there was never anything like that on my side of the family. I can't speak for Russell and his side though.'

'No, it's not inherited, or they don't think so, anyway. Just bad luck.'

'The worst. And the future? What can they do?'

'Medicines, lifestyle, dialysis. It all helps keep me ticking along, but it can't be reversed. Can't be cured. Only a transplant can do that. I have a friend, someone I met at the hospital, who's had one quite recently and it's given her a new lease of life.'

'That's good. It must give you hope.'

'Of course. I'd be a goner without hope, that's for sure. It's the one thing that keeps me going. Well, that and my kids, obviously.'

'They really are the most precious thing to us mums, aren't they? And the grandchildren when they start arriving. My Michael's having another baby, by the way. Well, Patsy is, to be precise about it. Lily's over the moon.'

'Ah, I bet she is.' The line went quiet for a moment. 'Oh, Geri, I didn't ask how your holiday went.'

'Lovely, thank you. And, yes, before you ask, I did tell your brother about you.'

'And?'

'Not as shocked as I had thought he might be. In fact, he was very understanding. I think having his own good news to tell us probably helped, and of course he's in no position to get all judgemental about something I did years ago, not after leaving our Ruby to cope with a toddler on her own when he ran off and left them.'

Geri could see William raising his eyebrows in surprise. It was not often that she criticised her own son, but there were some things she would never totally forgive him for.

'Beth...' She wasn't quite sure how to broach the subject, but it had to be done. 'There was something your Jack said to Ruby, about blood relatives being possible donors. Did you...?'

'Oh, God, Geri, no. Whatever Jack said, or implied, I have to put things straight. Yes, I admit the thought did cross my mind, way back before I found you, that it could be the answer, guilt-tripping some stranger into giving me what I needed, but no, I promise you, that's not why I came looking. Everything had changed by then. I had changed. As soon as I sat with that social worker and talked it through, as soon as I saw my birth records and your name on them it all became real to me. That you're actually my mother, that there were things about my own past I was longing to discover. I even went there, you know, to that baby home in Norfolk – well, it's a hotel now – just to get a feel for it, for you. Where it all began.'

'Did you?'

'Yes, and what I was looking for was my own story, my past, some sort of sense of belonging, not a kidney, I promise you.'

'I believe you, love. But, even so, I'd like to help you. I don't know if I'm too old, or if our blood groups match, or if I'm even brave enough to go through with it, but I'd like to get tested anyway. At least I'd know I've tried.' She looked across at William. His head was in his hands and he was shaking it, slowly.

'No need, Geri. Jack's insisting on being tested. It's not what I wanted but he's refusing to listen. And Tom too. So, it will be okay. I'm sure it will. And, if not, there's still the waiting list. I'm young enough. I have time on my side.'

'Well, three tests have to be better than two, surely? So, no arguments, okay? Count me in. Maybe Michael too, at some point, once he meets you. Tiny steps, but with all your family taking them together, who knows where they might lead?'

William had been walking around with a face like thunder all week.

'Well, nobody's forcing you to come with us,' Geraldine said as she checked the time of the train on the tickets she had just printed out.

'Well, I am coming, if only to make sure you don't do anything foolish.'

'There's really no need. It's just a chat to start with. Finding out what's involved. And a blood test, because there'll be no point in going any further if that part doesn't match up.'

'I know all that, but it's still a big step, and an emotional one, no matter what they tell you. If you can't help Beth, you'll feel guilty, I know you will. And if you can... then there could be weeks, months even, of more chats and more tests and some really tough decisions to be made. Oh God, I hate to think of you having to deal with any of this stuff on your own.'

'I won't be on my own though, will I? Not at this stage of the process anyway. Jack will be there too, and Ruby. And it's a chance to get the two of them in the same room again. I don't think things have been going too well between them lately.'

'Well, kissing and making up sounds all very well, but in a hospital room? Maybe not the ideal romantic location. And I still don't get why Ruby's going with you. Not just you matchmaking again, I hope.'

'Of course not. She just wanted to give me a bit of moral support, that's all.'

'Couldn't I have offered that?'

'Normally, yes, but not when you're so obviously against the whole idea. I'm not sure I could cope with you tutting and shaking your head all the way through the consultation. No, you stay here and look after Lily. Take her out somewhere. To see the animals at Sidell's maybe? She loves that place, and it will be closing down soon.'

'I've been thinking about that, actually. Ruby says the staff need advice, about raising the money, giving the place an overhaul, doing the books and everything, if they manage to take it over. What if I – *we* – were able to do a bit more than that?'

'Like what, exactly?'

'I was thinking about the money. You know, from the sale of the house. We always said we should do something useful with it, didn't we? Or with some of it, anyway.'

Geraldine stared at him and frowned. 'Useful, yes, but not buy a zoo if that's what you're thinking!'

'Not buy it, no. Or not all of it, and definitely not for ourselves. We're getting a bit long in the tooth to get out there working again day after day. I can't see us as zookeepers, out in all weathers, mucking out cages, can you? But we could consider investing, couldn't we? Silent partners, helping behind the scenes, trying to get the place profitable again. We both have business experience. I was thinking we could put some money in, act as backers, angels or whatever you want to call us. Something for Lily, as she grows up, and it might help keep young Ruby's friend in work, give her something to look forward to, stop her from trying anything stupid again.'

'That's good of you.' She reached for his hand and gave it a squeeze. 'I've always tried to help girls in need, you know that. Somewhere to live, a job, a bit of a confidence boost when they need it most. Payback for not being able to do it for Beth, I suppose. And I would never have met Ruby if I hadn't got involved in volunteering at the children's home.'

'Exactly. So, why not do it again? Give the sort of help that young Vicky needs. A loan, a leg-up, whatever. She understands the animals, we understand the accounts. It's a win–win partnership. I'm not talking about taking huge risks or ploughing in everything we've got. There'd be plenty left for that cruise, or Disneyland, or whatever you fancy. Besides, I feel I need something... to do, I suppose. A project to get my teeth into. I really enjoyed doing the am-dram show, making scenery and props and suchlike. I can just see myself down at the wildlife centre wielding a hammer or a paintbrush.'

'William, you haven't even seen the place. It's only small, admittedly, and I have to say it's quite charming in its way, but even so it probably needs a bit more than a lick of paint. A whole rebranding, from what I can gather. Dragging into the twenty-first century. And I'm not sure this is the time to discuss it. Which reminds me, you've very cleverly managed to change the subject. Beth, tomorrow, London...'

'Yes, I know. And I'm definitely coming with you. Lily can come too. Now, let me see what carriage you're in. I'm going to book us two more seats on the same train. You can go off and do your hospital stuff and have your posh afternoon tea – half the reason Ruby was so keen to go with you, I bet! – and Lily and I will make plans of our own and meet up with you again afterwards for the trip back. If we're going to have a go at running an animal place...'

'William! We have decided no such thing.'

'Not yet, but if we do – and I do mean *if*, so don't panic just yet – then I think it's time to find out how the big boys do it. So, it's a day at London Zoo for us.'

'Oh, she'll love that!'

'I know. And so will I. Having Lily to myself for a whole day, that'll be a first.'

'Don't fill her up with sweets and ice creams though, will you?'

'Why on earth not? If you lot can gorge yourselves at some posh London hotel, then you can hardly deny us a few treats, can you? And spoiling kids is what us grandads do!'

THIRTY-SEVEN

It didn't take Ruby and Geraldine long to find the hospital. They had sat together in a companionable near-silence on the Underground and then emerged into glorious sunshine that had them both shielding their eyes with their arms as they walked.

'Should have brought our sunglasses,' Geraldine said.

'Or hats.' Ruby linked her arm through Geraldine's. The streets were surprisingly busy, but then it was the school holidays and London always did draw the crowds.

'She said to meet her outside. Where is she?'

'Give her a few minutes, Geri. The appointment's not until eleven. We're early.'

'Let's sit then, shall we? Look, there's a spare bench over there.'

A couple of nurses in uniform were leaning against a wall, chatting, one of them smoking a cigarette.

'You wouldn't think they would, would you? Smoke like that. Not in their job.' Geraldine looked on disapprovingly.

'I guess even saints have their weaknesses, Geri. It's a stressful job. If it helps them cope...'

'You wouldn't say that if you'd watched someone die of cancer like my poor mum. Still, it's up to them, I suppose. Grown adults, able to make their own choices.'

'You're still mad at William, aren't you? For trying to stop you from making your choices? You hardly spoke to him on the train.'

'He was sitting two rows away. How could I?'

'Have it your own way. That man loves you to bits. You do know that, don't you?'

'Yes, of course. And I love him too. But...'

'Forget the buts, Geri. He's entitled to his opinions, and from where I'm standing, everything he's said is to try to protect you. What you're considering is a lot to take in. For him, and for all of us. We'd hate for anything to go wrong, for anything to happen to you.'

'Nothing's going to go wrong.'

Ruby bit her tongue. There was no point in arguing with Geri when she was in one of her stubborn moods, but at least she had been allowed to come along with her and offer some support, even if William had not. 'Look, here they come now.'

Beth was coming out of the main doors, one son on each side of her, arms linked just as hers and Geri's had been. Tom's nose was pretty much buried in his phone and Jack was wearing his nurse's uniform, as if he'd just popped down from the ward for a while, which he very likely had. That would probably explain why the three of them were coming from inside the hospital and not approaching from the street.

Ruby had only seen Tom once before and there had been so much to think about that day that she hadn't given him a lot of attention, but she was struck now by just how much he looked like Michael. Same colour hair, same jawline, same walk. There was no mistaking that they were related. Something inside her shivered, as if someone had walked over her grave. Michael.

Gone but never quite forgotten. She was never really sure how she felt about him these days. How quickly love had turned to hate and then eventually into a kind of indifference as the miles and the years had put more and more distance between them. She didn't want him back though, she knew that much for certain. And part of the reason for that was standing right there in front of her.

As Geraldine and Beth greeted each other with big smiles and hugs, and Tom concentrated on jabbing his thumb at the keypad on his phone, Jack stood silently and just looked at her, as if waiting for a cue.

'Jack.'

'Ruby.'

'I'm sorry...' They were both saying it at once, then both stopped abruptly and waited again. And then they laughed, at the sheer absurdity of it all.

'Can we put it behind us now? Our falling-out?' he said, turning his puppy dog eyes towards her until she could feel her resolve melting away.

'Falling-out? I don't know what you mean. A silly misunderstanding, that's all it was.'

'Absolutely. Never again, eh?' He leaned forward to kiss her on the cheek but she made a grab for him and pulled him in close. This was what she should have done in Brighton when he'd come down to apologise. If Vicky hadn't been in the house maybe she would have... No, it wasn't fair to put the blame on anyone else. It had been her own stubbornness that had held her back, even when he had held out an olive branch and offered to get tested, to try to save Geri from having to. Not that it had worked. It was Geri's stubbornness they had to deal with now. Together.

Jack kissed her lightly on the top of her head. She could feel the warmth of him, the watch pinned to the front of his uniform pressing against her. He smelled of soap and something vaguely medicinal.

'Get a room, you two.' Tom had put his phone in his pocket and was putting his fingers into his own throat, making sick gestures. Everybody laughed but, even as Jack pulled back, he kept his arm wrapped loosely across Ruby's shoulders.

'So, are we ready for this?' Beth pointed back towards the doors she had just emerged from.

'As we'll ever be.'

'Come on then. Let's get it over with, shall we?' Tom said, clapping his hands together and clearly trying to lighten the mood. 'Find out which one of us is going to do the deed.'

'It may not be any of you,' Beth said, cautiously. 'And I almost hope that it's not. The thought of any one of you...'

'Oh, stop it, Mum. We're here now, and what will be will be, okay?'

'Okay, love.' She put on a brave smile. 'But please, don't say anything to your sister. Not yet. I haven't told her where we are, or why. It's bad enough two of you having to go through all this, but at least I know one of my babies is safe. She's at your dad's today and none the wiser. Let's keep it that way until we have something definite to tell her, all right?'

'Do they have piggies, Grandad?' Lily tugged at William's hand as soon as they were through the gates of the zoo, eager to start exploring.

'I don't know. But I think we can do a bit better than pigs today, don't you? They have lots of animals here that you won't see at Sidell's. Big scary ones! Let's look at the signposts, shall we? Then we can see where everything is and decide what to see first.'

'Okay, Grandad.'

Oh, he did love it when she called him that.

Lily scrunched up her little face in thought. 'I want to see the lions and tigers and the elephants and polar bears. And all the penguins.'

'Right-o.'

'And the monkeys too, because they're funny, and I want to give them a banana.'

'I'm not sure we're allowed to do that, Lily. The keepers have to decide what the animals eat and when, so people don't give them the wrong food, or too much of it. We don't want them to get sick, do we? Or fat?'

Lily giggled, blowing out her cheeks and waddling on the spot, pretending to be a fat monkey.

'And those bananas are meant to be part of our packed lunch, remember? Granny made it specially for us so we didn't have to go buying hamburgers and chips.'

'But I like hamburgers and chips.'

'So do I, but maybe Granny's worried we might eat all the wrong food and get fat too!'

'I won't tell her if you don't.'

It was William's turn to laugh. Where on earth had she heard that expression? But she was right. This was a day for treats. Geri's sandwiches wouldn't go to waste. Feeding the zoo animals might be banned, but they could always throw the bread to the birds or the squirrels as they walked back through Regent's Park later.

'Okay, young lady. Shall we start with the gorillas, as they're not far away, and then work our way around to the tigers. We'll leave the penguins to last as it looks like they're right by the gift shop, and I'm sure there'll be a little something in there we can buy as a souvenir before we head for home.'

Lily nodded and slipped her hand into his as they set off

with the rest of the crowd down the path towards the gorilla enclosure.

William wondered what Geri and the others were doing now, if they were talking with the transplant co-ordinator, or perhaps having blood taken. Perhaps he should have swallowed his pride and gone with her. Not that she would have let him, while his feelings were so clear. Still, he knew he was never going to change her mind, so he might as well stop fighting her and just go with the flow. But he was here now, and looking forward to his day out with Lily. He would laugh with her at the antics of the animals, enjoy his burger, and maybe pick up a few tips for the animal park back home. Which attractions were the most popular, the choice of colours and fonts for the signs, and anything that could be provided cheaply but bring in extra people and extra money. A wooden adventure playground perhaps, or little bags of cheap food. He was sure Lily wouldn't be the only child eager to feed the animals. Quiz sheets with the answers hidden round the place. And anything interactive, of course. Buttons to press, flaps to lift, to reveal animal facts and secrets. Kids loved all that stuff. Already his imagination was running away with him, and way too quickly, but it had been ages since he'd felt really enthusiastic about anything except the am-dram show, and there wouldn't be another of those until the Christmas panto got underway. No, the more he thought about it, the more he was sure he wanted to get involved. All he had to do was persuade Geri, which could prove tricky. He knew only too well how stubborn she could be.

Beth was so pleased that they were all being seen together. As Elaine, the transplant co-ordinator, explained, this really was a family decision and, even if only one of them was considering becoming a donor, she would always have wanted to involve the others too.

'What happens before, during and for a long time after a transplant operation will inevitably affect all of you,' she told them. 'Not only medically, but emotionally, practically, sometimes financially too if someone needs time off work to recover, so it's far better to make sure you all have the full facts, and the opportunity to ask as many questions as you want to, right from the start.'

They sat in a small cosy room, in soft chairs with cushions and arms rather than the expected stacking plastic ones, arranged around a coffee table, which was already doing its job as cardboard cups of coffee and a plate of biscuits had been placed in front of them.

Elaine had come loaded up with files and leaflets, but mostly she left them untouched and just talked. She came across as knowledgeable but compassionate, as any good medical professional should be, and Beth instantly liked her.

'Giving an organ is a wonderful thing to do,' she said. 'The greatest gift, in my opinion, but none of you must feel in any way pressured or that, having offered it, you can't at any time change your minds and back out. Understand?' Elaine looked intently at each of them in turn. 'It will always be your decision, and we respect that at all stages. If you want to stop, for any reason at all, right up to the day you go into theatre, all you have to do is say.'

'Oh, no. I couldn't do that.' Geraldine had gone a bit pink and was shaking her head. 'That would be so unfair. Waving a lifeline like that and then snatching it away.'

Elaine reached forward and touched her hand. 'Just bear in mind what I've said, Mrs Munro. Your health, your well-being, are equally as important as the recipient's. Just remember that. After this initial chat, if any of you go forward into the living donor programme, then everything from then on will be strictly confidential, with one-to-one meetings, and anything you want to tell me or ask me will always be entirely between us, okay? There may be something we discover about your own current health or medical history that makes a difference and means we have to let you drop out, and of course there is no shame in having reservations, a change of heart, cold feet. At any stage. I'm not saying that you will, just that it's all right if you do.' She reached for a leaflet from her pile and laid it on the table, keeping her finger on it as she spoke. 'There is also a scheme you might like to think about if none of you turn out to be a match, whereby we can organise a... well, a swap, if you like. You donate to another family you might match up with and one of them donates to you. But that's not something for today...'

Everyone sat in silence, taking it all in. There was so much to think about. Beth nodded and gave Elaine a tentative smile as she felt Jack's hand close over hers, stopping her from reaching for the leaflet. There would be time to read that later, if it was needed. Maybe, if they were lucky today, it would not be.

'Now... the first thing we have to do is find out if any of you are possible matches. There are more detailed questionnaires, tests, scans and what-not that we will need to do over the coming weeks, or possibly months, but having the right blood group is imperative, the starting point if you like, so I'm going to ask the nurse to come in and take some blood from each of you now and then we'll go from there. It won't take too long to get the results, hopefully just an hour or so, so you can wait, or take a break and come back a little later. Or I'm more than happy to call you later if you'd rather leave. Nothing else will be done today anyway, but I will get back to all of you as soon as I can. I'm sure you're all anxious to know whether you can help Mrs Hogan.'

'Beth, please.'

Elaine smiled. 'Beth, yes, of course. And, once we get past this initial stage, I can make individual private appointments to see any of you who are able – and willing – to proceed. Okay?'

They all nodded as Elaine stood up and left the room.

'Maybe I should offer to have blood taken too?' Ruby said. 'I know I'm not actual family, but I feel I should...'

'No.' Beth shook her head vigorously. 'Nobody expects that of you, Ruby. You heard what Elaine said. No feeling obliged, or guilty, or any other such foolish notion. And you have a young child to think about. So, you can forget that idea right now. Don't you think I feel bad enough having to go cap in hand to my own kids, and to a mother I hardly know?'

'You didn't go cap in hand, Mum,' Tom said. 'You didn't ask at all. We volunteered.'

'Insisted, more like.' Jack reached for his coffee, which was now only lukewarm, and swallowed it in one.

'This is really happening, isn't it?' Tom was staring down at his feet, which were twitching about, making little tapping noises on the hard floor. 'It's like playing Russian roulette, waiting to see who gets the bullet.'

'But it's a game nobody's making you play, Tom.' Beth stood up and went to give him a cuddle, which he quickly shrugged off. 'You heard what she said. Nobody expects you to have to do this, least of all me.'

The door opened then and a young nurse came in, pushing a trolley laden with syringes and bottles and wipes.

'Right, then,' she said, cheerily. 'Who's first?'

'Me, if that's all right with the rest of you,' Jack said, standing up and offering his arm. 'I'm due back on the ward.'

'And there's somewhere I need to be too,' said Tom, without further explanation. Knowing him, Beth thought, there probably a girl involved. Or he was off to do a shift at the bar he was working in during the summer break from uni.

'That's fine. You boys go first. We're in no rush, are we, girls?'

'Not at all.' Geraldine checked her watch. 'We've got ages until our posh tea.'

'Too long.' Ruby laughed. 'My tummy's starting to rumble already. Must be the early start this morning.'

'We can nip out and get a snack somewhere maybe?' Beth tried not to look as the needle slipped into her eldest son's arm and the small bottle began to fill with blood. 'While we wait for the results. We are going to wait for them, aren't we?'

Geraldine and Ruby nodded enthusiastically. 'Of course,' they both said together.

'There's a shop just over the road,' the nurse said, giving Jack a pad of cotton wool to hold over the jab site while she sorted out a plaster. 'Cheaper than the canteen or the hospital shop, if it's just a sandwich you're after.'

'Thanks. We just might do that.'

'Right, who's next?' the nurse asked as Jack gave his mum a quick peck on the cheek and hurried back to work.

THIRTY-EIGHT

The street outside the hospital was busy, with a constant stream of buses and cars going past and hordes of pedestrians, either dawdling slowly and taking up the whole pavement or pushing past them in a hurry, so they could scarcely walk together without at least one of them having to hang back for a moment to let someone pass. Ruby soon spotted the sandwich shop over on the other side of the road. Although it was barely twelve o'clock, it already had a small queue inside, with a few people having to wait in line outside the open door. Most of them were in uniform, so it was clearly popular with the hospital staff.

'Should we bother?' Geraldine said as they stood at the kerb and waited for the signal to cross. 'The hospital shop might be quicker, or the canteen so we can have a sit down.'

'I can't see it taking long, Geri. It's not as if we're in that much of a rush and we're almost there now anyway. Nothing like a personal recommendation.' Ruby pointed to the queue. 'And that many hungry nurses can't be wrong.'

'Well, I don't know about you two, but I'm glad we came

out. I feel I needed a bit of fresh air.' Beth led the way across the road and they joined the end of the queue.

'Fresh? You must be joking.' Geri held her hand over her nose and pretended to cough. 'What with all these traffic fumes.'

'Just so long as the sandwiches are fresh,' Ruby joked, rubbing her tummy. 'I'm starving!'

Within five minutes they were at the front and selecting not only their preferred fillings but which of a choice of seven different breads or rolls they fancied too.

'Oh, I shouldn't have,' Beth said as they emerged back onto the street, clutching their paper bags. 'How am I going to manage my scones and jam later after stuffing myself with this lot?'

'It did all look yummy though, didn't it? I just couldn't resist that granary bread.' Ruby closed her eyes and made purring sounds, putting on her best ecstasy expression. 'And how is anyone meant to choose between the ham and the cheese when they both look that good?'

'Which is why you had both!'

The sign finally showed the little green man again and they followed the bustling crowd and stepped onto the crossing, still laughing. None of them saw the motorcycle speeding towards them. There was just a high-pitched squeal of brakes and the terrible sounds of scraping metal and spinning tyres and bouncing bodies as it hit full-on, scattering people and handbags and sandwiches all over the road.

THIRTY-NINE

'Jack.' The ward sister called him over to the desk, the phone held out in her hand. 'Call for you.'

'Must be time for the blood results. Sorry, is it okay...?'

'Yeah, sure. Don't take too long though. We are a bit short staffed today.'

'Course not. They should have just left a message on my mobile and I'd have picked it up at my next break. It's not as if it's urgent...'

'Tom? Where are you?'

Tom held his phone away from his ear and raised his eyebrows at the girl sitting next to him on the bus. Jack's voice sounded extra-loud and he was talking far too quickly. In fact, he sounded panicked, which was quite unlike him.

'Are you far away? Can you come back to the hospital? Now?'

Tom muttered to the girl, 'It's only my brother. What can be so bloody important? We're only having blood tests.'

'What's up, Jack?' he joked. 'Have they decided I'm the chosen one after all?'

William shifted his bottom on the bench and dug around in his back pocket for his mobile, hoping to retrieve it before it stopped ringing. It would be Geri, wanting to tell him how the meeting with the transplant woman had gone, and hopefully, please God, telling him she was not a match. Then they could put this whole ridiculous business behind them.

Lily was sitting beside him, licking at a 99 that she had far too easily persuaded him to buy for her, despite the fact that it would soon be time for lunch.

'Is that Granny?' she said, a trickle of vanilla ice cream running down the side of the cone and onto her fingers.

'Probably.' He grabbed at the phone and answered it quickly, without even looking at the screen. 'Hello?' He listened for a moment, feeling his face draining of colour, his hands starting to shake. 'No! No, she can't be... Yes, I'm on my way. I'll be as quick as I can.' He hung up and slipped the phone back into his pocket and turned towards Lily, her little face still all full of wonder and smeared with chocolate from the crumbling flake she had just bitten into. 'I'm sorry, Lily.' It was all he could do to stand up without wobbling, but he had charge of a child. He had to keep himself together. He took hold of her small sticky hand and pulled her gently to her feet. 'We have to go now.'

'But we haven't had our burger yet, or seen the penguins.'

'Another time, Lily. I promise.' He was already searching the internet for the number of a taxi firm. There was no time to lose. He had to get to that hospital. Geri needed him, now more than ever before.

As the taxi pulled up outside A&E, William guided Lily safely onto the pavement and paid the driver. A young woman came running towards him.

'Are you William?' she said, falling into step beside him as he hurried towards the sliding glass doors.

'Yes. And you are?'

'I'm Laura. I'm a nurse here. Oh, not involved in what's happened, sorry, so I can't give you an update. No, I'm Ruby's friend. Look, I'm sorry. I know you don't know me, but I'm here to take Lily. Ruby rang me and asked me to come over. She doesn't think...' She looked down at Lily and dropped her voice to a whisper. 'That this is really the place for her to be right now, if you know what I mean. So, we thought if she came home with me for a while, played with the twins, had something to eat... Best that we keep things as normal as possible, until we know...'

'Right. I see.'

'You haven't told her anything?'

William shook his head. Should he hand Lily over to this stranger? But then, she was right, of course. How could he even think of taking Lily inside, not knowing what he was about to encounter?

'Are you sure?'

'Of course. I don't live far from here. St Cuthbert's Vicarage. I'm still on maternity leave, there's nowhere else I have to be, so I'm more than happy to help, and she can stay as long as necessary. Look, call Ruby, please, if you're unsure. Check me out.'

'It's okay. I know who you are. Ruby talks about you, a lot. And she came to visit you not so long ago too, didn't she?' He bent down to Lily's level and forced a smile. 'Would you like to go and see Laura's babies, Lily? And have some lunch? We never did get that burger, did we?'

'Oh, I can run to a burger, no problem. Chips too, if you'd like.'

Lily peered up at William for reassurance, then slid her hand out of his and into Laura's.

'Yes, please. I like chips. And babies. My daddy and Patsy are going to have one soon and then I'll have a sister.'

'Or a brother, Lily.' William touched the top of her warm head. 'Be good now, and I'll see you later, okay?' He watched as they walked away, Lily chatting away as if she had known Laura all her life. Then he closed his eyes for a moment, took a deep breath and went inside.

Ruby was standing by the coffee machine in the reception area as he walked in. She was thumping at it, trying to get it to relinquish her change. 'Bloody thing,' she muttered, finally giving up and turning away, a cardboard cup of something vaguely brown and watery clutched in her hand. Was it the tea or the coffee button she had pressed? She really couldn't remember.

'Ruby...'

'Oh, William, I'm so glad you're here.' She moved towards him and leant her head down onto his chest, the tears brimming up and over, far beyond her control. 'What have they told you?'

'Nothing. I've only just walked in.' William eased her back and looked into her face. 'How bad is it, Ruby? Where is she?'

'Pretty bad, I think. They took her into theatre, but nobody's saying much yet. Come with me. Jack's here, and Tom. Neither of them had gone far when it happened, and they were called straight back. They've put us all in a little waiting room. And that's what we've been doing. Just waiting. Did Laura take Lily all right? I thought it was for the best...'

'Yes. She's gone away happy. None the wiser.'

'That's good.' She took a screwed-up tissue from up inside her sleeve and wiped it across her nose. 'I just wish I could say the same for the rest of us.'

They had arrived at a closed door marked 'Relatives Room'. William gazed at the sign. Something about it bothered him. He thought it was the absence of an apostrophe. For one ridiculous moment he stood there staring at it, debating in his mind whether it should go before or after the s.

'In here,' Ruby said, easing the door open and leading the way inside.

'Geri.' He could see her, half curled into a chair in the corner. 'Oh my God, Geri, I'm so pleased you're okay. If anything had happened to you...'

She opened her eyes as he stepped towards her, stood up slowly and let herself be held.

'Beth,' she said, her voice small and weak. 'It's Beth...'

'I know, love, I know.'

He held Geri close, lifted his head above hers and looked around the room. Beth's boys were both here, sitting silently, knees apart, staring at the floor.

'I'm so sorry,' he said. Well, what else was there to say?

They both nodded. Ruby walked forward and sat down next to Jack, handing him the drink she had just got from the machine. William watched as her fingers came to rest on Jack's knee and stayed there. So, they had made up. He was glad about that. The lad would need someone to look after him, care about him, through all of this. Nurses were pretty tough, they got to

335

see a lot of pain and suffering, but that probably wouldn't make a lot of difference when the patient was one of his own family. There was a plaster on Jack's arm, William noticed, in the crook of his elbow. They had had the blood tests then. He wanted to ask how it had gone, who matched and who didn't, but this really wasn't the time or the place.

'How did it happen, Geri?' William eased her back into her chair, pulled up another and sat beside her, clasping her hands in his.

'I'm not sure. Neither of us is sure.' She looked across at Ruby. 'It was all so quick, so sudden.'

'Oh God, Geri, were you hurt too?' Geraldine had a plaster on her arm, just like Jack's, but there was more. A dressing on her right knee, some bruising starting to show above it, and her hands looked grazed.

'I'm okay. Just a few cuts and scrapes.' She clutched tightly at his hands. 'Oh, it was awful, William. It still doesn't seem real somehow. One minute we were walking along together, and the next there was this awful noise, and something flew past us, over us, sort of through the middle of us. So fast, so fast... And then we were on the ground. There was shouting and screaming. I think someone had grabbed me and pulled me back, to get me out of the way. I don't know who it was, but they probably saved me from being hurt a lot more, whoever they were. I must try to find out... but I stumbled and landed badly, then lost my balance and fell, that's all. Nothing to worry about.' She rubbed idly at the bandage on her knee. 'I pulled myself up and tried to get to Beth. She was only a few feet away from me, but I couldn't even see her at first. She was down flat and already people were with her, checking her. There were others hurt too, or dazed, just sitting on the road, either crying or calling for help. Ruby was a step behind us, so it missed her, but even she says she didn't see it. Not properly. The lights were red. He should never have ploughed through them like that. Through us...' She looked across the room at the woman in the far corner. 'A motorbike. It didn't stop, William. It just didn't stop.'

'Brakes failed, maybe?'

'Who knows? That's his wife over there. And his son. The police have been in, but nobody really knows how it happened, or why. Not yet.'

'And Beth? You haven't told me what happened to Beth.'

Geraldine started to sob then. Big gulping sobs that made her shoulders shake.

'She just lay there. Totally still. On her back, with her head turned to one side. It was chaos. The crossing was busy, it was lunchtime, with lots of us trying to cross, both ways, squeezing past each other, bumping a bit, you know... and then suddenly there were people just knocked down, with no warning, others pushing, to try to escape it, and their belongings dropped and scattered all over the place, people trying to help, some getting in the way, some of them just looking, like it was a kind of sideshow.' She stopped and took a breath. 'I think most of us were okay really, a bit shaken, a bit battered, in shock I suppose, but Beth was in a bad way. Anyone could see that. She took the full brunt of it. There were people huddled around her, leaning over her. Somebody called for an ambulance, but she didn't move, William. Didn't open her eyes at all, not even when they were lifting her into the back of the ambulance, taking her away. Oh, please, God, let her be all right.'

After what seemed like hours, the door opened and all eyes looked up, expectantly.

A young doctor entered, wearing his white coat open, a stethoscope slung loosely around his neck, sombre-faced, and behind him a nurse who closed the door quietly and followed him across the room.

'Jack...'

Jack recognised the doctor, a colleague. 'Doctor Wilson.'

'And this is your brother?'

'Tom, yes.' Jack stood up, a little unsteadily, Tom just a pace behind him. 'Is there news?'

'I'm afraid there is.' The doctor placed his hand gently on Jack's arm. 'I'm so sorry, Jack – and Tom – but your mother never regained consciousness. Her head injury was simply too severe. We did all we could for her in theatre but, in the end, there was nothing we could do to save her. She's being kept breathing, for now, on a ventilator, so you can see her, take your time to say goodbye, but her brain function is...'

'I understand.' Jack had seen this so many times during his short nursing career, knew the score. Life support, the patient technically still alive, breathing through a machine, but in any real sense already gone. It was just delaying the inevitable. He knew that. He stood there, white-faced, shaking his head slowly, as he reached for his younger brother, trying to support him, give him the strength he was going to need to come through this. And Emily. How were they going to tell Emily?

It was Geraldine who broke the stillness as she let out a gasp, long and loud, that quickly morphed into a wail. 'No. No, not my Sandie. Not my baby. We'd only just found each other. I can't lose her again. I can't. Not so soon.'

'Mrs Munro. Geraldine...'

A third person had come in behind the others and was now standing at Geraldine's side, placing a comforting arm around her, talking in that same calm voice she had used so effectively earlier in the day.

'Elaine?' Geraldine looked confused. 'What are you doing

here? Have you come to tell me I'm a match? Because it's too late. I can't help her now.' Her voice cracked. 'None of us can.'

'I know. And I am so sorry.'

'Elaine?' William stared at the stranger. 'Forgive me, but I don't know who you are. Are you from the transplant team? I know my wife was being tested today, and I'm sorry, but I don't think she's up to this right now. Surely it can't matter anymore, whether she was a match or not. Can't it wait?'

Jack turned towards them. 'She's not here about finding an organ to save Mum,' he said, with the certainty of a nurse who had seen it all before and knew the signs. 'Not any more. Quite the opposite. They're keeping Mum ventilated, keeping her body functioning, for a reason. To keep her organs viable for donation, now that she's...' He struggled over finishing his sentence. 'Now that she's... dead.'

Geraldine was crying now, sobbing noisily, uncontrollably, into William's shoulder, and, beside him, Jack could feel Tom finally crumple as the enormity of what had just happened started to sink in. Only Ruby sat in silence, as if she had no idea what to say or do.

'It looks like she's made it to the top of the transplant list after all,' Jack said. 'But to give, rather than to take. Not what any of us expected when we came here today.'

'But her kidneys don't work,' Tom spluttered, sinking back into a chair as if his legs could no longer hold him up. 'What good can they possibly be...?'

'Kidneys, no. But she has a working heart, lungs, liver...'

'I'm so sorry,' Elaine said again. 'I know this is a terrible time to have to make decisions like this, but there's never a good time, and it's a decision that needs to be taken quickly.'

'Organ donation, the greatest gift of all, eh?' Jack nodded at Elaine. 'You were right when you called it that, and I know I speak for us all when I say it's definitely what Mum would have wanted. If she can't be saved, then at least she's able to help save someone else. Several someone elses. So, it's a yes. Obviously, it has to be a yes.' He choked back the tears that were threatening to burst out of him at any moment and reached for his brother's hand. 'Now, can we see her, please?'

William, Vicky and their band of new co-owners had spent every spare moment over the winter painting, mending and generally sprucing up the little animal park while it was closed to visitors, but had decided to leave the grand reopening until the spring. The weather was just about starting to get warmer now, after a long period of wind and rain, and although there was still a nip in the air, they wanted to get established and iron out any teething problems before the first of the season's tourists started arriving en masse at Easter. Weekend opening only to start with, and then, all being well, they would go all-out for seven days a week from the middle of April, when the school holidays began.

So, here they all were, owners, family, friends and visitors alike, waiting outside early on a Saturday morning for the gates of Sidell's to finally reopen. Not that it was called Sidell's anymore. This was a new beginning, and a new beginning demanded a new image, and definitely a new name.

As they all gathered for the small opening ceremony, a brand-new sign stood proudly above their heads, the words *Welcome to Sandie's* emblazoned across the centre in big red letters. Geraldine looked up at it and smiled. Her daughter may have officially been called Beth but to her she would always be Sandie...

The sign was massive, and definitely not one that any passing motorist would be able to miss. It was decorated with a glorious montage of pictures of just about every animal that visitors were likely to encounter inside, with a huge yellow sun positioned in the top corner, seeming to shine down over them all, bathing them in golden light.

From the moment she knew that the place was to be named after her mum, Emily had wanted to be involved. Living permanently with her father now, and with her share of her gran's house sale money sitting untouched in the bank to help secure her future, she was at last settling into her new life without her mum. Geraldine, of all people, knew what that felt like and was so glad that Emily had turned her grief into something positive and not let it swallow her up and turn her into some wayward rebel the way it had for her all those years ago.

Emily had done a fantastic job on the poster, gathering ideas, researching, poring over websites, art books and hundreds of animal photos, before painstakingly creating the final image, painting each animal by hand, stroke by careful stroke. It had certainly given her a much-needed project to focus her attention on, and it had so captured her imagination that she had told anyone who was prepared to listen that she was now determined to get herself into an art college and pursue a career in design, all thoughts of a future in hairdressing and make-up completely pushed aside. Somehow, Geraldine felt that Sandie... no, Beth, would have been pleased about that.

'Ready?' William whispered, slipping an arm around his wife's waist as he handed her the scissors.

Geraldine nodded. 'I still don't know why you want me to

cut the ribbon,' she said. 'I'm hardly a celebrity. We could have asked someone famous, like...'

'Like who, Geri? We don't know anybody famous. And, besides, I want it to be you. If it wasn't for your support, and your trust, when I took the reckless decision to plough so much of my money – *our* money – into this place, none of this would have happened.' He smiled, proudly. 'And look at it now. You'd hardly recognise the old place. It's given me a new lease of life, working here, planning, building, having something to really get my teeth into. I love it. The fresh air, the animals, the people.' He leant towards her and kissed her, hard, on the lips. 'And I love you.'

'You too.'

Geraldine stepped forward, lifted the big sharp shiny scissors and positioned them in the centre of the long strip of bright red fancy ribbon that Vicky had tied right across the front of the entrance. The difference she had seen in that girl in just a few months had been amazing. Her confidence was up, and she seemed so much happier, now that she had purpose again. Ruby had said she was moving back in with her parents too, her dad, reeling from her suicide attempt, having unexpectedly held out the proverbial olive branch and helped her raise her share of the funds needed to buy into this place. Geraldine was glad about that. It was only too clear how lonely and lost Vicky had been in the lead-up to her overdose. During her involvement with the children's home where she had first met Ruby, Geraldine had seen enough young girls struggling with their lives and it was a good feeling when she saw one pull herself back up and come out the other side.

She cleared her throat and began. 'It gives me great pleasure,' she said, shouting out her words in her best posh voice – God, she sounded like the Queen! – 'to declare Sandie's, this wonderful little animal park, officially open.' She almost added a 'God bless all who sail in her', but there was no champagne to smash, so she didn't. The scissors sliced through the ribbon as everyone cheered and Vicky rushed forward to unlock the gates and pop straight into the ticket booth inside, a stream of people already jostling to be first in the queue.

'Well, we did it.' William was back at Geraldine's side. 'All that hard work has finally paid off. Oh no, Geri, what have you done?' He lifted her hand as a small trickle of blood slipped down over her thumb.

'Good job the ribbon was red,' she joked. 'It's only a small cut and I don't think anybody noticed.'

'Here, Geri, let me find you a plaster.' Ruby was rummaging in her bag. 'I always carry a few. The joys of being in charge of a seven-year-old!'

'I've just checked Google, animal attractions in and around Brighton, and we're showing up on the first page.' Tom lifted his head from its almost permanent position bent over his phone. 'Must be all the keywords I dropped into the website. That should help people find us. Oh, and I'm definitely putting this on YouTube.' He held out the phone and replayed a short video clip of Geraldine cutting the ribbon, and herself.

'Must you? It's a bit embarrassing.'

'It's publicity, Geri. And it's funny, so it's the best kind.' He wandered away again, busily pressing at the keypad.

'You know, I don't understand half of what that boy says.' Geraldine laughed. 'But he's been such a help. They all have.'

'Nice to have family around us, isn't it?' William threw an arm across her shoulders and hugged her tight. 'Speaking of which, here comes your Michael. Late, as usual!'

'Blame that on the hotel breakfast.' Patsy laughed, arriving first as Michael followed behind with the pram. 'You try dragging your son away when it's all you can eat and they've got pancakes!'

'Hello, Patsy, love. And how is my little grandson today?' Geraldine peered into the pram, happy to see that the baby was wide awake. 'Can I hold him?'

'Be my guest. Make the most of him while you can. We're heading back to Portugal in three days.'

'Portugal?' Lily came hurtling towards her father and stepmother. She had been listening in again, but only getting half the story. 'Can we go and see him, Daddy? Please?'

Michael rubbed his eyes. He looked tired, as if he'd not had nearly enough sleep, which, with a young baby to care for, was highly likely. 'See who, sweetheart?' he said, lifting his daughter up into his arms.

'Portugal, of course. My piglet.'

'Not really a piglet any more, Lily,' William corrected her. 'He's grown pretty big over the winter, believe me!'

'Can we, Daddy? And can we buy a bag of stuff to feed him? And can I have an ice cream?'

'Yes to the pig, but not the ice cream, eh? It's a bit early in the day for that. Maybe later.'

'Says the man who's been gorging on pancakes and maple syrup since seven this morning!' Patsy laughed as she lifted baby Joe from his pram and handed him to his granny.

'This place is a bit out of town, isn't it?' Michael grumbled.

'Yes, but look on the bright side. We don't have room for a car park, so being so far away from the centre makes it easier for people to park in the street. And it's on the bus route too.'

'It's smaller than I imagined.' Michael pointed at a board behind him. 'I was just looking at the map over there. You could walk round the whole place in ten minutes.'

'Ah, but not if you stop at each enclosure to meet the animals. Vicky's got some talks lined up, and a couple of animal handling experiences for the kids. And then there's the shop and the café and the new playground.'

'You sound like an advert, Mum! You should have gone into marketing.'

'Oh, not me. It's just so easy to fall in love with this place, that's all. It may be small but it's perfectly formed, as they say. Just like this little one,' Geri said, marvelling at the baby's tiny fingers and tickling his tummy through his blanket.

'Go on, Michael, off you go.' Patsy gave her husband a gentle push. 'Spend some time with your daughter. I'm off to track down a nice cup of tea. Joe will be fine here with your mum.'

Everyone else had gone inside now, eager to start exploring the park's new features, the children eagerly grabbing free quiz sheets and pencils, a few of the adults already lining up for tea and cake. Only Geraldine, William and baby Joe remained at the gate, where the last shreds of the red ribbon still flapped in the breeze.

'Funny to think that this time last year I only had one grandchild,' Geraldine said, cuddling little Joe against her chest and rocking him gently from side to side. 'And now I have five.'

'You never know what life's going to throw at you, do you?' William replied. 'Who's going to turn up, what opportunities might come your way, when you might meet the love of your life...'

'I hope you mean me.' Geraldine laughed, although his eyes were very much trained on Ruby and Jack, having a sneaky smooch just yards away.

'Of course. You've given me the happiest four years of my life. So far. Although I'm sure there are many more wonderful years to come.'

'Not for my Sandie though. Sorry, I mean Beth. I still can't get used to that name, even now.'

'Life has its dark moments, Geri, as well as its good ones. At our age, we know that only too well. Look at this new virus thing. First China, now the world. Makes me worry every time I hear someone cough, but not a lot we can do about it, is there? But your Sandie... at least she was able to help save other lives. Several, from what Jack says.'

'I know. I wonder who they are though? Who were the people given her organs? Young or old, black or white, man or woman, living locally or miles away? It all seems such a lottery. And we could walk right past any one of them, couldn't we? Not knowing that a part of her is still there, working away inside another person's body.'

'We could, love, and that's what makes it so special, isn't it? That the gift she gave means she lives on, somewhere, somehow.'

'I'd love to know who has her heart though, wouldn't you? Whose chest it's beating in right now.'

'I think we already know where her heart is, Geri. It's right here, with all of us. Where it's always going to be, for as long as she's remembered and loved.'

'That could be for a very long time then,' Geraldine said, as she planted a kiss on the top of baby Joe's head, linked her arm through William's and followed the others inside.

THE END

ACKNOWLEDGEMENTS

When I was writing this story, Covid was all around us, forcing us to wear masks, closing our schools, and keeping us away from our friends and family. We watched helplessly as the TV reports brought us daily news of more restrictions and more deaths, and we all eagerly awaited, if not the cure, then at least the vaccine that would set us free. Yet I did not want Covid forcing its way into my novel. I knew there would be enough sickness and anguish in my fictional world without adding a pandemic to the mix, yet I could not ignore it and write as if it had never happened. That's why I decided to go back a few years and set the story pre-Covid, and to end it in the Spring of 2020, with just a hint in the final pages of what is lurking around the corner and about to change everything.

When it comes to saying thank you, I have to start with my readers, and all the reviewers and bloggers who do so much to support and promote authors. If you have read any of my fiction before, you may recognise a few things. In writing Geraldine and Beth's story, I have revisited a few of my favourite characters and settings. Ruby and little Lily first appeared, and Geraldine and William first met, in my earlier novel *Lily Alone* and I always liked the idea of coming back to Brighton to see what might have happened to them all a few years down the line. And to those who had grown fond of Agnes and her old cat Smudge, I apologise that somewhere between books I had to let them die!

My fictional Norfolk village of Shelling made its first

appearance in *Be Careful What You Wish For* and it was fun to have a few of the minor village characters pop up again in cameo roles this time around. The woman who runs the village shop turned out to be just as nosey as ever! And if you want to know what eventually happens to Beth's mum's house when the vet moves in, you can find out in my next novel, *The Three of Us*, due to be published later in 2024 and also featuring new characters with strong links to the village.

Novelists inevitably spend a lot of time alone, huddled over a screen or working out plots in their heads, so it is always great to have like-minded friends to meet up with and to be able to share writerly news. During the pandemic, that happened every month or so, weather permitting, as members of Phrase Writers, my local writers' group, sat several feet apart in my back garden, enjoying tea and cake and sharing words and wisdom. Thank you to Sheila, Richard, June, Megan, Kay and Marion for keeping those writing connections strong, whatever life threw at us. There were only ever six of us there at any one time though, obviously. We were never ones to break the rules!

Thanks also to Betsy, Shirley, Tara and all at Bloodhound Books for believing in, and loving, this book as much as I do. And to the cover designers who listened to my ideas and gave me everything I asked for and more. I so look forward to working with all of you again.

I must also mention, in this its 130th anniversary year, the wonderful Society of Women Writers and Journalists (SWWJ). I have been a proud member for well over twenty years and now hold a number of roles on its council, including organising all its writing competitions and taking care of social media. From the House of Lords to Jane Austen's house in the beautiful village of Chawton, the Society has chosen some fantastic venues in which to celebrate its anniversary, along with good food, fascinating speakers and lots of interesting and friendly company. If you write, whether professionally or just as a hobby, love meeting fellow writers, taking part in workshops and entering writing competitions, I recommend you take a look at all the SWWJ has to offer and think about joining. I feel sure you won't regret it. I never have.

Lastly, my family... Thank you to my husband Paul for accepting that I frequently disappear upstairs for hours at a time to pour what is going on in my head out through my fingers and onto a computer screen, and for just letting me get on with it. To my 95-year-old mum Betty, who has recently moved into a care home, and is sadly no longer the strong, independent woman or the avid reader she once was. Huge thanks to all the wonderful caring staff at Kingsley Court. In removing the daily responsibility and stress of trying to care for her myself, they have freed me to write again. To my daughters, Laura and Vicky, and a growing number of grandchildren. Hello to Penny, Olivia, Jenson, Amelia, new baby David, and the one still 'on the way'. Becoming a granny many times over can be tiring, but is an undeniably rewarding experience.

I have never suffered from kidney disease, had to give up a child, nor tried to track down a birth mother, so please forgive any gaps or errors in my research. In this novel I have tried to encapsulate the essence of what these emotional experiences may feel like, but inevitably there may be a few practical things I have left out, compressed or glossed over in order to tell a more engaging and compelling story. This is fiction after all, and I reserve the right to a little poetic licence!

The topic of organ donation is however a very sensitive one, something we don't like to think about until we have to, yet it can affect anyone at any time. There is nothing quite like a true story to inspire novelists and, although this novel was almost complete before I heard of her plight, I feel that I must mention a lady called Lyn Rowe who I once worked with in Hillingdon many moons ago and whose story I have recently been following on Facebook. Her urgent need for a kidney led to seven of her nearest and dearest volunteering to be tested as potential living donors, but unfortunately none was a match. Step forward her amazing son-in-law Joe Rees who tested in secret, found out he matched and, after more than two years of meetings, tests, scans and postponements, went on to donate one of his kidneys to Lyn last year, thus changing her life forever. Not a blood relation, but definitely the hero in her story. This novel is dedicated to him, and to all those like him. Living donation at its very best.

If anything in this novel has made you think about helping others through organ donation, particularly what might happen to your own organs after your death, then please talk to your loved ones NOW about your wishes, so the decisions are not left to them alone to make in their time of grief. Do you want your organs to be wasted? Buried or cremated with you? Your heart, lungs, kidneys, liver, pancreas, bowel, even your eyes? Or could they be used to change (or save) someone's life? Please don't leave it to chance. Registering your choices is easy and only takes a few moments. All you need to know is here: www. organdonation.nhs.uk

ABOUT THE AUTHOR

Vivien Brown was born and grew up in Middlesex and still lives there today, with her husband and two cats. Following an early career in banking and accountancy, the lure of working with words instead of numbers became too strong to resist and she went on to spend the happiest years of her working life reading with the under-fives in children's centres and libraries while writing short stories for women's magazines in her spare time. She went on to train as an adult education creative writing tutor and started writing novels, specialising in women's fiction with domestic drama and family relationships at its heart.

She is a past winner of the annual Mail on Sunday 'Best Opening to a Novel' competition and reached the shortlist again three years later, and was wined and dined on both occasions alongside the famous judges, Fay Weldon, John Mortimer, Sue Townsend and James Herbert, all incredibly friendly and supportive but sadly no longer with us.

Vivien is a fellow and honorary secretary of the Society of Women Writers and Journalists (SWWJ) where she oversees writing competitions and social media, and is a member of the Romantic Novelists' Association and a reader for its New Writers Scheme. She is also a regular tutor at the annual Swanwick Writers' Summer School.

Away from writing, Vivien loves playing with her grandchildren, watching and occasionally taking part in TV quiz shows, is an avid reader and reviewer of women's fiction, and enjoys the challenge of both solving and compiling cryptic crosswords.

A NOTE FROM THE PUBLISHER

Thank you for reading this book. If you enjoyed it please do consider leaving a review on Amazon to help others find it too.

We hate typos. All of our books have been rigorously edited and proofread, but sometimes mistakes do slip through. If you have spotted a typo, please do let us know and we can get it amended within hours.

info@bloodhoundbooks.com

Printed in Great Britain
by Amazon

41832358R00209